Phineas

Vol. II

Phineas Finn The Irish Member
Vol. II

by

Anthony Trollope

CAMBRIDGE
SCHOLARS
PUBLISHING

classic texts

Phineas Finn vol. II, by Anthony Trollope

This book in its current typographical format first published 2008 by

Cambridge Scholars Publishing

12 Back Chapman Street, Newcastle upon Tyne, NE6 2XX, UK

British Library Cataloguing in Publication Data
A catalogue record for this book is available from the British Library

ISBN (10): 1-84718-725-0, ISBN (13): 9781847187253

Contents

CHAPTER XXXVIII. The Duel

"I knew it was a duel;—bedad I did," said Laurence Fitzgibbon, standing at the corner of Orchard Street and Oxford Street, when Phineas had half told his story. "I was sure of it from the tone of your voice, my boy. We mustn't let it come off, that's all;—not if we can help it." Then Phineas was allowed to proceed and finish his story. "I don't see any way out of it; I don't, indeed," said Laurence. By this time Phineas had come to think that the duel was in very truth the best way out of the difficulty. It was a bad way out, but then it was a way;—and he could not see any other. "As for ill treating him, that's nonsense," said Laurence. "What are the girls to do, if one fellow mayn't come on as soon as another fellow is down? But then, you see, a fellow never knows when he's down himself, and therefore he thinks that he's ill used. I'll tell you what now. I shouldn't wonder if we couldn't do it on the sly,—unless one of you is stupid enough to hit the other in an awkward place. If you are certain of your hand now, the right shoulder is the best spot." Phineas felt very certain that he would not hit Lord Chiltern in an awkward place, although he was by no means sure of his hand. Let come what might, he would not aim at his adversary. But of this he had thought it proper to say nothing to Laurence Fitzgibbon.

And the duel did come off on the sly. The meeting in the drawing-room in Portman Square, of which mention was made in the last chapter, took place on a Wednesday afternoon. On the Thursday, Friday, Monday, and Tuesday following, the great debate on Mr. Mildmay's bill was continued, and at three on the Tuesday night the House divided. There was a majority in favour of the Ministers, not large enough to permit them to claim a triumph for their party, or even an ovation for themselves; but still sufficient to enable them to send their bill into committee. Mr. Daubeny and Mr. Turnbull had again joined their forces together in opposition to the ministerial measure. On the Thursday Phineas had shown himself in the House, but during the remainder of this interesting period he was absent from his place, nor was he seen at the clubs, nor did any man know of his whereabouts. I think that Lady Laura Kennedy was the first to miss him with any real sense of his absence. She would now go to Portman Square on the afternoon of every Sunday,—at which time her husband was attending the second service of his church,—and there she would receive those whom she called her father's guests. But as her father was never there on the Sundays, and as these gatherings had been created by herself, the reader will probably think that she was obeying her husband's behests in regard to the Sabbath after a very indifferent fashion. The reader may be quite sure, however, that Mr. Kennedy knew well what was being done in Portman Square. Whatever might be Lady Laura's faults, she did not commit the fault of disobeying her husband in secret. There were, probably, a few words on the subject; but we need not go very closely into that matter at the present moment.

On the Sunday which afforded some rest in the middle of the great Reform debate Lady Laura asked for Mr. Finn, and no one could answer her question. And then it was remembered that Laurence Fitzgibbon was also absent. Barrington Erle knew nothing of Phineas,—had heard nothing; but was able to say that Fitzgibbon had been with Mr. Ratler, the patronage secretary and liberal whip, early on Thursday, expressing his intention of absenting himself for two days. Mr. Ratler had been wroth, bidding him remain at his duty, and pointing out to him the great importance of the moment. Then Barrington Erle quoted Laurence Fitzgibbon's reply. "My boy," said Laurence to poor Ratler, "the path of duty leads but to the grave. All the same; I'll be in at the death, Ratler, my boy, as sure as the sun's in heaven." Not ten minutes after the telling of this little story, Fitzgibbon entered the room in Portman Square, and Lady Laura at once asked him after Phineas. "Bedad, Lady Laura, I have been out of town myself for two days, and I know nothing."

"Mr. Finn has not been with you, then?"

"With me! No,—not with me. I had a job of business of my own which took me over to Paris. And has Phinny fled too? Poor Ratler! I shouldn't wonder if it isn't an asylum he's in before the session is over."

Laurence Fitzgibbon certainly possessed the rare accomplishment of telling a lie with a good grace. Had any man called him a liar he would have considered himself to be not only insulted, but injured also. He believed himself to be a man of truth. There were, however, in his estimation certain subjects on which a man might depart as wide as the poles are asunder from truth without subjecting himself to any ignominy for falsehood. In dealing with a tradesman as to his debts, or with a rival as to a lady, or with any man or woman in defence of a lady's character, or in any such matter as that of a duel, Laurence believed that a gentleman was bound to lie, and that he would be no gentleman if he hesitated to do so. Not the slightest prick of conscience disturbed him when he told Lady Laura that he had been in Paris, and that he knew nothing of Phineas Finn. But, in truth, during the last day or two he had been in Flanders, and not in Paris, and had stood as second with his friend Phineas on the sands at Blankenberg, a little fishing-town some twelve miles distant from Bruges, and had left his friend since that at an hotel at Ostend,—with a wound just under the shoulder, from which a bullet had been extracted.

The manner of the meeting had been in this wise. Captain Colepepper and Laurence Fitzgibbon had held their meeting, and at this meeting Laurence had taken certain standing-ground on behalf of his friend, and in obedience to his friend's positive instruction;—which was this, that his friend could not abandon his right of addressing the young lady, should he hereafter ever think fit to do so. Let that be granted, and Laurence would do anything. But then that could not be granted, and Laurence could only shrug his shoulders. Nor would Laurence admit that his friend had been false. "The question lies in a nutshell," said Laurence, with that sweet Connaught brogue which always came to him when he desired to be effective;—"here it is. One gentleman tells another that he's sweet upon a young lady, but that the young lady has refused him, and always will refuse him, for ever and ever. That's the truth anyhow. Is the second gentleman bound by that not to address the young lady? I say he is not bound. It'd be a d—d hard tratement, Captain Colepepper, if a man's mouth and all the ardent affections of his heart were to be stopped in that manner! By Jases, I don't know who'd like to be the friend of any man if that's to be the way of it."

Captain Colepepper was not very good at an argument. "I think they'd better see each other," said Colepepper, pulling his thick grey moustache.

"If you choose to have it so, so be it. But I think it the hardest thing in the world;—I do indeed." Then they put their heads together in the most friendly way, and declared that the affair should, if possible, be kept private.

On the Thursday night Lord Chiltern and Captain Colepepper went over by Calais and Lille to Bruges. Laurence Fitzgibbon, with his friend Dr. O'Shaughnessy, crossed by the direct boat from Dover to Ostend. Phineas went to Ostend by Dover and Calais, but he took the day route on Friday. It had all been arranged among them, so that there might be no suspicion as to the job in hand. Even O'Shaughnessy and Laurence Fitzgibbon had left London by separate trains. They met on the sands at Blankenberg about nine o'clock on the Saturday morning, having reached that village in different vehicles from Ostend and Bruges, and had met quite unobserved amidst the sand-heaps. But one shot had been exchanged, and Phineas had been wounded in the right shoulder. He had proposed to exchange another shot with his left hand, declaring his capability of shooting quite as well with the left as with the right; but to this both Colepepper and Fitzgibbon had objected. Lord Chiltern had offered to shake hands with his late friend in a true spirit of friendship, if only his late friend would say that he did not intend to prosecute his suit with the young lady. In all these disputes the young lady's name was never mentioned. Phineas indeed had not once named Violet to Fitzgibbon, speaking of her always as the lady in question; and though Laurence correctly surmised the identity of the young lady, he never hinted that he had even guessed her name. I doubt whether Lord Chiltern had been so wary when alone with Captain Colepepper; but then Lord Chiltern was, when he spoke at all, a very plain-spoken man. Of course his lordship's late friend Phineas would give no such pledge, and therefore Lord Chiltern moved off the ground and back to Blankenberg and Bruges, and into Brussels, in still living enmity with our hero. Laurence and the doctor took Phineas back to Ostend, and though the bullet was then in his shoulder, Phineas made his way through Blankenberg after such a fashion that no one there knew what had occurred. Not a living soul, except the five concerned, was at that time aware that a duel had been fought among the sand-hills.

Laurence Fitzgibbon made his way to Dover by the Saturday night's boat, and was able to show himself in Portman Square on the Sunday. "Know anything about Phinny Finn?" he said afterwards to Barrington Erle, in answer to an inquiry from that anxious gentleman. "Not a word! I think you'd better send the town-crier round after him." Barrington, however, did not feel quite so well assured of Fitzgibbon's truth as Lady Laura had done.

Dr. O'Shaughnessy remained during the Sunday and Monday at Ostend with his patient, and the people at the inn only knew that Mr. Finn had sprained his shoulder badly; and on the Tuesday they came back to London again, via Calais and Dover. No bone had been broken, and Phineas, though his shoulder was very painful, bore the journey well. O'Shaughnessy had received a telegram on the Monday, telling him that the division would certainly take place on the Tuesday,—and on the Tuesday, at about ten in the evening, Phineas went down to the House. "By —, you're here," said Ratler, taking hold of him with an affection that was too warm. "Yes; I'm here," said Phineas, wincing in agony; "but be a little careful, there's a good fellow. I've been down in Kent and put my arm out."

"Put your arm out, have you?" said Ratler, observing the sling for the first time. "I'm sorry for that. But you'll stop and vote?"

"Yes;—I'll stop and vote. I've come up for the purpose. But I hope it won't be very late."

"There are both Daubeny and Gresham to speak yet, and at least three others. I don't suppose it will be much before three. But you're all right now. You can go down and smoke if you like!" In this way Phineas Finn spoke in the debate, and heard the end of it, voting for his party, and fought his duel with Lord Chiltern in the middle of it.

He did go and sit on a well-cushioned bench in the smoking-room, and then was interrogated by many of his friends as to his mysterious absence. He had, he said, been down in Kent, and had had an accident with his arm, by which he had been confined. When this questioner and that perceived that there was some little mystery in the matter, the questioners did not push their questions, but simply entertained their own surmises. One indiscreet questioner, however, did trouble Phineas sorely, declaring that there must have been some affair in which a woman had had a part, and asking after the young lady of Kent. This indiscreet questioner was Laurence Fitzgibbon, who, as Phineas thought, carried his spirit of intrigue a little too far. Phineas stayed and voted, and then he went painfully home to his lodgings.

How singular would it be if this affair of the duel should pass away, and no one be a bit the wiser but those four men who had been with him on the sands at Blankenberg! Again he wondered at his own luck. He had told himself that a duel with Lord Chiltern must create a quarrel between him and Lord Chiltern's relations, and also between him and Violet Effingham; that it must banish him from his comfortable seat for Loughton, and ruin him in regard to his political prospects. And now he had fought his duel, and was back in town,—and the thing seemed to have been a thing of nothing. He had not as yet seen Lady Laura or Violet, but he had no doubt but they both were as much in the dark as other people. The day might arrive, he thought, on which it would be pleasant for him to tell Violet Effingham what had occurred, but that day had not come as yet. Whither Lord Chiltern had gone, or what Lord Chiltern intended to do, he had not any idea; but he imagined that he should soon hear something of her brother from Lady Laura. That Lord Chiltern should say a word to Lady Laura of what had occurred,—or to any other person in the world,—he did not in the least suspect. There could be no man more likely to be reticent in such matters than Lord Chiltern,—or more sure to be guided by an almost exaggerated sense of what honour required of him. Nor did he doubt the discretion of his friend Fitzgibbon;—if only his friend might not damage the secret by being too discreet. Of the silence of the doctor and the captain he was by no means equally sure; but even though they should gossip, the gossiping would take so long a time in oozing out and becoming recognised information, as to have lost much of its power for injuring him. Were Lady Laura to hear at this moment that he had been over to Belgium, and had fought a duel with Lord Chiltern respecting Violet, she would probably feel herself obliged to quarrel with him; but no such obligation would rest on her, if in the course of six or nine months she should gradually have become aware that such an encounter had taken place.

Lord Chiltern, during their interview at the rooms in Great Marlborough Street, had said a word to him about the seat in Parliament;—had expressed some opinion that as he, Phineas Finn, was interfering with the views of the Standish family in regard to Miss Effingham, he ought not to keep the Standish seat, which had been conferred upon him in ignorance of any such intended interference. Phineas, as he thought of this, could not remember Lord Chiltern's words, but there was present to him an idea that such had been their purport. Was he bound, in circumstances as they now existed, to give up Loughton? He made up his mind that he was not so bound unless Lord Chiltern should demand from him that he should do so; but, nevertheless, he was uneasy in his position. It was quite true that the seat now was his for this session by all parliamentary law, even though the electors themselves might wish to be rid of him, and that Lord Brentford could not even open his mouth upon the matter in a tone more loud than that of a whisper. But Phineas, feeling that he had consented to accept the favour of a corrupt seat from Lord Brentford, felt also that he was bound to give up the spoil if it were demanded from him. If it were demanded from him, either by the father or the son, it should be given up at once.

On the following morning he found a leading article in the *People's Banner* devoted solely to himself. "During the late debate,"—so ran a passage in the leading article,—"Mr. Finn, Lord Brentford's Irish nominee for his pocket-borough at Loughton, did at last manage to stand on his legs and open his mouth. If we are not mistaken, this is Mr. Finn's third session in Parliament, and hitherto he has been unable to articulate three sentences, though he has on more than one occasion made the attempt. For what special merit this young man has been selected for aristocratic patronage we do not know,—but that there must be some merit recognisable by aristocratic eyes, we surmise. Three years ago he was a raw young Irishman, living in London as Irishmen only know how to live, earning nothing, and apparently without means; and then suddenly he bursts out as a member of Parliament and as the friend of Cabinet Ministers. The possession of one good gift must be acceded to the honourable member for Loughton,—he is a handsome young man, and looks to be as strong as a coal-porter. Can it be that his promotion has sprung from this? Be this as it may, we should like to know where he has been during his late mysterious absence from Parliament, and in what way he came by the wound in his arm. Even handsome young members of Parliament, fêted by titled ladies and their rich lords, are amenable to the laws,—to the laws of this country, and to the laws of any other which it may suit them to visit for a while!"

"Infamous scoundrel!" said Phineas to himself, as he read this. "Vile, low, disreputable blackguard!" It was clear enough, however, that Quintus Slide had found out something of his secret. If so, his only hope would rest on the fact that his friends were not likely to see the columns of the *People's Banner*.

CHAPTER XXXIX. Lady Laura is Told

By the time that Mr. Mildmay's great bill was going into committee Phineas was able to move about London in comfort,—with his arm, however, still in a sling. There had been nothing more about him and his wound in the *People's Banner*, and he was beginning to hope that that nuisance would also be allowed to die away. He had seen Lady Laura,—having dined in Grosvenor Place, where he had been petted to his heart's content. His dinner had been cut up for him, and his wound had been treated with the tenderest sympathy. And, singular to say, no questions were asked. He had been to Kent and had come by an accident. No more than that was told, and his dear sympathising friends were content to receive so much information, and to ask for no more. But he had not as yet seen Violet Effingham, and he was beginning to think that this romance about Violet might as well be brought to a close. He had not, however, as yet been able to go into crowded rooms, and unless he went out to large parties he could not be sure that he would meet Miss Effingham.

At last he resolved that he would tell Lady Laura the whole truth,—not the truth about the duel, but the truth about Violet Effingham, and ask for her assistance. When making this resolution, I think that he must have forgotten much that he had learned of his friend's character; and by making it, I think that he showed also that he had not learned as much as his opportunities might have taught him. He knew Lady Laura's obstinacy of purpose, he knew her devotion to her brother, and he knew also how desirous she had been that her brother should win Violet Effingham for himself. This knowledge should, I think, have sufficed to show him how improbable it was that Lady Laura should assist him in his enterprise. But beyond all this was the fact,—a fact as to the consequences of which Phineas himself was entirely blind, beautifully ignorant,—that Lady Laura had once condescended to love himself. Nay;—she had gone farther than this, and had ventured to tell him, even after her marriage, that the remembrance of some feeling that had once dwelt in her heart in regard to him was still a danger to her. She had warned him from Loughlinter, and then had received him in London;—and now he selected her as his confidante in this love affair! Had he not been beautifully ignorant and most modestly blind, he would surely have placed his confidence elsewhere.

It was not that Lady Laura Kennedy ever confessed to herself the existence of a vicious passion. She had, indeed, learned to tell herself that she could not love her husband; and once, in the excitement of such silent announcements to herself, she had asked herself whether her heart was quite a blank, and had answered herself by desiring Phineas Finn to absent himself from Loughlinter. During all the subsequent winter she had scourged herself inwardly for her own imprudence, her quite unnecessary folly in so doing. What! could not she, Laura Standish, who from her earliest years of girlish womanhood had resolved that she would use the world as men use it, and not as women do,—could not she have felt the slight shock of a passing tenderness for a handsome youth without allowing the feeling to be a rock before her big enough and sharp enough for the destruction of her entire barque? Could not she command, if not her heart, at any rate her mind, so that she might safely assure herself that, whether this man or any man was here or there, her course would be unaltered? What though Phineas Finn had been in the same house with her throughout all the winter, could not she have so lived with him on terms of friendship, that every deed and word and look of her friendship might have been open to her husband,—or open to all the world? She could have done so. She told herself that that was not,—need not have been her great calamity. Whether she could endure the dull, monotonous control of her slow but imperious lord,—or whether she must not rather tell him that it was not to be endured,—that was her trouble. So she told herself, and again admitted Phineas to her intimacy in London. But, nevertheless, Phineas, had he not been beautifully ignorant and most blind to his own achievements, would not have expected from Lady Laura Kennedy assistance with Miss Violet Effingham.

Phineas knew when to find Lady Laura alone, and he came upon her one day at the favourable hour. The two first clauses of the bill had been passed after twenty fights and endless divisions. Two points had been settled, as to which, however, Mr. Gresham had been driven to give way so far and to yield so much, that men declared that such a bill as the Government could consent to call its own could never be passed by that Parliament in that session. Immediately on his entrance into her room Lady Laura began about the third clause. Would the House let Mr. Gresham have his way about the—? Phineas stopped her at once. "My dear friend," he said, "I have come to you in a private trouble, and I want you to drop politics for half an hour. I have come to you for help."

"A private trouble, Mr. Finn! Is it serious?"

"It is very serious,—but it is no trouble of the kind of which you are thinking. But it is serious enough to take up every thought."

"Can I help you?"

"Indeed you can. Whether you will or no is a different thing."

"I would help you in anything in my power, Mr. Finn. Do you not know it?"

"You have been very kind to me!"

"And so would Mr. Kennedy."

"Mr. Kennedy cannot help me here."

"What is it, Mr. Finn?"

"I suppose I may as well tell you at once,—in plain language, I do not know how to put my story into words that shall fit it. I love Violet Effingham. Will you help me to win her to be my wife?"

"You love Violet Effingham!" said Lady Laura. And as she spoke the look of her countenance towards him was so changed that he became at once aware that from her no assistance might be expected. His eyes were not opened in any degree to the second reason above given for Lady Laura's opposition to his wishes, but he instantly perceived that she would still cling to that destination of Violet's hand which had for years past been the favourite scheme of her life. "Have you not always known, Mr. Finn, what have been our hopes for Violet?"

Phineas, though he had perceived his mistake, felt that he must go on with his cause. Lady Laura must know his wishes sooner or later, and it was as well that she should learn them in this way as in any other. "Yes;—but I have known also, from your brother's own lips,—and indeed from yours also, Lady Laura,—that Chiltern has been three times refused by Miss Effingham."

"What does that matter? Do men never ask more than three times?"

"And must I be debarred for ever while he prosecutes a hopeless suit?"

"Yes;—you of all men."

"Why so, Lady Laura?"

"Because in this matter you have been his chosen friend,—and mine. We have told you everything, trusting to you. We have believed in your honour. We have thought that with you, at any rate, we were safe." These words were very bitter to Phineas, and yet when he had written his letter at Loughton, he had intended to be so perfectly honest, chivalrously honest! Now Lady Laura spoke to him and looked at him as though he had been most basely false—most untrue to that noble friendship which had been lavished upon him by all her family. He felt that he would become the prey of her most injurious thoughts unless he could fully explain his ideas, and he felt, also, that the circumstances did not admit of his explaining them. He could not take up the argument on Violet's side, and show how unfair it would be to her that she should be debarred from the homage due to her by any man who really loved her, because Lord Chiltern chose to think that he still had a claim,—or at any rate a chance. And Phineas knew well of himself,—or thought that he knew well,—that he would not have interfered had there been any chance for Lord Chiltern. Lord Chiltern had himself told him more than once that there was no such chance. How was he to explain all this to Lady Laura? "Mr. Finn," said Lady Laura, "I can hardly believe this of you, even when you tell it me yourself."

"Listen to me, Lady Laura, for a moment."

"Certainly, I will listen. But that you should come to me for assistance! I cannot understand it. Men sometimes become harder than stones."

"I do not think that I am hard." Poor blind fool! He was still thinking only of Violet, and of the accusation made against him that he was untrue to his friendship for Lord Chiltern. Of that other accusation which could not be expressed in open words he understood nothing,—nothing at all as yet.

"Hard and false,—capable of receiving no impression beyond the outside husk of the heart."

"Oh, Lady Laura, do not say that. If you could only know how true I am in my affection for you all."

"And how do you show it?—by coming in between Oswald and the only means that are open to us of reconciling him to his father;—means that have been explained to you exactly as though you had been one of ourselves. Oswald has treated you as a brother in the matter, telling you everything, and this is the way you would repay him for his confidence!"

"Can I help it, that I have learnt to love this girl?"

"Yes, sir,—you can help it. What if she had been Oswald's wife;—would you have loved her then? Do you speak of loving a woman as if it were an affair of fate, over which you have no control? I doubt whether your passions are so strong as that. You had better put aside your love for Miss Effingham. I feel assured that it will never hurt you." Then some remembrance of what had passed between him and Lady Laura Standish near the falls of the Linter, when he first visited Scotland, came across his mind. "Believe me," she said with a smile, "this little wound in your heart will soon be cured."

He stood silent before her, looking away from her, thinking over it all. He certainly had believed himself to be violently in love with Lady Laura, and yet when he had just now entered her drawing-room, he had almost forgotten that there had been such a passage in his life. And he had believed that she had forgotten it,—even though she had counselled him not to come to Loughlinter within the last nine months! He had been a boy then, and had not known himself;—but now he was a man, and was proud of the intensity of his love. There came upon him some passing throb of pain from his shoulder, reminding him of the duel, and he was proud also of that. He had been willing to risk everything,—life, prospects, and position,—sooner than abandon the slight hope which was his of possessing Violet Effingham. And now he was told that this wound in his heart would soon be cured, and was told so by a woman to whom he had once sung a song of another passion. It is very hard to answer a woman in such circumstances, because her womanhood gives her so strong a ground of vantage! Lady Laura might venture to throw in his teeth the fickleness of his heart, but he could not in reply tell her that to change a love was better than to marry without love,—that to be capable of such a change showed no such inferiority of nature as did the capacity for such a marriage. She could hit him with her argument; but he could only remember his, and think how violent might be the blow he could inflict,—if it were not that she were a woman, and therefore guarded. "You will not help me then?" he said, when they had both been silent for a while.

"Help you? How should I help you?"

"I wanted no other help than this,—that I might have had an opportunity of meeting Violet here, and of getting from her some answer."

"Has the question then never been asked already?" said Lady Laura. To this Phineas made no immediate reply. There was no reason why he should show his whole hand to an adversary. "Why do you not go to Lady Baldock's house?" continued Lady Laura. "You are admitted there. You know Lady Baldock. Go and ask her to stand your friend with her niece. See what she will say to you. As far as I understand these matters, that is the fair, honourable, open way in which gentlemen are wont to make their overtures."

"I would make mine to none but to herself," said Phineas.

"Then why have you made it to me, sir?" demanded Lady Laura.

"I have come to you as I would to my sister."

"Your sister? Psha! I am not your sister, Mr. Finn. Nor, were I so, should I fail to remember that I have a dearer brother to whom my faith is pledged. Look here. Within the last three weeks Oswald has sacrificed everything to his father, because he was determined that Mr. Kennedy should have the money which he thought was due to my husband. He has enabled my father to do what he will with Saulsby. Papa will never hurt him;—I know that. Hard as papa is with him, he will never hurt Oswald's future position. Papa is too proud to do that. Violet has heard what Oswald has done; and now that he has nothing of his own to offer her for the future but his bare title, now that he has given papa power to do what he will with the property, I believe that she would accept him instantly. That is her disposition."

Phineas again paused a moment before he replied. "Let him try," he said.

"He is away,—in Brussels."

"Send to him, and bid him return. I will be patient, Lady Laura. Let him come and try, and I will bide my time. I confess that I have no right to interfere with him if there be a chance for him. If there is no chance, my right is as good as that of any other."

There was something in this which made Lady Laura feel that she could not maintain her hostility against this man on behalf of her brother;—and yet she could not force herself to be other than hostile to him. Her heart was sore, and it was he that had made it sore. She had lectured herself, schooling herself with mental sackcloth and ashes, rebuking herself with heaviest censures from day to day, because she had found herself to be in danger of regarding this man with a perilous love; and she had been constant in this work of penance till she had been able to assure herself that the sackcloth and ashes had done their work, and that the danger was past. "I like him still and love him well," she had said to herself with something almost of triumph, "but I have ceased to think of him as one who might have been my lover." And yet she was now sick and sore, almost beside herself with the agony of the wound, because this man whom she had been able to throw aside from her heart had also been able so to throw her aside. And she felt herself constrained to rebuke him with what bitterest words she might use. She had felt it easy to do this at first, on her brother's score. She had accused him of treachery to his friendship,—both as to Oswald and as to herself. On that she could say cutting words without subjecting herself to suspicion even from herself. But now this power was taken away from her, and still she wished to wound him. She desired to taunt him with his old fickleness, and yet to subject herself to no imputation. "Your right!" she said. "What gives you any right in the matter?"

"Simply the right of a fair field, and no favour."

"And yet you come to me for favour,—to me, because I am her friend. You cannot win her yourself, and think I may help you! I do not believe in your love for her. There! If there were no other reason, and I could help you, I would not, because I think your heart is a sham heart. She is pretty, and has money—"

"Lady Laura!"

"She is pretty, and has money, and is the fashion. I do not wonder that you should wish to have her. But, Mr. Finn, I believe that Oswald really loves her;—and that you do not. His nature is deeper than yours."

He understood it all now as he listened to the tone of her voice, and looked into the lines of her face. There was written there plainly enough that *spretœ injuria formœ* of which she herself was conscious, but only conscious. Even his eyes, blind as he had been, were opened,—and he knew that he had been a fool.

"I am sorry that I came to you," he said.

"It would have been better that you should not have done so," she replied.

"And yet perhaps it is well that there should be no misunderstanding between us."

"Of course I must tell my brother."

He paused but for a moment, and then he answered her with a sharp voice, "He has been told."

"And who told him?"

"I did. I wrote to him the moment that I knew my own mind. I owed it to him to do so. But my letter missed him, and he only learned it the other day."

"Have you seen him since?"

"Yes;—I have seen him."

"And what did he say? How did he take it? Did he bear it from you quietly?"

"No, indeed;" and Phineas smiled as he spoke.

"Tell me, Mr. Finn; what happened? What is to be done?"

"Nothing is to be done. Everything has been done. I may as well tell you all. I am sure that for the sake of me, as well as of your brother, you will keep our secret. He required that I should either give up my suit, or that I should,—fight him. As I could not comply with the one request, I found myself bound to comply with the other."

"And there has been a duel?"

"Yes;—there has been a duel. We went over to Belgium, and it was soon settled. He wounded me here in the arm."

"Suppose you had killed him, Mr. Finn?"

"That, Lady Laura, would have been a misfortune so terrible that I was bound to prevent it." Then he paused again, regretting what he had said. "You have surprised me, Lady Laura, into an answer that I should not have made. I may be sure,—may I not,—that my words will not go beyond yourself?"

"Yes;—you may be sure of that." This she said plaintively, with a tone of voice and demeanour of body altogether different from that which she lately bore. Neither of them knew what was taking place between them; but she was, in truth, gradually submitting herself again to this man's influence. Though she rebuked him at every turn for what he said, for what he had done, for what he proposed to do, still she could not teach herself to despise him, or even to cease to love him for any part of it. She knew it all now,—except that word or two which had passed between Violet and Phineas in the rides of Saulsby Park. But she suspected something even of that, feeling sure that the only matter on which Phineas would say nothing would be that of his own success,—if success there had been. "And so you and Oswald have quarrelled, and there has been a duel. That is why you were away?"

"That is why I was away."

"How wrong of you,—how very wrong! Had he been,—killed, how could you have looked us in the face again?"

"I could not have looked you in the face again."

"But that is over now. And were you friends afterwards?"

"No;—we did not part as friends. Having gone there to fight with him,—most unwillingly,—I could not afterwards promise him that I would give up Miss Effingham. You say she will accept him now. Let him come and try." She had nothing further to say,—no other argument to use. There was the soreness at her heart still present to her, making her wretched, instigating her to hurt him if she knew how to do so, in spite of her regard for him. But she felt that she was weak and powerless. She had shot her arrows at him,—all but one,—and if she used that, its poisoned point would wound herself far more surely than it would touch him. "The duel was very silly," he said. "You will not speak of it."

"No; certainly not."

"I am glad at least that I have told you everything."

"I do not know why you should be glad. I cannot help you."

"And you will say nothing to Violet?"

"Everything that I can say in Oswald's favour. I will say nothing of the duel; but beyond that you have no right to demand my secrecy with her. Yes; you had better go, Mr. Finn, for I am hardly well. And remember this,—If you can forget this little episode about Miss Effingham, so will I forget it also; and so will Oswald. I can promise for him." Then she smiled and gave him her hand, and he went.

She rose from her chair as he left the room, and waited till she heard the sound of the great door closing behind him before she again sat down. Then, when he was gone,—when she was sure that he was no longer there with her in the same house,—she laid her head down upon the arm of the sofa, and burst into a flood of tears. She was no longer angry with Phineas. There was no further longing in her heart for revenge. She did not now desire to injure him, though she had done so as long as he was with her. Nay,—she resolved instantly, almost instinctively, that Lord Brentford must know nothing of all this, lest the political prospects of the young member for Loughton should be injured. To have rebuked him, to rebuke him again and again, would be only fair,—would at least be womanly; but she would protect him from all material injury as far as her power of protection might avail. And why was she weeping now so bitterly? Of course she asked herself, as she rubbed away the tears with her hands,—Why should she weep? She was not weak enough to tell herself that she was weeping for any injury that had been done to Oswald. She got up suddenly from the sofa, and pushed away her hair from her face, and pushed away the tears from her cheeks, and then clenched her fists as she held them out at full length from her body, and stood, looking up with her eyes fixed upon the wall. "Ass!" she exclaimed. "Fool! Idiot! That I should not be able to crush it into nothing and have done with it! Why should he not have her? After all, he is better than Oswald. Oh,—is that you?" The door of the room had been opened while she was standing thus, and her husband had entered.

"Yes,—it is I. Is anything wrong?"

"Very much is wrong."

"What is it, Laura?"

"You cannot help me."

"If you are in trouble you should tell me what it is, and leave it to me to try to help you."

"Nonsense!" she said, shaking her head.

"Laura, that is uncourteous,—not to say undutiful also."

"I suppose it was,—both. I beg your pardon, but I could not help it."

"Laura, you should help such words to me."

"There are moments, Robert, when even a married woman must be herself rather than her husband's wife. It is so, though you cannot understand it."

"I certainly do not understand it."

"You cannot make a woman subject to you as a dog is so. You may have all the outside and as much of the inside as you can master. With a dog you may be sure of both."

"I suppose this means that you have secrets in which I am not to share."

"I have troubles about my father and my brother which you cannot share. My brother is a ruined man."

"Who ruined him?"

"I will not talk about it any more. I will not speak to you of him or of papa. I only want you to understand that there is a subject which must be secret to myself, and on which I may be allowed to shed tears,—if I am so weak. I will not trouble you on a matter in which I have not your sympathy." Then she left him, standing in the middle of the room, depressed by what had occurred,—but not thinking of it as of a trouble which would do more than make him uncomfortable for that day.

CHAPTER XL. Madame Max Goesler

Day after day, and clause after clause, the bill was fought in committee, and few men fought with more constancy on the side of the Ministers than did the member for Loughton. Troubled though he was by his quarrel with Lord Chiltern, by his love for Violet Effingham, by the silence of his friend Lady Laura,—for since he had told her of the duel she had become silent to him, never writing to him, and hardly speaking to him when she met him in society,—nevertheless Phineas was not so troubled but what he could work at his vocation. Now, when he would find himself upon his legs in the House, he would wonder at the hesitation which had lately troubled him so sorely. He would sit sometimes and speculate upon that dimness of eye, upon that tendency of things to go round, upon that obtrusive palpitation of heart, which had afflicted him so seriously for so long a time. The House now was no more to him than any other chamber, and the members no more than other men. He guarded himself from orations, speaking always very shortly,—because he believed that policy and good judgment required that he should be short. But words were very easy to him, and he would feel as though he could talk for ever. And there quickly came to him a reputation for practical usefulness. He was a man with strong opinions, who could yet be submissive. And no man seemed to know how his reputation had come. He had made one good speech after two or three failures. All who knew him, his whole party, had been aware of his failure; and his one good speech had been regarded by many as no very wonderful effort. But he was a man who was pleasant to other men,—not combative, not self-asserting beyond the point at which self-assertion ceases to be a necessity of manliness. Nature had been very good to him, making him comely inside and out,—and with this comeliness he had crept into popularity.

The secret of the duel was, I think, at this time, known to a great many men and women. So Phineas perceived; but it was not, he thought, known either to Lord Brentford or to Violet Effingham. And in this he was right. No rumour of it had yet reached the ears of either of these persons;—and rumour, though she flies so fast and so far, is often slow in reaching those ears which would be most interested in her tidings. Some dim report of the duel reached even Mr. Kennedy, and he asked his wife. "Who told you?" said she, sharply.

"Bonteen told me that it was certainly so."

"Mr. Bonteen always knows more than anybody else about everything except his own business."

"Then it is not true?"

Lady Laura paused,—and then she lied. "Of course it is not true. I should be very sorry to ask either of them, but to me it seems to be the most improbable thing in life." Then Mr. Kennedy believed that there had been no duel. In his wife's word he put absolute faith, and he thought that she would certainly know anything that her brother had done. As he was a man given to but little discourse, he asked no further questions about the duel either in the House or at the Clubs.

At first, Phineas had been greatly dismayed when men had asked him questions tending to elicit from him some explanation of the mystery;—but by degrees he became used to it, and as the tidings which had got abroad did not seem to injure him, and as the questionings were not pushed very closely, he became indifferent. There came out another article in the *People's Banner* in which Lord C—n and Mr. P—s F—n were spoken of as glaring examples of that aristocratic snobility,—that was the expressive word coined, evidently with great delight, for the occasion,—which the rotten state of London society in high quarters now produced. Here was a young lord, infamously notorious, quarrelling with one of his boon-companions, whom he had appointed to a private seat in the House of Commons, fighting duels, breaking the laws, scandalising the public,—and all this was done without punishment to the guilty! There were old stories afloat,—so said the article—of what in a former century had been done by Lord Mohuns and Mr. Bests; but now, in 186—, &c. &c. &c. And so the article went on. Any reader may fill in without difficulty the concluding indignation and virtuous appeal for reform in social morals as well as Parliament. But Phineas had so far progressed that he had almost come to like this kind of thing.

Certainly I think that the duel did him no harm in society. Otherwise he would hardly have been asked to a semi-political dinner at Lady Glencora Palliser's, even though he might have been invited to make one of the five hundred guests who were crowded into her saloons and staircases after the dinner was over. To have been one of the five hundred was nothing; but to be one of the sixteen was a great deal,—was indeed so much that Phineas, not understanding as yet the advantage of his own comeliness, was at a loss to conceive why so pleasant an honour was conferred upon him. There was no man among the eight men at the dinner-party not in Parliament,—and the only other except Phineas not attached to the Government was Mr. Palliser's great friend, John Grey, the member for Silverbridge. There were four Cabinet Ministers in the room,—the Duke, Lord Cantrip, Mr. Gresham, and the owner of the mansion. There was also Barrington Erle and young Lord Fawn, an Under-Secretary of State. But the wit and grace of the ladies present lent more of character to the party than even the position of the men. Lady Glencora Palliser herself was a host. There was no woman then in London better able to talk to a dozen people on a dozen subjects; and then, moreover, she was still in the flush of her beauty and the bloom of her youth. Lady Laura was there;—by what means divided from her husband Phineas could not imagine; but Lady Glencora was good at such divisions. Lady Cantrip had been allowed to come with her lord;—but, as was well understood, Lord Cantrip was not so manifestly a husband as was Mr. Kennedy. There are men who cannot guard themselves from the assertion of marital rights at most inappropriate moments. Now Lord Cantrip lived with his wife most happily; yet you should pass hours with him and her together, and hardly know that they knew each other. One of the Duke's daughters was there,—but not the Duchess, who was known to be heavy;—and there was the beauteous Marchioness of Hartletop. Violet Effingham was in the room also,—giving Phineas a blow at the heart as he saw her smile. Might it be that he could speak a word to her on this occasion? Mr. Grey had also brought his wife;—and then there was Madame Max Goesler. Phineas found that it was his fortune to take down to dinner,—not Violet Effingham, but Madame Max Goesler. And, when he was placed at dinner, on the other side of him there sat Lady Hartletop, who addressed the few words which she spoke exclusively to Mr. Palliser. There had been in former days matters difficult of arrangement between those two; but I think that those old passages had now been forgotten by them both. Phineas was, therefore, driven to depend exclusively on Madame Max Goesler for conversation, and he found that he was not called upon to cast his seed into barren ground.

Up to that moment he had never heard of Madame Max Goesler. Lady Glencora, in introducing them, had pronounced the lady's name so clearly that he had caught it with accuracy, but he could not surmise whence she had come, or why she was there. She was a woman probably something over thirty years of age. She had thick black hair, which she wore in curls,—unlike anybody else in the world,—in curls which hung down low beneath her face, covering, and perhaps intended to cover, a certain thinness in her cheeks which would otherwise have taken something from the charm of her countenance. Her eyes were large, of a dark blue colour, and very bright,—and she used them in a manner which is as yet hardly common with Englishwomen. She seemed to intend that you should know that she employed them to conquer you, looking as a knight may have looked in olden days who entered a chamber with his sword drawn from the scabbard and in his hand. Her forehead was broad and somewhat low. Her nose was not classically beautiful, being broader at the nostrils than beauty required, and, moreover, not perfectly straight in its line. Her lips were thin. Her teeth, which she endeavoured to show as little as possible, were perfect in form and colour. They who criticised her severely said, however, that they were too large. Her chin was well formed, and divided by a dimple which gave to her face a softness of grace which would otherwise have been much missed. But perhaps her great beauty was in the brilliant clearness of her dark complexion. You might almost fancy that you could see into it so as to read the different lines beneath the skin. She was somewhat tall, though by no means tall to a fault, and was so thin as to be almost meagre in her proportions. She always wore her dress close up to her neck, and never showed the bareness of her arms. Though she was the only woman so clad now present in the room, this singularity did not specially strike one, because in other respects her apparel was so rich and quaint as to make inattention to it impossible. The observer who did not observe very closely would perceive that Madame Max Goesler's dress was unlike the dress of other women, but seeing that it was unlike in make, unlike in colour, and unlike in material, the ordinary observer would not see also that it was unlike in form for any other purpose than that of maintaining its general peculiarity of character. In colour she was abundant, and yet the fabric of her garment was always black. My pen may not dare to describe the traceries of yellow and ruby silk which went in and out through the black lace, across her bosom, and round her neck, and over her shoulders, and along her arms, and down to the very ground at her feet, robbing the black stuff of all its sombre solemnity, and producing a brightness in which there was nothing gaudy. She wore no vestige of crinoline, and hardly anything that could be called a train. And the lace sleeves of her dress, with their bright traceries of silk, were fitted close to her arms; and round her neck she wore the smallest possible collar of lace, above which there was a short chain of Roman gold with a ruby pendant. And she had rubies in her ears, and a ruby brooch, and rubies in the bracelets on her arms. Such, as regarded the outward woman, was Madame Max Goesler; and Phineas, as he took his place by her side, thought that fortune for the nonce had done well with him,—only that he should have liked it so much better could he have been seated next to Violet Effingham!

I have said that in the matter of conversation his morsel of seed was not thrown into barren ground. I do not know that he can truly be said to have produced even a morsel. The subjects were all mooted by the lady, and so great was her fertility in discoursing that all conversational grasses seemed to grow with her spontaneously. "Mr. Finn," she said, "what would I not give to be a member of the British Parliament at such a moment as this!"

"Why at such a moment as this particularly?"

"Because there is something to be done, which, let me tell you, senator though you are, is not always the case with you."

"My experience is short, but it sometimes seems to me that there is too much to be done."

"Too much of nothingness, Mr. Finn. Is not that the case? But now there is a real fight in the lists. The one great drawback to the life of women is that they cannot act in politics."

"And which side would you take?"

"What, here in England?" said Madame Max Goesler,—from which expression, and from one or two others of a similar nature, Phineas was led into a doubt whether the lady were a countrywoman of his or not. "Indeed, it is hard to say. Politically I should want to out-Turnbull Mr. Turnbull, to vote for everything that could be voted for,—ballot, manhood suffrage, womanhood suffrage, unlimited right of striking, tenant right, education of everybody, annual parliaments, and the abolition of at least the bench of bishops."

"That is a strong programme," said Phineas.

"It is strong, Mr. Finn, but that's what I should like. I think, however, that I should be tempted to feel a dastard security in the conviction that I might advocate my views without any danger of seeing them carried out. For, to tell you the truth, I don't at all want to put down ladies and gentlemen."

"You think that they would go with the bench of bishops?"

"I don't want anything to go,—that is, as far as real life is concerned. There's that dear good Bishop of Abingdon is the best friend I have in the world,—and as for the Bishop of Dorchester, I'd walk from here to there to hear him preach. And I'd sooner hem aprons for them all myself than that they should want those pretty decorations. But then, Mr. Finn, there is such a difference between life and theory;—is there not?"

"And it is so comfortable to have theories that one is not bound to carry out," said Phineas.

"Isn't it? Mr. Palliser, do you live up to your political theories?" At this moment Mr. Palliser was sitting perfectly silent between Lady Hartletop and the Duke's daughter, and he gave a little spring in his chair as this sudden address was made to him. "Your House of Commons theories, I mean, Mr. Palliser. Mr. Finn is saying that it is very well to have far advanced ideas,—it does not matter how far advanced,—because one is never called upon to act upon them practically."

"That is a dangerous doctrine, I think," said Mr. Palliser.

"But pleasant,—so at least Mr. Finn says."

"It is at least very common," said Phineas, not caring to protect himself by a contradiction.

"For myself," said Mr. Palliser gravely, "I think I may say that I always am really anxious to carry into practice all those doctrines of policy which I advocate in theory."

During this conversation Lady Hartletop sat as though no word of it reached her ears. She did not understand Madame Max Goesler, and by no means loved her. Mr. Palliser, when he had made his little speech, turned to the Duke's daughter and asked some question about the conservatories at Longroyston.

"I have called forth a word of wisdom," said Madame Max Goesler, almost in a whisper.

"Yes," said Phineas, "and taught a Cabinet Minister to believe that I am a most unsound politician. You may have ruined my prospects for life, Madame Max Goesler."

"Let me hope not. As far as I can understand the way of things in your Government, the aspirants to office succeed chiefly by making themselves uncommonly unpleasant to those who are in power. If a man can hit hard enough he is sure to be taken into the Elysium of the Treasury bench,—not that he may hit others, but that he may cease to hit those who are there. I don't think men are chosen because they are useful."

"You are very severe upon us all."

"Indeed, as far as I can see, one man is as useful as another. But to put aside joking,—they tell me that you are sure to become a minister."

Phineas felt that he blushed. Could it be that people said of him behind his back that he was a man likely to rise high in political position? "Your informants are very kind," he replied awkwardly, "but I do not know who they are. I shall never get up in the way you describe,—that is, by abusing the men I support."

After that Madame Max Goesler turned round to Mr. Grey, who was sitting on the other side of her, and Phineas was left for a moment in silence. He tried to say a word to Lady Hartletop, but Lady Hartletop only bowed her head gracefully in recognition of the truth of the statement he made. So he applied himself for a while to his dinner.

"What do you think of Miss Effingham?" said Madame Max Goesler, again addressing him suddenly.

"What do I think about her?"

"You know her, I suppose."

"Oh yes, I know her. She is closely connected with the Kennedys, who are friends of mine."

"So I have heard. They tell me that scores of men are raving about her. Are you one of them?"

"Oh yes;—I don't mind being one of sundry scores. There is nothing particular in owning to that."

"But you admire her?"

"Of course I do," said Phineas.

"Ah, I see you are joking. I do amazingly. They say women never do admire women, but I most sincerely do admire Miss Effingham."

"Is she a friend of yours?"

"Oh no;—I must not dare to say so much as that. I was with her last winter for a week at Matching, and of course I meet her about at people's houses. She seems to me to be the most independent girl I ever knew in my life. I do believe that nothing would make her marry a man unless she loved him and honoured him, and I think it is so very seldom that you can say that of a girl."

"I believe so also," said Phineas. Then he paused a moment before he continued to speak. "I cannot say that I know Miss Effingham very intimately, but from what I have seen of her, I should think it very probable that she may not marry at all."

"Very probably," said Madame Max Goesler, who then again turned away to Mr. Grey.

Ten minutes after this, when the moment was just at hand in which the ladies were to retreat, Madame Max Goesler again addressed Phineas, looking very full into his face as she did so. "I wonder whether the time will ever come, Mr. Finn, in which you will give me an account of that day's journey to Blankenberg?"

"To Blankenberg!"

"Yes;—to Blankenberg. I am not asking for it now. But I shall look for it some day." Then Lady Glencora rose from her seat, and Madame Max Goesler went out with the others.

CHAPTER XLI. Lord Fawn

What had Madame Max Goesler to do with his journey to Blankenberg? thought Phineas, as he sat for a while in silence between Mr. Palliser and Mr. Grey; and why should she, who was a perfect stranger to him, have dared to ask him such a question? But as the conversation round the table, after the ladies had gone, soon drifted into politics and became general, Phineas, for a while, forgot Madame Max Goesler and the Blankenberg journey, and listened to the eager words of Cabinet Ministers, now and again uttering a word of his own, and showing that he, too, was as eager as others. But the session in Mr. Palliser's dining-room was not long, and Phineas soon found himself making his way amidst a throng of coming guests into the rooms above. His object was to meet Violet Effingham, but, failing that, he would not be unwilling to say a few more words to Madame Max Goesler.

He first encountered Lady Laura, to whom he had not spoken as yet, and, finding himself standing close to her for a while, he asked her after his late neighbour. "Do tell me one thing, Lady Laura;—who is Madame Max Goesler, and why have I never met her before?"

"That will be two things, Mr. Finn; but I will answer both questions as well as I can. You have not met her before, because she was in Germany last spring and summer, and in the year before that you were not about so much as you have been since. Still you must have seen her, I think. She is the widow of an Austrian banker, and has lived the greater part of her life at Vienna. She is very rich, and has a small house in Park Lane, where she receives people so exclusively that it has come to be thought an honour to be invited by Madame Max Goesler. Her enemies say that her father was a German Jew, living in England, in the employment of the Viennese bankers, and they say also that she has been married a second time to an Austrian Count, to whom she allows ever so much a year to stay away from her. But of all this, nobody, I fancy, knows anything. What they do know is that Madame Max Goesler spends seven or eight thousand a year, and that she will give no man an opportunity of even asking her to marry him. People used to be shy of her, but she goes almost everywhere now."

"She has not been at Portman Square?"

"Oh no; but then Lady Glencora is so much more advanced than we are! After all, we are but humdrum people, as the world goes now."

Then Phineas began to roam about the rooms, striving to find an opportunity of engrossing five minutes of Miss Effingham's attention. During the time that Lady Laura was giving him the history of Madame Max Goesler his eyes had wandered round, and he had perceived that Violet was standing in the further corner of a large lobby on to which the stairs opened,—so situated, indeed, that she could hardly escape, because of the increasing crowd, but on that very account almost impossible to be reached. He could see, also, that she was talking to Lord Fawn, an unmarried peer of something over thirty years of age, with an unrivalled pair of whiskers, a small estate, and a rising political reputation. Lord Fawn had been talking to Violet through the whole dinner, and Phineas was beginning to think that he should like to make another journey to Blankenberg, with the object of meeting his lordship on the sands. When Lady Laura had done speaking, his eyes were turned through a large open doorway towards the spot on which his idol was standing. "It is of no use, my friend," she said, touching his arm. "I wish I could make you know that it is of no use, because then I think you would be happier." To this Phineas made no answer, but went and roamed about the rooms. Why should it be of no use? Would Violet Effingham marry any man merely because he was a lord?

Some half-hour after this he had succeeded in making his way up to the place in which Violet was still standing, with Lord Fawn beside her. "I have been making such a struggle to get to you," he said.

"And now you are here, you will have to stay, for it is impossible to get out," she answered. "Lord Fawn has made the attempt half-a-dozen times, but has failed grievously."

"I have been quite contented," said Lord Fawn;—"more than contented."

Phineas felt that he ought to give some special reason to Miss Effingham to account for his efforts to reach her, but yet he had nothing special to say. Had Lord Fawn not been there, he would immediately have told her that he was waiting for an answer to the question he had asked her in Saulsby Park, but he could hardly do this in presence of the noble Under-Secretary of State. She received him with her pleasant genial smile, looking exactly as she had looked when he had parted from her on the morning after their ride. She did not show any sign of anger, or even of indifference at his approach. But still it was almost necessary that he should account for his search of her. "I have so longed to hear from you how you got on at Loughlinter," he said.

"Yes,—yes; and I will tell you something of it some day, perhaps. Why do you not come to Lady Baldock's?"

"I did not even know that Lady Baldock was in town."

"You ought to have known. Of course she is in town. Where did you suppose I was living? Lord Fawn was there yesterday, and can tell you that my aunt is quite blooming."

"Lady Baldock is blooming," said Lord Fawn; "certainly blooming;—that is, if evergreens may be said to bloom."

"Evergreens do bloom, as well as spring plants, Lord Fawn. You come and see her, Mr. Finn;—only you must bring a little money with you for the Female Protestant Unmarried Women's Emigration Society. That is my aunt's present hobby, as Lord Fawn knows to his cost."

"I wish I may never spend half-a-sovereign worse."

"But it is a perilous affair for me, as my aunt wants me to go out as a sort of leading Protestant unmarried female emigrant pioneer myself."

"You don't mean that," said Lord Fawn, with much anxiety.

"Of course you'll go," said Phineas. "I should, if I were you."

"I am in doubt," said Violet.

"It is such a grand prospect," said he. "Such an opening in life. So much excitement, you know; and such a useful career."

"As if there were not plenty of opening here for Miss Effingham," said Lord Fawn, "and plenty of excitement."

"Do you think there is?" said Violet. "You are much more civil than Mr. Finn, I must say." Then Phineas began to hope that he need not be afraid of Lord Fawn. "What a happy man you were at dinner!" continued Violet, addressing herself to Phineas.

"I thought Lord Fawn was the happy man."

"You had Madame Max Goesler all to yourself for nearly two hours, and I suppose there was not a creature in the room who did not envy you. I don't doubt that ever so much interest was made with Lady Glencora as to taking Madame Max down to dinner. Lord Fawn, I know, intrigued."

"Miss Effingham, really I must—contradict you."

"And Barrington Erle begged for it as a particular favour. The Duke, with a sigh, owned that it was impossible, because of his cumbrous rank; and Mr. Gresham, when it was offered to him, declared that he was fatigued with the business of the House, and not up to the occasion. How much did she say to you; and what did she talk about?"

"The ballot chiefly,—that, and manhood suffrage."

"Ah! she said something more than that, I am sure. Madame Max Goesler never lets any man go without entrancing him. If you have anything near your heart, Mr. Finn, Madame Max Goesler touched it, I am sure." Now Phineas had two things near his heart,—political promotion and Violet Effingham,—and Madame Max Goesler had managed to touch them both. She had asked him respecting his journey to Blankenberg, and had touched him very nearly in reference to Miss Effingham. "You know Madame Max Goesler, of course?" said Violet to Lord Fawn.

"Oh yes, I know the lady;—that is, as well as other people do. No one, I take it, knows much of her; and it seems to me that the world is becoming tired of her. A mystery is good for nothing if it remains always a mystery."

"And it is good for nothing at all when it is found out," said Violet.

"And therefore it is that Madame Max Goesler is a bore," said Lord Fawn.

"You did not find her a bore?" said Violet. Then Phineas, choosing to oppose Lord Fawn as well as he could on that matter, as on every other, declared that he had found Madame Max Goesler most delightful. "And beautiful,—is she not?" said Violet.

"Beautiful!" exclaimed Lord Fawn.

"I think her very beautiful," said Phineas.

"So do I," said Violet. "And she is a dear ally of mine. We were a week together last winter, and swore an undying friendship. She told me ever so much about Mr. Goesler."

"But she told you nothing of her second husband?" said Lord Fawn.

"Now that you have run into scandal, I shall have done," said Violet.

Half an hour after this, when Phineas was preparing to fight his way out of the house, he was again close to Madame Max Goesler. He had not found a single moment in which to ask Violet for an answer to his old question, and was retiring from the field discomfited, but not dispirited. Lord Fawn, he thought, was not a serious obstacle in his way. Lady Laura had told him that there was no hope for him; but then Lady Laura's mind on that subject was, he thought, prejudiced. Violet Effingham certainly knew what were his wishes, and knowing them, smiled on him and was gracious to him. Would she do so if his pretensions were thoroughly objectionable to her?

"I saw that you were successful this evening," said Madame Max Goesler to him.

"I was not aware of any success."

"I call it great success to be able to make your way where you will through such a crowd as there is here. You seem to me to be so stout a cavalier that I shall ask you to find my servant, and bid him get my carriage. Will you mind?" Phineas, of course, declared that he would be delighted. "He is a German, and not in livery. But if somebody will call out, he will hear. He is very sharp, and much more attentive than your English footmen. An Englishman hardly ever makes a good servant."

"Is that a compliment to us Britons?"

"No, certainly not. If a man is a servant, he should be clever enough to be a good one." Phineas had now given the order for the carriage, and, having returned, was standing with Madame Max Goesler in the cloak-room. "After all, we are surely the most awkward people in the world," she said. "You know Lord Fawn, who was talking to Miss Effingham just now. You should have heard him trying to pay me a compliment before dinner. It was like a donkey walking a minuet, and yet they say he is a clever man and can make speeches." Could it be possible that Madame Max Goesler's ears were so sharp that she had heard the things which Lord Fawn had said of her?

"He is a well-informed man," said Phineas.

"For a lord, you mean," said Madame Max Goesler. "But he is an oaf, is he not? And yet they say he is to marry that girl."

"I do not think he will," said Phineas, stoutly.

"I hope not, with all my heart; and I hope that somebody else may,—unless somebody else should change his mind. Thank you; I am so much obliged to you. Mind you come and call on me,—193, Park Lane. I dare say you know the little cottage." Then he put Madame Max Goesler into her carriage, and walked away to his club.

CHAPTER XLII. Lady Baldock does not Send a Card to Phineas Finn

Lady Baldock's house in Berkeley Square was very stately,—a large house with five front windows in a row, and a big door, and a huge square hall, and a fat porter in a round-topped chair;—but it was dingy and dull, and could not have been painted for the last ten years, or furnished for the last twenty. Nevertheless, Lady Baldock had "evenings," and people went to them,—though not such a crowd of people as would go to the evenings of Lady Glencora. Now Mr. Phineas Finn had not been asked to the evenings of Lady Baldock for the present season, and the reason was after this wise.

"Yes, Mr. Finn," Lady Baldock had said to her daughter, who, early in the spring, was preparing the cards. "You may send one to Mr. Finn, certainly."

"I don't know that he is very nice," said Augusta Boreham, whose eyes at Saulsby had been sharper perhaps than her mother's, and who had her suspicions.

But Lady Baldock did not like interference from her daughter. "Mr. Finn, certainly," she continued. "They tell me that he is a very rising young man, and he sits for Lord Brentford's borough. Of course he is a Radical, but we cannot help that. All the rising young men are Radicals now. I thought him very civil at Saulsby."

"But, mamma—"

"Well!"

"Don't you think that he is a little free with Violet?"

"What on earth do you mean, Augusta?"

"Have you not fancied that he is—fond of her?"

"Good gracious, no!"

"I think he is. And I have sometimes fancied that she is fond of him, too."

"I don't believe a word of it, Augusta,—not a word. I should have seen it if it was so. I am very sharp in seeing such things. They never escape me. Even Violet would not be such a fool as that. Send him a card, and if he comes I shall soon see." Miss Boreham quite understood her mother, though she could never master her,—and the card was prepared. Miss Boreham could never master her mother by her own efforts; but it was, I think, by a little intrigue on her part that Lady Baldock was mastered, and, indeed, altogether cowed, in reference to our hero, and that this victory was gained on that very afternoon in time to prevent the sending of the card.

When the mother and daughter were at tea, before dinner, Lord Baldock came into the room, and, after having been patted and petted and praised by his mother, he took up all the cards out of a china bowl and ran his eyes over them. "Lord Fawn!" he said, "the greatest ass in all London! Lady Hartletop! you know she won't come." "I don't see why she shouldn't come," said Lady Baldock;—"a mere country clergyman's daughter!" "Julius Cæsar Conway;—a great friend of mine, and therefore he always blackballs my other friends at the club. Lord Chiltern; I thought you were at daggers drawn with Chiltern." "They say he is going to be reconciled to his father, Gustavus, and I do it for Lord Brentford's sake. And he won't come, so it does not signify. And I do believe that Violet has really refused him." "You are quite right about his not coming," said Lord Baldock, continuing to read the cards; "Chiltern certainly won't come. Count Sparrowsky;—I wonder what you know about Sparrowsky that you should ask him here." "He is asked about, Gustavus; he is indeed," pleaded Lady Baldock. "I believe that Sparrowsky is a penniless adventurer. Mr. Monk; well, he is a Cabinet Minister. Sir Gregory Greeswing; you mix your people nicely at any rate. Sir Gregory Greeswing is the most old-fashioned Tory in England." "Of course we are not political, Gustavus." "Phineas Finn. They come alternately,—one and one.

"Mr. Finn is asked everywhere, Gustavus."

"I don't doubt it. They say he is a very good sort of fellow. They say also that Violet has found that out as well as other people."

"What do you mean, Gustavus?"

"I mean that everybody is saying that this Phineas Finn is going to set himself up in the world by marrying your niece. He is quite right to try it on, if he has a chance."

"I don't think he would be right at all," said Lady Baldock, with much energy. "I think he would be wrong,—shamefully wrong. They say he is the son of an Irish doctor, and that he hasn't a shilling in the world."

"That is just why he would be right. What is such a man to do, but to marry money? He's a deuced good-looking fellow, too, and will be sure to do it."

"He should work for his money in the city, then, or somewhere there. But I don't believe it, Gustavus; I don't, indeed."

"Very well. I only tell you what I hear. The fact is that he and Chiltern have already quarrelled about her. If I were to tell you that they have been over to Holland together and fought a duel about her, you wouldn't believe that."

"Fought a duel about Violet! People don't fight duels now, and I should not believe it."

"Very well. Then send your card to Mr. Finn." And, so saying, Lord Baldock left the room.

Lady Baldock sat in silence for some time toasting her toes at the fire, and Augusta Boreham sat by, waiting for orders. She felt pretty nearly sure that new orders would be given if she did not herself interfere. "You had better put by that card for the present, my dear," said Lady Baldock at last. "I will make inquiries. I don't believe a word of what Gustavus has said. I don't think that even Violet is such a fool as that. But if rash and ill-natured people have spoken of it, it may be as well to be careful."

"It is always well to be careful;—is it not, mamma?"

"Not but what I think it very improper that these things should be said about a young woman; and as for the story of the duel, I don't believe a word of it. It is absurd. I dare say that Gustavus invented it at the moment, just to amuse himself."

The card of course was not sent, and Lady Baldock at any rate put so much faith in her son's story as to make her feel it to be her duty to interrogate her niece on the subject. Lady Baldock at this period of her life was certainly not free from fear of Violet Effingham. In the numerous encounters which took place between them, the aunt seldom gained that amount of victory which would have completely satisfied her spirit. She longed to be dominant over her niece as she was dominant over her daughter; and when she found that she missed such supremacy, she longed to tell Violet to depart from out her borders, and be no longer niece of hers. But had she ever done so, Violet would have gone at the instant, and then terrible things would have followed. There is a satisfaction in turning out of doors a nephew or niece who is pecuniarily dependent, but when the youthful relative is richly endowed, the satisfaction is much diminished. It is the duty of a guardian, no doubt, to look after the ward; but if this cannot be done, the ward's money should at least be held with as close a fist as possible. But Lady Baldock, though she knew that she would be sorely wounded, poked about on her old body with the sharp lances of disobedience, and struck with the cruel swords of satire, if she took upon herself to scold or even to question Violet, nevertheless would not abandon the pleasure of lecturing and teaching. "It is my duty," she would say to herself, "and though it be taken in a bad spirit, I will always perform my duty." So she performed her duty, and asked Violet Effingham some few questions respecting Phineas Finn. "My dear," she said, "do you remember meeting a Mr. Finn at Saulsby?"

"A Mr. Finn, aunt! Why, he is a particular friend of mine. Of course I do, and he was at Saulsby. I have met him there more than once. Don't you remember that we were riding about together?"

"I remember that he was there, certainly; but I did not know that he was a special—friend."

"Most especial, aunt. A 1, I may say;—among young men, I mean."

Lady Baldock was certainly the most indiscreet of old women in such a matter as this, and Violet the most provoking of young ladies. Lady Baldock, believing that there was something to fear,—as, indeed, there was, much to fear,—should have been content to destroy the card, and to keep the young lady away from the young gentleman, if such keeping away was possible to her. But Miss Effingham was certainly very wrong to speak of any young man as being A 1. Fond as I am of Miss Effingham, I cannot justify her, and must acknowledge that she used the most offensive phrase she could find, on purpose to annoy her aunt.

"Violet," said Lady Baldock, bridling up, "I never heard such a word before from the lips of a young lady."

"Not as A 1? I thought it simply meant very good."

"A 1 is a nobleman," said Lady Baldock.

"No, aunt;—A 1 is a ship,—a ship that is very good," said Violet.

"And do you mean to say that Mr. Finn is,—is,—is,—very good?"

"Yes, indeed. You ask Lord Brentford, and Mr. Kennedy. You know he saved poor Mr. Kennedy from being throttled in the streets."

"That has nothing to do with it. A policeman might have done that."

"Then he would have been A 1 of policemen,—though A 1 does not mean a policeman."

"He would have done his duty, and so perhaps did Mr. Finn."

"Of course he did, aunt. It couldn't have been his duty to stand by and see Mr. Kennedy throttled. And he nearly killed one of the men, and took the other prisoner with his own hands. And he made a beautiful speech the other day. I read every word of it. I am so glad he's a Liberal. I do like young men to be Liberals." Now Lord Baldock was a Tory, as had been all the Lord Baldocks,—since the first who had been bought over from the Whigs in the time of George III at the cost of a barony.

"You have nothing to do with politics, Violet."

"Why shouldn't I have something to do with politics, aunt?"

"And I must tell you that your name is being very unpleasantly mentioned in connection with that of this young man because of your indiscretion."

"What indiscretion?" Violet, as she made her demand for a more direct accusation, stood quite upright before her aunt, looking the old woman full in the face,—almost with her arms akimbo.

"Calling him A 1, Violet."

"People have been talking about me and Mr. Finn, because I just now, at this very moment, called him A 1 to you! If you want to scold me about anything, aunt, do find out something less ridiculous than that."

"It was most improper language,—and if you used it to me, I am sure you would to others."

"To what others?"

"To Mr. Finn,—and those sort of people."

"Call Mr. Finn A 1 to his face! Well,—upon my honour I don't know why I should not. Lord Chiltern says he rides beautifully, and if we were talking about riding I might do so."

"You have no business to talk to Lord Chiltern about Mr. Finn at all."

"Have I not? I thought that perhaps the one sin might palliate the other. You know, aunt, no young lady, let her be ever so ill-disposed, can marry two objectionable young men,—at the same time."

"I said nothing about your marrying Mr. Finn."

"Then, aunt, what did you mean?"

"I meant that you should not allow yourself to be talked of with an adventurer, a young man without a shilling, a person who has come from nobody knows where in the bogs of Ireland."

"But you used to ask him here."

"Yes,—as long as he knew his place. But I shall not do so again. And I must beg you to be circumspect."

"My dear aunt, we may as well understand each other. I will not be circumspect, as you call it. And if Mr. Finn asked me to marry him to-morrow, and if I liked him well enough, I would take him,—even though he had been dug right out of a bog. Not only because I liked him,—mind! If I were unfortunate enough to like a man who was nothing, I would refuse him in spite of my liking,—because he was nothing. But this young man is not nothing. Mr. Finn is a fine fellow, and if there were no other reason to prevent my marrying him than his being the son of a doctor, and coming out of the bogs, that would not do so. Now I have made a clean breast to you as regards Mr. Finn; and if you do not like what I've said, aunt, you must acknowledge that you have brought it on yourself."

Lady Baldock was left for a time speechless. But no card was sent to Phineas Finn.

CHAPTER XLIII. Promotion

Phineas got no card from Lady Baldock, but one morning he received a note from Lord Brentford which was of more importance to him than any card could have been. At this time, bit by bit, the Reform Bill of the day had nearly made its way through the committee, but had been so mutilated as to be almost impossible of recognition by its progenitors. And there was still a clause or two as to the rearrangement of seats, respecting which it was known that there would be a combat,—probably combats,—carried on after the internecine fashion. There was a certain clipping of counties to be done, as to which it was said that Mr. Daubeny had declared that he would not yield till he was made to do so by the brute force of majorities;—and there was another clause for the drafting of certain superfluous members from little boroughs, and bestowing them on populous towns at which they were much wanted, respecting which Mr. Turnbull had proclaimed that the clause as it now stood was a faineant clause, capable of doing, and intended to do, no good in the proper direction; a clause put into the bill to gull ignorant folk who had not eyes enough to recognise the fact that it was faineant; a make-believe clause,—so said Mr. Turnbull,—to be detested on that account by every true reformer worse than the old Philistine bonds and Tory figments of representation, as to which there was at least no hypocritical pretence of popular fitness. Mr. Turnbull had been very loud and very angry,—had talked much of demonstrations among the people, and had almost threatened the House. The House in its present mood did not fear any demonstrations,—but it did fear that Mr. Turnbull might help Mr. Daubeny, and that Mr. Daubeny might help Mr. Turnbull. It was now May,—the middle of May,—and ministers, who had been at work on their Reform Bill ever since the beginning of the session, were becoming weary of it. And then, should these odious clauses escape the threatened Turnbull-Daubeny alliance,—then there was the House of Lords! "What a pity we can't pass our bills at the Treasury, and have done with them!" said Laurence Fitzgibbon. "Yes, indeed," replied Mr. Ratler. "For myself, I was never so tired of a session in my life. I wouldn't go through it again to be made,—no, not to be made Chancellor of the Exchequer."

Lord Brentford's note to Phineas Finn was as follows:—

House of Lords,
16th May, 186—.

My Dear Mr. Finn,

You are no doubt aware that Lord Bosanquet's death has taken Mr. Mottram into the Upper House, and that as he was Under-Secretary for the Colonies, and as the Under-Secretary must be in the Lower House, the vacancy must be filled up.

The heart of Phineas Finn at this moment was almost in his mouth. Not only to be selected for political employment, but to be selected at once for an office so singularly desirable! Under-Secretaries, he fancied, were paid two thousand a year. What would Mr. Low say now? But his great triumph soon received a check. "Mr. Mildmay has spoken to me on the subject," continued the letter, "and informs me that he has offered the place at the colonies to his old supporter, Mr. Laurence Fitzgibbon." Laurence Fitzgibbon!

I am inclined to think that he could not have done better, as Mr. Fitzgibbon has shown great zeal for his party. This will vacate the Irish seat at the Treasury Board, and I am commissioned by Mr. Mildmay to offer it to you. Perhaps you will do me the pleasure of calling on me to-morrow between the hours of eleven and twelve.

Yours very sincerely,   Brentford.

Phineas was himself surprised to find that his first feeling on reading this letter was one of dissatisfaction. Here were his golden hopes about to be realised,—hopes as to the realisation of which he had been quite despondent twelve months ago,—and yet he was uncomfortable because he was to be postponed to Laurence Fitzgibbon. Had the new Under-Secretary been a man whom he had not known, whom he had not learned to look down upon as inferior to himself, he would not have minded it,—would have been full of joy at the promotion proposed for himself. But Laurence Fitzgibbon was such a poor creature, that the idea of filling a place from which Laurence had risen was distasteful to him. "It seems to be all a matter of favour and convenience," he said to himself, "without any reference to the service." His triumph would have been so complete had Mr. Mildmay allowed him to go into the higher place at one leap. Other men who had made themselves useful had done so. In the first hour after receiving Lord Brentford's letter, the idea of becoming a Lord of the Treasury was almost displeasing to him. He had an idea that junior lordships of the Treasury were generally bestowed on young members whom it was convenient to secure, but who were not good at doing anything. There was a moment in which he thought that he would refuse to be made a junior lord.

But during the night cooler reflections told him that he had been very wrong. He had taken up politics with the express desire of getting his foot upon a rung of the ladder of promotion, and now, in his third session, he was about to be successful. Even as a junior lord he would have a thousand a year; and how long might he have sat in chambers, and have wandered about Lincoln's Inn, and have loitered in the courts striving to look as though he had business, before he would have earned a thousand a year! Even as a junior lord he could make himself useful, and when once he should be known to be a good working man, promotion would come to him. No ladder can be mounted without labour; but this ladder was now open above his head, and he already had his foot upon it.

At half-past eleven he was with Lord Brentford, who received him with the blandest smile and a pressure of the hand which was quite cordial. "My dear Finn," he said, "this gives me the most sincere pleasure,—the greatest pleasure in the world. Our connection together at Loughton of course makes it doubly agreeable to me."

"I cannot be too grateful to you, Lord Brentford."

"No, no; no, no. It is all your own doing. When Mr. Mildmay asked me whether I did not think you the most promising of the young members on our side in your House, I certainly did say that I quite concurred. But I should be taking too much on myself, I should be acting dishonestly, if I were to allow you to imagine that it was my proposition. Had he asked me to recommend, I should have named you; that I say frankly. But he did not. He did not. Mr. Mildmay named you himself. 'Do you think,' he said, 'that your friend Finn would join us at the Treasury?' I told him that I did think so. 'And do you not think,' said he, 'that it would be a useful appointment?' Then I ventured to say that I had no doubt whatever on that point;—that I knew you well enough to feel confident that you would lend a strength to the Liberal Government. Then there were a few words said about your seat, and I was commissioned to write to you. That was all."

Phineas was grateful, but not too grateful, and bore himself very well in the interview. He explained to Lord Brentford that of course it was his object to serve the country,—and to be paid for his services,—and that he considered himself to be very fortunate to be selected so early in his career for parliamentary place. He would endeavour to do his duty, and could safely say of himself that he did not wish to eat the bread of idleness. As he made this assertion, he thought of Laurence Fitzgibbon. Laurence Fitzgibbon had eaten the bread of idleness, and yet he was promoted. But Phineas said nothing to Lord Brentford about his idle friend. When he had made his little speech he asked a question about the borough.

"I have already ventured to write a letter to my agent at Loughton, telling him that you have accepted office, and that you will be shortly there again. He will see Shortribs and arrange it. But if I were you I should write to Shortribs and to

Grating,—after I had seen Mr. Mildmay. Of course you will not mention my name," And the Earl looked very grave as he uttered this caution.

"Of course I will not," said Phineas.

"I do not think you'll find any difficulty about the seat," said the peer. "There never has been any difficulty at Loughton yet. I must say that for them. And if we can scrape through with Clause 72 we shall be all right;—shall we not?" This was the clause as to which so violent an opposition was expected from Mr. Turnbull,—a clause as to which Phineas himself had felt that he would hardly know how to support the Government, in the event of the committee being pressed to a division upon it. Could he, an ardent reformer, a reformer at heart,—could he say that such a borough as Loughton should be spared;—that the arrangement by which Shortribs and Grating had sent him to Parliament, in obedience to Lord Brentford's orders, was in due accord with the theory of a representative legislature? In what respect had Gatton and Old Sarum been worse than Loughton? Was he not himself false to his principle in sitting for such a borough as Loughton? He had spoken to Mr. Monk, and Mr. Monk had told him that Rome was not built in a day,—and had told him also that good things were most valued and were more valuable when they came by instalments. But then Mr. Monk himself enjoyed the satisfaction of sitting for a popular Constituency. He was not personally pricked in the conscience by his own parliamentary position. Now, however, —now that Phineas had consented to join the Government, any such considerations as these must be laid aside. He could no longer be a free agent, or even a free thinker. He had been quite aware of this, and had taught himself to understand that members of Parliament in the direct service of the Government were absolved from the necessity of free-thinking. Individual free-thinking was incompatible with the position of a member of the Government, and unless such abnegation were practised, no government would be possible. It was of course a man's duty to bind himself together with no other men but those with whom, on matters of general policy, he could agree heartily;—but having found that he could so agree, he knew that it would be his duty as a subaltern to vote as he was directed. It would trouble his conscience less to sit for Loughton and vote for an objectionable clause as a member of the Government, than it would have done to give such a vote as an independent member. In so resolving, he thought that he was simply acting in accordance with the acknowledged rules of parliamentary government. And therefore, when Lord Brentford spoke of Clause 72, he could answer pleasantly, "I think we shall carry it; and, you see, in getting it through committee, if we can carry it by one, that is as good as a hundred. That's the comfort of close-fighting in committee. In the open House we are almost as much beaten by a narrow majority as by a vote against us."

"Just so; just so," said Lord Brentford, delighted to see that his young pupil,—as he regarded him,—understood so well the system of parliamentary management. "By-the-bye, Finn, have you seen Chiltern lately?"

"Not quite lately," said Phineas, blushing up to his eyes.

"Or heard from him?"

"No;—nor heard from him. When last I heard of him he was in Brussels."

"Ah,—yes; he is somewhere on the Rhine now. I thought that as you were so intimate, perhaps you corresponded with him. Have you heard that we have arranged about Lady Laura's money?"

"I have heard. Lady Laura has told me."

"I wish he would return," said Lord Brentford sadly,—almost solemnly. "As that great difficulty is over, I would receive him willingly, and make my house pleasant to him, if I can do so. I am most anxious that he should settle, and marry. Could you not write to him?" Phineas, not daring to tell Lord Brentford that he had quarrelled with Lord Chiltern,—feeling that if he did so everything would go wrong,—said that he would write to Lord Chiltern.

As he went away he felt that he was bound to get an answer from Violet Effingham. If it should be necessary, he was willing to break with Lord Brentford on that matter,—even though such breaking should lose him his borough and his place;—but not on any other matter.

CHAPTER XLIV. Phineas and his Friends

Our hero's friends were, I think, almost more elated by our hero's promotion than was our hero himself. He never told himself that it was a great thing to be a junior lord of the Treasury, though he acknowledged to himself that to have made a successful beginning was a very great thing. But his friends were loud in their congratulations,—or condolements as the case might be.

He had his interview with Mr. Mildmay, and, after that, one of his first steps was to inform Mrs. Bunce that he must change his lodgings. "The truth is, Mrs. Bunce, not that I want anything better; but that a better position will be advantageous to me, and that I can afford to pay for it." Mrs. Bunce acknowledged the truth of the argument, with her apron up to her eyes. "I've got to be so fond of looking after you, Mr. Finn! I have indeed," said Mrs. Bunce. "It is not just what you pays like, because another party will pay as much. But we've got so used to you, Mr. Finn,—haven't we?" Mrs. Bunce was probably not aware herself that the comeliness of her lodger had pleased her feminine eye, and touched her feminine heart. Had anybody said that Mrs. Bunce was in love with Phineas, the scandal would have been monstrous. And yet it was so,—after a fashion. And Bunce knew it,—after his fashion. "Don't be such an old fool," he said, "crying after him because he's six foot high." "I ain't crying after him because he's six foot high," whined the poor woman;—"but one does like old faces better than new, and a gentleman about one's place is pleasant." "Gentleman be d—d," said Bunce. But his anger was excited, not by his wife's love for Phineas, but by the use of an objectionable word.

Bunce himself had been on very friendly terms with Phineas, and they two had had many discussions on matters of politics, Bunce taking up the cudgels always for Mr. Turnbull, and generally slipping away gradually into some account of his own martyrdom. For he had been a martyr, having failed in obtaining any redress against the policeman who had imprisoned him so wrongfully. The *People's Banner* had fought for him manfully, and therefore there was a little disagreement between him and Phineas on the subject of that great organ of public opinion. And as Mr. Bunce thought that his lodger was very wrong to sit for Lord Brentford's borough, subjects were sometimes touched which were a little galling to Phineas.

Touching this promotion, Bunce had nothing but condolement to offer to the new junior lord. "Oh yes," said he, in answer to an argument from Phineas, "I suppose there must be lords, as you call 'em; though for the matter of that I can't see as they is of any mortal use."

"Wouldn't you have the Government carried on?"

"Government! Well; I suppose there must be government. But the less of it the better. I'm not against government;—nor yet against laws, Mr. Finn; though the less of them, too, the better. But what does these lords do in the Government? Lords indeed! I'll tell you what they do, Mr. Finn. They wotes; that's what they do! They wotes hard; black or white, white or black. Ain't that true? When you're a 'lord,' will you be able to wote against Mr. Mildmay to save your very soul?"

"If it comes to be a question of soul-saving, Mr. Bunce, I shan't save my place at the expense of my conscience."

"Not if you knows it, you mean. But the worst of it is that a man gets so thick into the mud that he don't know whether he's dirty or clean. You'll have to wote as you're told, and of course you'll think it's right enough. Ain't you been among Parliament gents long enough to know that that's the way it goes?"

"You think no honest man can be a member of the Government?"

"I don't say that, but I think honesty's a deal easier away from 'em. The fact is, Mr. Finn, it's all wrong with us yet, and will be till we get it nigher to the great American model. If a poor man gets into Parliament,—you'll excuse me, Mr. Finn, but I calls you a poor man."

"Certainly,—as a member of Parliament I am a very poor man."

"Just so,—and therefore what do you do? You goes and lays yourself out for government! I'm not saying as how you're anyways wrong. A man has to live. You has winning ways, and a good physiognomy of your own, and are as big as a life-guardsman." Phineas as he heard this doubtful praise laughed and blushed. "Very well; you makes your way with the big wigs, lords and earls and them like, and you gets returned for a rotten borough;—you'll excuse me, but that's about it, ain't it? —and then you goes in for government! A man may have a mission to govern, such as Washington and Cromwell and the like o' them. But when I hears of Mr. Fitzgibbon a-governing, why then I says,—d—n it all."

"There must be good and bad you know."

"We've got to change a deal yet, Mr. Finn, and we'll do it. When a young man as has liberal feelings gets into Parliament, he shouldn't be snapped up and brought into the governing business just because he's poor and wants a salary. They don't do it that way in the States; and they won't do it that way here long. It's the system as I hates, and not you, Mr. Finn. Well, good-bye, sir. I hope you'll like the governing business, and find it suits your health."

These condolements from Mr. Bunce were not pleasant, but they set him thinking. He felt assured that Bunce and Quintus Slide and Mr. Turnbull were wrong. Bunce was ignorant. Quintus Slide was dishonest. Turnbull was greedy of popularity. For himself, he thought that as a young man he was fairly well informed. He knew that he meant to be true in his vocation. And he was quite sure that the object nearest to his heart in politics was not self-aggrandisement, but the welfare of the people in general. And yet he could not but agree with Bunce that there was something wrong. When such men as Laurence Fitzgibbon were called upon to act as governors, was it not to be expected that the ignorant but still intelligent Bunces of the population should—"d—n it all"?

On the evening of that day he went up to Mrs. Low's, very sure that he should receive some encouragement from her and from her husband. She had been angry with him because he had put himself into a position in which money must be spent and none could be made. The Lows, especially Mrs. Low, had refused to believe that any success was within his reach. Now that he had succeeded, now that he was in receipt of a salary on which he could live and save money, he would be sure of sympathy from his old friends the Lows!

But Mrs. Low was as severe upon him as Mr. Bunce had been, and even from Mr. Low he could extract no real comfort. "Of course I congratulate you," said Mr. Low coldly.

"And you, Mrs. Low?"

"Well, you know, Mr. Finn, I think you have begun at the wrong end. I thought so before, and I think so still. I suppose I ought not to say so to a Lord of the Treasury, but if you ask me, what can I do?"

"Speak the truth out, of course."

"Exactly. That's what I must do. Well, the truth is, Mr. Finn, that I do not think it is a very good opening for a young man to be made what they call a Lord of the Treasury,—unless he has got a private fortune, you know, to support that kind of life."

"You see, Phineas, a ministry is such an uncertain thing," said Mr. Low.

"Of course it's uncertain;—but as I did go into the House, it's something to have succeeded."

"If you call that success," said Mrs. Low.

"You did intend to go on with your profession," said Mr. Low. He could not tell them that he had changed his mind, and that he meant to marry Violet Effingham, who would much prefer a parliamentary life for her husband to that of a working barrister. "I suppose that is all given up now," continued Mr. Low.

"Just for the present," said Phineas.

"Yes;—and for ever I fear," said Mrs. Low, "You'll never go back to real work after frittering away your time as a Lord of the Treasury. What sort of work must it be when just anybody can do it that it suits them to lay hold of? But of course a thousand a year is something, though a man may have it for only six months."

It came out in the course of the evening that Mr. Low was going to stand for the borough vacated by Mr. Mottram, at which it was considered that the Conservatives might possibly prevail. "You see, after all, Phineas," said Mr. Low, "that I am following your steps."

"Ah; you are going into the House in the course of your profession."

"Just so," said Mrs. Low.

"And are taking the first step towards being a Tory Attorney-General."

"That's as may be," said Mr. Low. "But it's the kind of thing a man does after twenty years of hard work. For myself, I really don't care much whether I succeed or fail. I should like to live to be a Vice-Chancellor. I don't mind saying as much as that to you. But I'm not at all sure that Parliament is the best way to the Equity Bench."

"But it is a grand thing to get into Parliament when you do it by means of your profession," said Mrs. Low.

Soon after that Phineas took his departure from the house, feeling sore and unhappy. But on the next morning he was received in Grosvenor Place with an amount of triumph which went far to compensate him. Lady Laura had written to him to call there, and on his arrival he found both Violet Effingham and Madame Max Goesler with his friend. When Phineas entered the room his first feeling was one of intense joy at seeing that Violet Effingham was present there. Then there was one of surprise that Madame Max Goesler should make one of the little party. Lady Laura had told him at Mr. Palliser's dinner-party that they, in Portman Square, had not as yet advanced far enough to receive Madame Max Goesler,—and yet here was the lady in Mr. Kennedy's drawing-room. Now Phineas would have thought it more likely that he should find her in Portman Square than in Grosvenor Place. The truth was that Madame Goesler had been brought by Miss Effingham,—with the consent, indeed, of Lady Laura, but with a consent given with much of hesitation. "What are you afraid of?" Violet had asked. "I am afraid of nothing," Lady Laura had answered; "but one has to choose one's acquaintance in accordance with rules which one doesn't lay down very strictly." "She is a clever woman," said Violet, "and everybody likes her; but if you think Mr. Kennedy would object, of course you are right." Then Lady Laura had consented, telling herself that it was not necessary that she should ask her husband's approval as to every new acquaintance she might form. At the same time Violet had been told that Phineas would be there, and so the party had been made up.

"'See the conquering hero comes,' said Violet in her cheeriest voice.

"I am so glad that Mr. Finn has been made a lord of something," said Madame Max Goesler. "I had the pleasure of a long political discussion with him the other night, and I quite approve of him."

"We are so much gratified, Mr. Finn," said Lady Laura. "Mr. Kennedy says that it is the best appointment they could have made, and papa is quite proud about it."

"You are Lord Brentford's member; are you not?" asked Madame Max Goesler. This was a question which Phineas did not quite like, and which he was obliged to excuse by remembering that the questioner had lived so long out of England as to be probably ignorant of the myths, and theories, and system, and working of the British Constitution. Violet Effingham, little as she knew of politics, would never have asked a question so imprudent.

But the question was turned off, and Phineas, with an easy grace, submitted himself to be petted, and congratulated, and purred over, and almost caressed by the three ladies, Their good-natured enthusiasm was at any rate better than the satire of Bunce, or the wisdom of Mrs. Low. Lady Laura had no misgivings as to Phineas being fit for governing, and Violet Effingham said nothing as to the short-lived tenure of ministers. Madame Max Goesler, though she had asked an indiscreet question, thoroughly appreciated the advantage of Government pay, and the prestige of Government power. "You are a lord now," she said, speaking, as was customary with her, with the slightest possible foreign accent, "and you will be a president soon, and then perhaps a secretary. The order of promotion seems odd, but I am told it is very pleasant."

"It is pleasant to succeed, of course," said Phineas, "let the success be ever so little."

"We knew you would succeed," said Lady Laura. "We were quite sure of it. Were we not, Violet?"

"You always said so, my dear. For myself I do not venture to have an opinion on such matters. Will you always have to go to that big building in the corner, Mr. Finn, and stay there from ten till four? Won't that be a bore?"

"We have a half-holiday on Saturday, you know," said Phineas.

"And do the Lords of the Treasury have to take care of the money?" asked Madame Max Goesler.

"Only their own; and they generally fail in doing that," said Phineas.

He sat there for a considerable time, wondering whether Mr. Kennedy would come in, and wondering also as to what Mr. Kennedy would say to Madame Max Goesler when he did come in. He knew that it was useless for him to expect any opportunity, then or there, of being alone for a moment with Violet Effingham. His only chance in that direction would be in some crowded room, at some ball at which he might ask her to dance with him; but it seemed that fate was very unkind to him, and that no such chance came in his way. Mr. Kennedy did not appear, and Madame Max Goesler with Violet went away, leaving Phineas still sitting with Lady Laura. Each of them said a kind word to him as they went. "I don't know whether I may dare to expect that a Lord of the Treasury will come and see me?" said Madame Max Goesler. Then Phineas made a second promise that he would call in Park Lane. Violet blushed as she remembered that she could not ask him to call at Lady Baldock's. "Good-bye, Mr. Finn," she said, giving him her hand. "I'm so very glad that they have chosen you; and I do hope that, as Madame Max says, they'll make you a secretary and a president, and everything else very quickly,—till it will come to your turn to be making other people." "He is very nice," said Madame Goesler to Violet as she took her place in the carriage. "He bears being petted and spoilt without being either awkward or conceited." "On the whole, he is rather nice," said Violet; "only he has not got a shilling in the world, and has to make himself before he will be anybody." "He must marry money, of course," said Madame Max Goesler.

"I hope you are contented?" said Lady Laura, rising from her chair and coming opposite to him as soon as they were alone.

"Of course I am contented."

"I was not,—when I first heard of it. Why did they promote that empty-headed countryman of yours to a place for which he was quite unfit? I was not contented. But then I am more ambitious for you than you are for yourself." He sat without answering her for awhile, and she stood waiting for his reply. "Have you nothing to say to me?" she asked.

"I do not know what to say. When I think of it all, I am lost in amazement. You tell me that you are not contented;—that you are ambitious for me. Why is it that you should feel any interest in the matter?"

"Is it not reasonable that we should be interested for our friends?"

"But when you and I last parted here in this room you were hardly my friend."

"Was I not? You wrong me there;—very deeply."

"I told you what was my ambition, and you resented it," said Phineas.

"I think I said that I could not help you, and I think I said also that I thought you would fail. I do not know that I showed much resentment. You see, I told her that you were here, that she might come and meet you. You know that I wished my brother should succeed. I wished it before I ever knew you. You cannot expect that I should change my wishes."

"But if he cannot succeed," pleaded Phineas.

"Who is to say that? Has a woman never been won by devotion and perseverance? Besides, how can I wish to see you go on with a suit which must sever you from my father, and injure your political prospects;—perhaps fatally injure them? It seems to me now that my father is almost the only man in London who has not heard of this duel."

"Of course he will hear of it. I have half made up my mind to tell him myself."

"Do not do that, Mr. Finn. There can be no reason for it. But I did not ask you to come here to-day to talk to you about Oswald or Violet. I have given you my advice about that, and I can do no more."

"Lady Laura, I cannot take it. It is out of my power to take it."

"Very well. The matter shall be what you members of Parliament call an open question between us. When papa asked you to accept this place at the Treasury, did it ever occur to you to refuse it?"

"It did;—for half an hour or so."

"I hoped you would,—and yet I knew that I was wrong. I thought that you should count yourself to be worth more than that, and that you should, as it were, assert yourself. But then it is so difficult to draw the line between proper self-assertion and proper self-denial;—to know how high to go up the table, and how low to go down. I do not doubt that you have been right,—only make them understand that you are not as other junior lords;—that you have been willing to be a junior lord, or anything else for a purpose; but that the purpose is something higher than that of fetching and carrying in Parliament for Mr. Mildmay and Mr. Palliser."

"I hope in time to get beyond fetching and carrying," said Phineas.

"Of course you will; and knowing that, I am glad that you are in office. I suppose there will be no difficulty about Loughton."

Then Phineas laughed. "I hear," said he, "that Mr. Quintus Slide, of the *People's Banner*, has already gone down to canvass the electors."

"Mr. Quintus Slide! To canvass the electors of Loughton!" and Lady Laura drew herself up and spoke of this unseemly intrusion on her father's borough, as though the vulgar man who had been named had forced his way into the very drawing-room in Portman Square. At that moment Mr. Kennedy came in. "Do you hear what Mr. Finn tells me?" she said. "He has heard that Mr. Quintus Slide has gone down to Loughton to stand against him."

"And why not?" said Mr. Kennedy.

"My dear!" ejaculated Lady Laura.

"Mr. Quintus Slide will no doubt lose his time and his money;—but he will gain the prestige of having stood for a borough, which will be something for him on the staff of the *People's Banner*," said Mr. Kennedy.

"He will get that horrid man Vellum to propose him," said Lady Laura.

"Very likely," said Mr. Kennedy. "And the less any of us say about it the better. Finn, my dear fellow, I congratulate you heartily. Nothing for a long time has given me greater pleasure than hearing of your appointment. It is equally honourable to yourself and to Mr. Mildmay. It is a great step to have gained so early."

Phineas, as he thanked his friend, could not help asking himself what his friend had done to be made a Cabinet Minister. Little as he, Phineas, himself had done in the House in his two sessions and a half, Mr. Kennedy had hardly done more in his fifteen or twenty. But then Mr. Kennedy was possessed of almost miraculous wealth, and owned half a county, whereas he, Phineas, owned almost nothing at all. Of course no Prime Minister would offer a junior lordship at the Treasury to a man with £30,000 a year. Soon after this Phineas took his leave. "I think he will do well," said Mr. Kennedy to his wife.

"I am sure he will do well," replied Lady Laura, almost scornfully.

"He is not quite such a black swan with me as he is with you; but still I think he will succeed, if he takes care of himself. It is astonishing how that absurd story of his duel with Chiltern has got about."

"It is impossible to prevent people talking," said Lady Laura.

"I suppose there was some quarrel, though neither of them will tell you. They say it was about Miss Effingham. I should hardly think that Finn could have any hopes in that direction."

"Why should he not have hopes?"

"Because he has neither position, nor money, nor birth," said Mr. Kennedy.

"He is a gentleman." said Lady Laura; "and I think he has position. I do not see why he should not ask any girl to marry him."

"There is no understanding you, Laura," said Mr. Kennedy, angrily. "I thought you had quite other hopes about Miss Effingham."

"So I have; but that has nothing to do with it. You spoke of Mr. Finn as though he would be guilty of some crime were he to ask Violet Effingham to be his wife. In that I disagree with you. Mr. Finn is—"

"You will make me sick of the name of Mr. Finn."

"I am sorry that I offend you by my gratitude to a man who saved your life." Mr. Kennedy shook his head. He knew that the argument used against him was false, but he did not know how to show that he knew that it was false. "Perhaps I had better not mention his name any more," continued Lady Laura.

"Nonsense!"

"I quite agree with you that it is nonsense, Robert."

"All I mean to say is, that if you go on as you do, you will turn his head and spoil him. Do you think I do not know what is going on among you?"

"And what is going on among us,—as you call it?"

"You are taking this young man up and putting him on a pedestal and worshipping him, just because he is well-looking, and rather clever and decently behaved. It's always the way with women who have nothing to do, and who cannot be made to understand that they should have duties. They cannot live without some kind of idolatry."

"Have I neglected my duty to you, Robert?"

"Yes,—you know you have;—in going to those receptions at your father's house on Sundays."

"What has that to do with Mr. Finn?"

"Psha!"

"I begin to think I had better tell Mr. Finn not to come here any more, since his presence is disagreeable to you. All the world knows how great is the service he did you, and it will seem to be very ridiculous. People will say all manner of things; but anything will be better than that you should go on as you have done,—accusing your wife of idolatry towards—a young man, because—he is—well-looking."

"I never said anything of the kind."

"You did, Robert."

"I did not. I did not speak more of you than of a lot of others."

"You accused me personally, saying that because of my idolatry I had neglected my duty; but really you made such a jumble of it all, with papa's visitors, and Sunday afternoons, that I cannot follow what was in your mind."

Then Mr. Kennedy stood for awhile, collecting his thoughts, so that he might unravel the jumble, if that were possible to him; but finding that it was not possible, he left the room, and closed the door behind him.

Then Lady Laura was left alone to consider the nature of the accusation which her husband had brought against her; or the nature rather of the accusation which she had chosen to assert that her husband had implied. For in her heart she knew that he had made no such accusation, and had intended to make none such. The idolatry of which he had spoken was the idolatry which a woman might show to her cat, her dog, her picture, her china, her furniture, her carriage and horses, or her pet maid-servant. Such was the idolatry of which Mr. Kennedy had spoken;—but was there no other worship in her heart, worse, more pernicious than that, in reference to this young man?

She had schooled herself about him very severely, and had come to various resolutions. She had found out and confessed to herself that she did not, and could not, love her husband. She had found out and confessed to herself that she did love, and could not help loving, Phineas Finn. Then she had resolved to banish him from her presence, and had gone the length of telling him so. After that she had perceived that she had been wrong, and had determined to meet him as she met other men,—and to conquer her love. Then, when this could not be done, when something almost like idolatry grew upon her, she determined that it should be the idolatry of friendship, that she would not sin even in thought, that there should be nothing in her heart of which she need be ashamed;—but that the one great object and purport of her life should be the promotion of this friend's welfare. She had just begun to love after this fashion, had taught herself to believe that she might combine something of the pleasure of idolatry towards her friend with a full complement of duty towards her husband, when Phineas came to her with his tale of love for Violet Effingham. The lesson which she got then was a very rough one,—so hard that at first she could not bear it. Her anger at his love for her brother's wished-for bride was lost in her dismay that Phineas should love any one after having once loved her. But by sheer force of mind she had conquered that dismay, that feeling of desolation at her heart, and had almost taught herself to hope that Phineas might succeed with Violet. He wished it,—and why should he not have what he wished,—he, whom she so fondly idolised? It was not his fault that he and she were not man and wife. She had chosen to arrange it otherwise, and was she not bound to assist him now in the present object of his reasonable wishes? She had got over in her heart that difficulty about her brother, but she could not quite conquer the other difficulty. She could not bring herself to plead his cause with Violet. She had not brought herself as yet to do it.

And now she was accused of idolatry for Phineas by her husband,—she with "a lot of others," in which lot Violet was of course included. Would it not be better that they two should be brought together? Would not her friend's husband still be her friend? Would she not then forget to love him? Would she not then be safer than she was now?

As she sat alone struggling with her difficulties, she had not as yet forgotten to love him,—nor was she as yet safe.

CHAPTER XLV. Miss Effingham's Four Lovers

One morning early in June Lady Laura called at Lady Baldock's house and asked for Miss Effingham. The servant was showing her into the large drawing-room, when she again asked specially for Miss Effingham. "I think Miss Effingham is there," said the man, opening the door. Miss Effingham was not there. Lady Baldock was sitting all alone, and Lady Laura perceived that she had been caught in the net which she specially wished to avoid. Now Lady Baldock had not actually or openly quarrelled with Lady Laura Kennedy or with Lord Brentford, but she had conceived a strong idea that her niece Violet was countenanced in all improprieties by the Standish family generally, and that therefore the Standish family was to be regarded as a family of enemies. There was doubtless in her mind considerable confusion on the subject, for she did not know whether Lord Chiltern or Mr. Finn was the suitor whom she most feared,—and she was aware, after a sort of muddled fashion, that the claims of these two wicked young men were antagonistic to each other. But they were both regarded by her as emanations from the same source of iniquity, and, therefore, without going deeply into the machinations of Lady Laura,—without resolving whether Lady Laura was injuring her by pressing her brother as a suitor upon Miss Effingham, or by pressing a rival of her brother,—still she became aware that it was her duty to turn a cold shoulder on those two houses in Portman Square and Grosvenor Place. But her difficulties in doing this were very great, and it may be said that Lady Baldock was placed in an unjust and cruel position. Before the end of May she had proposed to leave London, and to take her daughter and Violet down to Baddingham,—or to Brighton, if they preferred it, or to Switzerland. "Brighton in June!" Violet had exclaimed. "Would not a month among the glaciers be delightful!" Miss Boreham had said. "Don't let me keep you in town, aunt," Violet replied; "but I do not think I shall go till other people go. I can have a room at Laura Kennedy's house." Then Lady Baldock, whose position was hard and cruel, resolved that she would stay in town. Here she had in her hands a ward over whom she had no positive power, and yet in respect to whom her duty was imperative! Her duty was imperative, and Lady Baldock was not the woman to neglect her duty;—and yet she knew that the doing of her duty would all be in vain. Violet would marry a shoe-black out of the streets if she were so minded. It was of no use that the poor lady had provided herself with two strings, two most excellent strings, to her bow,—two strings either one of which should have contented Miss Effingham. There was Lord Fawn, a young peer, not very rich indeed,—but still with means sufficient for a wife, a rising man, and in every way respectable, although a Whig. And there was Mr. Appledom, one of the richest commoners in England, a fine Conservative too, with a seat in the House, and everything appropriate. He was fifty, but looked hardly more than thirty-five, and was,—so at least Lady Baldock frequently asserted,—violently in love with Violet Effingham. Why had not the law, or the executors, or the Lord Chancellor, or some power levied for the protection of the proprieties, made Violet absolutely subject to her guardian till she should be made subject to a husband?

"Yes, I think she is at home," said Lady Baldock, in answer to Lady Laura's inquiry for Violet. "At least, I hardly know. She seldom tells me what she means to do,—and sometimes she will walk out quite alone!" A most imprudent old woman was Lady Baldock, always opening her hand to her adversaries, unable to control herself in the scolding of people, either before their faces or behind their backs, even at moments in which such scolding was most injurious to her own cause. "However, we will see," she continued. Then the bell was rung, and in a few minutes Violet was in the room. In a few minutes more they were up-stairs together in Violet's own room, in spite of the openly-displayed wrath of Lady Baldock. "I almost wish she had never been born," said Lady Baldock to her daughter. "Oh, mamma, don't say that." "I certainly do wish that I had never seen her." "Indeed she has been a grievous trouble to you, mamma," said Miss Boreham, sympathetically.

"Brighton! What nonsense!" said Lady Laura.

"Of course it's nonsense. Fancy going to Brighton! And then they have proposed Switzerland. If you could only hear Augusta talking in rapture of a month among the glaciers! And I feel so ungrateful. I believe they would spend three months with me at any horrible place that I could suggest,—at Hong Kong if I were to ask it,—so intent are they on taking me away from metropolitan danger."

"But you will not go?"

"No!—I won't go. I know I am very naughty; but I can't help feeling that I cannot be good without being a fool at the same time. I must either fight my aunt, or give way to her. If I were to yield, what a life I should have;—and I should despise myself after all."

"And what is the special danger to be feared now?"

"I don't know;—you, I fancy. I told her that if she went, I should go to you. I knew that would make her stay."

"I wish you would come to me," said Lady Laura.

"I shouldn't think of it really,—not for any length of time."

"Why not?"

"Because I should be in Mr. Kennedy's way."

"You wouldn't be in his way in the least. If you would only be down punctually for morning prayers, and go to church with him on Sunday afternoon, he would be delighted to have you."

"What did he say about Madame Max coming?"

"Not a word. I don't think he quite knew who she was then. I fancy he has inquired since, by something he said yesterday."

"What did he say?"

"Nothing that matters;—only a word. I haven't come here to talk about Madame Max Goesler,—nor yet about Mr. Kennedy."

"Whom have you come to talk about?" asked Violet, laughing a little, with something of increased colour in her cheeks, though she could not be said to blush.

"A lover of course," said Lady Laura.

"I wish you would leave me alone with my lovers. You are as bad or worse than my aunt. She, at any rate, varies her prescription. She has become sick of poor Lord Fawn because he's a Whig."

"And who is her favourite now?"

"Old Mr. Appledom,—who is really a most unexceptionable old party, and whom I like of all things. I really think I could consent to be Mrs. Appledom, to get rid of my troubles,—if he did not dye his whiskers and have his coats padded."

"He'd give up those little things if you asked him."

"I shouldn't have the heart to do it. Besides, this isn't his time of the year for making proposals. His love fever, which is of a very low kind, and intermits annually, never comes on till the autumn. It is a rural malady, against which he is proof while among his clubs!"

"Well, Violet,—I am like your aunt."

"Like Lady Baldock?"

"In one respect. I, too, will vary my prescription."

"What do you mean, Laura?"

"Just this,—that if you like to marry Phineas Finn, I will say that you are right."

"Heaven and earth! And why am I to marry Phineas Finn?"

"Only for two reasons; because he loves you, and because—"

"No,—I deny it. I do not."

"I had come to fancy that you did."

"Keep your fancy more under control then. But upon my word I can't understand this. He was your great friend."

"What has that to do with it?" demanded Lady Laura.

"And you have thrown over your brother, Laura?"

"You have thrown him over. Is he to go on for ever asking and being refused?"

"I do not know why he should not," said Violet, "seeing how very little trouble it gives him. Half an hour once in six months does it all for him, allowing him time for coming and going in a cab."

"Violet, I do not understand you. Have you refused Oswald so often because he does not pass hours on his knees before you?"

"No, indeed! His nature would be altered very much for the worse before he could do that."

"Why do you throw it in his teeth then that he does not give you more of his time?"

"Why have you come to tell me to marry Mr. Phineas Finn? That is what I want to know. Mr. Phineas Finn, as far as I am aware, has not a shilling in the world,—except a month's salary now due to him from the Government. Mr. Phineas Finn I believe to be the son of a country doctor in Ireland,—with about seven sisters. Mr. Phineas Finn is a Roman Catholic. Mr. Phineas Finn is,—or was a short time ago,—in love with another lady; and Mr. Phineas Finn is not so much in love at this moment but what he is able to intrust his cause to an ambassador. None short of a royal suitor should ever do that with success."

"Has he never pleaded his cause to you himself?"

"My dear, I never tell gentlemen's secrets. It seems that if he has, his success was so trifling that he has thought he had better trust some one else for the future."

"He has not trusted me. He has not given me any commission."

"Then why have you come?"

"Because,—I hardly know how to tell his story. There have been things about Oswald which made it almost necessary that Mr. Finn should explain himself to me."

"I know it all;—about their fighting. Foolish young men! I am not a bit obliged to either of them,—not a bit. Only fancy, if my aunt knew it, what a life she would lead me! Gustavus knows all about it, and I feel that I am living at his mercy. Why were they so wrong-headed?"

"I cannot answer that,—though I know them well enough to be sure that Chiltern was the one in fault."

"It is so odd that you should have thrown your brother over."

"I have not thrown my brother over. Will you accept Oswald if he asks you again?"

"No," almost shouted Violet.

"Then I hope that Mr. Finn may succeed. I want him to succeed in everything. There;—you may know it all. He is my Phœbus Apollo."

"That is flattering to me,—looking at the position in which you desire to place your Phœbus at the present moment."

"Come, Violet, I am true to you, and let me have a little truth from you. This man loves you, and I think is worthy of you. He does not love me, but he is my friend. As his friend, and believing in his worth, I wish for his success beyond almost anything else in the world. Listen to me, Violet. I don't believe in those reasons which you gave me just now for not becoming this man's wife."

"Nor do I."

"I know you do not. Look at me. I, who have less of real heart than you, I who thought that I could trust myself to satisfy my mind and my ambition without caring for my heart, I have married for what you call position. My husband is very rich, and a Cabinet Minister, and will probably be a peer. And he was willing to marry me at a time when I had not a shilling of my own."

"He was very generous."

"He has asked for it since," said Lady Laura. "But never mind. I have not come to talk about myself;—otherwise than to bid you not do what I have done. All that you have said about this man's want of money and of family is nothing."

"Nothing at all," said Violet. "Mere words,—fit only for such people as my aunt."

"Well then?"

"Well?"

"If you love him—!"

"Ah! but if I do not? You are very close in inquiring into my secrets. Tell me, Laura;—was not this young Crichton once a lover of your own?"

"Psha! And do you think I cannot keep a gentleman's secret as well as you?"

"What is the good of any secret, Laura, when we have been already so open? He tried his 'prentice hand on you; and then he came to me. Let us watch him, and see who'll be the third. I too like him well enough to hope that he'll land himself safely at last."

CHAPTER XLVI. The Mousetrap

Phineas had certainly no desire to make love by an ambassador,—at second-hand. He had given no commission to Lady Laura, and was, as the reader is aware, quite ignorant of what was being done and said on his behalf. He had asked no more from Lady Laura than an opportunity of speaking for himself, and that he had asked almost with a conviction that by so asking he would turn his friend into an enemy. He had read but little of the workings of Lady Laura's heart towards himself, and had no idea of the assistance she was anxious to give him. She had never told him that she was willing to sacrifice her brother on his behalf, and, of course, had not told him that she was willing also to sacrifice herself. Nor, when she wrote to him one June morning and told him that Violet would be found in Portman Square, alone, that afternoon,—naming an hour, and explaining that Miss Effingham would be there to meet herself and her father, but that at such an hour she would be certainly alone,—did he even then know how much she was prepared to do for him. The short note was signed "L.," and then there came a long postscript. "Ask for me," she said in a postscript. "I shall be there later, and I have told them to bid you wait. I can give you no hope of success, but if you choose to try,—you can do so. If you do not come, I shall know that you have changed your mind. I shall not think the worse of you, and your secret will be safe with me. I do that which you have asked me to do,—simply because you have asked it. Burn this at once,—because I ask it." Phineas destroyed the note, tearing it into atoms, the moment that he had read it and re-read it. Of course he would go to Portman Square at the hour named. Of course he would take his chance. He was not buoyed up by much of hope;—but even though there were no hope, he would take his chance.

When Lord Brentford had first told Phineas of his promotion, he had also asked the new Lord of the Treasury to make a certain communication on his behalf to his son. This Phineas had found himself obliged to promise to do;—and he had done it. The letter had been difficult enough to write,—but he had written it. After having made the promise, he had found himself bound to keep it.

"DEAR LORD CHILTERN," he had commenced, "I will not think that there was anything in our late encounter to prevent my so addressing you. I now write at the instance of your father, who has heard nothing of our little affair." Then he explained at length Lord Brentford's wishes as he understood them. "Pray come home," he said, finishing his letter. "Touching V. E., I feel that I am bound to tell you that I still mean to try my fortune, but that I have no ground for hoping that my fortune will be good. Since the day on the sands, I have never met her but in society. I know you will be glad to hear that my wound was nothing; and I think you will be glad to hear that I have got my foot on to the ladder of promotion.—Yours always,   PHINEAS FINN."

Now he had to try his fortune,—that fortune of which he had told Lord Chiltern that he had no reason for hoping that it would be good. He went direct from his office at the Treasury to Portman Square, resolving that he would take no trouble as to his dress, simply washing his hands and brushing his hair as though he were going down to the House, and he knocked at the Earl's door exactly at the hour named by Lady Laura.

"Miss Effingham," he said, "I am so glad to find you alone."

"Yes," she said, laughing. "I am alone,—a poor unprotected female. But I fear nothing. I have strong reason for believing that Lord Brentford is somewhere about. And Pomfret the butler, who has known me since I was a baby, is a host in himself."

"With such allies you can have nothing to fear," he replied, attempting to carry on her little jest.

"Nor even without them, Mr. Finn. We unprotected females in these days are so self-reliant that our natural protectors fall off from us, finding themselves to be no longer wanted. Now with you,—what can I fear?"

"Nothing,—as I hope."

"There used to be a time, and that not so long ago either, when young gentlemen and ladies were thought to be very dangerous to each other if they were left alone. But propriety is less rampant now, and upon the whole virtue and morals, with discretion and all that kind of thing, have been the gainers. Don't you think so?"

"I am sure of it."

"All the same, but I don't like to be caught in a trap, Mr. Finn."

"In a trap?"

"Yes;—in a trap. Is there no trap here? If you will say so, I will acknowledge myself to be a dolt, and will beg your pardon."

"I hardly know what you call a trap."

"You were told that I was here?"

He paused a moment before he replied. "Yes, I was told."

"I call that a trap."

"Am I to blame?"

"I don't say that you set it,—but you use it."

"Miss Effingham, of course I have used it. You must know,—I think you must know that I have that to say to you which has made me long for such an opportunity as this."

"And therefore you have called in the assistance of your friend."

"It is true."

"In such matters you should never talk to any one, Mr. Finn. If you cannot fight your own battle, no one can fight it for you."

"Miss Effingham, do you remember our ride at Saulsby?"

"Very well;—as if it were yesterday."

"And do you remember that I asked you a question which you have never answered?"

"I did answer it,—as well as I knew how, so that I might tell you a truth without hurting you."

"It was necessary,—is necessary that I should be hurt sorely, or made perfectly happy. Violet Effingham, I have come to you to ask you to be my wife;—to tell you that I love you, and to ask for your love in return. Whatever may be my fate, the question must be asked, and an answer must be given. I have not hoped that you should tell me that you loved me—"

"For what then have you hoped?"

"For not much, indeed;—but if for anything, then for some chance that you might tell me so hereafter."

"If I loved you, I would tell you so now,—instantly. I give you my word of that."

"Can you never love me?"

"What is a woman to answer to such a question? No;—I believe never. I do not think I shall ever wish you to be my husband. You ask me to be plain, and I must be plain."

"Is it because—?" He paused, hardly knowing what the question was which he proposed to himself to ask.

"It is for no because,—for no cause except that simple one which should make any girl refuse any man whom she did not love. Mr. Finn, I could say pleasant things to you on any other subject than this,—because I like you."

"I know that I have nothing to justify my suit."

"You have everything to justify it;—at least I am bound to presume that you have. If you love me,—you are justified."

"You know that I love you."

"I am sorry that it should ever have been so,—very sorry. I can only hope that I have not been in fault."

"Will you try to love me?"

"No;—why should I try? If any trying were necessary, I would try rather not to love you. Why should I try to do that which would displease everybody belonging to me? For yourself, I admit your right to address me,—and tell you frankly that it would not be in vain, if I loved you. But I tell you as frankly that such a marriage would not please those whom I am bound to try to please."

He paused a moment before he spoke further. "I shall wait," he said, "and come again."

"What am I to say to that? Do not tease me, so that I be driven to treat you with lack of courtesy. Lady Laura is so much attached to you, and Mr. Kennedy, and Lord Brentford,—and indeed I may say, I myself also, that I trust there may be nothing to mar our good fellowship. Come, Mr. Finn,—say that you will take an answer, and I will give you my hand."

"Give it me," said he. She gave him her hand, and he put it up to his lips and pressed it. "I will wait and come again," he said. "I will assuredly come again." Then he turned from her and went out of the house. At the corner of the square he saw Lady Laura's carriage, but did not stop to speak to her. And she also saw him.

"So you have had a visitor here," said Lady Laura to Violet.

"Yes;—I have been caught in the trap."

"Poor mouse! And has the cat made a meal of you?"

"I fancy he has, after his fashion. There be cats that eat their mice without playing,—and cats that play with their mice, and then eat them; and cats again which only play with their mice, and don't care to eat them. Mr. Finn is a cat of the latter kind, and has had his afternoon's diversion."

"You wrong him there."

"I think not, Laura. I do not mean to say that he would not have liked me to accept him. But, if I can see inside his bosom, such a little job as that he has now done will be looked back upon as one of the past pleasures of his life;—not as a pain."

CHAPTER XLVII. Mr. Mildmay's Bill

It will be necessary that we should go back in our story for a very short period in order that the reader may be told that Phineas Finn was duly re-elected at Loughton after his appointment at the Treasury Board. There was some little trouble at Loughton, and something more of expense than he had before encountered. Mr. Quintus Slide absolutely came down, and was proposed by Mr. Vellum for the borough. Mr. Vellum being a gentleman learned in the law, and hostile to the interests of the noble owner of Saulsby, was able to raise a little trouble against our hero. Mr. Slide was proposed by Mr. Vellum, and seconded by Mr. Vellum's clerk,—though, as it afterwards appeared, Mr. Vellum's clerk was not in truth an elector,—and went to the poll like a man. He received three votes, and at twelve o'clock withdrew. This in itself could hardly have afforded compensation for the expense which Mr. Slide or his backers must have encountered;—but he had an opportunity of making a speech, every word of which was reported in the *People's Banner*; and if the speech was made in the language given in the report, Mr. Slide was really possessed of some oratorical power. Most of those who read the speech in the columns of the *People's Banner* were probably not aware how favourable an opportunity of retouching his sentences in type had been given to Mr. Slide by the fact of his connection with the newspaper. The speech had been very severe upon our hero; and though the speaker had been so hooted and pelted at Loughton as to have been altogether inaudible,—so maltreated that in point of fact he had not been able to speak above a tenth part of his speech at all,—nevertheless the speech did give Phineas a certain amount of pain. Why Phineas should have read it who can tell? But who is there that abstains from reading that which is printed in abuse of himself?

In the speech as it was printed Mr. Slide declared that he had no thought of being returned for the borough. He knew too well how the borough was managed, what slaves the electors were;—how they groaned under a tyranny from which hitherto they had been unable to release themselves. Of course the Earl's nominee, his lacquey, as the honourable gentleman might be called, would be returned. The Earl could order them to return whichever of his lacqueys he pleased.—There is something peculiarly pleasing to the democratic ear in the word lacquey! Any one serving a big man, whatever the service may be, is the big man's lacquey in the *People's Banner*.—The speech throughout was very bitter. Mr. Phineas Finn, who had previously served in Parliament as the lacquey of an Irish earl, and had been turned off by him, had now fallen into the service of the English earl, and was the lacquey chosen for the present occasion. But he, Quintus Slide, who boasted himself to be a man of the people,—he could tell them that the days of their thraldom were coming to an end, and that their enfranchisement was near at hand. That friend of the people, Mr. Turnbull, had a clause in his breeches-pocket which he would either force down the unwilling throat of Mr. Mildmay, or else drive the imbecile Premier from office by carrying it in his teeth. Loughton, as Loughton, must be destroyed, but it should be born again in a better birth as a part of a real electoral district, sending a real member, chosen by a real constituency, to a real Parliament. In those days,—and they would come soon,—Mr. Quintus Slide rather thought that Mr. Phineas Finn would be found "nowhere," and he rather thought also that when he showed himself again, as he certainly should do, in the midst of that democratic electoral district as the popular candidate for the honour of representing it in Parliament, that democratic electoral district would accord to him a reception very different from that which he was now receiving from the Earl's lacqueys in the parliamentary village of Loughton. A prettier bit of fiction than these sentences as composing a part of any speech delivered, or proposed to be delivered, at Loughton, Phineas thought he had never seen. And when he read at the close of the speech that though the Earl's hired bullies did their worst, the remarks of Mr. Slide were received by the people with reiterated cheering, he threw himself back in his chair at the Treasury and roared. The poor fellow had been three minutes on his legs, had received three rotten eggs, and one dead dog, and had retired. But not the half of the speech as printed in the *People's Banner* has been quoted. The sins of Phineas, who in spite of his inability to open his mouth in public had been made a Treasury hack by the aristocratic influence,—"by aristocratic influence not confined to the male sex,"—were described at great length, and in such language that Phineas for a while was fool enough to think that it would be his duty to belabour Mr. Slide with a horsewhip. This notion, however, did not endure long with him, and when Mr. Monk told him that things of that kind came as a matter of course, he was comforted.

But he found it much more difficult to obtain comfort when he weighed the arguments brought forward against the abominations of such a borough as that for which he sat, and reflected that if Mr. Turnbull brought forward his clause, he, Phineas Finn, would be bound to vote against the clause, knowing the clause to be right, because he was a servant of the Government. The arguments, even though they appeared in the *People's Banner*, were true arguments; and he had on one occasion admitted their truth to his friend Lady Laura,—in the presence of that great Cabinet Minister, her husband. "What business has such a man as that down there? Is there a single creature who wants him?" Lady Laura had said. "I don't suppose anybody does want Mr. Quintus Slide," Phineas had replied; "but I am disposed to think the electors should choose the man they do want, and that at present they have no choice left to them." "They are quite satisfied," said Lady Laura, angrily. "Then, Lady Laura," continued Phineas, "that alone should be sufficient to prove that their privilege of returning a member to Parliament is too much for them. We can't defend it." "It is defended by tradition," said Mr. Kennedy. "And by its great utility," said Lady Laura, bowing to the young member who was present, and forgetting that very useless old gentleman, her cousin, who had sat for the borough for many years. "In this country it doesn't do to go too fast," said Mr. Kennedy. "And then the mixture of vulgarity, falsehood, and pretence!" said Lady Laura, shuddering as her mind recurred to the fact that Mr. Quintus Slide had contaminated Loughton by his presence. "I am told that they hardly let him leave the place alive."

Whatever Mr. Kennedy and Lady Laura might think about Loughton and the general question of small boroughs, it was found by the Government, to their great cost, that Mr. Turnbull's clause was a reality. After two months of hard work, all questions of franchise had been settled, rating and renting, new and newfangled, fancy franchises and those which no one fancied, franchises for boroughs and franchises for counties, franchises single, dual, three-cornered, and four-sided,—by various clauses to which the Committee of the whole House had agreed after some score of divisions,—the matter of the franchise had been settled. No doubt there was the House of Lords, and there might yet be shipwreck. But it was generally believed that the Lords would hardly look at the bill,—that they would not even venture on an amendment. The Lords would only be too happy to let the matter be settled by the Commons themselves. But then, after the franchise, came redistribution. How sick of the subject were all members of the Government, no one could tell who did not see their weary faces. The whole House was sick, having been whipped into various lobbies, night after night, during the heat of the summer, for weeks past. Redistribution! Why should there be any redistribution? They had got, or would get, a beautiful franchise. Could they not see what that would do for them? Why redistribute anything? But, alas, it was too late to go back to so blessed an idea as that! Redistribution they must have. But there should be as little redistribution as possible. Men were sick of it all, and would not be *exigeant*. Something should be done for overgrown counties;—something for new towns which had prospered in brick and mortar. It would be easy to crush up a peccant borough or two,—a borough that had been discovered in its sin. And a few boroughs now blessed with two members might consent to be blessed only with one. Fifteen small clauses might settle the redistribution, in spite of Mr. Turnbull,—if only Mr. Daubeny would be good-natured.

Neither the weather, which was very hot, nor the tedium of the session, which had been very great, nor the anxiety of Ministers, which was very pressing, had any effect in impairing the energy of Mr. Turnbull. He was as instant, as oratorical, as hostile, as indignant about redistribution as he had been about the franchise. He had been sure then, and he was sure now, that Ministers desired to burke the question, to deceive the people, to produce a bill that should be no bill. He brought out his clause,—and made Loughton his instance. "Would the honourable gentleman who sat lowest on the Treasury bench,—who at this moment was in sweet confidential intercourse with the right honourable gentleman now President of the Board of Trade, who had once been a friend of the people,—would the young Lord of the Treasury get up in his place and tell them that no peer of Parliament had at present a voice in sending a member to their House of Commons,—that no peer would have a voice if this bill, as proposed by the Government, were passed in its present useless, ineffectual, conservative, and most dishonest form?"

Phineas, who replied to this, and who told Mr. Turnbull that he himself could not answer for any peers,—but that he thought it probable that most peers would, by their opinions, somewhat influence the opinions of some electors,—was thought to have got out of his difficulty very well. But there was the clause of Mr. Turnbull to be dealt with,—a clause directly disfranchising seven single-winged boroughs, of which Loughton was of course one,—a clause to which the Government must either submit or object. Submission would be certain defeat in one way, and objection would be as certain defeat in another,—if the gentlemen on the other side were not disposed to assist the ministers. It was said that the Cabinet was divided. Mr. Gresham and Mr. Monk were for letting the seven boroughs go. Mr. Mildmay could not bring himself to obey Mr. Turnbull, and Mr. Palliser supported him. When Mr. Mildmay was told that Mr. Daubeny would certainly go into the same lobby with Mr. Turnbull respecting the seven boroughs, he was reported to have said that in that case Mr. Daubeny must be prepared with a Government. Mr. Daubeny made a beautiful speech about the seven boroughs;—the seven sins, and seven stars, and seven churches, and seven lamps. He would make no party question of this. Gentlemen who usually acted with him would vote as their own sense of right or wrong directed them;—from which expression of a special sanction it was considered that these gentlemen were not accustomed to exercise the privilege now accorded to them. But in regarding the question as one of right and wrong, and in looking at what he believed to be both the wish of the country and its interests, he, Mr. Daubeny,—he, himself, being simply a humble member of that House,—must support the clause of the honourable gentleman. Almost all those to whom had been surrendered the privilege of using their own judgment for that occasion only, used it discreetly,—as their chief had used it himself,—and Mr. Turnbull carried his clause by a majority of fifteen. It was then 3 a.m., and Mr. Gresham, rising after the division, said that his right honourable friend the First Lord of the Treasury was too tired to return to the House, and had requested him to state that the Government would declare their purpose at 6 p.m. on the following evening.

Phineas, though he had made his little speech in answer to Mr. Turnbull with good-humoured flippancy, had recorded his vote in favour of the seven boroughs with a sore heart. Much as he disliked Mr. Turnbull, he knew that Mr. Turnbull was right in this. He had spoken to Mr. Monk on the subject, as it were asking Mr. Monk's permission to throw up his office, and vote against Mr. Mildmay. But Mr. Monk was angry with him, telling him that his conscience was of that restless, uneasy sort which is neither useful nor manly. "We all know," said Mr. Monk, "and none better than Mr. Mildmay, that we cannot justify such a borough as Loughton by the theory of our parliamentary representation,—any more than we can justify the fact that Huntingdonshire should return as many members as the East Riding. There must be compromises, and you should trust to others who have studied the matter more thoroughly than you, to say how far the compromise should go at the present moment."

"It is the influence of the peer, not the paucity of the electors," said Phineas.

"And has no peer any influence in a county? Would you disfranchise Westmoreland? Believe me, Finn, if you want to be useful, you must submit yourself in such matters to those with whom you act."

Phineas had no answer to make, but he was not happy in his mind. And he was the less happy, perhaps, because he was very sure that Mr. Mildmay would be beaten. Mr. Low in these days harassed him sorely. Mr. Low was very keen against such boroughs as Loughton, declaring that Mr. Daubeny was quite right to join his standard to that of Mr. Turnbull on such an issue. Mr. Low was the reformer now, and Phineas found himself obliged to fight a losing battle on behalf of an acknowledged abuse. He never went near Bunce; but, unfortunately for him, Bunce caught him once in the street and showed him no mercy. "Slide was a little 'eavy on you in the *Banner* the other day,—eh, Mr. Finn?—too 'eavy, as I told him."

"Mr. Slide can be just as heavy as he pleases, Bunce."

"That's in course. The press is free, thank God,—as yet. But it wasn't any good rattling away at the Earl's little borough when it's sure to go. Of course it'll go, Mr. Finn."

"I think it will."

"The whole seven on 'em. The 'ouse couldn't but do it. They tell me it's all Mr. Mildmay's own work, sticking out for keeping on 'em. He's very old, and so we'll forgive him. But he must go, Mr. Finn."

"We shall know all about that soon, Bunce."

"If you don't get another seat, Mr. Finn, I suppose we shall see you back at the Inn. I hope we may. It's better than being member for Loughton, Mr. Finn;—you may be sure of that." And then Mr. Bunce passed on.

Mr. Turnbull carried his clause, and Loughton was doomed. Loughton and the other six deadly sins were anathematized, exorcised, and finally got rid of out of the world by the voices of the gentlemen who had been proclaiming the beauty of such pleasant vices all their lives, and who in their hearts hated all changes that tended towards popular representation. But not the less was Mr. Mildmay beaten; and, in accordance with the promise made by his first lieutenant immediately after the vote was taken, the Prime Minister came forward on the next evening and made his statement. He had already put his resignation into the hands of Her Majesty, and Her Majesty had graciously accepted it. He was very old, and felt that the time had come in which it behoved him to retire into that leisure which he thought he had, perhaps, earned. He had hoped to carry this bill as the last act of his political life; but he was too old, too stiff, as he said, in his prejudices, to bend further than he had bent already, and he must leave the completion of the matter in other hands. Her Majesty had sent for Mr. Gresham, and Mr. Gresham had already seen Her Majesty. Mr. Gresham and his other colleagues, though they dissented from the clause which had been carried by the united efforts of gentlemen opposite to him, and of gentlemen below him on his own side of the House, were younger men than he, and would, for the country's sake,—and for the sake of Her Majesty,—endeavour to carry the bill through. There would then, of course, be a dissolution, and the future Government would, no doubt, depend on the choice of the country. From all which it was understood that Mr. Gresham was to go on with the bill to a conclusion, whatever might be the divisions carried against him, and that a new Secretary of State for Foreign Affairs must be chosen. Phineas understood, also, that he had lost his seat at Loughton. For the borough of Loughton there would never again be an election. "If I had been Mr. Mildmay, I would have thrown the bill up altogether," Lord Brentford said afterwards; "but of course it was not for me to interfere."

The session was protracted for two months after that,—beyond the time at which grouse should have been shot,—and by the 23rd of August became the law of the land. "I shall never get over it," said Mr. Ratler to Mr. Finn, seated one terribly hot evening on a bench behind the Cabinet Ministers,—"never. I don't suppose such a session for work was ever known before. Think what it is to have to keep men together in August, with the thermometer at 81 degrees, and the river stinking like,—like the very mischief." Mr. Ratler, however, did not die.

On the last day of the session Laurence Fitzgibbon resigned. Rumours reached the ears of Phineas as to the cause of this, but no certain cause was told him. It was said that Lord Cantrip had insisted upon it, Laurence having by mischance been called upon for some official statement during an unfortunate period of absence. There was, however, a mystery about it;—but the mystery was not half so wonderful as the triumph to Phineas, when Mr. Gresham offered him the place.

"But I shall have no seat," said Phineas.

"We shall none of us have seats to-morrow," said Mr. Gresham.

"But I shall be at a loss to find a place to stand for."

"The election will not come on till November, and you must look about you. Both Mr. Monk and Lord Brentford seem to think you will be in the House."

And so the bill was carried, and the session was ended.

CHAPTER XLVIII. "The Duke"

By the middle of September there was assembled a large party at Matching Priory, a country mansion belonging to Mr. Plantagenet Palliser. The men had certainly been chosen in reference to their political feelings and position,—for there was not a guest in the house who had voted for Mr. Turnbull's clause, or the wife or daughter, or sister of any one who had so voted. Indeed, in these days politics ran so high that among politicians all social gatherings were brought together with some reference to the state of parties. Phineas was invited, and when he arrived at Matching he found that half the Cabinet was there. Mr. Kennedy was not there, nor was Lady Laura. Mr. Monk was there, and the Duke,—with the Duchess, and Mr. Gresham, and Lord Thrift; Mrs. Max Goesler was there also, and Mrs. Bonteen,—Mr. Bonteen being detained somewhere out of the way; and Violet Effingham was expected in two days, and Lord Chiltern at the end of the week. Lady Glencora took an opportunity of imparting this latter information to Phineas very soon after his arrival; and Phineas, as he watched her eye and her mouth while she spoke, was quite sure that Lady Glencora knew the story of the duel. "I shall be delighted to see him again," said Phineas. "That is all right," said Lady Glencora. There were also there Mr. and Mrs. Grey, who were great friends of the Pallisers,—and on the very day on which Phineas reached Matching, at half an hour before the time for dressing, the Duke of Omnium arrived. Now, Mr. Palliser was the Duke's nephew and heir,—and the Duke of Omnium was a very great person indeed. I hardly know why it should have been so, but the Duke of Omnium was certainly a greater man in public estimation than the other duke then present,—the Duke of St. Bungay. The Duke of St. Bungay was a useful man, and had been so all his life, sitting in Cabinets and serving his country, constant as any peer in the House of Lords, always ready to take on his own shoulders any troublesome work required of him, than whom Mr. Mildmay, and Mr. Mildmay's predecessor at the head of the liberal party, had had no more devoted adherent. But the Duke of Omnium had never yet done a day's work on behalf of his country. They both wore the Garter, the Duke of St. Bungay having earned it by service, the Duke of Omnium having been decorated with the blue ribbon,—because he was Duke of Omnium. The one was a moral, good man, a good husband, a good father, and a good friend. The other,—did not bear quite so high a reputation. But men and women thought but little of the Duke of St. Bungay, while the other duke was regarded with an almost reverential awe. I think the secret lay in the simple fact that the Duke of Omnium had not been common in the eyes of the people. He had contrived to envelope himself in something of the ancient mystery of wealth and rank. Within three minutes of the Duke's arrival Mrs. Bonteen, with an air of great importance, whispered a word to Phineas. "He has come. He arrived exactly at seven!"

"Who has come?" Phineas asked.

"The Duke of Omnium!" she said, almost reprimanding him by her tone of voice for his indifference. "There has been a great doubt whether or no he would show himself at last. Lady Glencora told me that he never will pledge himself. I am so glad he has come."

"I don't think I ever saw him," said Phineas.

"Oh, I have seen him,—a magnificent-looking man! I think it is so very nice of Lady Glencora getting him to meet us. It is very rarely that he will join in a great party, but they say Lady Glencora can do anything with him since the heir was born. I suppose you have heard all about that."

"No," said Phineas; "I have heard nothing of the heir, but I know that there are three or four babies."

"There was no heir, you know, for a year and a half, and they were all *au désespoir*; and the Duke was very nearly quarrelling with his nephew; and Mr. Palliser—; you know it had very nearly come to a separation."

"I don't know anything at all about it," said Phineas, who was not very fond of the lady who was giving him the information.

"It is so, I can assure you; but since the boy was born Lady Glencora can do anything with the Duke. She made him go to Ascot last spring, and he presented her with the favourite for one of the races on the very morning the horse ran. They say he gave three thousand pounds for him."

"And did Lady Glencora win?"

"No;—the horse lost; and Mr. Palliser has never known what to do with him since. But it was very pretty of the Duke;—was it not?"

Phineas, though he had intended to show to Mrs. Bonteen how little he thought about the Duke of Omnium,—how small was his respect for a great peer who took no part in politics,—could not protect himself from a certain feeling of anxiety as to the aspect and gait and words of the man of whom people thought so much, of whom he had heard so often, and of whom he had seen so little. He told himself that the Duke of Omnium should be no more to him than any other man, but yet the Duke of Omnium was more to him than other men. When he came down into the drawing-room he was angry with himself, and stood apart;—and was then angry with himself again because he stood apart. Why should he make a difference in his own bearing because there was such a man in the company? And yet he could not avoid it. When he entered the room the Duke was standing in a large bow-window, and two or three ladies and two or three men were standing round him. Phineas would not go near the group, telling himself that he would not approach a man so grand as was the Duke of Omnium. He saw Madame Max Goesler among the party, and after a while he saw her retreat. As she retreated, Phineas knew that some words from Madame Max Goesler had not been received with the graciousness which she had expected. There was the prettiest smile in the world on the lady's face, and she took a corner on a sofa with an air of perfect satisfaction. But yet Phineas knew that she had received a wound.

"I called twice on you in London," said Phineas, coming up close to her, "but was not fortunate enough to find you!"

"Yes;—but you came so late in the season as to make it impossible that there should be any arrangements for our meeting. What can any woman do when a gentleman calls on her in August?"

"I came in July."

"Yes, you did; on the 31st. I keep the most accurate record of all such things, Mr. Finn. But let us hope that we may have better luck next year. In the meantime, we can only enjoy the good things that are going."

"Socially, or politically, Madame Goesler?"

"Oh, socially. How can I mean anything else when the Duke of Omnium is here? I feel so much taller at being in the same house with him. Do not you? But you are a spoilt child of fortune, and perhaps you have met him before."

"I think I once saw the back of a hat in the park, and somebody told me that the Duke's head was inside it."

"And you have never seen him but that once?"

"Never but that once,—till now."

"And do not you feel elated?"

"Of course I do. For what do you take me, Madame Goesler?"

"I do,—immensely. I believe him to be a fool, and I never heard of his doing a kind act to anybody in my life."

"Not when he gave the racehorse to Lady Glencora?"

"I wonder whether that was true. Did you ever hear of such an absurdity? As I was saying, I don't think he ever did anything for anybody;—but then, you know, to be Duke of Omnium! It isn't necessary,—is it,—that a Duke of Omnium should do anything except be Duke of Omnium?"

At this moment Lady Glencora came up to Phineas, and took him across to the Duke. The Duke had expressed a desire to be introduced to him. Phineas, half-pleased and half-disgusted, had no alternative, and followed Lady Glencora. The Duke shook hands with him, and made a little bow, and said something about the garrotters, which Phineas, in his confusion, did not quite understand. He tried to reply as he would have replied to anybody else, but the weight of the Duke's majesty was too much for him, and he bungled. The Duke made another little bow, and in a moment was speaking a word of condescension to some other favoured individual. Phineas retreated altogether disgusted,—hating the Duke, but hating himself worse; but he would not retreat in the direction of Madame Max Goesler. It might suit that lady to take an instant little revenge for her discomfiture, but it did not suit him to do so. The question with him would be, whether in some future part of his career it might not be his duty to assist in putting down Dukes of Omnium.

At dinner Phineas sat between Mrs. Bonteen and the Duchess of St. Bungay, and did not find himself very happy. At the other end of the table the Duke,—the great Duke, was seated at Lady Glencora's right hand, and on his other side Fortune had placed Madame Max Goesler. The greatest interest which Phineas had during the dinner was in watching the operations,—the triumphantly successful operations of that lady. Before dinner she had been wounded by the Duke. The Duke had not condescended to accord the honour of his little bow of graciousness to some little flattering morsel of wit which the lady had uttered on his behoof. She had said a sharp word or two in her momentary anger to Phineas; but when Fortune was so good to her in that matter of her place at dinner, she was not fool enough to throw away her chance. Throughout the soup and fish she was very quiet. She said a word or two after her first glass of champagne. The Duke refused two dishes, one after another, and then she glided into conversation. By the time that he had his roast mutton before him she was in full play, and as she eat her peach, the Duke was bending over her with his most gracious smile.

"Didn't you think the session was very long, Mr. Finn?" said the Duchess to Phineas.

"Very long indeed, Duchess," said Phineas, with his attention still fixed on Madame Max Goesler.

"The Duke found it very troublesome."

"I daresay he did," said Phineas. That duke and that duchess were no more than any other man and any other man's wife. The session had not been longer to the Duke of St. Bungay than to all the public servants. Phineas had the greatest possible respect for the Duke of St. Bungay, but he could not take much interest in the wailings of the Duchess on her husband's behalf.

"And things do seem to be so very uncomfortable now," said the Duchess,—thinking partly of the resignation of Mr. Mildmay, and partly of the fact that her own old peculiar maid who had lived with her for thirty years had retired into private life.

"Not so very bad, Duchess, I hope," said Phineas, observing that at this moment Madame Max Goesler's eyes were brilliant with triumph. Then there came upon him a sudden ambition,—that he would like to "cut out" the Duke of Omnium in the estimation of Madame Max Goesler. The brightness of Madame Max Goesler's eyes had not been thrown away upon our hero.

Violet Effingham came at the appointed time, and, to the surprise of Phineas, was brought to Matching by Lord Brentford. Phineas at first thought that it was intended that the Earl and his son should meet and make up their quarrel at Mr. Palliser's house. But Lord Brentford stayed only one night, and Phineas on the next morning heard the whole history of his coming and going from Violet. "I have almost been on my knees to him to stay," she said. "Indeed, I did go on my knees,—actually on my knees."

"And what did he say?"

"He put his arm round me and kissed me, and,—and,—I cannot tell you all that he said. But it ended in this,—that if Chiltern can be made to go to Saulsby, fatted calves without stint will be killed. I shall do all I can to make him go; and so must you, Mr. Finn. Of course that silly affair in foreign parts is not to make any difference between you two."

Phineas smiled, and said he would do his best, and looked up into her face, and was just able to talk to her as though things were going comfortably with him. But his heart was very cold. As Violet had spoken to him about Lord Chiltern there had come upon him, for the first time,—for the first time since he had known that Lord Chiltern had been refused,—an idea, a doubt, whether even yet Violet might not become Lord Chiltern's wife. His heart was very sad, but he struggled on,—declaring that it was incumbent on them both to bring together the father and son.

"I am so glad to hear you say so, Mr. Finn," said Violet. "I really do believe that you can do more towards it than any one else. Lord Chiltern would think nothing of my advice,—would hardly speak to me on such a subject. But he respects you as well as likes you, and not the less because of what has occurred."

How was it that Violet should know aught of the respect or liking felt by this rejected suitor for that other suitor,—who had also been rejected? And how was it that she was thus able to talk of one of them to the other, as though neither of them had ever come forward with such a suit? Phineas felt his position to be so strange as to be almost burdensome. He had told Violet, when she had refused him, very plainly, that he should come again to her, and ask once more for the great gift which he coveted. But he could not ask again now. In the first place, there was that in her manner which made him sure that were he to do so, he would ask in vain; and then he felt that she was placing a special confidence in him, against which he would commit a sin were he to use her present intimacy with him for the purposes of making love. They two were to put their shoulders together to help Lord Chiltern, and while doing so he could not continue a suit which would be felt by both of them to be hostile to Lord Chiltern. There might be opportunity for a chance word, and if so the chance word should be spoken; but he could not make a deliberate attack, such as he had made in Portman Square. Violet also probably understood that she had not now been caught in a mousetrap.

The Duke was to spend four days at Matching, and on the third day,—the day before Lord Chiltern was expected,—he was to be seen riding with Madame Max Goesler by his side. Madame Max Goesler was known as a perfect horsewoman,—one indeed who was rather fond of going a little fast on horseback, and who rode well to hounds. But the Duke seldom moved out of a walk, and on this occasion Madame Max was as steady in her seat and almost as slow as the mounted ghost in *Don Juan*. But it was said by some there, especially by Mrs. Bonteen, that the conversation between them was not slow. And on the next morning the Duke and Madame Max Goesler were together again before luncheon, standing on a terrace at the back of the house, looking down on a party who were playing croquet on the lawn.

"Do you never play?" said the Duke.

"Oh yes;—one does everything a little."

"I am sure you would play well. Why do you not play now?"

"No;—I shall not play now."

"I should like to see you with your mallet."

"I am sorry your Grace cannot be gratified. I have played croquet till I am tired of it, and have come to think it is only fit for boys and girls. The great thing is to give them opportunities for flirting, and it does that."

"And do you never flirt, Madame Goesler?"

"Never at croquet, Duke."

"And what with you is the choicest time?"

"That depends on so many things,—and so much on the chosen person. What do you recommend?"

"Ah,—I am so ignorant. I can recommend nothing."

"What do you say to a mountain-top at dawn on a summer day?" asked Madame Max Goesler.

"You make me shiver," said the Duke.

"Or a boat on a lake on a summer evening, or a good lead after hounds with nobody else within three fields, or the bottom of a salt-mine, or the deck of an ocean steamer, or a military hospital in time of war, or a railway journey from Paris to Marseilles?"

"Madame Max Goesler, you have the most uncomfortable ideas."

"I have no doubt your Grace has tried each of them,—successfully. But perhaps, after all, a comfortable chair over a good fire, in a pretty room, beats everything."

"I think it does,—certainly," said the Duke. Then he whispered something at which Madame Max Goesler blushed and smiled, and immediately after that she followed those who had already gone in to lunch.

Mrs. Bonteen had been hovering round the spot on the terrace on which the Duke and Madame Max Goesler had been standing, looking on with envious eyes, meditating some attack, some interruption, some excuse for an interpolation, but her courage had failed her and she had not dared to approach. The Duke had known nothing of the hovering propinquity of Mrs. Bonteen, but Madame Goesler had seen and had understood it all.

"Dear Mrs. Bonteen," she said afterwards, "why did you not come and join us? The Duke was so pleasant."

"Two is company, and three is none," said Mrs. Bonteen, who in her anger was hardly able to choose her words quite as well as she might have done had she been more cool.

"Our friend Madame Max has made quite a new conquest," said Mrs. Bonteen to Lady Glencora.

"I am so pleased," said Lady Glencora, with apparently unaffected delight. "It is such a great thing to get anybody to amuse my uncle. You see everybody cannot talk to him, and he will not talk to everybody."

"He talked enough to her in all conscience," said Mrs. Bonteen, who was now more angry than ever.

CHAPTER XLIX. The Duellists Meet

Lord Chiltern arrived, and Phineas was a little nervous as to their meeting. He came back from shooting on the day in question, and was told by the servant that Lord Chiltern was in the house. Phineas went into the billiard-room in his knickerbockers, thinking probably that he might be there, and then into the drawing-room, and at last into the library,—but Lord Chiltern was not to be found. At last he came across Violet.

"Have you seen him?" he asked.

"Yes;—he was with me half an hour since, walking round the gardens."

"And how is he? Come;—tell me something about him."

"I never knew him to be more pleasant. He would give no promise about Saulsby, but he did not say that he would not go."

"Does he know that I am here?"

"Yes;—I told him so. I told him how much pleasure I should have in seeing you two together,—as friends."

"And what did he say?"

"He laughed, and said you were the best fellow in the world. You see I am obliged to be explicit."

"But why did he laugh?" Phineas asked.

"He did not tell me, but I suppose it was because he was thinking of a little trip he once took to Belgium, and he perceived that I knew all about it."

"I wonder who told you. But never mind. I do not mean to ask any questions. As I do not like that our first meeting should be before all the people in the drawing-room, I will go to him in his own room."

"Do, do;—that will be so nice of you."

Phineas sent his card up by a servant, and in a few minutes was standing with his hand on the lock of Lord Chiltern's door. The last time he had seen this man, they had met with pistols in their hands to shoot at each other, and Lord Chiltern had in truth done his very best to shoot his opponent. The cause of quarrel was the same between them as ever. Phineas had not given up Violet, and had no intention of giving her up. And he had received no intimation whatever from his rival that there was to be a truce between them. Phineas had indeed written in friendship to Lord Chiltern, but he had received no answer;—and nothing of certainty was to be gathered from the report which Violet had just made. It might well be that Lord Chiltern would turn upon him now in his wrath, and that there would be some scene which in a strange house would be obviously objectionable. Nevertheless he had resolved that even that would be better than a chance encounter among strangers in a drawing-room. So the door was opened and the two men met.

"Well, old fellow," said Lord Chiltern, laughing. Then all doubt was over, and in a moment Phineas was shaking his former,—and present friend, warmly by the hand. "So we've come to be an Under-Secretary have we?—and all that kind of thing."

"I had to get into harness,—when the harness offered itself," said Phineas.

"I suppose so. It's a deuce of a bore, isn't it?"

"I always liked work, you know."

"I thought you liked hunting better. You used to ride as if you did. There's Bonebreaker back again in the stable for you. That poor fool who bought him could do nothing with him, and I let him have his money back."

"I don't see why you should have done that."

"Because I was the biggest fool of the two. Do you remember when that brute got me down under the bank in the river? That was about the nearest touch I ever had. Lord bless me;—how he did squeeze me! So here you are;—staying with the Pallisers,—one of a Government party I suppose. But what are you going to do for a seat, my friend?"

"Don't talk about that yet, Chiltern."

"A sore subject,—isn't it? I think they have been quite right, you know, to put Loughton into the melting-pot,—though I'm sorry enough for your sake."

"Quite right," said Phineas.

"And yet you voted against it, old chap? But, come; I'm not going to be down upon you. So my father has been here?"

"Yes;—he was here for a day or two."

"Violet has just been telling me. You and he are as good friends as ever?"

"I trust we are."

"He never heard of that little affair?" And Lord Chiltern nodded his head, intending to indicate the direction of Blankenberg.

"I do not think he has yet."

"So Violet tells me. Of course you know that she has heard all about it."

"I have reason to suppose as much."

"And so does Laura."

"I told her myself," said Phineas.

"The deuce you did! But I daresay it was for the best. It's a pity you had not proclaimed it at Charing Cross, and then nobody would have believed a word about it. Of course my father will hear it some day."

"You are going to Saulsby, I hope, Chiltern?"

"That question is easier asked than answered. It is quite true that the great difficulty has been got over. Laura has had her money. And if my father will only acknowledge that he has wronged me throughout, from beginning to end, I will go to Saulsby to-morrow;—and would cut you out at Loughton the next day, only that Loughton is not Loughton any longer."

"You cannot expect your father to do that."

"No;—and therefore there is a difficulty. So you've had that awfully ponderous Duke here. How did you get on with him?"

"Admirably. He condescended to do something which he called shaking hands with me."

"He is the greatest old dust out," said Lord Chiltern, disrespectfully. "Did he take any notice of Violet?"

"Not that I observed."

"He ought not to be allowed into the same room with her." After that there was a short pause, and Phineas felt some hesitation in speaking of Miss Effingham to Lord Chiltern. "And how do you get on with her?" asked Lord Chiltern. Here was a question for a man to answer. The question was so hard to be answered, that Phineas did not at first make any attempt to answer it. "You know exactly the ground that I stand on," continued Lord Chiltern. "She has refused me three times. Have you been more fortunate?"

Lord Chiltern, as he asked his question, looked full into Finn's face in a manner that was irresistible. His look was not one of anger nor even of pride. It was not, indeed, without a strong dash of fun. But such as it was it showed Phineas that Lord Chiltern intended to have an answer. "No," said he at last, "I have not been more fortunate."

"Perhaps you have changed your mind," said his host.

"No;—I have not changed my mind," said Phineas, quickly.

"How stands it then? Come;—let us be honest to each other. I told you down at Willingford that I would quarrel with any man who attempted to cut me out with Violet Effingham. You made up your mind that you would do so, and therefore I quarrelled with you. But we can't always be fighting duels."

"I hope we may not have to fight another."

"No;—it would be absurd," said Lord Chiltern. "I rather think that what we did was absurd. But upon my life I did not see any other way out of it. However, that is over. How is it to be now?"

"What am I to say in answer to that?" asked Phineas.

"Just the truth. You have asked her, I suppose?"

"Yes;—I have asked her."

"And she has refused you?"

"Yes;—she has refused me."

"And you mean to ask her again?"

"I shall;—if I ever think that there is a chance. Indeed, Chiltern, I believe I shall whether I think that I have any chance or not."

"Then we start fairly, Finn. I certainly shall do so. I believe I once told you that I never would;—but that was long before I suspected that you would enter for the same plate. What a man says on such a matter when he is down in the mouth goes for nothing. Now we understand each other, and you had better go and dress. The bell rang nearly half an hour ago, and my fellow is hanging about outside the door."

The interview had in one respect been very pleasant to Phineas, and in another it had been very bitter. It was pleasant to him to know that he and Lord Chiltern were again friends. It was a delight to him to feel that this half-savage but high-spirited young nobleman, who had been so anxious to fight with him and to shoot him, was nevertheless ready to own that he had behaved well. Lord Chiltern had in fact acknowledged that though he had been anxious to blow out our hero's brains, he was aware all the time that our hero was a good sort of fellow. Phineas understood this, and felt that it was pleasant. But with this understanding, and accompanying this pleasure, there was a conviction in his heart that the distance between Lord Chiltern and Violet would daily grow to be less and still less,—and that Lord Chiltern could afford to be generous. If Miss Effingham could teach herself to be fond of Lord Chiltern, what had he, Phineas Finn, to offer in opposition to the claims of such a suitor?

That evening Lord Chiltern took Miss Effingham out to dinner. Phineas told himself that this was of course so arranged by Lady Glencora, with the express view of serving the Saulsby interest. It was almost nothing to him at the moment that Madame Max Goesler was intrusted to him. He had his ambition respecting Madame Max Goesler; but that for the time was in abeyance. He could hardly keep his eyes off Miss Effingham. And yet, as he well knew, his observation of her must be quite useless. He knew beforehand, with absolute accuracy, the manner in which she would treat her lover. She would be kind, genial, friendly, confidential, nay, affectionate; and yet her manner would mean nothing, would give no clue to her future decision either for or against Lord Chiltern. It was, as Phineas thought, a peculiarity with Violet Effingham that she could treat her rejected lovers as dear familiar friends immediately after her rejection of them.

"Mr. Finn," said Madame Max Goesler, "your eyes and ears are tell-tales of your passion."

"I hope not," said Phineas, "as I certainly do not wish that any one should guess how strong is my regard for you."

"That is prettily turned,—very prettily turned; and shows more readiness of wit than I gave you credit for under your present suffering. But of course we all know where your heart is. Men do not undertake perilous journeys to Belgium for nothing."

"That unfortunate journey to Belgium! But, dear Madame Max, really nobody knows why I went."

"You met Lord Chiltern there?"

"Oh yes;—I met Lord Chiltern there."

"And there was a duel?"

"Madame Max,—you must not ask me to criminate myself!"

"Of course there was, and of course it was about Miss Effingham, and of course the lady thinks herself bound to refuse both the gentlemen who were so very wicked, and of course—"

"Well,—what follows?"

"Ah! if you have not wit enough to see, I do not think it can be my duty to tell you. But I wished to caution you as a friend that your eyes and ears should be more under your command."

"You will go to Saulsby?" Violet said to Lord Chiltern.

"I cannot possibly tell as yet," said he, frowning.

"Then I can tell you that you ought to go. I do not care a bit for your frowns. What does the fifth commandment say?"

"If you have no better arguments than the commandments, Violet—"

"There can be none better. Do you mean to say that the commandments are nothing to you?"

"I mean to say that I shan't go to Saulsby because I am told in the twentieth chapter of Exodus to honour my father and mother,—and that I shouldn't believe anybody who told me that he did anything because of the commandments."

"Oh, Lord Chiltern!"

"People are so prejudiced and so used to humbug that for the most part they do not in the least know their own motives for what they do. I will go to Saulsby to-morrow,—for a reward."

"For what reward?" said Violet, blushing.

"For the only one in the world that could tempt me to do anything."

"You should go for the sake of duty. I should not even care to see you go, much as I long for it, if that feeling did not take you there."

It was arranged that Phineas and Lord Chiltern were to leave Matching together. Phineas was to remain at his office all October, and in November the general election was to take place. What he had hitherto heard about a future seat was most vague, but he was to meet Ratler and Barrington Erle in London, and it had been understood that Barrington Erle, who was now at Saulsby, was to make some inquiry as to that group of boroughs of which Loughton at this moment formed one. But as Loughton was the smallest of four boroughs, and as one of the four had for many years had a representative of its own, Phineas feared that no success would be found there. In his present agony he began to think that there might be a strong plea made for a few private seats in the House of Commons, and that the propriety of throwing Loughton into the melting-pot was, after all, open to question. He and Lord Chiltern were to return to London together, and Lord Chiltern, according to his present scheme, was to proceed at once to Willingford to look after the cub-hunting. Nothing that either Violet or Phineas could say to him would induce him to promise to go to Saulsby. When Phineas pressed it, he was told by Lord Chiltern that he was a fool for his pains,—by which Phineas understood perfectly well that when Lord Chiltern did go to Saulsby, he, Phineas, was to take that as strong evidence that everything was over for him as regarded Violet Effingham. When Violet expressed her eagerness that the visit should be made, she was stopped with an assurance that she could have it done at once if she pleased. Let him only be enabled to carry with him the tidings of his betrothal, and he would start for his father's house without an hour's delay. But this authority Violet would not give him. When he answered her after this fashion she could only tell him that he was ungenerous. "At any rate I am not false," he replied on one occasion. "What I say is the truth."

There was a very tender parting between Phineas and Madame Max Goesler. She had learned from him pretty nearly all his history, and certainly knew more of the reality of his affairs than any of those in London who had been his most staunch friends. "Of course you'll get a seat," she said as he took his leave of her. "If I understand it at all, they never throw over an ally so useful as you are."

"But the intention is that in this matter nobody shall any longer have the power of throwing over, or of not throwing over, anybody."

"That is all very well, my friend; but cakes will still be hot in the mouth, even though Mr. Daubeny turn purist, with Mr. Turnbull to help him. If you want any assistance in finding a seat you will not go to the *People's Banner*,—even yet."

"Certainly not to the *People's Banner*."

"I don't quite understand what the franchise is," continued Madame Max Goesler.

"Household in boroughs," said Phineas with some energy.

"Very well;—household in boroughs. I daresay that is very fine and very liberal, though I don't comprehend it in the least. And you want a borough. Very well. You won't go to the households. I don't think you will;—not at first, that is."

"Where shall I go then?"

"Oh,—to some great patron of a borough;—or to a club;—or perhaps to some great firm. The households will know nothing about it till they are told. Is not that it?"

"The truth is, Madame Max, I do not know where I shall go. I am like a child lost in a wood. And you may understand this;—if you do not see me in Park Lane before the end of January, I shall have perished in the wood."

"Then I will come and find you,—with a troop of householders. You will come. You will be there. I do not believe in death coming without signs. You are full of life." As she spoke, she had hold of his hand, and there was nobody near them.

They were in a little book-room inside the library at Matching, and the door, though not latched, was nearly closed. Phineas had flattered himself that Madame Goesler had retreated there in order that this farewell might be spoken without interruption. "And, Mr. Finn;—I wonder whether I may say one thing," she continued.

"You may say anything to me," he replied.

"No,—not in this country, in this England. There are things one may not say here,—that are tabooed by a sort of consent,—and that without any reason." She paused again, and Phineas was at a loss to think what was the subject on which she was about to speak. Could she mean—? No; she could not mean to give him any outward plain-spoken sign that she was attached to him. It was the peculiar merit of this man that he was not vain, though much was done to him to fill him with vanity; and as the idea crossed his brain, he hated himself because it had been there.

"To me you may say anything, Madame Goesler," he said,—"here in England, as plainly as though we were in Vienna."

"But I cannot say it in English," she said. Then in French, blushing and laughing as she spoke,—almost stammering in spite of her usual self-confidence,—she told him that accident had made her rich, full of money. Money was a drug with her. Money she knew was wanted, even for householders. Would he not understand her, and come to her, and learn from her how faithful a woman could be?

He still was holding her by the hand, and he now raised it to his lips and kissed it. "The offer from you," he said, "is as high-minded, as generous, and as honourable as its acceptance by me would be mean-spirited, vile, and ignoble. But whether I fail or whether I succeed, you shall see me before the winter is over."

CHAPTER L. Again Successful

Phineas also said a word of farewell to Violet before he left Matching, but there was nothing peculiar in her little speech to him, or in his to her. "Of course we shall see each other in London. Don't talk of not being in the House. Of course you will be in the House." Then Phineas had shaken his head and smiled. Where was he to find a requisite number of householders prepared to return him? But as he went up to London he told himself that the air of the House of Commons was now the very breath of his nostrils. Life to him without it would be no life. To have come within the reach of the good things of political life, to have made his mark so as to have almost insured future success, to have been the petted young official aspirant of the day,—and then to sink down into the miserable platitudes of private life, to undergo daily attendance in law-courts without a brief, to listen to men who had come to be much below him in estimation and social intercourse, to sit in a wretched chamber up three pairs of stairs at Lincoln's Inn, whereas he was now at this moment provided with a gorgeous apartment looking out into the Park from the Colonial Office in Downing Street, to be attended by a mongrel between a clerk and an errand boy at 17s. 6d. a week instead of by a private secretary who was the son of an earl's sister, and was petted by countesses' daughters innumerable,—all this would surely break his heart. He could have done it, so he told himself, and could have taken glory in doing it, had not these other things come in his way. But the other things had come. He had run the risk, and had thrown the dice. And now when the game was so nearly won, must it be that everything should be lost at last?

He knew that nothing was to be gained by melancholy looks at his club, or by show of wretchedness at his office. London was very empty; but the approaching elections still kept some there who otherwise would have been looking after the first flush of pheasants. Barrington Erle was there, and was not long in asking Phineas what were his views.

"Ah;—that is so hard to say. Ratler told me that he would be looking about."

"Ratler is very well in the House," said Barrington, "but he is of no use for anything beyond it. I suppose you were not brought up at the London University?"

"Oh no," said Phineas, remembering the glories of Trinity.

"Because there would have been an opening. What do you say to Stratford,—the new Essex borough?"

"Broadbury the brewer is there already!"

"Yes;—and ready to spend any money you like to name. Let me see. Loughton is grouped with Smotherem, and Walker is a deal too strong at Smotherem to hear of any other claim. I don't think we could dare to propose it. There are the Chelsea hamlets, but it will take a wack of money."

"I have not got a wack of money," said Phineas, laughing.

"That's the devil of it. I think, if I were you, I should hark back upon some place in Ireland. Couldn't you get Laurence to give you up his seat?"

"What! Fitzgibbon?"

"Yes. He has not a ghost of a chance of getting into office again. Nothing on earth would induce him to look at a paper during all those weeks he was at the Colonial Office; and when Cantrip spoke to him, all he said was, 'Ah, bother!' Cantrip did not like it, I can tell you."

"But that wouldn't make him give up his seat."

"Of course you'd have to arrange it." By which Phineas understood Barrington Erle to mean that he, Phineas, was in some way to give to Laurence Fitzgibbon some adequate compensation for the surrender of his position as a county member.

"I'm afraid that's out of the question," said Phineas. "If he were to go, I should not get it."

"Would you have a chance at Loughshane?"

"I was thinking of trying it," said Phineas.

"Of course you know that Morris is very ill." This Mr. Morris was the brother of Lord Tulla, and was the sitting member of Loughshane. "Upon my word I think I should try that. I don't see where we're to put our hands on a seat in England. I don't indeed." Phineas, as he listened to this, could not help thinking that Barrington Erle, though he had certainly expressed a great deal of solicitude, was not as true a friend as he used to be. Perhaps he, Phineas, had risen too fast, and Barrington Erle was beginning to think that he might as well be out of the way.

He wrote to his father, asking after the borough, and asking after the health of Mr. Morris. And in his letter he told his own story very plainly,—almost pathetically. He perhaps had been wrong to make the attempt which he had made. He began to believe that he had been wrong. But at any rate he had made it so far successfully, and failure now would be doubly bitter. He thought that the party to which he belonged must now remain in office. It would hardly be possible that a new election would produce a House of Commons favourable to a conservative ministry. And with a liberal ministry he, Phineas, would be sure of his place, and sure of an official income,—if only he could find a seat. It was all very true, and was almost pathetic. The old doctor, who was inclined to be proud of his son, was not unwilling to make a sacrifice. Mrs. Finn declared before her daughters that if there was a seat in all Ireland, Phineas ought to have it. And Mary Flood Jones stood by listening, and wondering what Phineas would do if he lost his seat. Would he come back and live in County Clare, and be like any other girl's lover? Poor Mary had come to lose her ambition, and to think that girls whose lovers stayed at home were the happiest. Nevertheless, she would have walked all the way to Lord Tulla's house and back again, might that have availed to get the seat for Phineas. Then there came an express over from Castlemorris. The doctor was wanted at once to see Mr. Morris. Mr. Morris was very bad with gout in his stomach. According to the messenger it was supposed that Mr. Morris was dying. Before Dr. Finn had had an opportunity of answering his son's letter, Mr. Morris, the late member for Loughshane, had been gathered to his fathers.

Dr. Finn understood enough of elections for Parliament, and of the nature of boroughs, to be aware that a candidate's chance of success is very much improved by being early in the field; and he was aware, also, that the death of Mr. Morris would probably create various aspirants for the honour of representing Loughshane. But he could hardly address the Earl on the subject while the dead body of the late member was lying in the house at Castlemorris. The bill which had passed in the late session for reforming the constitution of the House of Commons had not touched Ireland, a future measure having been promised to the Irish for their comfort; and Loughshane therefore was, as to Lord Tulla's influence, the same as it had ever been. He had not there the plenary power which the other lord had held in his hands in regard to Loughton;—but still the Castlemorris interest would go a long way. It might be possible to stand against it, but it would be much more desirable that the candidate should have it at his back. Dr. Finn was fully alive to this as he sat opposite to the old lord, saying now a word about the old lord's gout in his legs and arms, and then about the gout in the stomach, which had carried away to another world the lamented late member for the borough.

"Poor Jack!" said Lord Tulla, piteously. "If I'd known it, I needn't have paid over two thousand pounds for him last year;—need I, doctor?"

"No, indeed," said Dr. Finn, feeling that his patient might perhaps approach the subject of the borough himself.

"He never would live by any rule, you know," said the desolate brother.

"Very hard to guide;—was he not, my lord?"

"The very devil. Now, you see, I do do what I'm told pretty well,—don't I, doctor?"

"Sometimes."

"By George, I do nearly always. I don't know what you mean by sometimes. I've been drinking brandy-and-water till I'm sick of it, to oblige you, and you tell me about—sometimes. You doctors expect a man to be a slave. Haven't I kept it out of my stomach?"

"Thank God, yes."

"It's all very well thanking God, but I should have gone as poor Jack has gone, if I hadn't been the most careful man in the world. He was drinking champagne ten days ago;—would do it, you know." Lord Tulla could talk about himself and his own ailments by the hour together, and Dr. Finn, who had thought that his noble patient was approaching the subject of the borough, was beginning again to feel that the double interest of the gout that was present, and the gout that had passed away, would be too absorbing. He, however, could say but little to direct the conversation.

"Mr. Morris, you see, lived more in London than you do, and was subject to temptation."

"I don't know what you call temptation. Haven't I the temptation of a bottle of wine under my nose every day of my life?"

"No doubt you have."

"And I don't drink it. I hardly ever take above a glass or two of brown sherry. By George! when I think of it, I wonder at my own courage. I do, indeed."

"But a man in London, my lord—"

"Why the deuce would he go to London? By-the-bye, what am I to do about the borough now?"

"Let my son stand for it, if you will, my lord."

"They've clean swept away Brentford's seat at Loughton, haven't they? Ha, ha, ha! What a nice game for him,—to have been forced to help to do it himself! There's nobody on earth I pity so much as a radical peer who is obliged to work like a nigger with a spade to shovel away the ground from under his own feet. As for me, I don't care who sits for Loughshane. I did care for poor Jack while he was alive. I don't think I shall interfere any longer. I am glad it lasted Jack's time." Lord Tulla had probably already forgotten that he himself had thrown Jack over for the last session but one.

"Phineas, my lord," began the father, "is now Under-Secretary of State."

"Oh, I've no doubt he's a very fine fellow;—but you see, he's an out-and-out Radical."

"No, my lord."

"Then how can he serve with such men as Mr. Gresham and Mr. Monk? They've turned out poor old Mildmay among them, because he's not fast enough for them. Don't tell me."

"My anxiety, of course, is for my boy's prospects. He seems to have done so well in Parliament."

"Why don't he stand for Marylebone or Finsbury?"

"The money, you know, my lord!"

"I shan't interfere here, doctor. If he comes, and the people then choose to return him, I shall say nothing. They may do just as they please. They tell me Lambert St. George, of Mockrath, is going to stand. If he does, it's the d— piece of impudence I ever heard of. He's a tenant of my own, though he has a lease for ever; and his father never owned an acre of land in the county till his uncle died." Then the doctor knew that, with a little management, the lord's interest might be secured for his son.

Phineas came over and stood for the borough against Mr. Lambert St. George, and the contest was sharp enough. The gentry of the neighbourhood could not understand why such a man as Lord Tulla should admit a liberal candidate to succeed his brother. No one canvassed for the young Under-Secretary with more persistent zeal than did his father, who, when Phineas first spoke of going into Parliament, had produced so many good arguments against that perilous step. Lord Tulla's agent stood aloof,—desolate with grief at the death of the late member. At such a moment of family affliction, Lord Tulla, he declared, could not think of such a matter as the borough. But it was known that Lord Tulla was dreadfully jealous of Mr. Lambert St. George, whose property in that part of the county was now nearly equal to his own, and who saw much more company at Mockrath than was ever entertained at Castlemorris. A word from Lord Tulla,—so said the Conservatives of the county,—would have put Mr. St. George into the seat; but that word was not spoken, and the Conservatives of the neighbourhood swore that Lord Tulla was a renegade. The contest was very sharp, but our hero was returned by a majority of seventeen votes.

Again successful! As he thought of it he remembered stories of great generals who were said to have chained Fortune to the wheels of their chariots, but it seemed to him that the goddess had never served any general with such staunch obedience as she had displayed in his cause. Had not everything gone well with him;—so well, as almost to justify him in expecting that even yet Violet Effingham would become his wife? Dear, dearest Violet! If he could only achieve that, no general, who ever led an army across the Alps, would be his equal either in success or in the reward of success. Then he questioned himself as to what he would say to Miss Flood Jones on that very night. He was to meet dear little Mary Flood Jones that evening at a neighbour's house. His sister Barbara had so told him in a tone of voice which he quite understood to imply a caution. "I shall be so glad to see her," Phineas had replied.

"If there ever was an angel on earth, it is Mary," said Barbara Finn.

"I know that she is as good as gold," said Phineas.

"Gold!" replied Barbara,—"gold indeed! She is more precious than refined gold. But, Phineas, perhaps you had better not single her out for any special attention. She has thought it wisest to meet you."

"Of course," said Phineas. "Why not?"

"That is all, Phineas. I have nothing more to say. Men of course are different from girls."

"That's true, Barbara, at any rate."

"Don't laugh at me, Phineas, when I am thinking of nothing but of you and your interests, and when I am making all manner of excuses for you because I know what must be the distractions of the world in which you live." Barbara made more than one attempt to renew the conversation before the evening came, but Phineas thought that he had had enough of it. He did not like being told that excuses were made for him. After all, what had he done? He had once kissed Mary Flood Jones behind the door.

"I am so glad to see you, Mary," he said, coming and taking a chair by her side. He had been specially warned not to single Mary out for his attention, and yet there was the chair left vacant as though it were expected that he would fall into it.

"Thank you. We did not happen to meet last year, did we,—Mr. Finn?"

"Do not call me Mr. Finn, Mary."

"You are such a great man now!"

"Not at all a great man. If you only knew what little men we understrappers are in London you would hardly speak to me."

"But you are something—of State now;—are you not?"

"Well;—yes. That's the name they give me. It simply means that if any member wants to badger some one in the House about the Colonies, I am the man to be badgered. But if there is any credit to be had, I am not the man who is to have it."

"But it is a great thing to be in Parliament and in the Government too."

"It is a great thing for me, Mary, to have a salary, though it may only be for a year or two. However, I will not deny that it is pleasant to have been successful."

"It has been very pleasant to us, Phineas. Mamma has been so much rejoiced."

"I am so sorry not to see her. She is at Floodborough, I suppose."

"Oh, yes;—she is at home. She does not like coming out at night in winter. I have been staying here you know for two days, but I go home to-morrow."

"I will ride over and call on your mother." Then there was a pause in the conversation for a moment. "Does it not seem odd, Mary, that we should see so little of each other?"

"You are so much away, of course."

"Yes;—that is the reason. But still it seems almost unnatural. I often wonder when the time will come that I shall be quietly at home again. I have to be back in my office in London this day week, and yet I have not had a single hour to myself since I have been at Killaloe. But I will certainly ride over and see your mother. You will be at home on Wednesday I suppose."

"Yes,—I shall be at home."

Upon that he got up and went away, but again in the evening he found himself near her. Perhaps there is no position more perilous to a man's honesty than that in which Phineas now found himself;—that, namely, of knowing himself to be quite loved by a girl whom he almost loves himself. Of course he loved Violet Effingham; and they who talk best of love protest that no man or woman can be in love with two persons at once. Phineas was not in love with Mary Flood Jones; but he would have liked to take her in his arms and kiss her;—he would have liked to gratify her by swearing that she was dearer to him than all the world; he would have liked to have an episode,—and did, at the moment, think that it might be possible to have one life in London and another life altogether different at Killaloe. "Dear Mary," he said as he pressed her hand that night, "things will get themselves settled at last, I suppose." He was behaving very ill to her, but he did not mean to behave ill.

He rode over to Floodborough, and saw Mrs. Flood Jones. Mrs. Flood Jones, however, received him very coldly; and Mary did not appear. Mary had communicated to her mother her resolutions as to her future life. "The fact is, mamma, I love him. I cannot help it. If he ever chooses to come for me, here I am. If he does not, I will bear it as well as I can. It may be very mean of me, but it's true."

CHAPTER LI. Troubles at Loughlinter

There was a dull house at Loughlinter during the greater part of this autumn. A few men went down for the grouse shooting late in the season; but they stayed but a short time, and when they went Lady Laura was left alone with her husband. Mr. Kennedy had explained to his wife, more than once, that though he understood the duties of hospitality and enjoyed the performance of them, he had not married with the intention of living in a whirlwind. He was disposed to think that the whirlwind had hitherto been too predominant, and had said so very plainly with a good deal of marital authority. This autumn and winter were to be devoted to the cultivation of proper relations between him and his wife. "Does that mean Darby and Joan?" his wife had asked him, when the proposition was made to her. "It means mutual regard and esteem," replied Mr. Kennedy in his most solemn tone, "and I trust that such mutual regard and esteem between us may yet be possible." When Lady Laura showed him a letter from her brother, received some weeks after this conversation, in which Lord Chiltern expressed his intention of coming to Loughlinter for Christmas, he returned the note to his wife without a word. He suspected that she had made the arrangement without asking him, and was angry; but he would not tell her that her brother would not be welcome at his house. "It is not my doing," she said, when she saw the frown on his brow.

"I said nothing about anybody's doing," he replied.

"I will write to Oswald and bid him not come, if you wish it. Of course you can understand why he is coming."

"Not to see me, I am sure," said Mr. Kennedy.

"Nor me," replied Lady Laura. "He is coming because my friend Violet Effingham will be here."

"Miss Effingham! Why was I not told of this? I knew nothing of Miss Effingham's coming."

"Robert, it was settled in your own presence last July."

"I deny it."

Then Lady Laura rose up, very haughty in her gait and with something of fire in her eye, and silently left the room. Mr. Kennedy, when he found himself alone, was very unhappy. Looking back in his mind to the summer weeks in London, he remembered that his wife had told Violet that she was to spend her Christmas at Loughlinter, that he himself had given a muttered assent and that Violet,—as far as he could remember,—had made no reply. It had been one of those things which are so often mentioned, but not settled. He felt that he had been strictly right in denying that it had been "settled" in his presence;—but yet he felt that he had been wrong in contradicting his wife so peremptorily. He was a just man, and he would apologise for his fault; but he was an austere man, and would take back the value of his apology in additional austerity. He did not see his wife for some hours after the conversation which has been narrated, but when he did meet her his mind was still full of the subject. "Laura", he said, "I am sorry that I contradicted you."

"I am quite used to it, Robert."

"No;—you are not used to it." She smiled and bowed her head. "You wrong me by saying that you are used to it." Then he paused a moment, but she said not a word,—only smiled and bowed her head again. "I remember," he continued, "that something was said in my presence to Miss Effingham about her coming here at Christmas. It was so slight, however, that it had passed out of my memory till recalled by an effort. I beg your pardon."

"That is unnecessary, Robert."

"It is, dear."

"And do you wish that I should put her off,—or put Oswald off,—or both? My brother never yet has seen me in your house."

"And whose fault has that been?"

"I have said nothing about anybody's fault, Robert. I merely mentioned a fact. Will you let me know whether I shall bid him stay away?"

"He is welcome to come,—only I do not like assignations for love-making."

"Assignations!"

"Clandestine meetings. Lady Baldock would not wish it."

"Lady Baldock! Do you think that Violet would exercise any secrecy in the matter,—or that she will not tell Lady Baldock that Oswald will be here,—as soon as she knows it herself?"

"That has nothing to do with it."

"Surely, Robert, it must have much to do with it. And why should not these two young people meet? The acknowledged wish of all the family is that they should marry each other. And in this matter, at any rate, my brother has behaved extremely well." Mr. Kennedy said nothing further at the time, and it became an understanding that Violet Effingham was to be a month at Loughlinter, staying from the 20th of December to the 20th of January, and that Lord Chiltern was to come there for Christmas,—which with him would probably mean three days.

Before Christmas came, however, there were various other sources of uneasiness at Loughlinter. There had been, as a matter of course, great anxiety as to the elections. With Lady Laura this anxiety had been very strong, and even Mr. Kennedy had been warmed with some amount of fire as the announcements reached him of the successes and of the failures. The English returns came first,—and then the Scotch, which were quite as interesting to Mr. Kennedy as the English. His own seat was quite safe,—was not contested; but some neighbouring seats were sources of great solicitude. Then, when this was over, there were the tidings from Ireland to be received; and respecting one special borough in Ireland, Lady Laura evinced more solicitude than her husband approved. There was much danger for the domestic bliss of the house of Loughlinter, when things came to such a pass, and such words were spoken, as the election at Loughshane produced.

"He is in," said Lady Laura, opening a telegram.

"Who is in?" said Mr. Kennedy, with that frown on his brow to which his wife was now well accustomed. Though he asked the question, he knew very well who was the hero to whom the telegram referred.

"Our friend Phineas Finn," said Lady Laura, speaking still with an excited voice,—with a voice that was intended to display excitement. If there was to be a battle on this matter, there should be a battle. She would display all her anxiety for her young friend, and fling it in her husband's face if he chose to take it as an injury. What,—should she endure reproach from her husband because she regarded the interests of the man who had saved his life, of the man respecting whom she had suffered so many heart-struggles, and as to whom she had at last come to the conclusion that he should ever be regarded as a second brother, loved equally with the elder brother? She had done her duty by her husband,—so at least she had assured herself;—and should he dare to reproach her on this subject, she would be ready for the battle. And now the battle came. "I am glad of this," she said, with all the eagerness she could throw into her voice. "I am, indeed,—and so ought you to be." The husband's brow grew blacker and blacker, but still he said nothing. He had long been too proud to be jealous, and was now too proud to express his jealousy,—if only he could keep the expression back. But his wife would not leave the subject. "I am so thankful for this," she said, pressing the telegram between her hands. "I was so afraid he would fail!"

"You over-do your anxiety on such a subject," at last he said, speaking very slowly.

"What do you mean, Robert? How can I be over-anxious? If it concerned any other dear friend that I have in the world, it would not be an affair of life and death. To him it is almost so. I would have walked from here to London to get him his election." And as she spoke she held up the clenched fist of her left hand, and shook it, while she still held the telegram in her right hand.

"Laura, I must tell you that it is improper that you should speak of any man in those terms;—of any man that is a stranger to your blood."

"A stranger to my blood! What has that to do with it? This man is my friend, is your friend;—saved your life, has been my brother's best friend, is loved by my father,—and is loved by me, very dearly. Tell me what you mean by improper!"

"I will not have you love any man,—very dearly."

"Robert!"

"I tell you that I will have no such expressions from you. They are unseemly, and are used only to provoke me."

"Am I to understand that I am insulted by an accusation? If so, let me beg at once that I may be allowed to go to Saulsby. I would rather accept your apology and retractation there than here."

"You will not go to Saulsby, and there has been no accusation, and there will be no apology. If you please there will be no more mention of Mr. Finn's name between us, for the present. If you will take my advice you will cease to think of him extravagantly;—and I must desire you to hold no further direct communication with him."

"I have held no communication with him," said Lady Laura, advancing a step towards him. But Mr. Kennedy simply pointed to the telegram in her hand, and left the room. Now in respect to this telegram there had been an unfortunate mistake. I am not prepared to say that there was any reason why Phineas himself should not have sent the news of his success to Lady Laura; but he had not done so. The piece of paper which she still held crushed in her hand was in itself very innocent. "Hurrah for the Loughshanes. Finny has done the trick." Such were the words written on the slip, and they had been sent to Lady Laura by her young cousin, the clerk in the office who acted as private secretary to the Under-Secretary of State. Lady Laura resolved that her husband should never see those innocent but rather undignified words. The occasion had become one of importance, and such words were unworthy of it. Besides, she would not condescend to defend herself by bringing forward a telegram as evidence in her favour. So she burned the morsel of paper.

Lady Laura and Mr. Kennedy did not meet again till late that evening. She was ill, she said, and would not come down to dinner. After dinner she wrote him a note. "DEAR ROBERT, I think you must regret what you said to me. If so, pray let me have a line from you to that effect. Yours affectionately, L." When the servant handed it to him, and he had read it, he smiled and thanked the girl who had brought it, and said he would see her mistress just now. Anything would be better than that the servants should know that there was a quarrel. But every servant in the house had known all about it for the last three hours. When the door was closed and he was alone, he sat fingering the note, thinking deeply how he should answer it, or whether he would answer it at all. No; he would not answer it;—not in writing. He would give his wife no written record of his humiliation. He had not acted wrongly. He had said nothing more than now, upon mature consideration, he thought that the circumstances demanded. But yet he felt that he must in some sort withdraw the accusation which he had made. If he did not withdraw it, there was no knowing what his wife might do. About ten in the evening he went up to her and made his little speech. "My dear, I have come to answer your note."

"I thought you would have written to me a line."

"I have come instead, Laura. Now, if you will listen to me for one moment, I think everything will be made smooth."

"Of course I will listen," said Lady Laura, knowing very well that her husband's moment would be rather tedious, and resolving that she also would have her moment afterwards.

"I think you will acknowledge that if there be a difference of opinion between you and me as to any question of social intercourse, it will be better that you should consent to adopt my opinion."

"You have the law on your side."

"I am not speaking of the law."

"Well;—go on, Robert. I will not interrupt you if I can help it."

"I am not speaking of the law. I am speaking simply of convenience, and of that which you must feel to be right. If I wish that your intercourse with any person should be of such or such a nature it must be best that you should comply with my wishes." He paused for her assent, but she neither assented nor dissented. "As far as I can understand the position of a man and wife in this country, there is no other way in which life can be made harmonious."

"Life will not run in harmonies."

"I expect that ours shall be made to do so, Laura. I need hardly say to you that I intend to accuse you of no impropriety of feeling in reference to this young man."

"No, Robert; you need hardly say that. Indeed, to speak my own mind, I think that you need hardly have alluded to it. I might go further, and say that such an allusion is in itself an insult,—an insult now repeated after hours of deliberation,—an insult which I will not endure to have repeated again. If you say another word in any way suggesting the possibility of improper relations between me and Mr. Finn, either as to deeds or thoughts, as God is above me, I will write to both my father and my brother, and desire them to take me from your house. If you wish me to remain here, you had better be careful!" As she was making this speech, her temper seemed to rise, and to become hot, and then hotter, till it glowed with a red heat. She had been cool till the word insult, used by herself, had conveyed back to her a strong impression of her own wrong,—or perhaps I should rather say a strong feeling of the necessity of becoming indignant. She was standing as she spoke, and the fire flashed from her eyes, and he quailed before her. The threat which she had held out to him was very dreadful to him. He was a man terribly in fear of the world's good opinion, who lacked the courage to go through a great and harassing trial in order that something better might come afterwards. His married life had been unhappy. His wife had not submitted either to his will or to his ways. He had that great desire to enjoy his full rights, so strong in the minds of weak, ambitious men, and he had told himself that a wife's obedience was one of those rights which he could not abandon without injury to his self-esteem. He had thought about the matter, slowly, as was his wont, and had resolved that he would assert himself. He had asserted himself, and his wife told him to his face that she would go away and leave him. He could detain her legally, but he could not do even that without the fact of such forcible detention being known to all the world. How was he to answer her now at this moment, so that she might not write to her father, and so that his self-assertion might still be maintained?

"Passion, Laura, can never be right."

"Would you have a woman submit to insult without passion? I at any rate am not such a woman." Then there was a pause for a moment. "If you have nothing else to say to me, you had better leave me. I am far from well, and my head is throbbing."

He came up and took her hand, but she snatched it away from him. "Laura," he said, "do not let us quarrel."

"I certainly shall quarrel if such insinuations are repeated."

"I made no insinuation."

"Do not repeat them. That is all."

He was cowed and left her, having first attempted to get out of the difficulty of his position by making much of her alleged illness, and by offering to send for Dr. Macnuthrie. She positively refused to see Dr. Macnuthrie, and at last succeeded in inducing him to quit the room.

This had occurred about the end of November, and on the 20th of December Violet Effingham reached Loughlinter. Life in Mr. Kennedy's house had gone quietly during the intervening three weeks, but not very pleasantly. The name of Phineas Finn had not been mentioned. Lady Laura had triumphed; but she had no desire to acerbate her husband by any unpalatable allusion to her victory. And he was quite willing to let the subject die away, if only it would die. On some other matters he continued to assert himself, taking his wife to church twice every Sunday, using longer family prayers than she approved, reading an additional sermon himself every Sunday evening, calling upon her for weekly attention to elaborate household accounts, asking for her personal assistance in much local visiting, initiating her into his favourite methods of family life in the country, till sometimes she almost longed to talk again about Phineas Finn, so that there might be a rupture, and she might escape. But her husband asserted himself within bounds, and she submitted, longing for the coming of Violet Effingham. She could not write to her father and beg to be taken away, because her husband would read a sermon to her on Sunday evening.

To Violet, very shortly after her arrival, she told her whole story. "This is terrible," said Violet. "This makes me feel that I never will be married."

"And yet what can a woman become if she remain single? The curse is to be a woman at all."

"I have always felt so proud of the privileges of my sex," said Violet.

"I never have found them," said the other; "never. I have tried to make the best of its weaknesses, and this is what I have come to! I suppose I ought to have loved some man."

"And did you never love any man?"

"No;—I think I never did,—not as people mean when they speak of love. I have felt that I would consent to be cut in little pieces for my brother,—because of my regard for him."

"Ah, that is nothing."

"And I have felt something of the same thing for another,—a longing for his welfare, a delight to hear him praised, a charm in his presence,—so strong a feeling for his interest, that were he to go to wrack and ruin, I too, should, after a fashion, be wracked and ruined. But it has not been love either."

"Do I know whom you mean? May I name him? It is Phineas Finn."

"Of course it is Phineas Finn."

"Did he ever ask you,—to love him?"

"I feared he would do so, and therefore accepted Mr. Kennedy's offer almost at the first word."

"I do not quite understand your reasoning, Laura."

"I understand it. I could have refused him nothing in my power to give him, but I did not wish to be his wife."

"And he never asked you?"

Lady Laura paused a moment, thinking what reply she should make;—and then she told a fib. "No; he never asked me." But Violet did not believe the fib. Violet was quite sure that Phineas had asked Lady Laura Standish to be his wife. "As far as I can see," said Violet, "Madame Max Goesler is his present passion."

"I do not believe it in the least," said Lady Laura, firing up.

"It does not much matter," said Violet.

"It would matter very much. You know, you,—you; you know whom he loves. And I do believe that sooner or later you will be his wife."

"Never."

"Yes, you will. Had you not loved him you would never have condescended to accuse him about that woman."

"I have not accused him. Why should he not marry Madame Max Goesler? It would be just the thing for him. She is very rich."

"Never. You will be his wife."

"Laura, you are the most capricious of women. You have two dear friends, and you insist that I shall marry them both. Which shall I take first?"

"Oswald will be here in a day or two, and you can take him if you like it. No doubt he will ask you. But I do not think you will."

"No; I do not think I shall. I shall knock under to Mr. Mill, and go in for women's rights, and look forward to stand for some female borough. Matrimony never seemed to me to be very charming, and upon my word it does not become more alluring by what I find at Loughlinter."

It was thus that Violet and Lady Laura discussed these matters together, but Violet had never showed to her friend the cards in her hand, as Lady Laura had shown those which she held. Lady Laura had in fact told almost everything that there was to tell,—had spoken either plainly with true words, or equally plainly with words that were not true. Violet Effingham had almost come to love Phineas Finn;—but she never told her friend that it was so. At one time she had almost made up her mind to give herself and all her wealth to this adventurer. He was a better man, she thought, than Lord Chiltern; and she had come to persuade herself that it was almost imperative on her to take the one or the other. Though she could talk about remaining unmarried, she knew that that was practically impossible. All those around her,—those of the Baldock as well as those of the Brentford faction,—would make such a life impossible to her. Besides, in such a case what could she do? It was all very well to talk of disregarding the world and of setting up a house for herself;—but she was quite aware that that project could not be used further than for the purpose of scaring her amiable aunt. And if not that,—then could she content herself to look forward to a joint life with Lady Baldock and Augusta Boreham? She might, of course, oblige her aunt by taking Lord Fawn, or oblige her aunt equally by taking Mr. Appledom; but she was strongly of opinion that either Lord Chiltern or Phineas would be preferable to these. Thinking over it always she had come to feel that it must be either Lord Chiltern or Phineas; but she had never whispered her thought to man or woman. On her journey to Loughlinter, where she then knew that she was to meet Lord Chiltern, she endeavoured to persuade herself that it should be Phineas. But Lady Laura had marred it all by that ill-told fib. There had been a moment before in which Violet had felt that Phineas had sacrificed something of that truth of love for which she gave him credit to the glances of Madame Goesler's eyes; but she had rebuked herself for the idea, accusing herself not only of a little jealousy, but of foolish vanity. Was he, whom she had rejected, not to speak to another woman? Then came the blow from Lady Laura, and Violet knew that it was a blow. This gallant lover, this young Crichton, this unassuming but ardent lover, had simply taken up with her as soon as he had failed with her friend. Lady Laura had been most enthusiastic in her expressions of friendship. Such platonic regards might be all very well. It was for Mr. Kennedy to look to that. But, for herself, she felt that such expressions were hardly compatible with her ideas of having her lover all to herself. And then she again remembered Madame Goesler's bright blue eyes.

Lord Chiltern came on Christmas eve, and was received with open arms by his sister, and with that painful, irritating affection which such a girl as Violet can show to such a man as Lord Chiltern, when she will not give him that other affection for which his heart is panting. The two men were civil to each other,—but very cold. They called each other Kennedy and Chiltern, but even that was not done without an effort. On the Christmas morning Mr. Kennedy asked his brother-in-law to go to church. "It's a kind of thing I never do," said Lord Chiltern. Mr. Kennedy gave a little start, and looked a look of horror. Lady Laura showed that she was unhappy. Violet Effingham turned away her face, and smiled.

As they walked across the park Violet took Lord Chiltern's part. "He only means that he does not go to church on Christmas day."

"I don't know what he means," said Mr. Kennedy.

"We need not speak of it," said Lady Laura.

"Certainly not," said Mr. Kennedy.

"I have been to church with him on Sundays myself," said Violet, perhaps not reflecting that the practices of early years had little to do with the young man's life at present.

Christmas day and the next day passed without any sign from Lord Chiltern, and on the day after that he was to go away. But he was not to leave till one or two in the afternoon. Not a word had been said between the two women, since he had been in the house, on the subject of which both of them were thinking. Very much had been said of the expediency of his going to Saulsby, but on this matter he had declined to make any promise. Sitting in Lady Laura's room, in the presence of both of them, he had refused to do so. "I am bad to drive," he said, turning to Violet, "and you had better not try to drive me."

"Why should not you be driven as well as another?" she answered, laughing.

CHAPTER LII. The First Blow

Lord Chiltern, though he had passed two entire days in the house with Violet without renewing his suit, had come to Loughlinter for the express purpose of doing so, and had his plans perfectly fixed in his own mind. After breakfast on that last morning he was up-stairs with his sister in her own room, and immediately made his request to her. "Laura," he said, "go down like a good girl, and make Violet come up here." She stood a moment looking at him and smiled. "And, mind," he continued, "you are not to come back yourself. I must have Violet alone."

"But suppose Violet will not come? Young ladies do not generally wait upon young men on such occasions."

"No;—but I rank her so high among young women, that I think she will have common sense enough to teach her that, after what has passed between us, I have a right to ask for an interview, and that it may be more conveniently had here than in the wilderness of the house below."

Whatever may have been the arguments used by her friend, Violet did come. She reached the door all alone, and opened it bravely. She had promised herself, as she came along the passages, that she would not pause with her hand on the lock for a moment. She had first gone to her own room, and as she left it she had looked into the glass with a hurried glance, and had then rested for a moment,—thinking that something should be done, that her hair might be smoothed, or a ribbon set straight, or the chain arranged under her brooch. A girl would wish to look well before her lover, even when she means to refuse him. But her pause was but for an instant, and then she went on, having touched nothing. She shook her head and pressed her hands together, and went on quick and opened the door,—almost with a little start. "Violet, this is very good of you," said Lord Chiltern, standing with his back to the fire, and not moving from the spot.

"Laura has told me that you thought I would do as much as this for you, and therefore I have done it."

"Thanks, dearest. It is the old story, Violet, and I am so bad at words!"

"I must have been bad at words too, as I have not been able to make you understand."

"I think I have understood. You are always clear-spoken, and I, though I cannot talk, am not muddle-pated. I have understood. But while you are single there must be yet hope;—unless, indeed, you will tell me that you have already given yourself to another man."

"I have not done that."

"Then how can I not hope? Violet, I would if I could tell you all my feelings plainly. Once, twice, thrice, I have said to myself that I would think of you no more. I have tried to persuade myself that I am better single than married."

"But I am not the only woman."

"To me you are,—absolutely, as though there were none other on the face of God's earth. I live much alone; but you are always with me. Should you marry any other man, it will be the same with me still. If you refuse me now I shall go away,—and live wildly."

"Oswald, what do you mean?"

"I mean that I will go to some distant part of the world, where I may be killed or live a life of adventure. But I shall do so simply in despair. It will not be that I do not know how much better and greater should be the life at home of a man in my position."

"Then do not talk of going."

"I cannot stay. You will acknowledge, Violet, that I have never lied to you. I am thinking of you day and night. The more indifferent you show yourself to me, the more I love you. Violet, try to love me." He came up to her, and took her by both her hands, and tears were in his eyes. "Say you will try to love me."

"It is not that," said Violet, looking away, but still leaving her hands with him.

"It is not what, dear?"

"What you call,—trying."

"It is that you do not wish to try?"

"Oswald, you are so violent, so headstrong. I am afraid of you,—as is everybody. Why have you not written to your father, as we have asked you?"

"I will write to him instantly, now, before I leave the room, and you shall dictate the letter to him. By heavens, you shall!" He had dropped her hands when she called him violent; but now he took them again, and still she permitted it. "I have postponed it only till I had spoken to you once again."

"No, Lord Chiltern, I will not dictate to you."

"But will you love me?" She paused and looked down, having even now not withdrawn her hands from him. But I do not think he knew how much he had gained. "You used to love me,—a little," he said.

"Indeed,—indeed, I did."

"And now? Is it all changed now?"

"No," she said, retreating from him.

"How is it, then? Violet, speak to me honestly. Will you be my wife?" She did not answer him, and he stood for a moment looking at her. Then he rushed at her, and, seizing her in his arms, kissed her all over,—her forehead, her lips, her cheeks, then both her hands, and then her lips again. "By G—, she is my own!" he said. Then he went back to the rug before the fire, and stood there with his back turned to her. Violet, when she found herself thus deserted, retreated to a sofa, and sat herself down. She had no negative to produce now in answer to the violent assertion which he had pronounced as to his own success. It was true. She had doubted, and doubted,—and still doubted. But now she must doubt no longer. Of one thing she was quite sure. She could love him. As things had now gone, she would make him quite happy with assurances on that subject. As to that other question,—that fearful question, whether or not she could trust him,—on that matter she had better at present say nothing, and think as little, perhaps, as might be. She had taken the jump, and therefore why should she not be gracious to him? But how was she to be gracious to a lover who stood there with his back turned to her?

After the interval of a minute or two he remembered himself, and turned round. Seeing her seated, he approached her, and went down on both knees close at her feet. Then he took her hands again, for the third time, and looked up into her eyes.

"Oswald, you on your knees!" she said.

"I would not bend to a princess," he said, "to ask for half her throne; but I will kneel here all day, if you will let me, in thanks for the gift of your love. I never kneeled to beg for it."

"This is the man who cannot make speeches."

"I think I could talk now by the hour, with you for a listener."

"Oh, but I must talk too."

"What will you say to me?"

"Nothing while you are kneeling. It is not natural that you should kneel. You are like Samson with his locks shorn, or Hercules with a distaff."

"Is that better?" he said, as he got up and put his arm round her waist.

"You are in earnest?" she asked.

"In earnest. I hardly thought that that would be doubted. Do you not believe me?"

"I do believe you. And you will be good?"

"Ah,—I do not know that."

"Try, and I will love you so dearly. Nay, I do love you dearly. I do. I do."

"Say it again."

"I will say it fifty times,—till your ears are weary with it";—and she did say it to him, after her own fashion, fifty times.

"This is a great change," he said, getting up after a while and walking about the room.

"But a change for the better;—is it not, Oswald?"

"So much for the better that I hardly know myself in my new joy. But, Violet, we'll have no delay,—will we? No shilly-shallying. What is the use of waiting now that it's settled?"

"None in the least, Lord Chiltern. Let us say,—this day twelvemonth."

"You are laughing at me, Violet."

"Remember, sir, that the first thing you have to do is to write to your father."

He instantly went to the writing-table and took up paper and pen. "Come along," he said. "You are to dictate it." But this she refused to do, telling him that he must write his letter to his father out of his own head, and out of his own heart. "I cannot write it," he said, throwing down the pen. "My blood is in such a tumult that I cannot steady my hand."

"You must not be so tumultuous, Oswald, or I shall have to live in a whirlwind."

"Oh, I shall shake down. I shall become as steady as an old stager. I'll go as quiet in harness by-and-by as though I had been broken to it a four-year-old. I wonder whether Laura could not write this letter."

"I think you should write it yourself, Oswald."

"If you bid me I will."

"Bid you indeed! As if it was for me to bid you. Do you not know that in these new troubles you are undertaking you will have to bid me in everything, and that I shall be bound to do your bidding? Does it not seem to be dreadful? My wonder is that any girl can ever accept any man."

"But you have accepted me now."

"Yes, indeed."

"And you repent?"

"No, indeed, and I will try to do your biddings;—but you must not be rough to me, and outrageous, and fierce,—will you, Oswald?"

"I will not at any rate be like Kennedy is with poor Laura."

"No;—that is not your nature."

"I will do my best, dearest. And you may at any rate be sure of this, that I will love you always. So much good of myself, if it be good, I can say."

"It is very good," she answered; "the best of all good words. And now I must go. And as you are leaving Loughlinter I will say good-bye. When am I to have the honour and felicity of beholding your lordship again?"

"Say a nice word to me before I am off, Violet."

"I,—love,—you,—better,—than all the world beside; and I mean,—to be your wife,—some day. Are not those twenty nice words?"

He would not prolong his stay at Loughlinter, though he was asked to do so both by Violet and his sister, and though, as he confessed himself, he had no special business elsewhere. "It is no use mincing the matter. I don't like Kennedy, and I don't like being in his house," he said to Violet. And then he promised that there should be a party got up at Saulsby before the winter was over. His plan was to stop that night at Carlisle, and write to his father from thence. "Your blood, perhaps, won't be so tumultuous at Carlisle," said Violet. He shook his head and went on with his plans. He would then go on to London and down to Willingford, and there wait for his father's answer. "There is no reason why I should lose more of the hunting than necessary." "Pray don't lose a day for me," said Violet. As soon as he heard from his father, he would do his father's bidding. "You will go to Saulsby," said Violet; "you can hunt at Saulsby, you know."

"I will go to Jericho if he asks me, only you will have to go with me." "I thought we were to go to,—Belgium," said Violet.

"And so that is settled at last," said Violet to Laura that night.

"I hope you do not regret it."

"On the contrary, I am as happy as the moments are long."

"My fine girl!"

"I am happy because I love him. I have always loved him. You have known that."

"Indeed, no."

"But I have, after my fashion. I am not tumultuous, as he calls himself. Since he began to make eyes at me when he was nineteen—"

"Fancy Oswald making eyes!"

"Oh, he did, and mouths too. But from the beginning, when I was a child, I have known that he was dangerous, and I have thought that he would pass on and forget me after a while. And I could have lived without him. Nay, there have been moments when I thought I could learn to love some one else."

"Poor Phineas, for instance."

"We will mention no names. Mr. Appledom, perhaps, more likely. He has been my most constant lover, and then he would be so safe! Your brother, Laura, is dangerous. He is like the bad ice in the parks where they stick up the poles. He has had a pole stuck upon him ever since he was a boy."

"Yes;—give a dog a bad name and hang him."

"Remember that I do not love him a bit the less on that account;—perhaps the better. A sense of danger does not make me unhappy, though the threatened evil may be fatal. I have entered myself for my forlorn hope, and I mean to stick to it. Now I must go and write to his worship. Only think,—I never wrote a love-letter yet!"

Nothing more shall be said about Miss Effingham's first love-letter, which was, no doubt, creditable to her head and heart; but there were two other letters sent by the same post from Loughlinter which shall be submitted to the reader, as they will assist the telling of the story. One was from Lady Laura Kennedy to her friend Phineas Finn, and the other from Violet to her aunt, Lady Baldock. No letter was written to Lord Brentford, as it was thought desirable that he should receive the first intimation of what had been done from his son.

Respecting the letter to Phineas, which shall be first given, Lady Laura thought it right to say a word to her husband. He had been of course told of the engagement, and had replied that he could have wished that the arrangement could have been made elsewhere than at his house, knowing as he did that Lady Baldock would not approve of it. To this Lady Laura had made no reply, and Mr. Kennedy had condescended to congratulate the bride-elect. When Lady Laura's letter to Phineas was completed she took care to put it into the letter-box in the presence of her husband. "I have written to Mr. Finn," she said, "to tell him of this marriage."

"Why was it necessary that he should be told?"

"I think it was due to him,—from certain circumstances."

"I wonder whether there was any truth in what everybody was saying about their fighting a duel?" asked Mr. Kennedy. His wife made no answer, and then he continued—"You told me of your own knowledge that it was untrue."

"Not of my own knowledge, Robert."

"Yes;—of your own knowledge." Then Mr. Kennedy walked away, and was certain that his wife had deceived him about the duel. There had been a duel, and she had known it; and yet she had told him that the report was a ridiculous fabrication. He never forgot anything. He remembered at this moment the words of the falsehood, and the look of her face as she told it. He had believed her implicitly, but he would never believe her again. He was one of those men who, in spite of their experience of the world, of their experience of their own lives, imagine that lips that have once lied can never tell the truth.

Lady Laura's letter to Phineas was as follows:

Loughlinter,
December 28th, 186—.

My Dear Friend,

Violet Effingham is here, and Oswald has just left us. It is possible that you may see him as he passes through London. But, at any rate, I think it best to let you know immediately that she has accepted him,—at last. If there be any pang in this to you, be sure that I will grieve for you. You will not wish me to say that I regret that which was the dearest wish of my heart before I knew you. Lately, indeed, I have been torn in two ways. You will understand what I mean, and I believe I need say nothing more;—except this, that it shall be among my prayers that you may obtain all things that may tend to make you happy, honourable, and of high esteem.

Your most sincere friend   Laura Kennedy.

Even though her husband should read the letter, there was nothing in that of which she need be ashamed. But he did not read the letter. He simply speculated as to its contents, and inquired within himself whether it would not be for the welfare of the world in general, and for the welfare of himself in particular, that husbands should demand to read their wives' letters.

And this was Violet's letter to her aunt:—

MY DEAR AUNT,

The thing has come at last, and all your troubles will be soon over;—for I do believe that all your troubles have come from your unfortunate niece. At last I am going to be married, and thus take myself off your hands. Lord Chiltern has just been here, and I have accepted him. I am afraid you hardly think so well of Lord Chiltern as I do; but then, perhaps, you have not known him so long. You do know, however, that there has been some difference between him and his father. I think I may take upon myself to say that now, upon his engagement, this will be settled. I have the inexpressible pleasure of feeling sure that Lord Brentford will welcome me as his daughter-in-law. Tell the news to Augusta with my best love. I will write to her in a day or two. I hope my cousin Gustavus will condescend to give me away. Of course there is nothing fixed about time;—but I should say, perhaps, in nine years.

Your affectionate niece,   VIOLET EFFINGHAM.

Loughlinter, Friday.

"What does she mean about nine years?" said Lady Baldock in her wrath.

"She is joking," said the mild Augusta.

"I believe she would—joke, if I were going to be buried," said Lady Baldock.

CHAPTER LIII. Showing How Phineas Bore the Blow

When Phineas received Lady Laura Kennedy's letter, he was sitting in his gorgeous apartment in the Colonial Office. It was gorgeous in comparison with the very dingy room at Mr. Low's to which he had been accustomed in his early days,—and somewhat gorgeous also as compared with the lodgings he had so long inhabited in Mr. Bunce's house. The room was large and square, and looked out from three windows on to St. James's Park. There were in it two very comfortable arm-chairs and a comfortable sofa. And the office table at which he sat was of old mahogany, shining brightly, and seemed to be fitted up with every possible appliance for official comfort. This stood near one of the windows, so that he could sit and look down upon the park. And there was a large round table covered with books and newspapers. And the walls of the room were bright with maps of all the colonies. And there was one very interesting map,—but not very bright,—showing the American colonies, as they used to be. And there was a little inner closet in which he could brush his hair and wash his hands; and in the room adjoining there sat,—or ought to have sat, for he was often absent, vexing the mind of Phineas,—the Earl's nephew, his private secretary. And it was all very gorgeous. Often as he looked round upon it, thinking of his old bedroom at Killaloe, of his little garrets at Trinity, of the dingy chambers in Lincoln's Inn, he would tell himself that it was very gorgeous. He would wonder that anything so grand had fallen to his lot.

The letter from Scotland was brought to him in the afternoon, having reached London by some day-mail from Glasgow. He was sitting at his desk with a heap of papers before him referring to a contemplated railway from Halifax, in Nova Scotia, to the foot of the Rocky Mountains. It had become his business to get up the subject, and then discuss with his principal, Lord Cantrip, the expediency of advising the Government to lend a company five million of money, in order that this railway might be made. It was a big subject, and the contemplation of it gratified him. It required that he should look forward to great events, and exercise the wisdom of a statesman. What was the chance of these colonies being swallowed up by those other regions,—once colonies,—of which the map that hung in the corner told so eloquent a tale? And if so, would the five million ever be repaid? And if not swallowed up, were the colonies worth so great an adventure of national money? Could they repay it? Would they do so? Should they be made to do so? Mr. Low, who was now a Q.C. and in Parliament, would not have greater subjects than this before him, even if he should come to be Solicitor General. Lord Cantrip had specially asked him to get up this matter,—and he was getting it up sedulously. Once in nine years the harbour of Halifax was blocked up by ice. He had just jotted down the fact, which was material, when Lady Laura's letter was brought to him. He read it, and putting it down by his side very gently, went back to his maps as though the thing would not so trouble his mind as to disturb his work. He absolutely wrote, automatically, certain words of a note about the harbour, after he had received the information. A horse will gallop for some scores of yards, after his back has been broken, before he knows of his great ruin;—and so it was with Phineas Finn. His back was broken, but, nevertheless, he galloped, for a yard or two. "Closed in 1860–61 for thirteen days." Then he began to be aware that his back was broken, and that the writing of any more notes about the ice in Halifax harbour was for the present out of the question. "I think it best to let you know immediately that she has accepted him." These were the words which he read the oftenest. Then it was all over! The game was played out, and all his victories were as nothing to him. He sat for an hour in his gorgeous room thinking of it, and various were the answers which he gave during the time to various messages;—but he would see nobody. As for the colonies, he did not care if they revolted to-morrow. He would have parted with every colony belonging to Great Britain to have gotten the hand of Violet Effingham for himself. Now,—now at this moment, he told himself with oaths that he had never loved any one but Violet Effingham.

There had been so much to make such a marriage desirable! I should wrong my hero deeply were I to say that the weight of his sorrow was occasioned by the fact that he had lost an heiress. He would never have thought of looking for Violet Effingham had he not first learned to love her. But as the idea opened itself out to him, everything had seemed to be so suitable. Had Miss Effingham become his wife, the mouths of the Lows and of the Bunces would have been stopped altogether. Mr. Monk would have come to his house as his familiar guest, and he would have been connected with half a score of peers. A seat in Parliament would be simply his proper place, and even Under-Secretaryships of State might soon come to be below him. He was playing a great game, but hitherto he had played it with so much success,—with such wonderful luck! that it had seemed to him that all things were within his reach. Nothing more had been wanting to him than Violet's hand for his own comfort, and Violet's fortune to support his position; and these, too, had almost seemed to be within his grasp. His goddess had indeed refused him,—but not with disdain. Even Lady Laura had talked of his marriage as not improbable. All the world, almost, had heard of the duel; and all the world had smiled, and seemed to think that in the real fight Phineas Finn would be the victor,—that the lucky pistol was in his hands. It had never occurred to any one to suppose,—as far as he could see,—that he was presuming at all, or pushing himself out of his own sphere, in asking Violet Effingham to be his wife. No;—he would trust his luck, would persevere, and would succeed. Such had been his resolution on that very morning,—and now there had come this letter to dash him to the ground.

There were moments in which he declared to himself that he would not believe the letter,—not that there was any moment in which there was in his mind the slightest spark of real hope. But he would tell himself that he would still persevere. Violet might have been driven to accept that violent man by violent influence,—or it might be that she had not in truth accepted him, that Chiltern had simply so asserted. Or, even if it were so, did women never change their minds? The manly thing would be to persevere to the end. Had he not before been successful, when success seemed to be as far from him? But he could buoy himself up with no real hope. Even when these ideas were present to his mind, he knew,—he knew well,—at those very moments, that his back was broken.

Some one had come in and lighted the candles and drawn down the blinds while he was sitting there, and now, as he looked at his watch, he found that it was past five o'clock. He was engaged to dine with Madame Max Goesler at eight, and in his agony he half-resolved that he would send an excuse. Madame Max would be full of wrath, as she was very particular about her little dinner-parties;—but, what did he care now about the wrath of Madame Max Goesler? And yet only this morning he had been congratulating himself, among his other successes, upon her favour, and had laughed inwardly at his own falseness,—his falseness to Violet Effingham,—as he did so. He had said something to himself jocosely about lovers' perjuries, the remembrance of which was now very bitter to him. He took up a sheet of note-paper and scrawled an excuse to Madame Goesler. News from the country, he said, made it impossible that he should go out to-night. But he did not send the note. At about half-past five he opened the door of his private secretary's room and found the young man fast asleep, with a cigar in his mouth. "Halloa, Charles," he said.

"All right!" Charles Standish was a first cousin of Lady Laura's, and, having been in the office before Phineas had joined it, and being a great favourite with his cousin, had of course become the Under-Secretary's private secretary. "I'm all here," said Charles Standish, getting up and shaking himself.

"I am going. Just tie up those papers,—exactly as they are. I shall be here early to-morrow, but I shan't want you before twelve. Good night, Charles."

"Ta, ta," said his private secretary, who was very fond of his master, but not very respectful,—unless upon express occasions.

Then Phineas went out and walked across the park; but as he went he became quite aware that his back was broken. It was not the less broken because he sang to himself little songs to prove to himself that it was whole and sound. It was broken, and it seemed to him now that he never could become an Atlas again, to bear the weight of the world upon his shoulders. What did anything signify? All that he had done had been part of a game which he had been playing throughout, and now he had been beaten in his game. He absolutely ignored his old passion for Lady Laura as though it had never been, and regarded himself as a model of constancy,—as a man who had loved, not wisely perhaps, but much too well,—and who must now therefore suffer a living death. He hated Parliament. He hated the Colonial Office. He hated his friend Mr. Monk; and he especially hated Madame Max Goesler. As to Lord Chiltern,—he believed that Lord Chiltern had obtained his object by violence. He would see to that! Yes;—let the consequences be what they might, he would see to that!

He went up by the Duke of York's column, and as he passed the Athenaeum he saw his chief, Lord Cantrip, standing under the portico talking to a bishop. He would have gone on unnoticed, had it been possible; but Lord Cantrip came down to him at once. "I have put your name down here," said his lordship.

"What's the use?" said Phineas, who was profoundly indifferent at this moment to all the clubs in London.

"It can't do any harm, you know. You'll come up in time. And if you should get into the ministry, they'll let you in at once."

"Ministry!" ejaculated Phineas. But Lord Cantrip took the tone of voice as simply suggestive of humility, and suspected nothing of that profound indifference to all ministers and ministerial honours which Phineas had intended to express. "By-the-bye," said Lord Cantrip, putting his arm through that of the Under-Secretary, "I wanted to speak to you about the guarantees. We shall be in the devil's own mess, you know—" And so the Secretary of State went on about the Rocky Mountain Railroad, and Phineas strove hard to bear his burden with his broken back. He was obliged to say something about the guarantees, and the railway, and the frozen harbour,—and something especially about the difficulties which would be found, not in the measures themselves, but in the natural pugnacity of the Opposition. In the fabrication of garments for the national wear, the great thing is to produce garments that shall, as far as possible, defy hole-picking. It may be, and sometimes is, the case, that garments so fabricated will be good also for wear. Lord Cantrip, at the present moment, was very anxious and very ingenious in the stopping of holes; and he thought that perhaps his Under-Secretary was too much prone to the indulgence of large philanthropical views without sufficient thought of the hole-pickers. But on this occasion, by the time that he reached Brooks's, he had been enabled to convince his Under-Secretary, and though he had always thought well of his Under-Secretary, he thought better of him now than ever he had done. Phineas during the whole time had been meditating what he could do to Lord Chiltern when they two should meet. Could he take him by the throat and smite him? "I happen to know that Broderick is working as hard at the matter as we are," said Lord Cantrip, stopping opposite to the club. "He moved for papers, you know, at the end of last session." Now Mr. Broderick was a gentleman in the House looking for promotion in a Conservative Government, and of course would oppose any measure that could be brought forward by the Cantrip-Finn Colonial Administration. Then Lord Cantrip slipped into the club, and Phineas went on alone.

A spark of his old ambition with reference to Brooks's was the first thing to make him forget his misery for a moment. He had asked Lord Brentford to put his name down, and was not sure whether it had been done. The threat of Mr. Broderick's opposition had been of no use towards the strengthening of his broken back, but the sight of Lord Cantrip hurrying in at the coveted door did do something. "A man can't cut his throat or blow his brains out," he said to himself; "after all, he must go on and do his work. For hearts will break, yet brokenly live on." Thereupon he went home, and after sitting for an hour over his own fire, and looking wistfully at a little treasure which he had,—a treasure obtained by some slight fraud at Saulsby, and which he now chucked into the fire, and then instantly again pulled out of it, soiled but unscorched,—he dressed himself for dinner, and went out to Madame Max Goesler's. Upon the whole, he was glad that he had not sent the note of excuse. A man must live, even though his heart be broken, and living he must dine.

Madame Max Goesler was fond of giving little dinners at this period of the year, before London was crowded, and when her guests might probably not be called away by subsequent social arrangements. Her number seldom exceeded six or eight, and she always spoke of these entertainments as being of the humblest kind. She sent out no big cards. She preferred to catch her people as though by chance, when that was possible. "Dear Mr. Jones. Mr. Smith is coming to tell me about some sherry on Tuesday. Will you come and tell me too? I daresay you know as much about it." And then there was a studious absence of parade. The dishes were not very numerous. The bill of fare was simply written out once, for the mistress, and so circulated round the table. Not a word about the things to be eaten or the things to be drunk was ever spoken at the table,—or at least no such word was ever spoken by Madame Goesler. But, nevertheless, they who knew anything about dinners were aware that Madame Goesler gave very good dinners indeed. Phineas Finn was beginning to flatter himself that he knew something about dinners, and had been heard to assert that the soups at the cottage in Park Lane were not to be beaten in London. But he cared for no soup to-day, as he slowly made his way up Madame Goesler's staircase.

There had been one difficulty in the way of Madame Goesler's dinner-parties which had required some patience and great ingenuity in its management. She must either have ladies, or she must not have them. There was a great allurement in the latter alternative; but she knew well that if she gave way to it, all prospect of general society would for her be closed,—and for ever. This had been in the early days of her widowhood in Park Lane. She cared but little for women's society; but she knew well that the society of gentlemen without women would not be that which she desired. She knew also that she might as effectually crush herself and all her aspirations by bringing to her house indifferent women,—women lacking something either in character, or in position, or in talent,—as by having none at all. Thus there had been a great difficulty, and sometimes she had thought that the thing could not be done at all. "These English are so stiff, so hard, so heavy!" And yet she would not have cared to succeed elsewhere than among the English. By degrees, however, the thing was done. Her prudence equalled her wit, and even suspicious people had come to acknowledge that they could not put their fingers on anything wrong. When Lady Glencora Palliser had once dined at the cottage in Park Lane, Madame Max Goesler had told herself that henceforth she did not care what the suspicious people said. Since that the Duke of Omnium had almost promised that he would come. If she could only entertain the Duke of Omnium she would have done everything.

But there was no Duke of Omnium there to-night. At this time the Duke of Omnium was, of course, not in London. But Lord Fawn was there; and our old friend Laurence Fitzgibbon, who had—resigned his place at the Colonial Office; and there were Mr. and Mrs. Bonteen. They, with our hero, made up the party. No one doubted for a moment to what source Mr. Bonteen owed his dinner. Mrs. Bonteen was good-looking, could talk, was sufficiently proper, and all that kind of thing,—and did as well as any other woman at this time of year to keep Madame Max Goesler in countenance. There was never any sitting after dinner at the cottage; or, I should rather say, there was never any sitting after Madame Goesler went; so that the two ladies could not weary each other by being alone together. Mrs. Bonteen understood quite well that she was not required there to talk to her hostess, and was as willing as any woman to make herself agreeable to the gentlemen she might meet at Madame Goesler's table. And thus Mr. and Mrs. Bonteen not unfrequently dined in Park Lane.

"Now we have only to wait for that horrible man, Mr. Fitzgibbon," said Madame Max Goesler, as she welcomed Phineas. "He is always late."

"What a blow for me!" said Phineas.

"No,—you are always in good time. But there is a limit beyond which good time ends, and being shamefully late at once begins. But here he is." And then, as Laurence Fitzgibbon entered the room, Madame Goesler rang the bell for dinner.

Phineas found himself placed between his hostess and Mr. Bonteen, and Lord Fawn was on the other side of Madame Goesler. They were hardly seated at the table before some one stated it as a fact that Lord Brentford and his son were reconciled. Now Phineas knew, or thought that he knew, that this could not as yet be the case; and indeed such was not the case, though the father had already received the son's letter. But Phineas did not choose to say anything at present about Lord Chiltern.

"How odd it is," said Madame Goesler; "how often you English fathers quarrel with your sons!"

"How often we English sons quarrel with our fathers rather," said Lord Fawn, who was known for the respect he had always paid to the fifth commandment.

"It all comes from entail and primogeniture, and old-fashioned English prejudices of that kind," said Madame Goesler. "Lord Chiltern is a friend of yours, Mr. Finn, I think."

"They are both friends of mine," said Phineas.

"Ah, yes; but you,—you,—you and Lord Chiltern once did something odd together. There was a little mystery, was there not?"

"It is very little of a mystery now," said Fitzgibbon.

"It was about a lady;—was it not?" said Mrs. Bonteen, affecting to whisper to her neighbour.

"I am not at liberty to say anything on the subject," said Fitzgibbon; "but I have no doubt Phineas will tell you."

"I don't believe this about Lord Brentford," said Mr. Bonteen. "I happen to know that Chiltern was down at Loughlinter three days ago, and that he passed through London yesterday on his way to the place where he hunts. The Earl is at Saulsby. He would have gone to Saulsby if it were true."

"It all depends upon whether Miss Effingham will accept him," said Mrs. Bonteen, looking over at Phineas as she spoke.

As there were two of Violet Effingham's suitors at table, the subject was becoming disagreeably personal; and the more so, as every one of the party knew or surmised something of the facts of the case. The cause of the duel at Blankenberg had become almost as public as the duel, and Lord Fawn's courtship had not been altogether hidden from the public eye. He on the present occasion might probably be able to carry himself better than Phineas, even presuming him to be equally eager in his love,—for he knew nothing of the fatal truth. But he was unable to hear Mrs. Bonteen's statement with indifference, and showed his concern in the matter by his reply. "Any lady will be much to be pitied," he said, "who does that. Chiltern is the last man in the world to whom I would wish to trust the happiness of a woman for whom I cared."

"Chiltern is a very good fellow," said Laurence Fitzgibbon.

"Just a little wild," said Mrs. Bonteen.

"And never had a shilling in his pocket in his life," said her husband.

"I regard him as simply a madman," said Lord Fawn.

"I do so wish I knew him," said Madame Max Goesler. "I am fond of madmen, and men who haven't shillings, and who are a little wild, Could you not bring him here, Mr. Finn?"

Phineas did not know what to say, or how to open his mouth without showing his deep concern. "I shall be happy to ask him if you wish it," he replied, as though the question had been put to him in earnest; "but I do not see so much of Lord Chiltern as I used to do."

"You do not believe that Violet Effingham will accept him?" asked Mrs. Bonteen.

He paused a moment before he spoke, and then made his answer in a deep solemn voice,—with a seriousness which he was unable to repress. "She has accepted him," he said.

"Do you mean that you know it?" said Madame Goesler.

"Yes;—I mean that I know it."

Had anybody told him beforehand that he would openly make this declaration at Madame Goesler's table, he would have said that of all things it was the most impossible. He would have declared that nothing would have induced him to speak of Violet Effingham in his existing frame of mind, and that he would have had his tongue cut out before he spoke of her as the promised bride of his rival. And now he had declared the whole truth of his own wretchedness and discomfiture. He was well aware that all of them there knew why he had fought the duel at Blankenberg;—all, that is, except perhaps Lord Fawn. And he felt as he made the statement as to Lord Chiltern that he blushed up to his forehead, and that his voice was strange, and that he was telling the tale of his own disgrace. But when the direct question had been asked him he had been unable to refrain from answering it directly. He had thought of turning it off with some jest or affectation of drollery, but had failed. At the moment he had been unable not to speak the truth.

"I don't believe a word of it," said Lord Fawn,—who also forgot himself.

"I do believe it, if Mr. Finn says so," said Mrs. Bonteen, who rather liked the confusion she had caused.

"But who could have told you, Finn?" asked Mr. Bonteen.

"His sister, Lady Laura, told me so," said Phineas.

"Then it must be true," said Madame Goesler.

"It is quite impossible," said Lord Fawn. "I think I may say that I know that it is impossible. If it were so, it would be a most shameful arrangement. Every shilling she has in the world would be swallowed up." Now, Lord Fawn in making his proposals had been magnanimous in his offers as to settlements and pecuniary provisions generally.

For some minutes after that Phineas did not speak another word, and the conversation generally was not so brisk and bright as it was expected to be at Madame Goesler's. Madame Max Goesler herself thoroughly understood our hero's position, and felt for him. She would have encouraged no questionings about Violet Effingham had she thought that they would have led to such a result, and now she exerted herself to turn the minds of her guests to other subjects. At last she succeeded; and after a while, too, Phineas himself was able to talk. He drank two or three glasses of wine, and dashed away into politics, taking the earliest opportunity in his power of contradicting Lord Fawn very plainly on one or two matters. Laurence Fitzgibbon was of course of opinion that the ministry could not stay in long. Since he had left the Government the ministers had made wonderful mistakes, and he spoke of them quite as an enemy might speak. "And yet, Fitz," said Mr. Bonteen, "you used to be so staunch a supporter."

"I have seen the error of my way, I can assure you," said Laurence.

"I always observe," said Madame Max Goesler, "that when any of you gentlemen resign,—which you usually do on some very trivial matter,—the resigning gentleman becomes of all foes the bitterest. Somebody goes on very well with his friends, agreeing most cordially about everything, till he finds that his public virtue cannot swallow some little detail, and then he resigns. Or some one, perhaps, on the other side has attacked him, and in the *mêlée* he is hurt, and so he resigns. But when he has resigned, and made his parting speech full of love and gratitude, I know well after that where to look for the bitterest hostility to his late friends. Yes, I am beginning to understand the way in which politics are done in England."

All this was rather severe upon Laurence Fitzgibbon; but he was a man of the world, and bore it better than Phineas had borne his defeat.

The dinner, taken altogether, was not a success, and so Madame Goesler understood. Lord Fawn, after he had been contradicted by Phineas, hardly opened his mouth. Phineas himself talked rather too much and rather too loudly; and Mrs. Bonteen, who was well enough inclined to flatter Lord Fawn, contradicted him. "I made a mistake," said Madame Goesler afterwards, "in having four members of Parliament who all of them were or had been in office. I never will have two men in office together again." This she said to Mrs. Bonteen. "My dear Madame Max," said Mrs. Bonteen, "your resolution ought to be that you will never again have two claimants for the same young lady."

In the drawing-room up-stairs Madame Goesler managed to be alone for three minutes with Phineas Finn. "And it is as you say, my friend?" she asked. Her voice was plaintive and soft, and there was a look of real sympathy in her eyes. Phineas almost felt that if they two had been quite alone he could have told her everything, and have wept at her feet.

"Yes," he said, "it is so."

"I never doubted it when you had declared it. May I venture to say that I wish it had been otherwise?"

"It is too late now, Madame Goesler. A man of course is a fool to show that he has any feelings in such a matter. The fact is, I heard it just before I came here, and had made up my mind to send you an excuse. I wish I had now."

"Do not say that, Mr. Finn."

"I have made such an ass of myself."

"In my estimation you have done yourself honour. But if I may venture to give you counsel, do not speak of this affair again as though you had been personally concerned in it. In the world now-a-days the only thing disgraceful is to admit a failure."

"And I have failed."

"But you need not admit it, Mr. Finn. I know I ought not to say as much to you."

"I, rather, am deeply indebted to you. I will go now, Madame Goesler, as I do not wish to leave the house with Lord Fawn."

"But you will come and see me soon." Then Phineas promised that he would come soon; and felt as he made the promise that he would have an opportunity of talking over his love with his new friend at any rate without fresh shame as to his failure.

Laurence Fitzgibbon went away with Phineas, and Mr. Bonteen, having sent his wife away by herself, walked off towards the clubs with Lord Fawn. He was very anxious to have a few words with Lord Fawn. Lord Fawn had evidently been annoyed by Phineas, and Mr. Bonteen did not at all love the young Under-Secretary. "That fellow has become the most consummate puppy I ever met," said he, as he linked himself on to the lord, "Monk, and one or two others among them, have contrived to spoil him altogether."

"I don't believe a word of what he said about Lord Chiltern," said Lord Fawn.

"About his marriage with Miss Effingham?"

"It would be such an abominable shame to sacrifice the girl," said Lord Fawn. "Only think of it. Everything is gone. The man is a drunkard, and I don't believe he is any more reconciled to his father than you are. Lady Laura Kennedy must have had some object in saying so."

"Perhaps an invention of Finn's altogether," said Mr. Bonteen. "Those Irish fellows are just the men for that kind of thing."

"A man, you know, so violent that nobody can hold him," said Lord Fawn, thinking of Chiltern.

"And so absurdly conceited," said Mr. Bonteen, thinking of Phineas.

"A man who has never done anything, with all his advantages in the world,—and never will."

"He won't hold his place long," said Mr. Bonteen.

"Whom do you mean?"

"Phineas Finn."

"Oh, Mr. Finn. I was talking of Lord Chiltern. I believe Finn to be a very good sort of a fellow, and he is undoubtedly clever. They say Cantrip likes him amazingly. He'll do very well. But I don't believe a word of this about Lord Chiltern." Then Mr. Bonteen felt himself to be snubbed, and soon afterwards left Lord Fawn alone.

CHAPTER LIV. Consolation

On the day following Madame Goesler's dinner party, Phineas, though he was early at his office, was not able to do much work, still feeling that as regarded the realities of the world, his back was broken. He might no doubt go on learning, and, after a time, might be able to exert himself in a perhaps useful, but altogether uninteresting kind of way, doing his work simply because it was there to be done,—as the carter or the tailor does his;—and from the same cause, knowing that a man must have bread to live. But as for ambition, and the idea of doing good, and the love of work for work's sake,—as for the elastic springs of delicious and beneficent labour,—all that was over for him. He would have worked from day till night, and from night till day, and from month till month throughout the year to have secured for Violet Effingham the assurance that her husband's position was worthy of her own. But now he had no motive for such work as this. As long as he took the public pay, he would earn it; and that was all.

On the next day things were a little better with him. He received a note in the morning from Lord Cantrip saying that they two were to see the Prime Minister that evening, in order that the whole question of the railway to the Rocky Mountains might be understood, and Phineas was driven to his work. Before the time of the meeting came he had once more lost his own identity in great ideas of colonial welfare, and had planned and peopled a mighty region on the Red River, which should have no sympathy with American democracy. When he waited upon Mr. Gresham in the afternoon he said nothing about the mighty region; indeed, he left it to Lord Cantrip to explain most of the proposed arrangements,—speaking only a word or two here and there as occasion required. But he was aware that he had so far recovered as to be able to save himself from losing ground during the interview.

"He's about the first Irishman we've had that has been worth his salt," said Mr. Gresham to his colleague afterwards.

"That other Irishman was a terrible fellow," said Lord Cantrip, shaking his head.

On the fourth day after his sorrow had befallen him, Phineas went again to the cottage in Park Lane. And in order that he might not be balked in his search for sympathy he wrote a line to Madame Goesler to ask if she would be at home. "I will be at home from five to six,—and alone.—M. M. G." That was the answer from Marie Max Goesler, and Phineas was of course at the cottage a few minutes after five. It is not, I think, surprising that a man when he wants sympathy in such a calamity as that which had now befallen Phineas Finn, should seek it from a woman. Women sympathise most effectually with men, as men do with women. But it is, perhaps, a little odd that a man when he wants consolation because his heart has been broken, always likes to receive it from a pretty woman. One would be disposed to think that at such a moment he would be profoundly indifferent to such a matter, that no delight could come to him from female beauty, and that all he would want would be the softness of a simply sympathetic soul. But he generally wants a soft hand as well, and an eye that can be bright behind the mutual tear, and lips that shall be young and fresh as they express their concern for his sorrow. All these things were added to Phineas when he went to Madame Goesler in his grief.

"I am so glad to see you," said Madame Max.

"You are very good-natured to let me come."

"No;—but it is so good of you to trust me. But I was sure you would come after what took place the other night. I saw that you were pained, and I was so sorry for it."

"I made such a fool of myself."

"Not at all. And I thought that you were right to tell them when the question had been asked. If the thing was not to be kept a secret, it was better to speak it out. You will get over it quicker in that way than in any other. I have never seen the young lord, myself."

"Oh, there is nothing amiss about him. As to what Lord Fawn said, the half of it is simply exaggeration, and the other half is misunderstood."

"In this country it is so much to be a lord," said Madame Goesler.

Phineas thought a moment of that matter before he replied. All the Standish family had been very good to him, and Violet Effingham had been very good. It was not the fault of any of them that he was now wretched and back-broken. He had meditated much on this, and had resolved that he would not even think evil of them. "I do not in my heart believe that that has had anything to do with it," he said.

"But it has, my friend,—always. I do not know your Violet Effingham."

"She is not mine."

"Well;—I do not know this Violet that is not yours. I have met her, and did not specially admire her. But then the tastes of men and women about beauty are never the same. But I know she is one that always lives with lords and countesses. A girl who always lived with countesses feels it to be hard to settle down as a plain Mistress."

"She has had plenty of choice among all sorts of men. It was not the title. She would not have accepted Chiltern unless she had—. But what is the use of talking of it?"

"They had known each other long?"

"Oh, yes,—as children. And the Earl desired it of all things."

"Ah;—then he arranged it."

"Not exactly. Nobody could arrange anything for Chiltern,—nor, as far as that goes, for Miss Effingham. They arranged it themselves, I fancy."

"You had asked her?"

"Yes;—twice. And she had refused him more than twice. I have nothing for which to blame her; but yet I had thought,—I had thought—"

"She is a jilt then?"

"No;—I will not let you say that of her. She is no jilt. But I think she has been strangely ignorant of her own mind. What is the use of talking of it, Madame Goesler?"

"None;—only sometimes it is better to speak a word, than to keep one's sorrow to oneself."

"So it is;—and there is not one in the world to whom I can speak such a word, except yourself. Is not that odd? I have sisters, but they have never heard of Miss Effingham, and would be quite indifferent."

"Perhaps they have some other favourites."

"Ah;—well. That does not matter, And my best friend here in London is Lord Chiltern's own sister."

"She knew of your attachment?"

"Oh, yes."

"And she told you of Miss Effingham's engagement. Was she glad of it?"

"She has always desired the marriage. And yet I think she would have been satisfied had it been otherwise. But of course her heart must be with her brother. I need not have troubled myself to go to Blankenberg after all."

"It was for the best, perhaps. Everybody says you behaved so well."

"I could not but go, as things were then."

"What if you had—shot him?"

"There would have been an end of everything. She would never have seen me after that. Indeed I should have shot myself next, feeling that there was nothing else left for me to do."

"Ah;—you English are so peculiar. But I suppose it is best not to shoot a man. And, Mr. Finn, there are other ladies in the world prettier than Miss Violet Effingham. No;—of course you will not admit that now. Just at this moment, and for a month or two, she is peerless, and you will feel yourself to be of all men the most unfortunate. But you have the ball at your feet. I know no one so young who has got the ball at his feet so well. I call it nothing to have the ball at your feet if you are born with it there. It is so easy to be a lord if your father is one before you,—and so easy to marry a pretty girl if you can make her a countess. But to make yourself a lord, or to be as good as a lord, when nothing has been born to you,—that I call very much. And there are women, and pretty women too, Mr. Finn, who have spirit enough to understand this, and to think that the man, after all, is more important than the lord." Then she sang the old well-worn verse of the Scotch song with wonderful spirit, and with a clearness of voice and knowledge of music for which he had hitherto never given her credit.

> "A prince can mak' a belted knight,
>   A marquis, duke, and a' that;
> But an honest man's aboon his might,
>   Guid faith he mauna fa' that."

"I did not know that you sung, Madame Goesler."

"Only now and then when something specially requires it. And I am very fond of Scotch songs. I will sing to you now if you like it." Then she sang the whole song,—"A man's a man for a' that," she said as she finished. "Even though he cannot get the special bit of painted Eve's flesh for which his heart has had a craving." Then she sang again:—

> "There are maidens in Scotland more lovely by far,
>   Who would gladly be bride to the young Lochinvar."

"But young Lochinvar got his bride," said Phineas.

"Take the spirit of the lines, Mr. Finn, which is true; and not the tale as it is told, which is probably false. I often think that Jock of Hazledean, and young Lochinvar too, probably lived to repent their bargains. We will hope that Lord Chiltern may not do so."

"I am sure he never will."

"That is all right. And as for you, do you for a while think of your politics, and your speeches, and your colonies, rather than of your love. You are at home there, and no Lord Chiltern can rob you of your success. And if you are down in the mouth, come to me, and I will sing you a Scotch song. And, look you, the next time I ask you to dinner I will promise you that Mrs. Bonteen shall not be here. Good-bye." She gave him her hand, which was very soft, and left it for a moment in his, and he was consoled.

Madame Goesler, when she was alone, threw herself on to her chair and began to think of things. In these days she would often ask herself what in truth was the object of her ambition, and the aim of her life. Now at this moment she had in her hand a note from the Duke of Omnium. The Duke had allowed himself to say something about a photograph, which had justified her in writing to him,—or which she had taken for such justification. And the Duke had replied. "He would not," he said, "lose the opportunity of waiting upon her in person which the presentation of the little gift might afford him." It would be a great success to have the Duke of Omnium at her house,—but to what would the success reach? What was her definite object,—or had she any? In what way could she make herself happy? She could not say that she was happy yet. The hours with her were too long and the days too many.

The Duke of Omnium should come,—if he would. And she was quite resolved as to this,—that if the Duke did come she would not be afraid of him. Heavens and earth! What would be the feelings of such a woman as her, were the world to greet her some fine morning as Duchess of Omnium! Then she made up her mind very resolutely on one subject. Should the Duke give her any opportunity she would take a very short time in letting him know what was the extent of her ambition.

CHAPTER LV. Lord Chiltern at Saulsby

Lord Chiltern did exactly as he said he would do. He wrote to his father as he passed through Carlisle, and at once went on to his hunting at Willingford. But his letter was very stiff and ungainly, and it may be doubted whether Miss Effingham was not wrong in refusing the offer which he had made to her as to the dictation of it. He began his letter, "My Lord," and did not much improve the style as he went on with it. The reader may as well see the whole letter;—

> Railway Hotel,
> Carlisle,
> December 27, 186—.

My Lord,

I am now on my way from Loughlinter to London, and write this letter to you in compliance with a promise made by me to my sister and to Miss Effingham. I have asked Violet to be my wife, and she has accepted me, and they think that you will be pleased to hear that this has been done. I shall be, of course, obliged, if you will instruct Mr. Edwards to let me know what you would propose to do in regard to settlements. Laura thinks that you will wish to see both Violet and myself at Saulsby. For myself, I can only say that, should you desire me to come, I will do so on receiving your assurance that I shall be treated neither with fatted calves nor with reproaches. I am not aware that I have deserved either.

I am, my lord, yours affect., CHILTERN.

P.S.—My address will be "The Bull, Willingford."

That last word, in which he half-declared himself to be joined in affectionate relations to his father, caused him a world of trouble. But he could find no term for expressing, without a circumlocution which was disagreeable to him, exactly that position of feeling towards his father which really belonged to him. He would have written "yours with affection," or "yours with deadly enmity," or "yours with respect," or "yours with most profound indifference," exactly in accordance with the state of his father's mind, if he had only known what was that state. He was afraid of going beyond his father in any offer of reconciliation, and was firmly fixed in his resolution that he would never be either repentant or submissive in regard to the past. If his father had wishes for the future, he would comply with them if he could do so without unreasonable inconvenience, but he would not give way a single point as to things done and gone. If his father should choose to make any reference to them, his father must prepare for battle.

The Earl was of course disgusted by the pertinacious obstinacy of his son's letter, and for an hour or two swore to himself that he would not answer it. But it is natural that the father should yearn for the son, while the son's feeling for the father is of a very much weaker nature. Here, at any rate, was that engagement made which he had ever desired. And his son had made a step, though it was so very unsatisfactory a step, towards reconciliation. When the old man read the letter a second time, he skipped that reference to fatted calves which had been so peculiarly distasteful to him, and before the evening had passed he had answered his son as follows;—

Saulsby,
December 29, 186—.

My Dear Chiltern,

I have received your letter, and am truly delighted to hear that dear Violet has accepted you as her husband. Her fortune will be very material to you, but she herself is better than any fortune. You have long known my opinion of her. I shall be proud to welcome her as a daughter to my house.

I shall of course write to her immediately, and will endeavour to settle some early day for her coming here. When I have done so, I will write to you again, and can only say that I will endeavour to make Saulsby comfortable to you.

Your affectionate father,   Brentford.

Richards, the groom, is still here. You had perhaps better write to him direct about your horses.

 By the middle of February arrangements had all been made, and Violet met her lover at his father's house. She in the meantime had been with her aunt, and had undergone a good deal of mild unceasing persecution. "My dear Violet," said her aunt to her on her arrival at Baddingham, speaking with a solemnity that ought to have been terrible to the young lady, "I do not know what to say to you."

"Say 'how d'you do?' aunt," said Violet.

"I mean about this engagement," said Lady Baldock, with an increase of awe-inspiring severity in her voice.

"Say nothing about it at all, if you don't like it," said Violet.

"How can I say nothing about it? How can I be silent? Or how am I to congratulate you?"

"The least said, perhaps, the soonest mended," and Violet smiled as she spoke.

"That is very well, and if I had no duty to perform, I would be silent. But, Violet, you have been left in my charge. If I see you shipwrecked in life, I shall ever tell myself that the fault has been partly mine."

"Nay, aunt, that will be quite unnecessary. I will always admit that you did everything in your power to—to—to—make me run straight, as the sporting men say."

"Sporting men! Oh, Violet."

"And you know, aunt, I still hope that I shall be found to have kept on the right side of the posts. You will find that poor Lord Chiltern is not so black as he is painted."

"But why take anybody that is black at all?"

"I like a little shade in the picture, aunt."

"Look at Lord Fawn."

"I have looked at him."

"A young nobleman beginning a career of useful official life, that will end in—; there is no knowing what it may end in."

"I daresay not;—but it never could have begun or ended in my being Lady Fawn."

"And Mr. Appledom!"

"Poor Mr. Appledom. I do like Mr. Appledom. But, you see, aunt, I like Lord Chiltern so much better. A young woman will go by her feelings."

"And yet you refused him a dozen times."

"I never counted the times, aunt; but not quite so many as that."

The same thing was repeated over and over again during the month that Miss Effingham remained at Baddingham, but Lady Baldock had no power of interfering, and Violet bore her persecution bravely. Her future husband was generally spoken of as "that violent young man," and hints were thrown out as to the personal injuries to which his wife might be possibly subjected. But the threatened bride only laughed, and spoke of these coming dangers as part of the general lot of married women. "I daresay, if the truth were known, my uncle Baldock did not always keep his temper," she once said. Now, the truth was, as

Violet well knew, that "my uncle Baldock" had been dumb as a sheep before the shearers in the hands of his wife, and had never been known to do anything improper by those who had been most intimate with him even in his earlier days. "Your uncle Baldock, miss," said the outraged aunt, "was a nobleman as different in his manner of life from Lord Chiltern as chalk from cheese." "But then comes the question, which is the cheese?" said Violet. Lady Baldock would not argue the question any further, but stalked out of the room.

Lady Laura Kennedy met them at Saulsby, having had something of a battle with her husband before she left her home to do so. When she told him of her desire to assist at this reconciliation between her father and brother, he replied by pointing out that her first duty was at Loughlinter, and before the interview was ended had come to express an opinion that that duty was very much neglected. She in the meantime had declared that she would go to Saulsby, or that she would explain to her father that she was forbidden by her husband to do so. "And I also forbid any such communication," said Mr. Kennedy. In answer to which, Lady Laura told him that there were some marital commands which she should not consider it to be her duty to obey. When matters had come to this pass, it may be conceived that both Mr. Kennedy and his wife were very unhappy. She had almost resolved that she would take steps to enable her to live apart from her husband; and he had begun to consider what course he would pursue if such steps were taken. The wife was subject to her husband by the laws both of God and man; and Mr. Kennedy was one who thought much of such laws. In the meantime, Lady Laura carried her point and went to Saulsby, leaving her husband to go up to London and begin the session by himself.

Lady Laura and Violet were both at Saulsby before Lord Chiltern arrived, and many were the consultations which were held between them as to the best mode in which things might be arranged. Violet was of opinion that there had better be no arrangement, that Lord Chiltern should be allowed to come in and take his father's hand, and sit down to dinner,—and that so things should fall into their places. Lady Laura was rather in favour of some scene. But the interview had taken place before either of them were able to say a word. Lord Chiltern, on his arrival, had gone immediately to his father, taking the Earl very much by surprise, and had come off best in the encounter.

"My lord," said he, walking up to his father with his hand out, "I am very glad to come back to Saulsby." He had written to his sister to say that he would be at Saulsby on that day, but had named no hour. He now appeared between ten and eleven in the morning, and his father had as yet made no preparation for him,—had arranged no appropriate words. He had walked in at the front door, and had asked for the Earl. The Earl was in his own morning-room,—a gloomy room, full of dark books and darker furniture, and thither Lord Chiltern had at once gone. The two women still were sitting together over the fire in the breakfast-room, and knew nothing of his arrival.

"Oswald!" said his father, "I hardly expected you so early."

"I have come early. I came across country, and slept at Birmingham. I suppose Violet is here."

"Yes, she is here,—and Laura. They will be very glad to see you. So am I." And the father took the son's hand for the second time.

"Thank you, sir," said Lord Chiltern, looking his father full in the face.

"I have been very much pleased by this engagement," continued the Earl.

"What do you think I must be, then?" said the son, laughing. "I have been at it, you know, off and on, ever so many years; and have sometimes thought I was quite a fool not to get it out of my head. But I couldn't get it out of my head. And now she talks as though it were she who had been in love with me all the time!"

"Perhaps she was," said the father.

"I don't believe it in the least. She may be a little so now."

"I hope you mean that she always shall be so."

"I shan't be the worst husband in the world, I hope; and I am quite sure I shan't be the best. I will go and see her now. I suppose I shall find her somewhere in the house. I thought it best to see you first."

"Stop half a moment, Oswald," said the Earl. And then Lord Brentford did make something of a shambling speech, in which he expressed a hope that they two might for the future live together on friendly terms, forgetting the past. He ought to have been prepared for the occasion, and the speech was poor and shambling. But I think that it was more useful than it might have been, had it been uttered roundly and with that paternal and almost majestic effect which he would have achieved had he been thoroughly prepared. But the roundness and the majesty would have gone against the grain with his son, and there would have been a danger of some outbreak. As it was, Lord Chiltern smiled, and muttered some word about things being "all right," and then made his way out of the room. "That's a great deal better than I had hoped," he said to himself; "and it has all come from my going in without being announced." But there was still a fear upon him that his father even yet might prepare a speech, and speak it, to the great peril of their mutual comfort.

His meeting with Violet was of course pleasant enough. Now that she had succumbed, and had told herself and had told him that she loved him, she did not scruple to be as generous as a maiden should be who has acknowledged herself to be conquered, and has rendered herself to the conqueror. She would walk with him and ride with him, and take a lively interest in the performances of all his horses, and listen to hunting stories as long as he chose to tell them. In all this, she was so good and so loving that Lady Laura was more than once tempted to throw in her teeth her old, often-repeated assertions, that she was not prone to be in love,—that it was not her nature to feel any ardent affection for a man, and that, therefore, she would probably remain unmarried. "You begrudge me my little bits of pleasure," Violet said, in answer to one such attack. "No;—but it is so odd to see you, of all women, become so love-lorn," "I am not love-lorn," said Violet, "but I like the freedom of telling him everything and of hearing everything from him, and of having him for my own best friend. He might go away for twelve months, and I should not be unhappy, believing, as I do, that he would be true to me." All of which set Lady Laura thinking whether her friend had not been wiser than she had been. She had never known anything of that sort of friendship with her husband which already seemed to be quite established between these two.

In her misery one day Lady Laura told the whole story of her own unhappiness to her brother, saying nothing of Phineas Finn,—thinking nothing of him as she told her story, but speaking more strongly perhaps than she should have done, of the terrible dreariness of her life at Loughlinter, and of her inability to induce her husband to alter it for her sake.

"Do you mean that he,—ill-treats you?" said the brother, with a scowl on his face which seemed to indicate that he would like no task better than that of resenting such ill-treatment.

"He does not beat me, if you mean that."

"Is he cruel to you? Does he use harsh language?"

"He never said a word in his life either to me or, as I believe, to any other human being, that he would think himself bound to regret."

"What is it then?"

"He simply chooses to have his own way, and his way cannot be my way. He is hard, and dry, and just, and dispassionate, and he wishes me to be the same. That is all."

"I tell you fairly, Laura, as far as I am concerned, I never could speak to him. He is antipathetic to me. But then I am not his wife."

"I am;—and I suppose I must bear it."

"Have you spoken to my father?"

"No."

"Or to Violet?"

"Yes."

"And what does she say?"

"What can she say? She has nothing to say. Nor have you. Nor, if I am driven to leave him, can I make the world understand why I do so. To be simply miserable, as I am, is nothing to the world."

"I could never understand why you married him."

"Do not be cruel to me, Oswald."

"Cruel! I will stick by you in any way that you wish. If you think well of it, I will go off to Loughlinter to-morrow, and tell him that you will never return to him. And if you are not safe from him here at Saulsby, you shall go abroad with us. I am sure Violet would not object. I will not be cruel to you."

But in truth neither of Lady Laura's councillors was able to give her advice that could serve her. She felt that she could not leave her husband without other cause than now existed, although she felt, also, that to go back to him was to go back to utter wretchedness. And when she saw Violet and her brother together there came to her dreams of what might have been her own happiness had she kept herself free from those terrible bonds in which she was now held a prisoner. She could not get out of her heart the remembrance of that young man who would have been her lover, if she would have let him,—of whose love for herself she had been aware before she had handed herself over as a bale of goods to her unloved, unloving husband. She had married Mr. Kennedy because she was afraid that otherwise she might find herself forced to own that she loved that other man who was then a nobody;—almost nobody. It was not Mr. Kennedy's money that had bought her. This woman in regard to money had shown herself to be as generous as the sun. But in marrying Mr. Kennedy she had maintained herself in her high position, among the first of her own people,—among the first socially and among the first politically. But had she married Phineas,—had she become Lady Laura Finn,—there would have been a great descent. She could not have entertained the leading men of her party. She would not have been on a level with the wives and daughters of Cabinet Ministers. She might, indeed, have remained unmarried! But she knew that had she done so,—had she so resolved,—that which she called her fancy would have been too strong for her. She would not have remained unmarried. At that time it was her fate to be either Lady Laura Kennedy or Lady Laura Finn. And she had chosen to be Lady Laura Kennedy. To neither Violet Effingham nor to her brother could she tell one half of the sorrow which afflicted her.

"I shall go back to Loughlinter," she said to her brother.

"Do not, unless you wish it," he answered.

"I do not wish it. But I shall do it. Mr. Kennedy is in London now, and has been there since Parliament met, but he will be in Scotland again in March, and I will go and meet him there. I told him that I would do so when I left."

"But you will go up to London?"

"I suppose so. I must do as he tells me, of course. What I mean is, I will try it for another year."

"If it does not succeed, come to us."

"I cannot say what I will do. I would die if I knew how. Never be a tyrant, Oswald; or at any rate, not a cold tyrant. And remember this, there is no tyranny to a woman like telling her of her duty. Talk of beating a woman! Beating might often be a mercy."

Lord Chiltern remained ten days at Saulsby, and at last did not get away without a few unpleasant words with his father,—or without a few words that were almost unpleasant with his mistress. On his first arrival he had told his sister that he should go on a certain day, and some intimation to this effect had probably been conveyed to the Earl. But when his son told him one evening that the post-chaise had been ordered for seven o'clock the next morning, he felt that his son was ungracious and abrupt. There were many things still to be said, and indeed there had been no speech of any account made at all as yet.

"That is very sudden," said the Earl.

"I thought Laura had told you."

"She has not told me a word lately. She may have said something before you came here. What is there to hurry you?"

"I thought ten days would be as long as you would care to have me here, and as I said that I would be back by the first, I would rather not change my plans."

"You are going to hunt?"

"Yes;—I shall hunt till the end of March."

"You might have hunted here, Oswald." But the son made no sign of changing his plans; and the father, seeing that he would not change them, became solemn and severe. There were a few words which he must say to his son,—something of a speech that he must make;—so he led the way into the room with the dark books and the dark furniture, and pointed to a great deep arm-chair for his son's accommodation. But as he did not sit down himself, neither did Lord Chiltern. Lord Chiltern understood very well how great is the advantage of a standing orator over a sitting recipient of his oratory, and that advantage he would not give to his father. "I had hoped to have an opportunity of saying a few words to you about the future," said the Earl.

"I think we shall be married in July," said Lord Chiltern.

"So I have heard;—but after that. Now I do not want to interfere, Oswald, and of course the less so, because Violet's money will to a great degree restore the inroads which have been made upon the property."

"It will more than restore them altogether."

"Not if her estate be settled on a second son, Oswald, and I hear from Lady Baldock that that is the wish of her relations."

"She shall have her own way,—as she ought. What that way is I do not know. I have not even asked about it. She asked me, and I told her to speak to you."

"Of course I should wish it to go with the family property. Of course that would be best."

"She shall have her own way,—as far as I am concerned."

"But it is not about that, Oswald, that I would speak. What are your plans of life when you are married?"

"Plans of life?"

"Yes;—plans of life. I suppose you have some plans. I suppose you mean to apply yourself to some useful occupation?"

"I don't know really, sir, that I am of much use for any purpose." Lord Chiltern laughed as he said this, but did not laugh pleasantly.

"You would not be a drone in the hive always?"

"As far as I can see, sir, we who call ourselves lords generally are drones."

"I deny it," said the Earl, becoming quite energetic as he defended his order. "I deny it utterly. I know no class of men who do work more useful or more honest. Am I a drone? Have I been so from my youth upwards? I have always worked, either in the one House or in the other, and those of my fellows with whom I have been most intimate have worked also. The same career is open to you."

"You mean politics?"

"Of course I mean politics."

"I don't care for politics. I see no difference in parties."

"But you should care for politics, and you should see a difference in parties. It is your duty to do so. My wish is that you should go into Parliament."

"I can't do that, sir."

"And why not?"

"In the first place, sir, you have not got a seat to offer me. You have managed matters among you in such a way that poor little Loughton has been swallowed up. If I were to canvass the electors of Smotherem, I don't think that many would look very sweet on me."

"There is the county, Oswald."

"And whom am I to turn out? I should spend four or five thousand pounds, and have nothing but vexation in return for it. I had rather not begin that game, and indeed I am too old for Parliament. I did not take it up early enough to believe in it."

All this made the Earl very angry, and from these things they went on to worse things. When questioned again as to the future, Lord Chiltern scowled, and at last declared that it was his idea to live abroad in the summer for his wife's recreation, and somewhere down in the shires during the winter for his own. He would admit of no purpose higher than recreation, and when his father again talked to him of a nobleman's duty, he said that he knew of no other special duty than that of not exceeding his income. Then his father made a longer speech than before, and at the end of it Lord Chiltern simply wished him good night. "It's getting late, and I've promised to see Violet before I go to bed. Good-bye." Then he was off, and Lord Brentford was left there, standing with his back to the fire.

After that Lord Chiltern had a discussion with Violet, which lasted nearly half the night; and during the discussion she told him more than once that he was wrong. "Such as I am you must take me, or leave me," he said, in anger. "Nay; there is no choice now," she answered. "I have taken you, and I will stick by you,—whether you are right or wrong. But when I think you wrong, I shall say so." He swore to her as he pressed her to his heart that she was the finest, grandest, sweetest woman that ever the world had produced. But still there was present on his palate, when he left her, the bitter taste of her reprimand.

CHAPTER LVI. What the People in Marylebone Thought

Phineas Finn, when the session began, was still hard at work upon his Canada bill, and in his work found some relief for his broken back. He went into the matter with all his energy, and before the debate came on, knew much more about the seven thousand inhabitants of some hundreds of thousands of square miles at the back of Canada, than he did of the people of London or of County Clare. And he found some consolation also in the good-nature of Madame Goesler, whose drawing-room was always open to him. He could talk freely now to Madame Goesler about Violet, and had even ventured to tell her that once, in old days, he had thought of loving Lady Laura Standish. He spoke of those days as being very old; and then he perhaps said some word to her about dear little Mary Flood Jones. I think that there was not much in his career of which he did not say something to Madame Goesler, and that he received from her a good deal of excellent advice and encouragement in the direction of his political ambition. "A man should work," she said,—"and you do work. A woman can only look on, and admire and long. What is there that I can do? I can learn to care for these Canadians, just because you care for them. If it was the beavers that you told me of, I should have to care for the beavers." Then Phineas of course told her that such sympathy from her was all and all to him. But the reader must not on this account suppose that he was untrue in his love to Violet Effingham. His back was altogether broken by his fall, and he was quite aware that such was the fact. Not as yet, at least, had come to him any remotest idea that a cure was possible.

Early in March he heard that Lady Laura was up in town, and of course he was bound to go to her. The information was given to him by Mr. Kennedy himself, who told him that he had been to Scotland to fetch her. In these days there was an acknowledged friendship between these two, but there was no intimacy. Indeed, Mr. Kennedy was a man who was hardly intimate with any other man. With Phineas he now and then exchanged a few words in the lobby of the House, and when they chanced to meet each other, they met as friends. Mr. Kennedy had no strong wish to see again in his house the man respecting whom he had ventured to caution his wife; but he was thoughtful; and thinking over it all, he found it better to ask him there. No one must know that there was any reason why Phineas should not come to his house; especially as all the world knew that Phineas had protected him from the garrotters. "Lady Laura is in town now," he said; "you must go and see her before long." Phineas of course promised that he would go.

In these days Phineas was beginning to be aware that he had enemies,—though he could not understand why anybody should be his enemy now that Violet Effingham had decided against him. There was poor Laurence Fitzgibbon, indeed, whom he had superseded at the Colonial Office, but Laurence Fitzgibbon, to give merit where merit was due, felt no animosity against him at all. "You're welcome, me boy; you're welcome,—as far as yourself goes. But as for the party, bedad, it's rotten to the core, and won't stand another session. Mind, it's I who tell you so." And the poor idle Irishman, in so speaking, spoke the truth as well as he knew it. But the Ratlers and the Bonteens were Finn's bitter foes, and did not scruple to let him know that such was the case. Barrington Erle had scruples on the subject, and in a certain mildly apologetic way still spoke well of the young man, whom he had himself first introduced into political life only four years since;—but there was no earnestness or cordiality in Barrington Erle's manner, and Phineas knew that his first staunch friend could no longer be regarded as a pillar of support. But there was a set of men, quite as influential,—so Phineas thought,—as the busy politicians of the club, who were very friendly to him. These were men, generally of high position, of steady character,—hard workers,—who thought quite as much of what a man did in his office as what he said in the House. Lords Cantrip, Thrift, and Fawn were of this class,—and they were all very courteous to Phineas. Envious men began to say of him that he cared little now for any one of the party who had not a handle to his name, and that he preferred to live with lords and lordlings. This was hard upon him, as the great political ambition of his life was to call Mr. Monk his friend; and he would sooner have acted with Mr. Monk than with any other man in the Cabinet. But though Mr. Monk had not deserted him, there had come to be little of late in common between the two. His life was becoming that of a parliamentary official rather than that of a politician;—whereas, though Mr. Monk was in office, his public life was purely political. Mr. Monk had great ideas of his own which he intended to hold, whether by holding them he might remain in office or be forced out of office; and he was indifferent as to the direction which things in this respect might take with him. But Phineas, who had achieved his declared object in getting into place, felt that he was almost constrained to adopt the views of others, let them be what they might. Men spoke to him, as though his parliamentary career were wholly at the disposal of the Government,—as though he were like a proxy in Mr. Gresham's pocket,—with this difference, that when directed to get up and speak on a subject he was bound to do so. This annoyed him, and he complained to Mr. Monk; but Mr. Monk only shrugged his shoulders and told him that he must make his choice. He soon discovered Mr. Monk's meaning. "If you choose to make Parliament a profession,—as you have chosen,—you can have no right even to think of independence. If the country finds you out when you are in Parliament, and then invites you to office, of course the thing is different. But the latter is a slow career, and probably would not have suited you." That was the meaning of what Mr. Monk said to him. After all, these official and parliamentary honours were greater when seen at a distance than he found them to be now that he possessed them. Mr. Low worked ten hours a day, and could rarely call a day his own; but, after all, with all this work, Mr. Low was less of a slave, and more independent, than was he, Phineas Finn, Under-Secretary of State, the friend of Cabinet Ministers, and Member of Parliament since his twenty-fifth year! He began to dislike the House, and to think it a bore to sit on the Treasury bench;—he, who a few years since had regarded Parliament as the British heaven on earth, and who, since he had been in Parliament, had looked at that bench with longing envious eyes. Laurence Fitzgibbon, who seemed to have as much to eat and drink as ever, and a bed also to lie on, could come and go in the House as he pleased, since his—resignation.

And there was a new trouble coming. The Reform Bill for England had passed; but now there was to be another Reform Bill for Ireland. Let them pass what bill they might, this would not render necessary a new Irish election till the entire House should be dissolved. But he feared that he would be called upon to vote for the abolition of his own borough,—and for other points almost equally distasteful to him. He knew that he would not be consulted,—but would be called upon to vote, and perhaps to speak; and was certain that if he did so, there would be war between him and his constituents. Lord Tulla had already communicated to him his ideas that, for certain excellent reasons, Loughshane ought to be spared. But this evil was, he hoped, a distant one. It was generally thought that, as the English Reform Bill had been passed last year, and as the Irish bill, if carried, could not be immediately operative, the doing of the thing might probably be postponed to the next session.

When he first saw Lady Laura he was struck by the great change in her look and manner. She seemed to him to be old and worn, and he judged her to be wretched,—as she was. She had written to him to say that she would be at her father's house on such and such a morning, and he had gone to her there. "It is of no use your coming to Grosvenor Place," she said. "I see nobody there, and the house is like a prison." Later in the interview she told him not to come and dine there, even though Mr. Kennedy should ask him.

"And why not?" he demanded.

"Because everything would be stiff, and cold, and uncomfortable. I suppose you do not wish to make your way into a lady's house if she asks you not." There was a sort of smile on her face as she said this, but he could perceive that it was a very bitter smile. "You can easily excuse yourself."

"Yes, I can excuse myself."

"Then do so. If you are particularly anxious to dine with Mr. Kennedy, you can easily do so at your club." In the tone of her voice, and the words she used, she hardly attempted to conceal her dislike of her husband.

"And now tell me about Miss Effingham," he said.

"There is nothing for me to tell."

"Yes there is;—much to tell. You need not spare me. I do not pretend to deny to you that I have been hit hard,—so hard, that I have been nearly knocked down; but it will not hurt me now to hear of it all. Did she always love him?"

"I cannot say. I think she did after her own fashion."

"I sometimes think women would be less cruel," he said, "if they knew how great is the anguish they can cause."

"Has she been cruel to you?"

"I have nothing to complain of. But if she loved Chiltern, why did she not tell him so at once? And why—"

"This is complaining, Mr. Finn."

"I will not complain. I would not even think of it, if I could help it. Are they to be married soon?"

"In July;—so they now say."

"And where will they live?"

"Ah! no one can tell. I do not think that they agree as yet as to that. But if she has a strong wish Oswald will yield to it. He was always generous."

"I would not even have had a wish,—except to have her with me."

There was a pause for a moment, and then Lady Laura answered him with a touch of scorn in her voice,—and with some scorn, too, in her eye:—"That is all very well, Mr. Finn; but the season will not be over before there is some one else."

"There you wrong me."

"They tell me that you are already at Madame Goesler's feet."

"Madame Goesler!"

"What matters who it is as long as she is young and pretty, and has the interest attached to her of something more than ordinary position? When men tell me of the cruelty of women, I think that no woman can be really cruel because no man is capable of suffering. A woman, if she is thrown aside, does suffer."

"Do you mean to tell me, then, that I am indifferent to Miss Effingham?" When he thus spoke, I wonder whether he had forgotten that he had ever declared to this very woman to whom he was speaking, a passion for herself.

"Psha!"

"It suits you, Lady Laura, to be harsh to me, but you are not speaking your thoughts."

Then she lost all control of herself, and poured out to him the real truth that was in her. "And whose thoughts did you speak when you and I were on the braes of Loughlinter? Am I wrong in saying that change is easy to you, or have I grown to be so old that you can talk to me as though those far-away follies ought to be forgotten? Was it so long ago? Talk of love! I tell you, sir, that your heart is one in which love can have no durable hold. Violet Effingham! There may be a dozen Violets after her, and you will be none the worse." Then she walked away from him to the window, and he stood still, dumb, on the spot that he had occupied. "You had better go now," she said, "and forget what has passed between us. I know that you are a gentleman, and that you will forget it." The strong idea of his mind when he heard all this was the injustice of her attack,—of the attack as coming from her, who had all but openly acknowledged that she had married a man whom she had not loved because it suited her to escape from a man whom she did love. She was reproaching him now for his fickleness in having ventured to set his heart upon another woman, when she herself had been so much worse than fickle,—so profoundly false! And yet he could not defend himself by accusing her. What would she have had of him? What would she have proposed to him, had he questioned her as to his future, when they were together on the braes of Loughlinter? Would she not have bid him to find some one else whom he could love? Would she then have suggested to him the propriety of nursing his love for herself,—for her who was about to become another man's wife,—for her after she should have become another man's wife? And yet because he had not done so, and because she had made herself wretched by marrying a man whom she did not love, she reproached him!

He could not tell her of all this, so he fell back for his defence on words which had passed between them since the day when they had met on the braes. "Lady Laura," he said, "it is only a month or two since you spoke to me as though you wished that Violet Effingham might be my wife."

"I never wished it. I never said that I wished it. There are moments in which we try to give a child any brick on the chimney top for which it may whimper." Then there was another silence which she was the first to break. "You had better go," she said. "I know that I have committed myself, and of course I would rather be alone."

"And what would you wish that I should do?"

"Do?" she said. "What you do can be nothing to me."

"Must we be strangers, you and I, because there was a time in which we were almost more than friends?"

"I have spoken nothing about myself, sir,—only as I have been drawn to do so by your pretence of being love-sick. You can do nothing for me,—nothing,—nothing. What is it possible that you should do for me? You are not my father, or my brother." It is not to be supposed that she wanted him to fall at her feet. It is to be supposed that had he done so her reproaches would have been hot and heavy on him; but yet it almost seemed to him as though he had no other alternative. No! —He was not her father or her brother;—nor could he be her husband. And at this very moment, as she knew, his heart was sore with love for another woman. And yet he hardly knew how not to throw himself at her feet, and swear, that he would return now and for ever to his old passion, hopeless, sinful, degraded as it would be.

"I wish it were possible for me to do something," he said, drawing near to her.

"There is nothing to be done," she said, clasping her hands together. "For me nothing. I have before me no escape, no hope, no prospect of relief, no place of consolation. You have everything before you. You complain of a wound! You have at least shown that such wounds with you are capable of cure. You cannot but feel that when I hear your wailings, I must be impatient. You had better leave me now, if you please."

"And are we to be no longer friends?" he asked.

"As far as friendship can go without intercourse, I shall always be your friend."

Then he went, and as he walked down to his office, so intent was he on that which had just passed that he hardly saw the people as he met them, or was aware of the streets through which his way led him. There had been something in the later words which Lady Laura had spoken that had made him feel almost unconsciously that the injustice of her reproaches was not so great as he had at first felt it to be, and that she had some cause for her scorn. If her case was such as she had so plainly described it, what was his plight as compared with hers? He had lost his Violet, and was in pain. There must be much of suffering before him. But though Violet were lost, the world was not all blank before his eyes. He had not told himself, even in his dreariest moments, that there was before him "no escape, no hope, no prospect of relief, no place of consolation." And then he began to think whether this must in truth be the case with Lady Laura. What if Mr. Kennedy were to die? What in such case as that would he do? In ten or perhaps in five years time might it not be possible for him to go through the ceremony of falling upon his knees, with stiffened joints indeed, but still with something left of the ardour of his old love, of his oldest love of all?

As he was thinking of this he was brought up short in his walk as he was entering the Green Park beneath the Duke's figure, by Laurence Fitzgibbon. "How dare you not be in your office at such an hour as this, Finn, me boy,—or, at least, not in the House,—or serving your masters after some fashion?" said the late Under-Secretary.

"So I am. I've been on a message to Marylebone, to find what the people there think about the Canadas."

"And what do they think about the Canadas in Marylebone?"

"Not one man in a thousand cares whether the Canadians prosper or fail to prosper. They care that Canada should not go to the States, because,—though they don't love the Canadians, they do hate the Americans. That's about the feeling in Marylebone,—and it's astonishing how like the Maryleboners are to the rest of the world."

"Dear me, what a fellow you are for an Under-Secretary! You've heard the news about little Violet."

"What news?"

"She has quarrelled with Chiltern, you know."

"Who says so?"

"Never mind who says so, but they tell me it's true. Take an old friend's advice, and strike while the iron's hot."

Phineas did not believe what he had heard, but though he did not believe it, still the tidings set his heart beating. He would have believed it less perhaps had he known that Laurence had just received the news from Mrs. Bonteen.

CHAPTER LVII. The Top Brick of the Chimney

Madame Max Goesler was a lady who knew that in fighting the battles which fell to her lot, in arranging the social difficulties which she found in her way, in doing the work of the world which came to her share, very much more care was necessary,—and care too about things apparently trifling,—than was demanded by the affairs of people in general. And this was not the case so much on account of any special disadvantage under which she laboured, as because she was ambitious of doing the very uttermost with those advantages which she possessed. Her own birth had not been high, and that of her husband, we may perhaps say, had been very low. He had been old when she had married him, and she had had little power of making any progress till he had left her a widow. Then she found herself possessed of money, certainly; of wit,—as she believed; and of a something in her personal appearance which, as she plainly told herself, she might perhaps palm off upon the world as beauty. She was a woman who did not flatter herself, who did not strongly believe in herself, who could even bring herself to wonder that men and women in high position should condescend to notice such a one as her. With all her ambition, there was a something of genuine humility about her; and with all the hardness she had learned there was a touch of womanly softness which would sometimes obtrude itself upon her heart. When she found a woman really kind to her, she would be very kind in return. And though she prized wealth, and knew that her money was her only rock of strength, she could be lavish with it, as though it were dirt.

But she was highly ambitious, and she played her game with great skill and great caution. Her doors were not open to all callers;—were shut even to some who find but few doors closed against them;—were shut occasionally to those whom she most specially wished to see within them. She knew how to allure by denying, and to make the gift rich by delaying it. We are told by the Latin proverb that he who gives quickly gives twice; but I say that she who gives quickly seldom gives more than half. When in the early spring the Duke of Omnium first knocked at Madame Max Goesler's door, he was informed that she was not at home. The Duke felt very cross as he handed his card out from his dark green brougham,—on the panel of which there was no blazon to tell the owner's rank. He was very cross. She had told him that she was always at home between four and six on a Thursday. He had condescended to remember the information, and had acted upon it,—and now she was not at home! She was not at home, though he had come on a Thursday at the very hour she had named to him. Any duke would have been cross, but the Duke of Omnium was particularly cross. No;—he certainly would give himself no further trouble by going to the cottage in Park Lane. And yet Madame Max Goesler had been in her own drawing-room, while the Duke was handing out his card from the brougham below.

On the next morning there came to him a note from the cottage,—such a pretty note!—so penitent, so full of remorse,—and, which was better still, so laden with disappointment, that he forgave her.

My Dear Duke,

I hardly know how to apologise to you, after having told you that I am always at home on Thursdays; and I was at home yesterday when you called. But I was unwell, and I had told the servant to deny me, not thinking how much I might be losing. Indeed, indeed, I would not have given way to a silly headache, had I thought that your Grace would have been here. I suppose that now I must not even hope for the photograph.

Yours penitently,   Marie M. G.

The note-paper was very pretty note-paper, hardly scented, and yet conveying a sense of something sweet, and the monogram was small and new, and fantastic without being grotesque, and the writing was of that sort which the Duke, having much experience, had learned to like,—and there was something in the signature which pleased him. So he wrote a reply,—

Dear Madame Max Goesler,

I will call again next Thursday, or, if prevented, will let you know.

Yours faithfully,   O.

When the green brougham drew up at the door of the cottage on the next Thursday, Madame Goesler was at home, and had no headache.

She was not at all penitent now. She had probably studied the subject, and had resolved that penitence was more alluring in a letter than when acted in person. She received her guest with perfect ease, and apologised for the injury done to him in the preceding week, with much self-complacency. "I was so sorry when I got your card," she said; "and yet I am so glad now that you were refused."

"If you were ill," said the Duke, "it was better."

"I was horribly ill, to tell the truth;—as pale as a death's head, and without a word to say for myself. I was fit to see no one."

"Then of course you were right."

"But it flashed upon me immediately that I had named a day, and that you had been kind enough to remember it. But I did not think you came to London till the March winds were over."

"The March winds blow everywhere in this wretched island, Madame Goesler, and there is no escaping them. Youth may prevail against them; but on me they are so potent that I think they will succeed in driving me out of my country. I doubt whether an old man should ever live in England if he can help it."

The Duke certainly was an old man, if a man turned of seventy be old;—and he was a man too who did not bear his years with hearty strength. He moved slowly, and turned his limbs, when he did turn them, as though the joints were stiff in their sockets. But there was nevertheless about him a dignity of demeanour, a majesty of person, and an upright carriage which did not leave an idea of old age as the first impress on the minds of those who encountered the Duke of Omnium. He was tall and moved without a stoop; and though he moved slowly, he had learned to seem so to do because it was the proper kind of movement for one so high up in the world as himself. And perhaps his tailor did something for him. He had not been long under Madame Max Goesler's eyes before she perceived that his tailor had done a good deal for him. When he alluded to his own age and to her youth, she said some pleasant little word as to the difference between oak-trees and currant-bushes; and by that time she was seated comfortably on her sofa, and the Duke was on a chair before her,—just as might have been any man who was not a Duke.

After a little time the photograph was brought forth from his Grace's pocket. That bringing out and giving of photographs, with the demand for counter photographs, is the most absurd practice of the day. "I don't think I look very nice, do I?" "Oh yes,—very nice, but a little too old; and certainly you haven't got those spots all over your forehead. These are the remarks which on such occasions are the most common. It may be said that to give a photograph or to take a photograph without the utterance of some words which would be felt by a bystander to be absurd, is almost an impossibility. At this moment there was no bystander, and therefore the Duke and the lady had no need for caution. Words were spoken that were very absurd. Madame Goesler protested that the Duke's photograph was more to her than the photographs of all the world beside; and the Duke declared that he would carry the lady's picture next to his heart,—I am afraid he said for ever and ever. Then he took her hand and pressed it, and was conscious that for a man over seventy years of age he did that kind of thing very well.

"You will come and dine with me, Duke?" she said, when he began to talk of going.

"I never dine out."

"That is just the reason you should dine with me. You shall meet nobody you do not wish to meet."

"I would so much rather see you in this way,—I would indeed. I do dine out occasionally, but it is at big formal parties, which I cannot escape without giving offence."

"And you cannot escape my little not formal party,—without giving offence." She looked into his face as she spoke, and he knew that she meant it. And he looked into hers, and thought that her eyes were brighter than any he was in the habit of seeing in these latter days. "Name your own day, Duke. Will a Sunday suit you?"

"If I must come—"

"You must come." As she spoke her eyes sparkled more and more, and her colour went and came, and she shook her curls till they emitted through the air the same soft feeling of a perfume that her note had produced. Then her foot peeped out from beneath the black and yellow drapery of her dress, and the Duke saw that it was perfect. And she put out her finger and touched his arm as she spoke. Her hand was very fair, and her fingers were bright with rich gems. To men such as the Duke, a hand, to be quite fair, should be bright with rich gems. "You must come," she said,—not imploring him now but commanding him.

"Then I will come," he answered, and a certain Sunday was fixed.

The arranging of the guests was a little difficulty, till Madame Goesler begged the Duke to bring with him Lady Glencora Palliser, his nephew's wife. This at last he agreed to do. As the wife of his nephew and heir, Lady Glencora was to the Duke all that a woman could be. She was everything that was proper as to her own conduct, and not obtrusive as to his. She did not bore him, and yet she was attentive. Although in her husband's house she was a fierce politician, in his house she was simply an attractive woman. "Ah; she is very clever," the Duke once said, "she adapts herself. If she were to go from any one place to any other, she would be at home in both." And the movement of his Grace's hand as he spoke seemed to indicate the widest possible sphere for travelling and the widest possible scope for adaptation. The dinner was arranged, and went off very pleasantly. Madame Goesler's eyes were not quite so bright as they were during that morning visit, nor did she touch her guest's arm in a manner so alluring. She was very quiet, allowing her guests to do most of the talking. But the dinner and the flowers and the wine were excellent, and the whole thing was so quiet that the Duke liked it. "And now you must come and dine with me," the Duke said as he took his leave. "A command to that effect will be one which I certainly shall not disobey," whispered Madame Goesler.

"I am afraid he is going to get fond of that woman." These words were spoken early on the following morning by Lady Glencora to her husband, Mr. Palliser.

"He is always getting fond of some woman, and he will to the end," said Mr. Palliser.

"But this Madame Max Goesler is very clever."

"So they tell me. I have generally thought that my uncle likes talking to a fool the best."

"Every man likes a clever woman the best," said Lady Glencora, "if the clever woman only knows how to use her cleverness."

"I'm sure I hope he'll be amused," said Mr. Palliser innocently. "A little amusement is all that he cares for now."

"Suppose you were told some day that he was going—to be married?" said Lady Glencora.

"My uncle married!"

"Why not he as well as another?"

"And to Madame Goesler?"

"If he be ever married it will be to some such woman."

"There is not a man in all England who thinks more of his own position than my uncle," said Mr. Palliser somewhat proudly,—almost with a touch of anger.

"That is all very well, Plantagenet, and true enough in a kind of way. But a child will sacrifice all that it has for the top brick of the chimney, and old men sometimes become children. You would not like to be told some morning that there was a little Lord Silverbridge in the world." Now the eldest son of the Duke of Omnium, when the Duke of Omnium had a son, was called the Earl of Silverbridge; and Mr. Palliser, when this question was asked him, became very pale. Mr. Palliser knew well how thoroughly the cunning of the serpent was joined to the purity of the dove in the person of his wife, and he was sure that there was cause for fear when she hinted at danger.

"Perhaps you had better keep your eye upon him," he said to his wife.

"And upon her," said Lady Glencora.

When Madame Goesler dined at the Duke's house in St. James's Square there was a large party, and Lady Glencora knew that there was no need for apprehension then. Indeed Madame Goesler was no more than any other guest, and the Duke hardly spoke to her. There was a Duchess there,—the Duchess of St. Bungay, and old Lady Hartletop, who was a dowager marchioness,—an old lady who pestered the Duke very sorely,—and Madame Max Goesler received her reward, and knew that she was receiving it, in being asked to meet these people. Would not all these names, including her own, be blazoned to the world in the columns of the next day's *Morning Post?* There was no absolute danger here, as Lady Glencora knew; and Lady Glencora, who was tolerant and begrudged nothing to Madame Max except the one thing, was quite willing to meet the lady at such a grand affair as this. But the Duke, even should he become ever so childish a child in his old age, still would have that plain green brougham at his command, and could go anywhere in that at any hour in the day. And then Madame Goesler was so manifestly a clever woman. A Duchess of Omnium might be said to fill,—in the estimation, at any rate, of English people,—the highest position in the world short of royalty. And the reader will remember that Lady Glencora intended to be a Duchess of Omnium herself,—unless some very unexpected event should intrude itself. She intended also that her little boy, her fair-haired, curly-pated, bold-faced little boy, should be Earl of Silverbridge when the sand of the old man should have run itself out. Heavens, what a blow would it be, should some little wizen-cheeked half-monkey baby, with black brows, and yellow skin, be brought forward and shown to her some day as the heir! What a blow to herself;—and what a blow to all England! "We can't prevent it if he chooses to do it," said her husband, who had his budget to bring forward that very night, and who in truth cared more for his budget than he did for his heirship at that moment. "But we must prevent it," said Lady Glencora. "If I stick to him by the tail of his coat, I'll prevent it." At the time when she thus spoke, the dark green brougham had been twice again brought up at the door in Park Lane.

And the brougham was standing there a third time. It was May now, the latter end of May, and the park opposite was beautiful with green things, and the air was soft and balmy, as it will be sometimes even in May, and the flowers in the balcony were full of perfume, and the charm of London,—what London can be to the rich,—was at its height. The Duke was sitting in Madame Goesler's drawing-room, at some distance from her, for she had retreated. The Duke had a habit of taking her hand, which she never would permit for above a few seconds. At such times she would show no anger, but would retreat.

"Marie," said the Duke, "you will go abroad when the summer is over." As an old man he had taken the privilege of calling her Marie, and she had not forbidden it.

Yes, probably; to Vienna. I have property in Vienna you know, which must be looked after.

"Do not mind Vienna this year. Come to Italy."

"What; in summer, Duke?"

"The lakes are charming in August. I have a villa on Como which is empty now, and I think I shall go there. If you do not know the Italian lakes, I shall be so happy to show them to you."

"I know them well, my lord. When I was young I was on the Maggiore almost alone. Some day I will tell you a history of what I was in those days."

"You shall tell it me there."

"No, my lord, I fear not. I have no villa there."

"Will you not accept the loan of mine? It shall be all your own while you use it."

"My own,—to deny the right of entrance to its owner?"

"If it so pleases you."

"It would not please me. It would so far from please me that I will never put myself in a position that might make it possible for me to require to do so. No, Duke; it behoves me to live in houses of my own. Women of whom more is known can afford to be your guests."

"Marie, I would have no other guest than you."

"It cannot be so, Duke."

"And why not?"

"Why not? Am I to be put to the blush by being made to answer such a question as that? Because the world would say that the Duke of Omnium had a new mistress, and that Madame Goesler was the woman. Do you think that I would be any man's mistress;—even yours? Or do you believe that for the sake of the softness of a summer evening on an Italian lake, I would give cause to the tongues of the women here to say that I was such a thing? You would have me lose all that I have gained by steady years of sober work for the sake of a week or two of dalliance such as that! No, Duke; not for your dukedom!"

How his Grace might have got through his difficulty had they been left alone, cannot be told. For at this moment the door was opened, and Lady Glencora Palliser was announced.

CHAPTER LVIII. Rara Avis in Terris

"Come and see the country and judge for yourself," said Phineas.

"I should like nothing better," said Mr. Monk.

"It has often seemed to me that men in Parliament know less about Ireland than they do of the interior of Africa," said Phineas.

"It is seldom that we know anything accurately on any subject that we have not made matter of careful study," said Mr. Monk, "and very often do not do so even then. We are very apt to think that we men and women understand one another; but most probably you know nothing even of the modes of thought of the man who lives next door to you."

"I suppose not."

"There are general laws current in the world as to morality. 'Thou shalt not steal,' for instance. That has necessarily been current as a law through all nations. But the first man you meet in the street will have ideas about theft so different from yours, that, if you knew them as you know your own, you would say that this law and yours were not even founded on the same principle. It is compatible with this man's honesty to cheat you in a matter of horseflesh, with that man's in a traffic of railway shares, with that other man's as to a woman's fortune; with a fourth's anything may be done for a seat in Parliament, while the fifth man, who stands high among us, and who implores his God every Sunday to write that law on his heart, spends every hour of his daily toil in a system of fraud, and is regarded as a pattern of the national commerce!"

Mr. Monk and Phineas were dining together at Mr. Monk's house, and the elder politician of the two in this little speech had recurred to certain matters which had already been discussed between them. Mr. Monk was becoming somewhat sick of his place in the Cabinet, though he had not as yet whispered a word of his sickness to any living ears; and he had begun to pine for the lost freedom of a seat below the gangway. He had been discussing political honesty with Phineas, and hence had come the sermon of which I have ventured to reproduce the concluding denunciations.

Phineas was fond of such discussions and fond of holding them with Mr. Monk,—in this matter fluttering like a moth round a candle. He would not perceive that as he had made up his mind to be a servant of the public in Parliament, he must abandon all idea of independent action; and unless he did so he could be neither successful as regarded himself, or useful to the public whom he served. Could a man be honest in Parliament, and yet abandon all idea of independence? When he put such questions to Mr. Monk he did not get a direct answer. And indeed the question was never put directly. But the teaching which he received was ever of a nature to make him uneasy. It was always to this effect: "You have taken up the trade now, and seem to be fit for success in it. You had better give up thinking about its special honesty." And yet Mr. Monk would on an occasion preach to him such a sermon as that which he had just uttered! Perhaps there is no question more difficult to a man's mind than that of the expediency or inexpediency of scruples in political life. Whether would a candidate for office be more liable to rejection from a leader because he was known to be scrupulous, or because he was known to be the reverse?

"But putting aside the fourth commandment and all the theories, you will come to Ireland?" said Phineas.

"I shall be delighted."

"I don't live in a castle, you know."

"I thought everybody did live in a castle in Ireland," said Mr. Monk. "They seemed to do when I was there twenty years ago. But for myself, I prefer a cottage."

This trip to Ireland had been proposed in consequence of certain ideas respecting tenant-right which Mr. Monk was beginning to adopt, and as to which the minds of politicians were becoming moved. It had been all very well to put down Fenianism, and Ribandmen, and Repeal,—and everything that had been put down in Ireland in the way of rebellion for the last seventy-five years. England and Ireland had been apparently joined together by laws of nature so fixed, that even politicians liberal as was Mr. Monk,—liberal as was Mr. Turnbull,—could not trust themselves to think that disunion could be for the good of the Irish. They had taught themselves that it certainly could not be good for the English. But if it was incumbent on England to force upon Ireland the maintenance of the Union for her own sake, and for England's sake, because England could not afford independence established so close against her own ribs,—it was at any rate necessary to England's character that the bride thus bound in a compulsory wedlock should be endowed with all the best privileges that a wife can enjoy. Let her at least not be a kept mistress. Let it be bone of my bone and flesh of my flesh, if we are to live together in the married state. Between husband and wife a warm word now and then matters but little, if there be a thoroughly good understanding at bottom. But let there be that good understanding at bottom. What about this Protestant Church; and what about this tenant-right? Mr. Monk had been asking himself these questions for some time past. In regard to the Church, he had long made up his mind that the Establishment in Ireland was a crying sin. A man had married a woman whom he knew to be of a religion different from his own, and then insisted that his wife should say that she believed those things which he knew very well that she did not believe. But, as Mr. Monk well knew, the subject of the Protestant Endowments in Ireland was so difficult that it would require almost more than human wisdom to adjust it. It was one of those matters which almost seemed to require the interposition of some higher power,—the coming of some apparently chance event,—to clear away the evil; as a fire comes, and pestilential alleys are removed; as a famine comes, and men are driven from want and ignorance and dirt to seek new homes and new thoughts across the broad waters; as a war comes, and slavery is banished from the face of the earth. But in regard to tenant-right, to some arrangement by which a tenant in Ireland might be at least encouraged to lay out what little capital he might have in labour or money without being at once called upon to pay rent for that outlay which was his own, as well as for the land which was not his own,—Mr. Monk thought that it was possible that if a man would look hard enough he might perhaps be able to see his way as to that. He had spoken to two of his colleagues on the subject, the two men in the Cabinet whom he believed to be the most thoroughly honest in their ideas as public servants, the Duke and Mr. Gresham. There was so much to be done;—and then so little was known upon the subject! "I will endeavour to study it," said Mr. Monk. "If you can see your way, do;" said Mr. Gresham,—"but of course we cannot bind ourselves." "I should be glad to see it named in the Queen's speech at the beginning of the next session," said Mr. Monk. "That is a long way off as yet," said Mr. Gresham, laughing. "Who will be in then, and who will be out?" So the matter was disposed of at the time, but Mr. Monk did not abandon his idea. He rather felt himself the more bound to cling to it because he received so little encouragement. What was a seat in the Cabinet to him that he should on that account omit a duty? He had not taken up politics as a trade. He had sat far behind the Treasury bench or below the gangway for many a year, without owing any man a shilling,—and could afford to do so again.

But it was different with Phineas Finn, as Mr. Monk himself understood;—and, understanding this, he felt himself bound to caution his young friend. But it may be a question whether his cautions did not do more harm than good. "I shall be delighted," he said, "to go over with you in August, but I do not think that if I were you, I would take up this matter."

"And why not? You don't want to fight the battle singlehanded?"

"No; I desire no such glory, and would wish to have no better lieutenant than you. But you have a subject of which you are really fond, which you are beginning to understand, and in regard to which you can make yourself useful."

"You mean this Canada business?"

"Yes;—and that will grow to other matters as regards the colonies. There is nothing so important to a public man as that he should have his own subject;—the thing which he understands, and in respect of which he can make himself really useful."

"Then there comes a change."

"Yes;—and the man who has half learned how to have a ship built without waste is sent into opposition, and is then brought back to look after regiments, or perhaps has to take up that beautiful subject, a study of the career of India. But, nevertheless, if you have a subject, stick to it at any rate as long as it will stick to you."

"But," said Phineas, "if a man takes up his own subject, independent of the Government, no man can drive him from it."

"And how often does he do anything? Look at the annual motions which come forward in the hands of private men,—Maynooth and the ballot for instance. It is becoming more and more apparent every day that all legislation must be carried by the Government, and must be carried in obedience to the expressed wish of the people. The truest democracy that ever had a chance of living is that which we are now establishing in Great Britain."

"Then leave tenant-right to the people and the Cabinet. Why should you take it up?"

Mr. Monk paused a moment or two before he replied. "If I choose to run a-muck, there is no reason why you should follow me. I am old and you are young. I want nothing from politics as a profession, and you do. Moreover, you have a congenial subject where you are, and need not disturb yourself. For myself, I tell you, in confidence, that I cannot speak so comfortably of my own position."

"We will go and see, at any rate," said Phineas.

"Yes," said Mr. Monk, "we will go and see." And thus, in the month of May, it was settled between them that, as soon as the session should be over, and the incidental work of his office should allow Phineas to pack up and be off, they two should start together for Ireland. Phineas felt rather proud as he wrote to his father and asked permission to bring home with him a Cabinet Minister as a visitor. At this time the reputation of Phineas at Killaloe, as well in the minds of the Killaloeians generally as in those of the inhabitants of the paternal house, stood very high indeed. How could a father think that a son had done badly when before he was thirty years of age he was earning £2,000 a year? And how could a father not think well of a son who had absolutely paid back certain moneys into the paternal coffers? The moneys so repaid had not been much; but the repayment of any such money at Killaloe had been regarded as little short of miraculous. The news of Mr. Monk's coming flew about the town, about the county, about the diocese, and all people began to say all good things about the old doctor's only son. Mrs. Finn had long since been quite sure that a real black swan had been sent forth out of her nest. And the sisters Finn, for some time past, had felt in all social gatherings they stood quite on a different footing than formerly because of their brother. They were asked about in the county, and two of them had been staying only last Easter with the Molonys,—the Molonys of Poldoodie! How should a father and a mother and sisters not be grateful to such a son, to such a brother, to such a veritable black swan out of the nest! And as for dear little Mary Flood Jones, her eyes became suffused with tears as in her solitude she thought how much out of her reach this swan was flying. And yet she took joy in his swanhood, and swore that she would love him still;—that she would love him always. Might he bring home with him to Killaloe, Mr. Monk, the Cabinet Minister! Of course he might. When Mrs. Finn first heard of this august arrival, she felt as though she would like to expend herself in entertaining, though but an hour, the whole cabinet.

Phineas, during the spring, had, of course, met Mr. Kennedy frequently in and about the House, and had become aware that Lady Laura's husband, from time to time, made little overtures of civility to him,—taking him now and again by the button-hole, walking home with him as far as their joint paths allowed, and asking him once or twice to come and dine in Grosvenor Place. These little advances towards a repetition of the old friendship Phineas would have avoided altogether, had it been possible. The invitation to Mr. Kennedy's house he did refuse, feeling himself positively bound to do so by Lady Laura's command, let the consequences be what they might. When he did refuse, Mr. Kennedy would assume a look of displeasure and leave him, and Phineas would hope that the work was done. Then there would come another encounter, and the invitation would be repeated. At last, about the middle of May, there came another note. "Dear Finn, will you dine with us on Wednesday, the 28th? I give you a long notice, because you seem to have so many appointments. Yours always, Robert Kennedy." He had no alternative. He must refuse, even though double the notice had been given. He could only think that Mr. Kennedy was a very obtuse man and one who would not take a hint, and hope that he might succeed at last. So he wrote an answer, not intended to be conciliatory. "MY DEAR KENNEDY, I am sorry to say that I am engaged on the 28th. Yours always, PHINEAS FINN." At this period he did his best to keep out of Mr. Kennedy's way, and would be very cunning in his manoeuvres that they should not be alone together. It was difficult, as they sat on the same bench in the House, and consequently saw each other almost every day of their lives. Nevertheless, he thought that with a little cunning he might prevail, especially as he was not unwilling to give so much of offence as might assist his own object. But when Mr.

Kennedy called upon him at his office the day after he had written the above note, he had no means of escape.

"I am sorry you cannot come to us on the 28th," Mr. Kennedy said, as soon as he was seated.

Phineas was taken so much by surprise that all his cunning failed him. "Well, yes," said he; "I was very sorry;—very sorry indeed."

"It seems to me, Finn, that you have had some reason for avoiding me of late. I do not know that I have done anything to offend you."

"Nothing on earth," said Phineas.

"I am wrong, then, in supposing that anything beyond mere chance has prevented you from coming to my house?" Phineas felt that he was in a terrible difficulty, and he felt also that he was being rather ill-used in being thus cross-examined as to his reasons for not going to a gentleman's dinner. He thought that a man ought to be allowed to choose where he would go and where he would not go, and that questions such as these were very uncommon. Mr. Kennedy was sitting opposite to him, looking more grave and more sour than usual;—and now his own countenance also became a little solemn. It was impossible that he should use Lady Laura's name, and yet he must, in some way, let his persecuting friend know that no further invitation would be of any use;—that there was something beyond mere chance in his not going to Grosvenor Place. But how was he to do this? The difficulty was so great that he could not see his way out of it. So he sat silent with a solemn face. Mr. Kennedy then asked him another question, which made the difficulty ten times greater. "Has my wife asked you not to come to our house?"

It was necessary now that he should make a rush and get out of his trouble in some way. "To tell you the truth, Kennedy, I don't think she wants to see me there."

"That does not answer my question. Has she asked you not to come?"

"She said that which left on my mind an impression that she would sooner that I did not come."

"What did she say?"

"How can I answer such a question as that, Kennedy? Is it fair to ask it?"

"Quite fair,—I think."

"I think it quite unfair, and I must decline to answer it. I cannot imagine what you expect to gain by cross-questioning me in this way. Of course no man likes to go to a house if he does not believe that everybody there will make him welcome."

"You and Lady Laura used to be great friends."

"I hope we are not enemies now. But things will occur that cause friendships to grow cool."

"Have you quarrelled with her father?"

"With Lord Brentford?—no."

"Or with her brother,—since the duel I mean?"

"Upon my word and honour I cannot stand this, and I will not. I have not as yet quarrelled with anybody; but I must quarrel with you, if you go on in this way. It is quite unusual that a man should be put through his facings after such a fashion, and I must beg that there may be an end of it."

"Then I must ask Lady Laura."

"You can say what you like to your own wife of course. I cannot hinder you."

Upon that Mr. Kennedy formally shook hands with him, in token that there was no positive breach between them,—as two nations may still maintain their alliance, though they have made up their minds to hate each other, and thwart each other at every turn,—and took his leave. Phineas, as he sat at his window, looking out into the park, and thinking of what had passed, could not but reflect that, disagreeable as Mr. Kennedy had been to him, he would probably make himself much more disagreeable to his wife. And, for himself, he thought that he had got out of the scrape very well by the exhibition of a little mock anger.

CHAPTER LIX. The Earl's Wrath

The reader may remember that a rumour had been conveyed to Phineas,—a rumour indeed which reached him from a source which he regarded as very untrustworthy,—that Violet Effingham had quarrelled with her lover. He would probably have paid no attention to the rumour, beyond that which necessarily attached itself to any tidings as to a matter so full of interest to him, had it not been repeated to him in another quarter. "A bird has told me that your Violet Effingham has broken with her lover," Madame Goesler said to him one day. "What bird?" he asked. "Ah, that I cannot tell you. But this I will confess to you, that these birds which tell us news are seldom very credible,—and are often not very creditable, You must take a bird's word for what it may be worth. It is said that they have quarrelled. I daresay, if the truth were known, they are billing and cooing in each other's arms at this moment."

Phineas did not like to be told of their billing and cooing,—did not like to be told even of their quarrelling. Though they were to quarrel, it would do him no good. He would rather that nobody should mention their names to him;—so that his back, which had been so utterly broken, might in process of time get itself cured. From what he knew of Violet he thought it very improbable that, even were she to quarrel with one lover, she would at once throw herself into the arms of another. And he did feel, too, that there would be some meanness in taking her, were she willing to be so taken. But, nevertheless, these rumours, coming to him in this way from different sources, almost made it incumbent on him to find out the truth. He began to think that his broken back was not cured;—that perhaps, after all, it was not in the way of being cured, And was it not possible that there might be explanations? Then he went to work and built castles in the air, so constructed as to admit of the possibility of Violet Effingham becoming his wife.

This had been in April, and at that time all that he knew of Violet was, that she was not yet in London. And he thought that he knew the same as to Lord Chiltern. The Earl had told him that Chiltern was not in town, nor expected in town as yet; and in saying so had seemed to express displeasure against his son. Phineas had met Lady Baldock at some house which he frequented, and had been quite surprised to find himself graciously received by the old woman. She had said not a word of Violet, but had spoken of Lord Chiltern,—mentioning his name in bitter wrath. "But he is a friend of mine," said Phineas, smiling. "A friend indeed! Mr. Finn. I know what sort of a friend. I don't believe that you are his friend. I am afraid he is not worthy of having any friend." Phineas did not quite understand from this that Lady Baldock was signifying to him that, badly as she had thought of him as a suitor for her niece, she would have preferred him,—especially now when people were beginning to speak well of him,—to that terrible young man, who, from his youth upwards, had been to her a cause of fear and trembling. Of course it was desirable that Violet should marry an elder son, and a peer's heir. All that kind of thing, in Lady Baldock's eyes, was most desirable. But, nevertheless, anything was better than Lord Chiltern. If Violet would not take Mr. Appledom or Lord Fawn, in heaven's name let her take this young man, who was kind, worthy, and steady, who was civilised in his manners, and would no doubt be amenable in regard to settlements. Lady Baldock had so far fallen in the world that she would have consented to make a bargain with her niece,—almost any bargain, so long as Lord Chiltern was excluded. Phineas did not quite understand all this; but when Lady Baldock asked him to come to Berkeley Square, he perceived that help was being proffered to him where he certainly had not looked for help.

He was frequently with Lord Brentford, who talked to him constantly on matters connected with his parliamentary life. After having been the intimate friend of the daughter and of the son, it now seemed to be his lot to be the intimate friend of the father. The Earl had constantly discussed with him his arrangements with his son, and had lately expressed himself as only half satisfied with such reconciliation as had taken place. And Phineas could perceive that from day to day the Earl was less and less satisfied. He would complain bitterly of his son,—complain of his silence, complain of his not coming to London, complain of his conduct to Violet, complain of his idle indifference to anything like proper occupation; but he had never as yet said a word to show that there had been any quarrel between Violet and her lover, and Phineas had felt that he could not ask the question. "Mr. Finn," said the Earl to him one morning, as soon as he entered the room, "I have just heard a story which has almost seemed to me to be incredible." The nobleman's manner was very stern, and the fact that he called his young friend "Mr. Finn", showed at once that something was wrong.

"What is it you have heard, my lord?" said Phineas.

"That you and Chiltern went over,—last year to,—Belgium, and fought,—a duel there!"

Now it must have been the case that, in the set among which they all lived,—Lord Brentford and his son and daughter and Phineas Finn,—the old lord was the only man who had not heard of the duel before this. It had even penetrated to the dull ears of Mr. Kennedy, reminding him, as it did so, that his wife had,—told him a lie! But it was the fact that no rumour of the duel had reached the Earl till this morning.

"It is true," said Phineas.

"I have never been so much shocked in my life;—never. I had no idea that you had any thought of aspiring to the hand of Miss Effingham." The lord's voice as he said this was very stern.

"As I aspired in vain, and as Chiltern has been successful, that need not now be made a reproach against me."

"I do not know what to think of it, Mr. Finn. I am so much surprised that I hardly know what to say. I must declare my opinion at once, that you behaved,—very badly."

"I do not know how much you know, my lord, and how much you do not know; and the circumstances of the little affair do not permit me to be explicit about them; but, as you have expressed your opinion so openly you must allow me to express mine, and to say that, as far as I can judge of my own actions, I did not behave badly at all."

"Do you intend to defend duelling, sir?"

"No. If you mean to tell me that a duel is of itself sinful, I have nothing to say. I suppose it is. My defence of myself merely goes to the manner in which this duel was fought, and the fact that I fought it with your son."

"I cannot conceive how you can have come to my house as my guest, and stood upon my interest for my borough, when you at the time were doing your very best to interpose yourself between Chiltern and the lady whom you so well knew I wished to become his wife." Phineas was aware that the Earl must have been very much moved indeed when he thus permitted himself to speak of "his" borough. He said nothing now, however, though the Earl paused;—and then the angry lord went on. "I must say that there was something,—something almost approaching to duplicity in such conduct."

"If I were to defend myself by evidence, Lord Brentford, I should have to go back to exact dates,—and dates not of facts which I could verify, but dates as to my feelings which could not be verified,—and that would be useless. I can only say that I believe I know what the honour and truth of a gentleman demand,—even to the verge of self-sacrifice, and that I have done nothing that ought to place my character as a gentleman in jeopardy. If you will ask your son, I think he will tell you the same."

"I have asked him. It was he who told me of the duel."

"When did he tell you, my lord?"

"Just now; this morning." Thus Phineas learned that Lord Chiltern was at this moment in the house,—or at least in London.

"And did he complain of my conduct?"

"I complain of it, sir. I complain of it very bitterly. I placed the greatest confidence in you, especially in regard to my son's affairs, and you deceived me." The Earl was very angry, and was more angry from the fact that this young man who had offended him, to whom he had given such vital assistance when assistance was needed, had used that assistance to its utmost before his sin was found out. Had Phineas still been sitting for Loughton, so that the Earl could have said to him, "You are now bound to retreat from this borough because you have offended me, your patron," I think that he would have forgiven the offender and allowed him to remain in his seat. There would have been a scene, and the Earl would have been pacified. But now the offender was beyond his reach altogether, having used the borough as a most convenient stepping-stone over his difficulties, and having so used it just at the time when he was committing this sin. There was a good fortune about Phineas which added greatly to the lord's wrath. And then, to tell the truth, he had not that rich consolation for which Phineas gave him credit. Lord Chiltern had told him that morning that the engagement between him and Violet was at an end. "You have so preached to her, my lord, about my duties," the son had said to his father, "that she finds herself obliged to give me your sermons at second hand, till I can bear them no longer." But of this Phineas knew nothing as yet. The Earl, however, was so imprudent in his anger that before this interview was over he had told the whole story. "Yes;—you deceived me," he continued; "and I can never trust you again."

"Was it for me, my lord, to tell you of that which would have increased your anger against your own son? When he wanted me to fight was I to come, like a sneak at school, and tell you the story? I know what you would have thought of me had I done so. And when it was over was I to come and tell you then? Think what you yourself would have done when you were young, and you may be quite sure that I did the same. What have I gained? He has got all that he wanted; and you have also got all that you wanted;—and I have helped you both. Lord Brentford, I can put my hand on my heart and say that I have been honest to you."

"I have got nothing that I wanted," said the Earl in his despair.

"Lord Chiltern and Miss Effingham will be man and wife."

"No;—they will not. He has quarrelled with her. He is so obstinate that she will not bear with him."

Then it was all true, even though the rumours had reached him through Laurence Fitzgibbon and Madame Max Goesler. "At any rate, my lord, that has not been my fault," he said, after a moment's hesitation. The Earl was walking up and down the room, angry with himself at his own mistake in having told the story, and not knowing what further to say to his visitor. He had been in the habit of talking so freely to Phineas about his son that he could hardly resist the temptation of doing so still; and yet it was impossible that he could swallow his anger and continue in the same strain. "My lord," said Phineas, after a while, "I can assure you that I grieve that you should be grieved. I have received so much undeserved favour from your family, that I owe you a debt which I can never pay. I am sorry that you should be angry with me now; but I hope that a time may come when you will think less severely of my conduct."

He was about to leave the room when the Earl stopped him. "Will you give me your word," said the Earl, "that you will think no more of Miss Effingham?" Phineas stood silent, considering how he might answer this proposal, resolving that nothing should bring him to such a pledge as that suggested while there was yet a ledge for hope to stand on. "Say that, Mr. Finn, and I will forgive everything."

"I cannot acknowledge that I have done anything to be forgiven."

"Say that," repeated the Earl, "and everything shall be forgotten."

"There need be no cause for alarm, my lord," said Phineas. "You may be sure that Miss Effingham will not think of me."

"Will you give me your word?"

"No, my lord;—certainly not. You have no right to ask it, and the pursuit is open to me as to any other man who may choose to follow it. I have hardly a vestige of a hope of success. It is barely possible that I should succeed. But if it be true that Miss Effingham be disengaged, I shall endeavour to find an opportunity of urging my suit. I would give up everything that I have, my seat in Parliament, all the ambition of my life, for the barest chance of success. When she had accepted your son, I desisted,—of course. I have now heard, from more sources than one, that she or he or both of them have changed their minds. If this be so, I am free to try again." The Earl stood opposite to him, scowling at him, but said nothing. "Good morning, my lord."

"Good morning, sir."

"I am afraid it must be good-bye, for some long days to come."

"Good morning, sir," And the Earl as he spoke rang the bell. Then Phineas took up his hat and departed.

As he walked away his mind filled itself gradually with various ideas, all springing from the words which Lord Brentford had spoken. What account had Lord Chiltern given to his father of the duel? Our hero was a man very sensitive as to the good opinion of others, and in spite of his bold assertion of his own knowledge of what became a gentleman, was beyond measure solicitous that others should acknowledge his claim at any rate to that title. He thought that he had been generous to Lord Chiltern; and as he went back in his memory over almost every word that had been spoken in the interview that had just passed, he fancied that he was able to collect evidence that his antagonist at Blankenberg had not spoken ill of him. As to the charge of deceit which the Earl had made against him, he told himself that the Earl had made it in anger. He would not even think hardly of the Earl who had been so good a friend to him, but he believed in his heart that the Earl had made the accusation out of his wrath and not out of his judgment. "He cannot think that I have been false to him," Phineas said to himself. But it was very sad to him that he should have to quarrel with all the family of the Standishes, as he could not but feel that it was they who had put him on his feet. It seemed as though he were never to see Lady Laura again except when they chanced to meet in company,—on which occasions he simply bowed to her. Now the Earl had almost turned him out of his house. And though there had been to a certain extent a reconciliation between him and Lord Chiltern, he in these days never saw the friend who had once put him upon Bonebreaker; and now,—now that Violet Effingham was again free,—how was it possible to avoid some renewal of enmity between them? He would, however, endeavour to see Lord Chiltern at once.

And then he thought of Violet,—of Violet again free, of Violet as again a possible wife for himself, of Violet to whom he might address himself at any rate without any scruple as to his own unworthiness. Everybody concerned, and many who were not concerned at all, were aware that he had been among her lovers, and he thought that he could perceive that those who interested themselves on the subject, had regarded him as the only horse in the race likely to run with success against Lord Chiltern. She herself had received his offers without scorn, and had always treated him as though he were a favoured friend, though not favoured as a lover. And now even Lady Baldock was smiling upon him, and asking him to her house as though the red-faced porter in the hall in Berkeley Square had never been ordered to refuse him a moment's admission inside the doors. He had been very humble in speaking of his own hopes to the Earl, but surely there might be a chance. What if after all the little strain which he had had in his back was to be cured after such a fashion as this! When he got to his lodgings, he found a card from Lady Baldock, informing him that Lady Baldock would be at home on a certain night, and that there would be music. He could not go to Lady Baldock's on the night named, as it would be necessary that he should be in the House;—nor did he much care to go there, as Violet Effingham was not in town. But he would call and explain, and endeavour to curry favour in that way.

He at once wrote a note to Lord Chiltern, which he addressed to Portman Square. "As you are in town, can we not meet? Come and dine with me at the — Club on Saturday." That was the note. After a few days he received the following answer, dated from the "Bull" at Willingford. Why on earth should Chiltern be staying at the "Bull" at Willingford in May?

The old Shop at W—,
Friday.

DEAR PHINEAS,

I can't dine with you, because I am down here, looking after the cripples, and writing a sporting novel. They tell me I ought to do something, so I am going to do that. I hope you don't think I turned informer against you in telling the Earl of our pleasant little meeting on the sands. It had become necessary, and you are too much of a man to care much for any truth being told. He was terribly angry both with me and with you; but the fact is, he is so blindly unreasonable that one cannot regard his anger. I endeavoured to tell the story truly, and, so told, it certainly should not have injured you in his estimation. But it did. Very sorry, old fellow, and I hope you'll get over it. It is a good deal more important to me than to you.

Yours,   C.

There was not a word about Violet. But then it was hardly to be expected that there should be words about Violet. It was not likely that a man should write to his rival of his own failure. But yet there was a flavour of Violet in the letter which would not have been there, so Phineas thought, if the writer had been despondent. The pleasant little meeting on the sands had been convened altogether in respect of Violet. And the telling of the story to the Earl must have arisen from discussions about Violet. Lord Chiltern must have told his father that Phineas was his rival. Could the rejected suitor have written on such a subject in such a strain to such a correspondent if he had believed his own rejection to be certain? But then Lord Chiltern was not like anybody else in the world, and it was impossible to judge of him by one's experience of the motives of others.

Shortly afterwards Phineas did call in Berkeley Square, and was shown up at once into Lady Baldock's drawing-room. The whole aspect of the porter's countenance was changed towards him, and from this, too, he gathered good auguries This had surprised him; but his surprise was far greater, when, on entering the room, he found Violet Effingham there alone. A little fresh colour came to her face as she greeted him, though it cannot be said that she blushed. She behaved herself admirably, not endeavouring to conceal some little emotion at thus meeting him, but betraying none that was injurious to her composure. "I am so glad to see you, Mr. Finn," she said. "My aunt has just left me, and will be back directly."

He was by no means her equal in his management of himself on the occasion; but perhaps it may be acknowledged that his position was the more difficult of the two. He had not seen her since her engagement had been proclaimed to the world, and now he had heard from a source which was not to be doubted, that it had been broken off. Of course there was nothing to be said on that matter. He could not have congratulated her in the one case, nor could he either congratulate her or condole with her on the other. And yet he did not know how to speak to her as though no such events had occurred. "I did not know that you were in town," he said.

"I only came yesterday. I have been, you know, at Rome with the Effinghams; and since that I have been—; but, indeed, I have been such a vagrant that I cannot tell you of all my comings and goings. And you,—you are hard at work!"

"Oh yes;—always."

"That is right. I wish I could be something, if it were only a stick in waiting, or a door-keeper. It is so good to be something." Was it some such teaching as this that had jarred against Lord Chiltern's susceptibilities, and had seemed to him to be a repetition of his father's sermons?

"A man should try to be something," said Phineas.

"And a woman must be content to be nothing,—unless Mr. Mill can pull us through! And now, tell me,—have you seen Lady Laura?"

"Not lately."

"Nor Mr. Kennedy?"

"I sometimes see him in the House." The visit to the Colonial Office of which the reader has been made aware had not at that time as yet been made.

"I am sorry for all that," she said. Upon which Phineas smiled and shook his head. "I am very sorry that there should be a quarrel between you two."

"There is no quarrel."

"I used to think that you and he might do so much for each other,—that is, of course, if you could make a friend of him."

"He is a man of whom it is very hard to make a friend," said Phineas, feeling that he was dishonest to Mr. Kennedy in saying so, but thinking that such dishonesty was justified by what he owed to Lady Laura.

"Yes;—he is hard, and what I call ungenial. We won't say anything about him,—will we? Have you seen much of the Earl?" This she asked as though such a question had no reference whatever to Lord Chiltern.

"Oh dear,—alas, alas!"

"You have not quarrelled with him too?"

"He has quarrelled with me. He has heard, Miss Effingham, of what happened last year, and he thinks that I was wrong."

"Of course you were wrong, Mr. Finn."

"Very likely. To him I chose to defend myself, but I certainly shall not do so to you. At any rate, you did not think it necessary to quarrel with me."

"I ought to have done so. I wonder why my aunt does not come." Then she rang the bell.

"Now I have told you all about myself," said he; "you should tell me something of yourself."

"About me? I am like the knife-grinder, who had no story to tell,—none at least to be told. We have all, no doubt, got our little stories, interesting enough to ourselves."

"But your story, Miss Effingham," he said, "is of such intense interest to me." At that moment, luckily, Lady Baldock came into the room, and Phineas was saved from the necessity of making a declaration at a moment which would have been most inopportune.

Lady Baldock was exceedingly gracious to him, bidding Violet use her influence to persuade him to come to the gathering. "Persuade him to desert his work to come and hear some fiddlers!" said Miss Effingham. "Indeed I shall not, aunt. Who can tell but what the colonies might suffer from it through centuries, and that such a lapse of duty might drive a province or two into the arms of our mortal enemies?"

"Herr Moll is coming," said Lady Baldock, "and so is Signor Scrubi, and Pjinskt, who, they say, is the greatest man living on the flageolet. Have you ever heard Pjinskt, Mr. Finn?" Phineas never had heard Pjinskt. "And as for Herr Moll, there is nothing equal to him, this year, at least." Lady Baldock had taken up music this season, but all her enthusiasm was unable to shake the conscientious zeal of the young Under-Secretary of State. At such a gathering he would have been unable to say a word in private to Violet Effingham.

CHAPTER LX. Madame Goesler's Politics

It may be remembered that when Lady Glencora Palliser was shown into Madame Goesler's room, Madame Goesler had just explained somewhat forcibly to the Duke of Omnium her reasons for refusing the loan of his Grace's villa at Como. She had told the Duke in so many words that she did not mean to give the world an opportunity of maligning her, and it would then have been left to the Duke to decide whether any other arrangements might have been made for taking Madame Goesler to Como, had he not been interrupted. That he was very anxious to take her was certain. The green brougham had already been often enough at the door in Park Lane to make his Grace feel that Madame Goesler's company was very desirable,—was, perhaps, of all things left for his enjoyment, the one thing the most desirable. Lady Glencora had spoken to her husband of children crying for the top brick of the chimney. Now it had come to this, that in the eyes of the Duke of Omnium Marie Max Goesler was the top brick of the chimney. She had more wit for him than other women,—more of that sort of wit which he was capable of enjoying. She had a beauty which he had learned to think more alluring than other beauty. He was sick of fair faces, and fat arms, and free necks. Madame Goesler's eyes sparkled as other eyes did not sparkle, and there was something of the vagueness of mystery in the very blackness and gloss and abundance of her hair,—as though her beauty was the beauty of some world which he had not yet known. And there was a quickness and yet a grace of motion about her which was quite new to him. The ladies upon whom the Duke had of late most often smiled had been somewhat slow,—perhaps almost heavy,—though, no doubt, graceful withal. In his early youth he remembered to have seen, somewhere in Greece, such a houri as was this Madame Goesler. The houri in that case had run off with the captain of a Russian vessel engaged in the tallow trade; but not the less was there left on his Grace's mind some dreamy memory of charms which had impressed him very strongly when he was simply a young Mr. Palliser, and had had at his command not so convenient a mode of sudden abduction as the Russian captain's tallow ship. Pressed hard by such circumstances as these, there is no knowing how the Duke might have got out of his difficulties had not Lady Glencora appeared upon the scene.

Since the future little Lord Silverbridge had been born, the Duke had been very constant in his worship of Lady Glencora, and as, from year to year, a little brother was added, thus making the family very strong and stable, his acts of worship had increased; but with his worship there had come of late something almost of dread,—something almost of obedience, which had made those who were immediately about the Duke declare that his Grace was a good deal changed. For, hitherto, whatever may have been the Duke's weaknesses, he certainly had known no master. His heir, Plantagenet Palliser, had been always subject to him. His other relations had been kept at such a distance as hardly to be more than recognised; and though his Grace no doubt had had his intimacies, they who had been intimate with him had either never tried to obtain ascendancy, or had failed. Lady Glencora, whether with or without a struggle, had succeeded, and people about the Duke said that the Duke was much changed. Mr. Fothergill,—who was his Grace's man of business, and who was not a favourite with Lady Glencora,—said that he was very much changed indeed. Finding his Grace so much changed, Mr. Fothergill had made a little attempt at dictation himself, but had receded with fingers very much scorched in the attempt. It was indeed possible that the Duke was becoming in the slightest degree weary of Lady Glencora's thraldom, and that he thought that Madame Max Goesler might be more tender with him. Madame Max Goesler, however, intended to be tender only on one condition.

When Lady Glencora entered the room, Madame Goesler received her beautifully. "How lucky that you should have come just when his Grace is here!" she said.

"I saw my uncle's carriage, and of course I knew it," said Lady Glencora.

"Then the favour is to him," said Madame Goesler, smiling.

"No, indeed; I was coming. If my word is to be doubted in that point, I must insist on having the servant up; I must, certainly. I told him to drive to this door, as far back as Grosvenor Street. Did I not, Planty?" Planty was the little Lord Silverbridge as was to be, if nothing unfortunate intervened, who was now sitting on his granduncle's knee.

"Dou said to the little house in Park Lane," said the boy.

"Yes,—because I forgot the number."

"And it is the smallest house in Park Lane, so the evidence is complete," said Madame Goesler. Lady Glencora had not cared much for evidence to convince Madame Goesler, but she had not wished her uncle to think that he was watched and hunted down. It might be necessary that he should know that he was watched, but things had not come to that as yet.

"How is Plantagenet?" asked the Duke.

"Answer for papa," said Lady Glencora to her child.

"Papa is very well, but he almost never comes home."

"He is working for his country," said the Duke. "Your papa is a busy, useful man, and can't afford time to play with a little boy as I can."

"But papa is not a duke."

"He will be some day, and that probably before long, my boy. He will be a duke quite as soon as he wants to be a duke. He likes the House of Commons better than the strawberry leaves, I fancy. There is not a man in England less in a hurry than he is."

"No, indeed," said Lady Glencora.

"How nice that is," said Madame Goesler.

"And I ain't in a hurry either,—am I, mamma?" said the little future Lord Silverbridge.

"You are a wicked little monkey," said his grand-uncle, kissing him. At this moment Lady Glencora was, no doubt, thinking how necessary it was that she should be careful to see that things did turn out in the manner proposed,—so that people who had waited should not be disappointed; and the Duke was perhaps thinking that he was not absolutely bound to his nephew by any law of God or man; and Madame Max Goesler,—I wonder whether her thoughts were injurious to the prospects of that handsome bold-faced little boy.

Lady Glencora rose to take her leave first. It was not for her to show any anxiety to force the Duke out of the lady's presence. If the Duke were resolved to make a fool of himself, nothing that she could do would prevent it. But she thought that this little inspection might possibly be of service, and that her uncle's ardour would be cooled by the interruption to which he had been subjected. So she went, and immediately afterwards the Duke followed her. The interruption had, at any rate, saved him on that occasion from making the highest bid for the pleasure of Madame Goesler's company at Como. The Duke went down with the little boy in his hand, so that there was not an opportunity for a single word of interest between the gentleman and the lady.

Madame Goesler, when she was alone, seated herself on her sofa, tucking her feet up under her as though she were seated somewhere in the East, pushed her ringlets back roughly from her face, and then placed her two hands to her sides so that her thumbs rested lightly on her girdle. When alone with something weighty on her mind she would sit in this form for the hour together, resolving, or trying to resolve, what should be her conduct. She did few things without much thinking, and though she walked very boldly, she walked warily. She often told herself that such success as she had achieved could not have been achieved without much caution. And yet she was ever discontented with herself, telling herself that all that she had done was nothing, or worse than nothing. What was it all, to have a duke and to have lords dining with her, to dine with lords or with a duke itself, if life were dull with her, and the hours hung heavy! Life with her was dull, and the hours did hang heavy. And what if she caught this old man, and became herself a duchess,—caught him by means of his weakness, to the inexpressible dismay of all those who were bound to him by ties of blood,—would that make her life happier, or her hours less tedious? That prospect of a life on the Italian lakes with an old man tied to her side was not so charming in her eyes as it was in those of the Duke. Were she to succeed, and to be blazoned forth to the world as Duchess of Omnium, what would she have gained?

She perfectly understood the motive of Lady Glencora's visit, and thought that she would at any rate gain something in the very triumph of baffling the manoeuvres of so clever a woman. Let Lady Glencora throw her ægis before the Duke, and it would be something to carry off his Grace from beneath the protection of so thick a shield. The very flavour of the contest was pleasing to Madame Goesler. But, the victory gained, what then would remain to her? Money she had already; position, too, she had of her own. She was free as air, and should it suit her at any time to go off to some lake of Como in society that would personally be more agreeable to her than that of the Duke of Omnium, there was nothing to hinder her for a moment. And then came a smile over her face,—but the saddest smile,—as she thought of one with whom it might be pleasant to look at the colour of Italian skies and feel the softness of Italian breezes. In feigning to like to do this with an old man, in acting the raptures of love on behalf of a worn-out duke who at the best would scarce believe in her acting, there would not be much delight for her. She had never yet known what it was to have anything of the pleasure of love. She had grown, as she often told herself, to be a hard, cautious, selfish, successful woman, without any interference or assistance from such pleasure. Might there not be yet time left for her to try it without selfishness,—with an absolute devotion of self,—if only she could find the right companion? There was one who might be such a companion, but the Duke of Omnium certainly could not be such a one.

But to be Duchess of Omnium! After all, success in this world is everything;—is at any rate the only thing the pleasure of which will endure. There was the name of many a woman written in a black list within Madame Goesler's breast,—written there because of scorn, because of rejected overtures, because of deep social injury; and Madame Goesler told herself often that it would be a pleasure to her to use the list, and to be revenged on those who had ill-used and scornfully treated her. She did not readily forgive those who had injured her. As Duchess of Omnium she thought that probably she might use that list with efficacy. Lady Glencora had treated her well, and she had no such feeling against Lady Glencora. As Duchess of Omnium she would accept Lady Glencora as her dearest friend, if Lady Glencora would admit it. But if it should be necessary that there should be a little duel between them, as to which of them should take the Duke in hand, the duel must of course be fought. In a matter so important, one woman would of course expect no false sentiment from another. She and Lady Glencora would understand each other;—and no doubt, respect each other.

I have said that she would sit there resolving, or trying to resolve. There is nothing in the world so difficult as that task of making up one's mind. Who is there that has not longed that the power and privilege of selection among alternatives should be taken away from him in some important crisis of his life, and that his conduct should be arranged for him, either this way or that, by some divine power if it were possible,—by some patriarchal power in the absence of divinity,—or by chance even, if nothing better than chance could be found to do it? But no one dares to cast the die, and to go honestly by the hazard. There must be the actual necessity of obeying the die, before even the die can be of any use. As it was, when Madame Goesler had sat there for an hour, till her legs were tired beneath her, she had not resolved. It must be as her impulse should direct her when the important moment came. There was not a soul on earth to whom she could go for counsel, and when she asked herself for counsel, the counsel would not come.

Two days afterwards the Duke called again. He would come generally on a Thursday,—early, so that he might be there before other visitors; and he had already quite learned that when he was there other visitors would probably be refused admittance. How Lady Glencora had made her way in, telling the servant that her uncle was there, he had not understood. That visit had been made on the Thursday, but now he came on the Saturday,—having, I regret to say, sent down some early fruit from his own hot-houses,—or from Covent Garden,—with a little note on the previous day. The grapes might have been pretty well, but the note was injudicious. There were three lines about the grapes, as to which there was some special history, the vine having been brought from the garden of some villa in which some ill-used queen had lived and died; and then there was a postscript in one line to say that the Duke would call on the following morning. I do not think that he had meant to add this when he began his note; but then children, who want the top brick, want it so badly, and cry for it so perversely!

Of course Madame Goesler was at home. But even then she had not made up her mind. She had made up her mind only to this,—that he should be made to speak plainly, and that she would take time for her reply. Not even with such a gem as the Duke's coronet before her eyes, would she jump at it. Where there was so much doubt, there need at least be no impatience.

"You ran away the other day, Duke, because you could not resist the charm of that little boy," she said, laughing.

"He is a dear little boy,—but it was not that," he answered.

"Then what was it? Your niece carried you off in a whirl-wind. She was come and gone, taking you with her, in half a minute."

"She had disturbed me when I was thinking of something," said the Duke.

"Things shouldn't be thought of,—not so deeply as that." Madame Goesler was playing with a bunch of his grapes now, eating one or two from a small china plate which had stood upon the table, and he thought that he had never seen a woman so graceful and yet so natural. "Will you not eat your own grapes with me? They are delicious;—flavoured with the poor queen's sorrows." He shook his head, knowing that it did not suit his gastric juices to have to deal with fruit eaten at odd times. "Never think, Duke. I am convinced that it does no good. It simply means doubting, and doubt always leads to error. The safest way in the world is to do nothing."

"I believe so," said the Duke.

"Much the safest. But if you have not sufficient command over yourself to enable you to sit in repose, always quiet, never committing yourself to the chance of any danger,—then take a leap in the dark; or rather many leaps. A stumbling horse regains his footing by persevering in his onward course. As for moving cautiously, that I detest."

"And yet one must think;—for instance, whether one will succeed or not."

"Take that for granted always. Remember, I do not recommend motion at all. Repose is my idea of life;—repose and grapes."

The Duke sat for a while silent, taking his repose as far as the outer man was concerned, looking at his top brick of the chimney, as from time to time she ate one of his grapes. Probably she did not eat above half-a-dozen of them altogether, but he thought that the grapes must have been made for the woman, she was so pretty in the eating of them. But it was necessary that he should speak at last. "Have you been thinking of coming to Como?" he said.

"I told you that I never think."

"But I want an answer to my proposition."

"I thought I had answered your Grace on that question." Then she put down the grapes, and moved herself on her chair, so that she sat with her face turned away from him.

"But a request to a lady may be made twice."

"Oh, yes. And I am grateful, knowing how far it is from your intention to do me any harm. And I am somewhat ashamed of my warmth on the other day. But still there can be but one answer. There are delights which a woman must deny herself, let them be ever so delightful."

"I had thought,—" the Duke began, and then he stopped himself.

"Your Grace was saying that you thought,—"

"Marie, a man at my age does not like to be denied."

"What man likes to be denied anything by a woman at any age? A woman who denies anything is called cruel at once,—even though it be her very soul." She had turned round upon him now, and was leaning forward towards him from her chair, so that he could touch her if he put out his hand.

He put out his hand and touched her. "Marie," he said, "will you deny me if I ask?"

"Nay, my lord; how shall I say? There is many a trifle I would deny you. There is many a great gift I would give you willingly."

"But the greatest gift of all?"

"My lord, if you have anything to say, you must say it plainly. There never was a woman worse than I am at the reading of riddles."

"Could you endure to live in the quietude of an Italian lake with an old man?" Now he touched her again, and had taken her hand.

"No, my lord;—nor with a young one,—for all my days. But I do not know that age would guide me."

Then the Duke rose and made his proposition in form. "Marie, you know that I love you. Why it is that I at my age should feel so sore a love, I cannot say."

"So sore a love!"

"So sore, if it be not gratified. Marie, I ask you to be my wife."

"Duke of Omnium, this from you!"

"Yes, from me. My coronet is at your feet. If you will allow me to raise it, I will place it on your brow."

Then she went away from him, and seated herself at a distance. After a moment or two he followed her, and stood with his arm upon her shoulder. "You will give me an answer, Marie?"

"You cannot have thought of this, my lord."

"Nay; I have thought of it much."

"And your friends?"

"My dear, I may venture to please myself in this,—as in everything. Will you not answer me?"

"Certainly not on the spur of the moment, my lord. Think how high is the position you offer me, and how immense is the change you propose to me. Allow me two days, and I will answer you by letter. I am so fluttered now that I must leave you." Then he came to her, took her hand, kissed her brow, and opened the door for her.

CHAPTER LXI. Another Duel

It happened that there were at this time certain matters of business to be settled between the Duke of Omnium and his nephew Mr. Palliser, respecting which the latter called upon his uncle on the morning after the Duke had committed himself by his offer. Mr. Palliser had come by appointment made with Mr. Fothergill, the Duke's man of business, and had expected to meet Mr. Fothergill. Mr. Fothergill, however, was not with the Duke, and the uncle told the nephew that the business had been postponed. Then Mr. Palliser asked some question as to the reason of such postponement, not meaning much by his question,—and the Duke, after a moment's hesitation, answered him, meaning very much by his answer. "The truth is, Plantagenet, that it is possible that I may marry, and if so this arrangement would not suit me."

"Are you going to be married?" asked the astonished nephew.

"It is not exactly that,—but it is possible that I may do so. Since I proposed this matter to Fothergill, I have been thinking over it, and I have changed my mind. It will make but little difference to you; and after all you are a far richer man than I am."

"I am not thinking of money, Duke," said Plantagenet Palliser.

"Of what then were you thinking?"

"Simply of what you told me. I do not in the least mean to interfere."

"I hope not, Plantagenet."

"But I could not hear such a statement from you without some surprise. Whatever you do I hope will tend to make you happy."

So much passed between the uncle and the nephew, and what the uncle told to the nephew, the nephew of course told to his wife. "He was with her again, yesterday," said Lady Glencora, "for more than an hour. And he had been half the morning dressing himself before he went to her."

"He is not engaged to her, or he would have told me," said Plantagenet Palliser.

"I think he would, but there is no knowing. At the present moment I have only one doubt,—whether to act upon him or upon her."

"I do not see that you can do good by going to either."

"Well, we will see. If she be the woman I take her to be, I think I could do something with her. I have never supposed her to be a bad woman,—never. I will think of it." Then Lady Glencora left her husband, and did not consult him afterwards as to the course she would pursue. He had his budget to manage, and his speeches to make. The little affair of the Duke and Madame Goesler, she thought it best to take into her own hands without any assistance from him. "What a fool I was," she said to herself, "to have her down there when the Duke was at Matching!"

Madame Goesler, when she was left alone, felt that now indeed she must make up her mind. She had asked for two days. The intervening day was a Sunday, and on the Monday she must send her answer. She might doubt at any rate for this one night,—the Saturday night,—and sit playing, as it were, with the coronet of a duchess in her lap. She had been born the daughter of a small country attorney, and now a duke had asked her to be his wife,—and a duke who was acknowledged to stand above other dukes! Nothing at any rate could rob her of that satisfaction. Whatever resolution she might form at last, she had by her own resources reached a point of success in remembering which there would always be a keen gratification. It would be much to be Duchess of Omnium; but it would be something also to have refused to be a Duchess of Omnium. During that evening, that night, and the next morning, she remained playing with the coronet in her lap. She would not go to church. What good could any sermon do her while that bauble was dangling before her eyes? After church-time, about two o'clock, Phineas Finn came to her. Just at this period Phineas would come to her often;—sometimes full of a new decision to forget Violet Effingham altogether, at others minded to continue his siege let the hope of success be ever so small. He had now heard that Violet and Lord Chiltern had in truth quarrelled, and was of course anxious to be advised to continue the siege. When he first came in and spoke a word or two, in which there was no reference to Violet Effingham, there came upon Madame Goesler a strong wish to decide at once that she would play no longer with the coronet, that the gem was not worth the cost she would be called upon to pay for it. There was something in the world better for her than the coronet,—if only it might be had. But within ten minutes he had told her the whole tale about Lord Chiltern, and how he had seen Violet at Lady Baldock's,—and how there might yet be hope for him. What would she advise him to do? "Go home, Mr. Finn," she said, "and write a sonnet to her eyebrow. See if that will have any effect."

"Ah, well! It is natural that you should laugh at me; but somehow, I did not expect it from you."

"Do not be angry with me. What I mean is that such little things seem to influence this Violet of yours."

"Do they? I have not found that they do so."

"If she had loved Lord Chiltern she would not have quarrelled with him for a few words. If she had loved you, she would not have accepted Lord Chiltern. If she loves neither of you, she should say so. I am losing my respect for her."

"Do not say that, Madame Goesler. I respect her as strongly as I love her." Then Madame Goesler almost made up her mind that she would have the coronet. There was a substance about the coronet that would not elude her grasp.

Late that afternoon, while she was still hesitating, there came another caller to the cottage in Park Lane. She was still hesitating, feeling that she had as yet another night before her. Should she be Duchess of Omnium or not? All that she wished to be, she could not be;—but to be Duchess of Omnium was within her reach. Then she began to ask herself various questions. Would the Queen refuse to accept her in her new rank? Refuse! How could any Queen refuse to accept her? She had not done aught amiss in life. There was no slur on her name; no stain on her character. What though her father had been a small attorney, and her first husband a Jew banker! She had broken no law of God or man, had been accused of breaking no law, which breaking or which accusation need stand in the way of her being as good a duchess as any other woman! She was sitting thinking of this, almost angry with herself at the awe with which the proposed rank inspired her, when Lady Glencora was announced to her.

"Madame Goesler," said Lady Glencora, "I am very glad to find you."

"And I more than equally so, to be found," said Madame Goesler, smiling with all her grace.

"My uncle has been with you since I saw you last?"

"Oh yes;—more than once if I remember right. He was here yesterday at any rate."

"He comes often to you then?"

"Not so often as I would wish, Lady Glencora. The Duke is one of my dearest friends."

"It has been a quick friendship."

"Yes;—a quick friendship," said Madame Goesler. Then there was a pause for some moments which Madame Goesler was determined that she would not break. It was clear to her now on what ground Lady Glencora had come to her, and she was fully minded that if she could bear the full light of the god himself in all his glory, she would not allow herself to be scorched by any reflected heat coming from the god's niece. She thought she could endure anything that Lady Glencora might say; but she would wait and hear what might be said.

"I think, Madame Goesler, that I had better hurry on to my subject at once," said Lady Glencora, almost hesitating as she spoke, and feeling that the colour was rushing up to her cheeks and covering her brow. "Of course what I have to say will be disagreeable. Of course I shall offend you. And yet I do not mean it."

"I shall be offended at nothing, Lady Glencora, unless I think that you mean to offend me."

"I protest that I do not. You have seen my little boy."

"Yes, indeed. The sweetest child! God never gave me anything half so precious as that."

"He is the Duke's heir."

"So I understand."

"For myself, by my honour as a woman, I care nothing. I am rich and have all that the world can give me. For my husband, in this matter, I care nothing. His career he will make for himself, and it will depend on no title."

"Why all this to me, Lady Glencora? What have I to do with your husband's titles?"

"Much;—if it be true that there is an idea of marriage between you and the Duke of Omnium."

"Psha!" said Madame Goesler, with all the scorn of which she was mistress.

"It is untrue, then?" asked Lady Glencora.

"No;—it is not untrue. There is an idea of such a marriage."

"And you are engaged to him?"

"No;—I am not engaged to him."

"Has he asked you?"

"Lady Glencora, I really must say that such a cross-questioning from one lady to another is very unusual. I have promised not to be offended, unless I thought that you wished to offend me. But do not drive me too far."

"Madame Goesler, if you will tell me that I am mistaken, I will beg your pardon, and offer to you the most sincere friendship which one woman can give another."

"Lady Glencora, I can tell you nothing of the kind."

"Then it is to be so! And have you thought what you would gain?"

"I have thought much of what I should gain:—and something also of what I should lose."

"You have money."

"Yes, indeed; plenty,—for wants so moderate as mine."

"And position."

"Well, yes; a sort of position. Not such as yours, Lady Glencora. That, if it be not born to a woman, can only come to her from a husband. She cannot win it for herself."

"You are free as air, going where you like, and doing what you like."

"Too free, sometimes," said Madame Goesler.

"And what will you gain by changing all this simply for a title?"

"But for such a title, Lady Glencora! It may be little to you to be Duchess of Omnium, but think what it must be to me!"

"And for this you will not hesitate to rob him of all his friends, to embitter his future life, to degrade him among his peers,—"

"Degrade him! Who dares say that I shall degrade him? He will exalt me, but I shall no whit degrade him. You forget yourself, Lady Glencora."

"Ask any one. It is not that I despise you. If I did, would I offer you my hand in friendship? But an old man, over seventy, carrying the weight and burden of such rank as his, will degrade himself in the eyes of his fellows, if he marries a young woman without rank, let her be ever so clever, ever so beautiful. A Duke of Omnium may not do as he pleases, as may another man."

"It may be well, Lady Glencora, for other dukes, and for the daughters and heirs and cousins of other dukes, that his Grace should try that question. I will, if you wish it, argue this matter with you on many points, but I will not allow you to say that I should degrade any man whom I might marry. My name is as unstained as your own."

"I meant nothing of that," said Lady Glencora.

"For him;—I certainly would not willingly injure him. Who wishes to injure a friend? And, in truth, I have so little to gain, that the temptation to do him an injury, if I thought it one, is not strong. For your little boy, Lady Glencora, I think your fears are premature." As she said this, there came a smile over her face, which threatened to break from control and almost become laughter. "But, if you will allow me to say so, my mind will not be turned against this marriage half so strongly by any arguments you can use as by those which I can adduce myself. You have nearly driven me into it by telling me I should degrade his house. It is almost incumbent on me to prove that you are wrong. But you had better leave me to settle the matter in my own bosom. You had indeed."

After a while Lady Glencora did leave her,—to settle the matter within her own bosom,—having no other alternative.

CHAPTER LXII. The Letter That was Sent to Brighton

Monday morning came and Madame Goesler had as yet written no answer to the Duke of Omnium. Had not Lady Glencora gone to Park Lane on the Sunday afternoon, I think the letter would have been written on that day; but, whatever may have been the effect of Lady Glencora's visit, it so far disturbed Madame Goesler as to keep her from her writing-table. There was yet another night for thought, and then the letter should be written on the Monday morning.

When Lady Glencora left Madame Goesler she went at once to the Duke's house. It was her custom to see her husband's uncle on a Sunday, and she would most frequently find him just at this hour,—before he went up-stairs to dress for dinner. She usually took her boy with her, but on this occasion she went alone. She had tried what she could do with Madame Goesler, and she found that she had failed. She must now make her attempt upon the Duke. But the Duke, perhaps anticipating some attack of the kind, had fled. "Where is his Grace, Barker?" said Lady Glencora to the porter. "We do not know, your ladyship. His Grace went away yesterday evening with nobody but Lapoule." Lapoule was the Duke's French valet. Lady Glencora could only return home and consider in her own mind what batteries might yet be brought to bear upon the Duke, towards stopping the marriage, even after the engagement should have been made,—if it were to be made. Lady Glencora felt that such batteries might still be brought up as would not improbably have an effect on a proud, weak old man. If all other resources failed, royalty in some of its branches might be induced to make a request, and every august relation in the peerage should interfere. The Duke no doubt might persevere and marry whom he pleased,—if he were strong enough. But it requires much personal strength,—that standing alone against the well-armed batteries of all one's friends. Lady Glencora had once tried such a battle on her own behalf, and had failed. She had wished to be imprudent when she was young; but her friends had been too strong for her. She had been reduced, and kept in order, and made to run in a groove,—and was now, when she sat looking at her little boy with his bold face, almost inclined to think that the world was right, and that grooves were best. But if she had been controlled when she was young, so ought the Duke to be controlled now that he was old. It is all very well for a man or woman to boast that he,—or she,—may do what he likes with his own,—or with her own. But there are circumstances in which such self-action is ruinous to so many that coercion from the outside becomes absolutely needed. Nobody had felt the injustice of such coercion when applied to herself more sharply than had Lady Glencora. But she had lived to acknowledge that such coercion might be proper, and was now prepared to use it in any shape in which it might be made available. It was all very well for Madame Goesler to laugh and exclaim, "Psha!" when Lady Glencora declared her real trouble. But should it ever come to pass that a black-browed baby with a yellow skin should be shown to the world as Lord Silverbridge, Lady Glencora knew that her peace of mind would be gone for ever. She had begun the world desiring one thing, and had missed it. She had suffered much, and had then reconciled herself to other hopes. If those other hopes were also to be cut away from her, the world would not be worth a pinch of snuff to her. The Duke had fled, and she could do nothing to-day; but to-morrow she would begin with her batteries. And she herself had done the mischief! She had invited this woman down to Matching! Heaven and earth!—that such a man as the Duke should be such a fool! —The widow of a Jew banker! He, the Duke of Omnium,—and thus to cut away from himself, for the rest of his life, all honour, all peace of mind, all the grace of a noble end to a career which, if not very noble in itself, had received the praise of nobility! And to do this for a thin, black-browed, yellow-visaged woman with ringlets and devil's eyes, and a beard on her upper lip,—a Jewess,—a creature of whose habits of life and manners of thought they all were absolutely ignorant; who drank, possibly; who might have been a forger, for what any one knew; an adventuress who had found her way into society by her art and perseverance,—and who did not even pretend to have a relation in the world! That such a one should have influence enough to intrude herself into the house of Omnium, and blot the scutcheon, and,— what was worst of all,—perhaps be the mother of future dukes! Lady Glencora, in her anger, was very unjust to Madame Goesler, thinking all evil of her, accusing her in her mind of every crime, denying her all charm, all beauty. Had the Duke forgotten himself and his position for the sake of some fair girl with a pink complexion and grey eyes, and smooth hair, and a father, Lady Glencora thought that she would have forgiven it better. It might be that Madame Goesler would win her way to the coronet; but when she came to put it on, she should find that there were sharp thorns inside the lining of it. Not a woman worth the knowing in all London should speak to her;—nor a man either of those men with whom a Duchess of Omnium would wish to hold converse. She should find her husband rated as a doting fool, and herself rated as a scheming female adventuress. And it should go hard with Lady Glencora, if the Duke were not separated from his new Duchess before the end of the first year! In her anger Lady Glencora was very unjust.

The Duke, when he left his house without telling his household whither he was going, did send his address to,—the top brick of the chimney. His note, which was delivered at Madame Goesler's house late on the Sunday evening, was as follows:—"I am to have your answer on Monday. I shall be at Brighton. Send it by a private messenger to the Bedford Hotel there. I need not tell you with what expectation, with what hope, with what fear I shall await it.—O." Poor old man! He had run through all the pleasures of life too quickly, and had not much left with which to amuse himself. At length he had set his eyes on a top brick, and being tired of everything else, wanted it very sorely. Poor old man! How should it do him any good, even if he got it? Madame Goesler, when she received the note, sat with it in her hand, thinking of his great want. "And he would be tired of his new plaything after a month," she said to herself. But she had given herself to the next morning, and she would not make up her mind that night. She would sleep once more with the coronet of a duchess within her reach. She did do so; and woke in the morning with her mind absolutely in doubt. When she walked down to breakfast, all doubt was at an end. The time had come when it was necessary that she should resolve, and while her maid was brushing her hair for her she did make her resolution.

"What a thing it is to be a great lady," said the maid, who may probably have reflected that the Duke of Omnium did not come here so often for nothing.

"What do you mean by that, Lotta?"

"The women I know, madame, talk so much of their countesses, and ladyships, and duchesses. I would never rest till I had a title in this country, if I were a lady,—and rich and beautiful."

"And can the countesses, and the ladyships, and the duchesses do as they please?"

"Ah, madame;—I know not that."

"But I know. That will do, Lotta. Now leave me." Then Madame Goesler had made up her mind; but I do not know whether that doubt as to having her own way had much to do with it. As the wife of an old man she would probably have had much of her own way. Immediately after breakfast she wrote her answer to the Duke, which was as follows:—

Park Lane,
Monday.

My Dear Duke of Omnium,

I find so great a difficulty in expressing myself to your Grace in a written letter, that since you left me I have never ceased to wish that I had been less nervous, less doubting, and less foolish when you were present with me here in my room. I might then have said in one word what will take so many awkward words to explain.

Great as is the honour you propose to confer on me, rich as is the gift you offer me, I cannot accept it. I cannot be your Grace's wife. I may almost say that I knew it was so when you parted from me; but the surprise of the situation took away from me a part of my judgment, and made me unable to answer you as I should have done. My lord, the truth is, that I am not fit to be the wife of the Duke of Omnium. I should injure you; and though I should raise myself in name, I should injure myself in character. But you must not think, because I say this, that there is any reason why I should not be an honest man's wife. There is none. I have nothing on my conscience which I could not tell you,—or to another man; nothing that I need fear to tell to all the world. Indeed, my lord, there is nothing to tell but this,—that I am not fitted by birth and position to be the wife of the Duke of Omnium. You would have to blush for me, and that no man shall ever have to do on my account.

I will own that I have been ambitious, too ambitious, and have been pleased to think that one so exalted as you are, one whose high position is so rife in the eyes of all men, should have taken pleasure in my company. I will confess to a foolish woman's silly vanity in having wished to be known to be the friend of the Duke of Omnium. I am like the other moths that flutter near the light and have their wings burned. But I am wiser than they in this, that having been scorched, I know that I must keep my distance. You will easily believe that a woman, such as I am, does not refuse to ride in a carriage with your Grace's arms on the panels without a regret. I am no philosopher. I do not pretend to despise the rich things of the world, or the high things. According to my way of thinking a woman ought to wish to be Duchess of Omnium;—but she ought to wish also to be able to carry her coronet with a proper grace. As Madame Goesler I can live, even among my superiors, at my ease. As your Grace's wife, I should be easy no longer;—nor would your Grace.

You will think perhaps that what I write is heartless, that I speak altogether of your rank, and not at all of the affection you have shown me, or of that which I might possibly bear towards you. I think that when the first flush of passion is over in early youth men and women should strive to regulate their love, as they do their other desires, by their reason. I could love your Grace, fondly, as your wife, if I thought it well for your Grace or for myself that we should be man and wife. As I think it would be ill for both of us, I will restrain that feeling, and remember your Grace ever with the purest feeling of true friendship.

Before I close this letter, I must utter a word of gratitude. In the kind of life which I have led as a widow, a life which has been very isolated as regards true fellowship, it has been my greatest effort to obtain the good opinion of those among whom I have attempted to make my way. I may, perhaps, own to you now that I have had many difficulties. A woman who is alone in the world is ever regarded with suspicion. In this country a woman with a foreign name, with means derived from foreign sources, with a foreign history, is specially suspected. I have striven to live that down, and I have succeeded. But in my wildest dreams I never dreamed of such success as this,—that the Duke of Omnium should think me the worthiest of the worthy. You may be sure that I am not ungrateful,—that I never will be ungrateful. And I trust it will not derogate from your opinion of my worth, that I have known what was due to your Grace's highness.

I have the honour to be,
My Lord Duke,
Your most obliged and faithful servant,   MARIE MAX GOESLER.

"How many unmarried women in England are there would do the same?" she said to herself, as she folded the paper, and put it into an envelope, and sealed the cover. The moment that the letter was completed she sent it off, as she was directed to send it, so that there might be no possibility of repentance and subsequent hesitation. She had at last made up her mind, and she would stand by the making. She knew that there would come moments in which she would deeply regret the opportunity that she had lost,—the chance of greatness that she had flung away from her. But so would she have often regretted it, also, had she accepted the greatness. Her position was one in which there must be regret, let her decision have been what it might. But she had decided, and the thing was done. She would still be free,—Marie Max Goesler,—unless in abandoning her freedom she would obtain something that she might in truth prefer to it. When the letter was gone she sat disconsolate, at the window of an up-stairs room in which she had written, thinking much of the coronet, much of the name, much of the rank, much of that position in society which she had flattered herself she might have won for herself as Duchess of Omnium by her beauty, her grace, and her wit. It had not been simply her ambition to be a duchess, without further aim or object. She had fancied that she might have been such a duchess as there is never another, so that her fame might have been great throughout Europe, as a woman charming at all points. And she would have had friends, then,—real friends, and would not have lived alone as it was now her fate to do. And she would have loved her ducal husband, old though he was, and stiff with pomp and ceremony. She would have loved him, and done her best to add something of brightness to his life. It was indeed true that there was one whom she loved better; but of what avail was it to love a man who, when he came to her, would speak to her of nothing but of the charms which he found in another woman!

She had been sitting thus at her window, with a book in her hand, at which she never looked, gazing over the park which was now beautiful with its May verdure, when on a sudden a thought struck her. Lady Glencora Palliser had come to her, trying to enlist her sympathy for the little heir, behaving, indeed, not very well, as Madame Goesler had thought, but still with an earnest purpose which was in itself good. She would write to Lady Glencora and put her out of her misery. Perhaps there was some feeling of triumph in her mind as she returned to the desk from which her epistle had been sent to the Duke;—not of that triumph which would have found its gratification in boasting of the offer that had been made to her, but arising from a feeling that she could now show the proud mother of the bold-faced boy that though she would not pledge herself to any woman as to what she might do or not do, she was nevertheless capable of resisting such a temptation as would have been irresistible to many. Of the Duke's offer to her she would have spoken to no human being, had not this woman shown that the Duke's purpose was known at least to her, and now, in her letter, she would write no plain word of that offer. She would not state, in words intelligible to any one who might read, that the Duke had offered her his hand and his coronet. But she would write so that Lady Glencora should understand her. And she would be careful that there should be no word in the letter to make Lady Glencora think that she supposed herself to be unfit for the rank offered to her. She had been very humble in what she had written to the Duke, but she would not be at all humble in what she was about to write to the mother of the bold-faced boy. And this was the letter when it was written:—

MY DEAR LADY GLENCORA,

I venture to send you a line to put you out of your misery;—for you were very miserable when you were so good as to come here yesterday. Your dear little boy is safe from me;—and, what is more to the purpose, so are you and your husband,—and your uncle, whom, in truth, I love. You asked me a downright question which I did not then choose to answer by a downright answer. The downright answer was not at that time due to you. It has since been given, and as I like you too well to wish you to be in torment, I send you a line to say that I shall never be in the way of you or your boy.

And now, dear Lady Glencora, one word more. Should it ever again appear to you to be necessary to use your zeal for the protection of your husband or your child, do not endeavour to dissuade a woman by trying to make her think that she, by her alliance, would bring degradation into any house, or to any man. If there could have been an argument powerful with me, to make me do that which you wished to prevent, it was the argument which you used. But my own comfort, and the happiness of another person whom I value almost as much as myself, were too important to be sacrificed even to a woman's revenge. I take mine by writing to you and telling you that I am better and more rational and wiser than you took me to be.

If, after this, you choose to be on good terms with me, I shall be happy to be your friend. I shall want no further revenge. You owe me some little apology; but whether you make it or not, I will be contented, and will never do more than ask whether your darling's prospects are still safe. There are more women than one in the world, you know, and you must not consider yourself to be out of the wood because you have escaped from a single danger. If there arise another, come to me, and we will consult together.

Dear Lady Glencora, yours always sincerely,   Marie M. G.

There was a thing or two besides which she longed to say, laughing as she thought of them. But she refrained, and her letter, when finished, was as it is given above.

On the day following, Lady Glencora was again in Park Lane. When she first read Madame Goesler's letter, she felt herself to be annoyed and angry, but her anger was with herself rather than with her correspondent. Ever since her last interview with the woman whom she had feared, she had been conscious of having been indiscreet. All her feelings had been too violent, and it might well have been that she should have driven this woman to do the very thing that she was so anxious to avoid. "You owe me some little apology," Madame Goesler had said. It was true,—and she would apologise. Undue pride was not a part of Lady Glencora's character. Indeed, there was not enough of pride in her composition. She had been quite ready to hate this woman, and to fight her on every point as long as the danger existed; but she was equally willing to take the woman to her heart now that the danger was over. Apologise! Of course she would apologise. And she would make a friend of the woman if the woman wished it. But she would not have the woman and the Duke at Matching together again, lest, after all, there might be a mistake. She did not show Madame Goesler's letter to her husband, or tell him anything of the relief she had received. He had cared but little for the danger, thinking more of his budget than of the danger; and would be sufficiently at his ease if he heard no more rumours of his uncle's marriage. Lady Glencora went to Park Lane early on the Tuesday morning, but she did not take her boy with her. She understood that Madame Goesler might perhaps indulge in a little gentle raillery at the child's expense, and the mother felt that this might be borne the more easily if the child were not present.

"I have come to thank you for your letter, Madame Goesler," said Lady Glencora, before she sat down.

"Oh, come ye in peace here, or come ye in war, or to dance at our bridal?" said Madame Goesler, standing up from her chair and laughing, as she sang the lines.

"Certainly not to dance at your bridal," said Lady Glencora.

"Alas! no. You have forbidden the banns too effectually for that, and I sit here wearing the willow all alone. Why shouldn't I be allowed to get married as well as another woman, I wonder? I think you have been very hard upon me among you. But sit down, Lady Glencora. At any rate you come in peace."

"Certainly in peace, and with much admiration,—and a great deal of love and affection, and all that kind of thing, if you will only accept it."

"I shall be too proud, Lady Glencora;—for the Duke's sake, if for no other reason."

"And I have to make my apology."

"It was made as soon as your carriage stopped at my door with friendly wheels. Of course I understand. I can know how terrible it all was to you,—even though the dear little Plantagenet might not have been in much danger. Fancy what it would be to disturb the career of a Plantagenet! I am far too well read in history, I can assure you."

"I said a word for which I am sorry, and which I should not have said."

"Never mind the word. After all, it was a true word. I do not hesitate to say so now myself, though I will allow no other woman to say it,—and no man either. I should have degraded him,—and disgraced him." Madame Goesler now had dropped the bantering tone which she had assumed, and was speaking in sober earnest. "I, for myself, have nothing about me of which I am ashamed. I have no history to hide, no story to be brought to light to my discredit. But I have not been so born, or so placed by circumstances, as make me fit to be the wife of the Duke of Omnium. I should not have been happy, you know."

"You want nothing, dear Madame Goesler. You have all that society can give you."

"I do not know about that. I have much given to me by society, but there are many things that I want;—a bright-faced little boy, for instance, to go about with me in my carriage. Why did you not bring him, Lady Glencora?"

"I came out in my penitential sheet, and when one goes in that guise, one goes alone. I had half a mind to walk."

"You will bring him soon?"

"Oh, yes. He was very anxious to know the other day who was the beautiful lady with the black hair."

"You did not tell him that the beautiful lady with the black hair was a possible aunt, was a possible—? But we will not think any more of things so horrible."

"I told him nothing of my fears, you may be sure."

"Some day, when I am a very old woman, and when his father is quite an old duke, and when he has a dozen little boys and girls of his own, you will tell him the story. Then he will reflect what a madman his great-uncle must have been, to have thought of making a duchess out of such a wizened old woman as that."

They parted the best of friends, but Lady Glencora was still of opinion that if the lady and the Duke were to be brought together at Matching, or elsewhere, there might still be danger.

CHAPTER LXIII. Showing How the Duke Stood his Ground

Mr. Low the barrister, who had given so many lectures to our friend Phineas Finn, lectures that ought to have been useful, was now himself in the House of Commons, having reached it in the legitimate course of his profession. At a certain point of his career, supposing his career to have been sufficiently prosperous, it becomes natural to a barrister to stand for some constituency, and natural for him also to form his politics at that period of his life with a view to his further advancement, looking, as he does so, carefully at the age and standing of the various candidates for high legal office. When a man has worked as Mr. Low had worked, he begins to regard the bench wistfully, and to calculate the profits of a two years' run in the Attorney-Generalship. It is the way of the profession, and thus a proper and sufficient number of real barristers finds its way into the House. Mr. Low had been angry with Phineas because he, being a barrister, had climbed into it after another fashion, having taken up politics, not in the proper way as an assistance to his great profession, but as a profession in itself. Mr. Low had been quite sure that his pupil had been wrong in this, and that the error would at last show itself, to his pupil's cost. And Mrs. Low had been more sure than Mr. Low, having not unnaturally been jealous that a young whipper-snapper of a pupil,—as she had once called Phineas,—should become a Parliament man before her husband, who had worked his way up gallantly, in the usual course. She would not give way a jot even now,—not even when she heard that Phineas was going to marry this and that heiress. For at this period of his life such rumours were afloat about him, originating probably in his hopes as to Violet Effingham and his intimacy with Madame Goesler. "Oh, heiresses!" said Mrs. Low. "I don't believe in heiresses' money till I see it. Three or four hundred a year is a great fortune for a woman, but it don't go far in keeping a house in London. And when a woman has got a little money she generally knows how to spend it. He has begun at the wrong end, and they who do that never get themselves right at the last."

At this time Phineas had become somewhat of a fine gentleman, which made Mrs. Low the more angry with him. He showed himself willing enough to go to Mrs. Low's house, but when there he seemed to her to give himself airs. I think that she was unjust to him, and that it was natural that he should not bear himself beneath her remarks exactly as he had done when he was nobody. He had certainly been very successful. He was always listened to in the House, and rarely spoke except on subjects which belonged to him, or had been allotted to him as part of his business. He lived quite at his ease with people of the highest rank,—and those of his own mode of life who disliked him did so simply because they regarded with envy his too rapid rise. He rode upon a pretty horse in the park, and was careful in his dress, and had about him an air of comfortable wealth which Mrs. Low thought he had not earned. When her husband told her of his sufficient salary, she would shake her head and express her opinion that a good time was coming. By which she perhaps meant to imply a belief that a time was coming in which her husband would have a salary much better than that now enjoyed by Phineas, and much more likely to be permanent. The Radicals were not to have office for ever, and when they were gone, what then? "I don't suppose he saves a shilling," said Mrs. Low. "How can he, keeping a horse in the park, and hunting down in the country, and living with lords? I shouldn't wonder if he isn't found to be over head and ears in debt when things come to be looked into." Mrs. Low was fond of an assured prosperity, of money in the funds, and was proud to think that her husband lived in a house of his own. "£19 10s. ground-rent to the Portman estate is what we pay, Mr. Bunce," she once said to that gallant Radical, "and that comes of beginning at the right end. Mr. Low had nothing when he began the world, and I had just what made us decent the day we married. But he began at the right end, and let things go as they may he can't get a fall." Mr. Bunce and Mrs. Low, though they differed much in politics, sympathised in reference to Phineas.

"I never believes, ma'am, in nobody doing any good by getting a place," said Mr. Bunce. "Of course I don't mean judges and them like, which must be. But when a young man has ever so much a year for sitting in a big room down at Whitehall, and reading a newspaper with his feet up on a chair, I don't think it honest, whether he's a Parliament man or whether he ain't." Whence Mr. Bunce had got his notions as to the way in which officials at Whitehall pass their time, I cannot say; but his notions are very common notions. The British world at large is slow to believe that the great British housekeeper keeps no more cats than what kill mice.

Mr. Low, who was now frequently in the habit of seeing Phineas at the House, had somewhat changed his opinions, and was not so eager in condemning Phineas as was his wife. He had begun to think that perhaps Phineas had shown some knowledge of his own aptitudes in the career which he had sought, and was aware, at any rate, that his late pupil was somebody in the House of Commons. A man will almost always respect him whom those around him respect, and will generally look up to one who is evidently above himself in his own daily avocation. Now Phineas was certainly above Mr. Low in parliamentary reputation. He sat on a front bench. He knew the leaders of parties. He was at home amidst the forms of the House. He enjoyed something of the prestige of Government power. And he walked about familiarly with the sons of dukes and the brothers of earls in a manner which had its effect even on Mr. Low. Seeing these things Mr. Low could not maintain his old opinion as stoutly as did his wife. It was almost a privilege to Mr. Low to be intimate with Phineas Finn. How then could he look down upon him?

He was surprised, therefore, one day when Phineas discussed the matter with him fully. Phineas had asked him what would be his chance of success if even now he were to give up politics and take to the Bar as the means of earning his livelihood. "You would have uphill work at first, as a matter of course," said Mr. Low.

"But it might be done, I suppose. To have been in office would not be fatal to me?"

"No, not fatal, Nothing of the kind need be fatal. Men have succeeded, and have sat on the bench afterwards, who did not begin till they were past forty. You would have to live down a prejudice created against yourself; that is all. The attorneys do not like barristers who are anything else but barristers."

"The attorneys are very arbitrary, I know," said Phineas.

"Yes;—and there would be this against you—that it is so difficult for a man to go back to the verdure and malleability of pupildom, who has once escaped from the necessary humility of its conditions. You will find it difficult to sit and wait for business in a Vice-Chancellor's Court, after having had Vice-Chancellors, or men as big as Vice-Chancellors, to wait upon you."

"I do not think much of that."

"But others would think of it, and you would find that there were difficulties. But you are not thinking of it in earnest?"

"Yes, in earnest."

"Why so? I should have thought that every day had removed you further and further from any such idea."

"The ground I'm on at present is so slippery."

"Well, yes. I can understand that. But yet it is less slippery than it used to be."

"Ah;—you do not exactly see. What if I were to lose my seat?"

"You are safe at least for the next four years, I should say."

"Ah;—no one can tell. And suppose I took it into my head to differ from the Government?"

"You must not do that. You have put yourself into a boat with these men, and you must remain in the boat. I should have thought all that was easy to you."

"It is not so easy as it seems. The very necessity of sitting still in the boat is in itself irksome,—very irksome. And then there comes some crisis in which a man cannot sit still."

"Is there any such crisis at hand now?"

"I cannot say that;—but I am beginning to find that sitting still is very disagreeable to me. When I hear those fellows below having their own way, and saying just what they like, it makes me furious. There is Robson. He tried office for a couple of years, and has broken away; and now, by George, there is no man they think so much of as they do of Robson. He is twice the man he was when he sat on the Treasury Bench."

"He is a man of fortune;—is he not?"

"I suppose so. Of course he is, because he lives. He never earns anything. His wife had money."

"My dear Finn, that makes all the difference. When a man has means of his own he can please himself. Do you marry a wife with money, and then you may kick up your heels, and do as you like about the Colonial Office. When a man hasn't money, of course he must fit himself to the circumstances of a profession."

"Though his profession may require him to be dishonest."

"I did not say that."

"But I say it, my dear Low. A man who is ready to vote black white because somebody tells him, is dishonest. Never mind, old fellow. I shall pull through, I daresay. Don't go and tell your wife all this, or she'll be harder upon me than ever when she sees me." After that Mr. Low began to think that his wife's judgment in this matter had been better than his own.

Robson could do as he liked because he had married a woman with money. Phineas told himself that that game was also open to him. He, too, might marry money. Violet Effingham had money;—quite enough to make him independent were he married to her. And Madame Goesler had money;—plenty of money. And an idea had begun to creep upon him that Madame Goesler would take him were he to offer himself. But he would sooner go back to the Bar as the lowest pupil, sooner clean boots for barristers,—so he told himself,—than marry a woman simply because she had money, than marry any other woman as long as there was a chance that Violet might be won. But it was very desirable that he should know whether Violet might be won or not. It was now July, and everybody would be gone in another month. Before August would be over he was to start for Ireland with Mr. Monk, and he knew that words would be spoken in Ireland which might make it indispensable for him to be, at any rate, able to throw up his office. In these days he became more anxious than he used to be about Miss Effingham's fortune.

He had never spoken as yet to Lord Brentford since the day on which the Earl had quarrelled with him, nor had he ever been at the house in Portman Square. Lady Laura he met occasionally, and had always spoken to her. She was gracious to him, but there had been no renewal of their intimacy. Rumours had reached him that things were going badly with her and her husband; but when men repeated such rumours in his presence, he said little or nothing on the subject. It was not for him, at any rate, to speak of Lady Laura's unhappiness. Lord Chiltern he had seen once or twice during the last month, and they had met cordially as friends. Of course he could ask no question from Lord Chiltern as to Violet; but he did learn that his friend had again patched up some reconciliation with his father. "He has quarrelled with me, you know," said Phineas.

"I am very sorry, but what could I do? As things went, I was obliged to tell him."

"Do not suppose for a moment that I am blaming you. It is, no doubt, much better that he should know it all."

"And it cannot make much difference to you, I should say."

"One doesn't like to quarrel with those who have been kind to one," said Phineas.

"But it isn't your doing. He'll come right again after a time. When I can get my own affairs settled, you may be sure I'll do my best to bring him round. But what's the reason you never see Laura now?"

"What's the reason that everything goes awry?" said Phineas, bitterly.

"When I mentioned your name to Kennedy the other day, he looked as black as thunder. But it is not odd that any one should quarrel with him. I can't stand him. Do you know, I sometimes think that Laura will have to give it up. Then there will be another mess in the family!"

This was all very well as coming from Lord Chiltern; but there was no word about Violet, and Phineas did not know how to get a word from any one. Lady Laura could have told him everything, but he could not go to Lady Laura. He did go to Lady Baldock's house as often as he thought he could with propriety, and occasionally he saw Violet. But he could do no more than see her, and the days and weeks were passing by, and the time was coming in which he would have to go away, and be with her no more. The end of the season, which was always to other men,—to other working men such as our hero,—a period of pleasurable anticipation, to him was a time of sadness, in which he felt that he was not exactly like to, or even equal to, the men with whom he lived in London. In the old days, in which he was allowed to go to Loughlinter or to Saulsby, when all men and women were going to their Loughlinters and their Saulsbys, it was very well with him; but there was something melancholy to him in his yearly journey to Ireland. He loved his father and mother and sisters as well as do other men; but there was a falling off in the manner of his life which made him feel that he had been in some sort out of his own element in London. He would have liked to have shot grouse at Loughlinter, or pheasants at Saulsby, or to have hunted down at Willingford,—or better still, to have made love to Violet Effingham wherever Violet Effingham might have placed herself. But all this was closed to him now; and there would be nothing for him but to remain at Killaloe, or to return to his work in Downing Street, from August to February. Mr. Monk, indeed, was going with him for a few weeks; but even this association did not make up for that sort of society which he would have preferred.

The session went on very quietly. The question of the Irish Reform Bill was postponed till the next year, which was a great thing gained. He carried his bill about the Canada Railway, with sundry other small bills appertaining to it, through the House in a manner which redounded infinitely to his credit. There was just enough of opposition to give a zest to the work, and to make the affair conspicuous among the affairs of the year. As his chief was in the other house, the work fell altogether into his hands, so that he came to be conspicuous among Under-Secretaries. It was only when he said a word to any leaders of his party about other matters,—about Irish Tenant-right, for instance, which was beginning to loom very large, that he found himself to be snubbed. But there was no room for action this year in reference to Irish Tenant-right, and therefore any deep consideration of that discomfort might be legitimately postponed. If he did by chance open his mouth on the subject to Mr. Monk, even Mr. Monk discouraged him.

In the early days of July, when the weather was very hot, and people were beginning to complain of the Thames, and members were becoming thirsty after grouse, and the remaining days of parliamentary work were being counted up, there came to him news,—news that was soon known throughout the fashionable world,—that the Duke of Omnium was going to give a garden party at a certain villa residence on the banks of the Thames above Richmond. It was to be such a garden party as had never been seen before. And it would be the more remarkable because the Duke had never been known to do such a thing. The villa was called The Horns, and had, indeed, been given by the Duke to Lady Glencora on her marriage; but the party was to be the Duke's party, and The Horns, with all its gardens, conservatories, lawns, shrubberies, paddocks, boat-houses, and boats, was to be made bright and beautiful for the occasion. Scores of workmen were about the place through the three first weeks of July. The world at large did not at all know why the Duke was doing so unwonted a thing,—why he should undertake so new a trouble. But Lady Glencora knew, and Madame Goesler shrewdly guessed, the riddle. When Madame Goesler's unexpected refusal had reached his Grace, he felt that he must either accept the lady's refusal, or persevere. After a day's consideration, he resolved that he would accept it. The top brick of the chimney was very desirable; but perhaps it might be well that he should endeavour to live without it. Then, accepting this refusal, he must either stand his ground and bear the blow,—or he must run away to that villa at Como, or elsewhere. The running away seemed to him at first to be the better, or at least the more pleasant, course; but at last he determined that he would stand his ground and bear the blow. Therefore he gave his garden party at The Horns.

Who was to be invited? Before the first week in July was over, many a bosom in London was fluttering with anxiety on that subject. The Duke, in giving his short word of instruction to Lady Glencora, made her understand that he would wish her to be particular in her invitations. Her Royal Highness the Princess, and his Royal Highness the Prince, had both been so gracious as to say that they would honour his fête. The Duke himself had made out a short list, with not more than a dozen names. Lady Glencora was employed to select the real crowd,—the five hundred out of the ten thousand who were to be blessed. On the Duke's own private list was the name of Madame Goesler. Lady Glencora understood it all. When Madame Goesler got her card, she thought that she understood it too. And she thought also that the Duke was behaving in a gallant way.

There was, no doubt, much difficulty about the invitations, and a considerable amount of ill-will was created. And they who considered themselves entitled to be asked, and were not asked, were full of wrath against their more fortunate friends, instead of being angry with the Duke or with Lady Glencora, who had neglected them. It was soon known that Lady Glencora was the real dispenser of the favours, and I fancy that her ladyship was tired of her task before it was completed. The party was to take place on Wednesday, the 27th of July, and before the day had come, men and women had become so hardy in the combat that personal applications were made with unflinching importunity; and letters were written to Lady Glencora putting forward this claim and that claim with a piteous clamour. "No, that is too bad," Lady Glencora said to her particular friend, Mrs. Grey, when a letter came from Mrs. Bonteen, stating all that her husband had ever done towards supporting Mr. Palliser in Parliament,—and all that he ever would do. "She shan't have it, even though she could put Plantagenet into a minority to-morrow."

Mrs. Bonteen did not get a card; and when she heard that Phineas Finn had received one, her wrath against Phineas was very great. He was "an Irish adventurer," and she regretted deeply that Mr. Bonteen had ever interested himself in bringing such an upstart forward in the world of politics. But as Mr. Bonteen never had done anything towards bringing Phineas forward, there was not much cause for regret on this head. Phineas, however, got his card, and, of course, accepted the invitation.

The grounds were opened at four. There was to be an early dinner out in tents at five; and after dinner men and women were to walk about, or dance, or make love—or hay, as suited them. The haycocks, however, were ready prepared, while it was expected that they should bring the love with them. Phineas, knowing that he should meet Violet Effingham, took a great deal with him ready made.

For an hour and a half Lady Glencora kept her position in a saloon through which the guests passed to the grounds, and to every comer she imparted the information that the Duke was on the lawn;—to every comer but one. To Madame Goesler she said no such word. "So glad to see you, my dear," she said, as she pressed her friend's hand: "if I am not killed by this work, I'll make you out again by-and-by." Then Madame Goesler passed on, and soon found herself amidst a throng of acquaintance. After a few minutes she saw the Duke seated in an arm-chair, close to the river-bank, and she bravely went up to him, and thanked him for the invitation. "The thanks are due to you for gracing our entertainment," said the Duke, rising to greet her. There were a dozen people standing round, and so the thing was done without difficulty. At that moment there came a notice that their royal highnesses were on the ground, and the Duke, of course, went off to meet them. There was not a word more spoken between the Duke and Madame Goesler on that afternoon.

Phineas did not come till late,—till seven, when the banquet was over. I think he was right in this, as the banqueting in tents loses in comfort almost more than it gains in romance. A small picnic may be very well, and the distance previously travelled may give to a dinner on the ground the seeming excuse of necessity. Frail human nature must be supported,—and human nature, having gone so far in pursuit of the beautiful, is entitled to what best support the unaccustomed circumstances will allow. Therefore, out with the cold pies, out with the salads, and the chickens, and the champagne. Since no better may be, let us recruit human nature sitting upon this moss, and forget our discomforts in the glory of the verdure around us. And dear Mary, seeing that the cushion from the waggonet is small, and not wishing to accept the too generous offer that she should take it all for her own use, will admit a contact somewhat closer than the ordinary chairs of a dining-room render necessary. That in its way is very well;—but I hold that a banquet on narrow tables in a tent is displeasing.

Phineas strolled into the grounds when the tent was nearly empty, and when Lady Glencora, almost sinking beneath her exertions, was taking rest in an inner room. The Duke at this time was dining with their royal highnesses, and three or four others, specially selected, very comfortably within doors. Out of doors the world had begun to dance,—and the world was beginning to say that it would be much nicer to go and dance upon the boards inside as soon as possible. For, though of all parties a garden party is the nicest, everybody is always anxious to get out of the garden as quick as may be. A few ardent lovers of suburban picturesque effect were sitting beneath the haycocks, and four forlorn damsels were vainly endeavouring to excite the sympathy of manly youth by playing croquet in a corner. I am not sure, however, that the lovers beneath the haycocks and the players at croquet were not actors hired by Lady Glencora for the occasion.

Phineas had not been long on the lawn before he saw Lady Laura Kennedy. She was standing with another lady, and Barrington Erle was with them. "So you have been successful?" said Barrington, greeting him.

"Successful in what?"

"In what? In getting a ticket. I have had to promise three tide-waiterships, and to give deep hints about a bishopric expected to be vacant, before I got in. But what matters? Success pays for everything. My only trouble now is how I'm to get back to London."

Lady Laura shook hands with Phineas, and then as he was passing on, followed him for a step and whispered a word to him. "Mr. Finn," she said, "if you are not going yet, come back to me presently. I have something to say to you. I shall not be far from the river, and shall stay here for about an hour."

Phineas said that he would, and then went on, not knowing exactly where he was going. He had one desire,—to find Violet Effingham, but when he should find her he could not carry her off, and sit with her beneath a haycock.

CHAPTER LXIV. The Horns

While looking for Violet Effingham, Phineas encountered Madame Goesler, among a crowd of people who were watching the adventurous embarkation of certain daring spirits in a pleasure-boat. There were watermen there in the Duke's livery, ready to take such spirits down to Richmond or up to Teddington lock, and many daring spirits did take such trips,—to the great peril of muslins, ribbons, and starch, to the peril also of ornamental summer white garments, so that when the thing was over, the boats were voted to have been a bore.

"Are you going to venture?" said Phineas to the lady.

"I should like it of all things if I were not afraid for my clothes. Will you come?"

"I was never good upon the water. I should be sea-sick to a certainty. They are going down beneath the bridge too, and we should be splashed by the steamers. I don't think my courage is high enough." Thus Phineas excused himself, being still intent on prosecuting his search for Violet.

"Then neither will I," said Madame Goesler. "One dash from a peccant oar would destroy the whole symmetry of my dress. Look. That green young lady has already been sprinkled."

"But the blue young gentleman has been sprinkled also," said Phineas, "and they will be happy in a joint baptism." Then they strolled along the river path together, and were soon alone. "You will be leaving town soon, Madame Goesler?"

"Almost immediately."

"And where do you go?"

"Oh,—to Vienna. I am there for a couple of months every year, minding my business. I wonder whether you would know me, if you saw me;—sometimes sitting on a stool in a counting-house, sometimes going about among old houses, settling what must be done to save them from tumbling down. I dress so differently at such times, and talk so differently, and look so much older, that I almost fancy myself to be another person."

"Is it a great trouble to you?"

"No,—I rather like it. It makes me feel that I do something in the world."

"Do you go alone?"

"Quite alone. I take a German maid with me, and never speak a word to any one else on the journey."

"That must be very bad," said Phineas.

"Yes; it is the worst of it. But then I am so much accustomed to be alone. You see me in society, and in society only, and therefore naturally look upon me as one of a gregarious herd; but I am in truth an animal that feeds alone and lives alone. Take the hours of the year all through, and I am a solitary during four-fifths of them. And what do you intend to do?"

"I go to Ireland."

"Home to your own people. How nice! I have no people to go to. I have one sister, who lives with her husband at Riga. She is my only relation, and I never see her."

"But you have thousands of friends in England."

"Yes,—as you see them,"—and she turned and spread out her hands towards the crowded lawn, which was behind them. "What are such friends worth? What would they do for me?"

"I do not know that the Duke would do much," said Phineas laughing.

Madame Goesler laughed also. "The Duke is not so bad," she said. "The Duke would do as much as any one else. I won't have the Duke abused."

"He may be your particular friend, for what I know," said Phineas.

"Ah;—no. I have no particular friend. And were I to wish to choose one, I should think the Duke a little above me."

"Oh, yes;—and too stiff, and too old, and too pompous, and too cold, and too make-believe, and too gingerbread."

"Mr. Finn!"

"The Duke is all buckram, you know."

"Then why do you come to his house?"

"To see you, Madame Goesler."

"Is that true, Mr. Finn?"

"Yes;—it is true in its way. One goes about to meet those whom one likes, not always for the pleasure of the host's society. I hope I am not wrong because I go to houses at which I like neither the host nor the hostess." Phineas as he said this was thinking of Lady Baldock, to whom of late he had been exceedingly civil,—but he certainly did not like Lady Baldock.

"I think you have been too hard upon the Duke of Omnium. Do you know him well?"

"Personally? certainly not. Do you? Does anybody?"

"I think he is a gracious gentleman," said Madame Goesler, "and though I cannot boast of knowing him well, I do not like to hear him called buckram. I do not think he is buckram. It is not very easy for a man in his position to live so as to please all people. He has to maintain the prestige of the highest aristocracy in Europe."

"Look at his nephew, who will be the next Duke, and who works as hard as any man in the country. Will he not maintain it better? What good did the present man ever do?"

"You believe only in motion, Mr. Finn;—and not at all in quiescence. An express train at full speed is grander to you than a mountain with heaps of snow. I own that to me there is something glorious in the dignity of a man too high to do anything,—if only he knows how to carry that dignity with a proper grace. I think that there should be breasts made to carry stars."

"Stars which they have never earned," said Phineas.

"Ah;—well; we will not fight about it. Go and earn your star, and I will say that it becomes you better than any glitter on the coat of the Duke of Omnium." This she said with an earnestness which he could not pretend not to notice or not to understand. "I too may be able to see that the express train is really greater than the mountain."

"Though, for your own life, you would prefer to sit and gaze upon the snowy peaks?"

"No;—that is not so. For myself, I would prefer to be of use somewhere,—to some one, if it were possible. I strive sometimes."

"And I am sure successfully."

"Never mind. I hate to talk about myself. You and the Duke are fair subjects for conversation; you as the express train, who will probably do your sixty miles an hour in safety, but may possibly go down a bank with a crash."

"Certainly I may," said Phineas.

"And the Duke, as the mountain, which is fixed in its stateliness, short of the power of some earthquake, which shall be grander and more terrible than any earthquake yet known. Here we are at the house again. I will go in and sit down for a while."

"If I leave you, Madame Goesler, I will say good-bye till next winter."

"I shall be in town again before Christmas, you know. You will come and see me?"

"Of course I will."

"And then this love trouble of course will be over,—one way or the other;—will it not?"

"Ah!—who can say?"

"Faint heart never won fair lady. But your heart is never faint. Farewell."

Then he left her. Up to this moment he had not seen Violet, and yet he knew that she was to be there. She had herself told him that she was to accompany Lady Laura, whom he had already met. Lady Baldock had not been invited, and had expressed great animosity against the Duke in consequence. She had gone so far as to say that the Duke was a man at whose house a young lady such as her niece ought not to be seen. But Violet had laughed at this, and declared her intention of accepting the invitation. "Go," she had said; "of course I shall go. I should have broken my heart if I could not have got there." Phineas therefore was sure that she must be in the place. He had kept his eyes ever on the alert, and yet he had not found her. And now he must keep his appointment with Lady Laura Kennedy. So he went down to the path by the river, and there he found her seated close by the water's edge. Her cousin Barrington Erle was still with her, but as soon as Phineas joined them, Erle went away. "I had told him," said Lady Laura, "that I wished to speak to you, and he stayed with me till you came. There are worse men than Barrington a great deal."

"I am sure of that."

"Are you and he still friends, Mr. Finn?"

"I hope so. I do not see so much of him as I did when I had less to do."

"He says that you have got into altogether a different set."

"I don't know that. I have gone as circumstances have directed me, but I have certainly not intended to throw over so old and good a friend as Barrington Erle."

"Oh,—he does not blame you. He tells me that you have found your way among what he calls the working men of the party, and he thinks you will do very well,—if you can only be patient enough. We all expected a different line from you, you know,—more of words and less of deeds, if I may say so;—more of liberal oratory and less of government action; but I do not doubt that you are right."

"I think that I have been wrong," said Phineas. "I am becoming heartily sick of officialities."

"That comes from the fickleness about which papa is so fond of quoting his Latin. The ox desires the saddle. The charger wants to plough."

"And which am I?"

"Your career may combine the dignity of the one with the utility of the other. At any rate you must not think of changing now. Have you seen Mr. Kennedy lately?" She asked the question abruptly, showing that she was anxious to get to the matter respecting which she had summoned him to her side, and that all that she had said hitherto had been uttered as it were in preparation of that subject.

"Seen him? yes; I see him daily. But we hardly do more than speak,"

"Why not?" Phineas stood for a moment in silence, hesitating. "Why is it that he and you do not speak?"

"How can I answer that question, Lady Laura?"

"Do you know any reason? Sit down, or, if you please, I will get up and walk with you. He tells me that you have chosen to quarrel with him, and that I have made you do so. He says that you have confessed to him that I have asked you to quarrel with him."

"He can hardly have said that."

"But he has said it,—in so many words. Do you think that I would tell you such a story falsely?"

"Is he here now?"

"No;—he is not here. He would not come. I came alone."

"Is not Miss Effingham with you?"

"No;—she is to come with my father later. She is here no doubt, now. But answer my question, Mr. Finn;—unless you find that you cannot answer it. What was it that you did say to my husband?"

"Nothing to justify what he has told you."

"Do you mean to say that he has spoken falsely?"

"I mean to use no harsh word,—but I think that Mr. Kennedy when troubled in his spirit looks at things gloomily, and puts meaning upon words which they should not bear."

"And what has troubled his spirit?"

"You must know that better than I can do, Lady Laura. I will tell you all that I can tell you. He invited me to his house and I would not go, because you had forbidden me. Then he asked me some questions about you. Did I refuse because of you,—or of anything that you had said? If I remember right, I told him that I did fancy that you would not be glad to see me,—and that therefore I would rather stay away. What was I to say?"

"You should have said nothing."

"Nothing with him would have been worse than what I did say. Remember that he asked me the question point-blank, and that no reply would have been equal to an affirmation. I should have confessed that his suggestion was true."

"He could not then have twitted me with your words."

"If I have erred, Lady Laura, and brought any sorrow on you, I am indeed grieved."

"It is all sorrow. There is nothing but sorrow. I have made up my mind to leave him."

"Oh, Lady Laura!"

"It is very bad,—but not so bad, I think, as the life I am now leading. He has accused me—, of what do you think? He says that you are my lover!"

"He did not say that,—in those words?"

"He said it in words which made me feel that I must part from him."

"And how did you answer him?"

"I would not answer him at all. If he had come to me like a man,—not accusing me, but asking me,—I would have told him everything. And what was there to tell? I should have broken my faith to you, in speaking of that scene at Loughlinter, but women always tell such stories to their husbands when their husbands are good to them, and true, and just. And it is well that they should be told. But to Mr. Kennedy I can tell nothing. He does not believe my word."

"Not believe you, Lady Laura?"

"No! Because I did not blurt out to him all that story about your foolish duel,—because I thought it best to keep my brother's secret, as long as there was a secret to be kept, he told me that I had,—lied to him!"

"What!—with that word?"

"Yes,—with that very word. He is not particular about his words, when he thinks it necessary to express himself strongly. And he has told me since that because of that he could never believe me again. How is it possible that a woman should live with such a man?" But why did she come to him with this story,—to him whom she had been accused of entertaining as a lover;—to him who of all her friends was the last whom she should have chosen as the recipient for such a tale? Phineas as he thought how he might best answer her, with what words he might try to comfort her, could not but ask himself this question. "The moment that the word was out of his mouth," she went on to say, "I resolved that I would tell you. The accusation is against you as it is against me, and is equally false to both. I have written to him, and there is my letter."

"But you will see him again?"

"No;—I will go to my father's house. I have already arranged it. Mr. Kennedy has my letter by this time, and I go from hence home with my father."

"Do you wish that I should read the letter?"

"Yes,—certainly. I wish that you should read it. Should I ever meet him again, I shall tell him that you saw it."

They were now standing close upon the river's bank, at a corner of the grounds, and, though the voices of people sounded near to them, they were alone. Phineas had no alternative but to read the letter, which was as follows:—

After what you have said to me it is impossible that I should return to your house. I shall meet my father at the Duke of Omnium's, and have already asked him to give me an asylum. It is my wish to remain wherever he may be, either in town or in the country. Should I change my purpose in this, and change my residence, I will not fail to let you know where I go and what I propose to do. You I think must have forgotten that I was your wife; but I will never forget it.

You have accused me of having a lover. You cannot have expected that I should continue to live with you after such an accusation. For myself I cannot understand how any man can have brought himself to bring such a charge against his wife. Even had it been true the accusation should not have been made by your mouth to my ears.

That it is untrue I believe you must be as well aware as I am myself. How intimate I was with. Mr. Finn, and what were the limits of my intimacy with him you knew before I married you. After our marriage I encouraged his friendship till I found that there was something in it that displeased you,—and, after learning that, I discouraged it. You have said that he is my lover, but you have probably not defined for yourself that word very clearly. You have felt yourself slighted because his name has been mentioned with praise;—and your jealousy has been wounded because you have thought that I have regarded him as in some way superior to yourself. You have never really thought that he was my lover,—that he spoke words to me which others might not hear, that he claimed from me aught that a wife may not give, that he received aught which a friend should not receive. The accusation has been a coward's accusation.

I shall be at my father's to-night, and to-morrow I will get you to let my servant bring to me such things as are my own,—my clothes, namely, and desk, and a few books. She will know what I want. I trust you may be happier without a wife, than ever you have been with me. I have felt almost daily since we were married that you were a man who would have been happier without a wife than with one.

Yours affectionately,   LAURA KENNEDY.

"It is at any rate true," she said, when Phineas had read the letter.

"True! Doubtless it is true," said Phineas, "except that I do not suppose he was ever really angry with me, or jealous, or anything of the sort,—because I got on well. It seems absurd even to think it."

"There is nothing too absurd for some men. I remember your telling me that he was weak, and poor, and unworthy. I remember your saying so when I first thought that he might become my husband. I wish I had believed you when you told me so. I should not have made such a shipwreck of myself as I have done. That is all I had to say to you. After what has passed between us I did not choose that you should hear how I was separated from my husband from any lips but my own. I will go now and find papa. Do not come with me. I prefer being alone." Then he was left standing by himself, looking down upon the river as it glided by. How would it have been with both of them if Lady Laura had accepted him three years ago, when she consented to join her lot with that of Mr. Kennedy, and had rejected him? As he stood he heard the sound of music from the house, and remembered that he had come there with the one sole object of seeing Violet Effingham. He had known that he would meet Lady Laura, and it had been in his mind to break through that law of silence which she had imposed upon him, and once more to ask her to assist him,—to implore her for the sake of their old friendship to tell him whether there might yet be for him any chance of success. But in the interview which had just taken place it had been impossible for him to speak a word of himself or of Violet.

To her, in her great desolation, he could address himself on no other subject than that of her own misery. But not the less when she was talking to him of her own sorrow, of her regret that she had not listened to him when in years past he had spoken slightingly of Mr. Kennedy, was he thinking of Violet Effingham. Mr. Kennedy had certainly mistaken the signs of things when he had accused his wife by saying that Phineas was her lover. Phineas had soon got over that early feeling; and as far as he himself was concerned had never regretted Lady Laura's marriage.

He remained down by the water for a few minutes, giving Lady Laura time to escape, and then he wandered across the grounds towards the house. It was now about nine o'clock, and though there were still many walking about the grounds, the crowd of people were in the rooms. The musicians were ranged out on a verandah, so that their music might have been available for dancing within or without; but the dancers had found the boards pleasanter than the lawn, and the Duke's garden party was becoming a mere ball, with privilege for the dancers to stroll about the lawn between the dances. And in this respect the fun was better than at a ball,—that let the engagements made for partners be what they might, they could always be broken with ease. No lady felt herself bound to dance with a cavalier who was displeasing to her; and some gentlemen were left sadly in the lurch. Phineas felt himself to be very much in the lurch, even after he had discovered Violet Effingham standing up to dance with Lord Fawn.

He bided his time patiently, and at last he found his opportunity. "Would she dance with him?" She declared that she intended to dance no more, and that she had promised to be ready to return home with Lord Brentford before ten o'clock. "I have pledged myself not to be after ten," she said, laughing. Then she put her hand upon his arm, and they stepped out upon the terrace together. "Have you heard anything?" she asked him, almost in a whisper.

"Yes," he said. "I have heard what you mean. I have heard it all."

"Is it not dreadful?"

"I fear it is the best thing she can do. She has never been happy with him."

"But to be accused after that fashion,—by her husband!" said Violet. "One can hardly believe it in these days. And of all women she is the last to deserve such accusation."

"The very last," said Phineas, feeling that the subject was one upon which it was not easy for him to speak.

"I cannot conceive to whom he can have alluded," said Violet. Then Phineas began to understand that Violet had not heard the whole story; but the difficulty of speaking was still very great.

"It has been the result of ungovernable temper," he said.

"But a man does not usually strive to dishonour himself because he is in a rage. And this man is incapable of rage. He must be cursed with one of those dark gloomy minds in which love always leads to jealousy. She will never return to him."

"One cannot say. In many respects it would be better that she should," said Phineas.

"She will never return to him," repeated Violet,—"never. Would you advise her to do so?"

"How can I say? If one were called upon for advice, one would think so much before one spoke."

"I would not,—not for a minute. What! to be accused of that! How are a man and woman to live together after there have been such words between them? Poor Laura! What a terrible end to all her high hopes! Do you not grieve for her?"

They were now at some distance from the house, and Phineas could not but feel that chance had been very good to him in giving him his opportunity. She was leaning on his arm, and they were alone, and she was speaking to him with all the familiarity of old friendship. "I wonder whether I may change the subject," said he, "and ask you a word about yourself?"

"What word?" she said sharply.

"I have heard—"

"What have you heard?"

"Simply this,—that you are not now as you were six months ago. Your marriage was then fixed for June."

"It has been unfixed since then," she said.

"Yes;—it has been unfixed. I know it. Miss Effingham, you will not be angry with me if I say that when I heard it was so, something of a hope,—no, I must not call it a hope,—something that longed to form itself into hope returned to my breast, and from that hour to this has been the only subject on which I have cared to think."

"Lord Chiltern is your friend, Mr. Finn?"

"He is so, and I do not think that I have ever been untrue to my friendship for him."

"He says that no man has ever had a truer friend. He will swear to that in all companies. And I, when it was allowed to me to swear with him, swore it too. As his friend, let me tell you one thing,—one thing which I would never tell to any other man,—one thing which I know I may tell you in confidence. You are a gentleman, and will not break my confidence?"

"I think I will not."

"I know you will not, because you are a gentleman. I told Lord Chiltern in the autumn of last year that I loved him. And I did love him. I shall never have the same confession to make to another man. That he and I are not now,—on those loving terms,—which once existed, can make no difference in that. A woman cannot transfer her heart. There have been things which have made me feel,—that I was perhaps mistaken,—in saying that I would be,—his wife. But I said so, and cannot now give myself to another. Here is Lord Brentford, and we will join him." There was Lord Brentford with Lady Laura on his arm, very gloomy,—resolving on what way he might be avenged on the man who had insulted his daughter. He took but little notice of Phineas as he resumed his charge of Miss Effingham; but the two ladies wished him good night.

"Good night, Lady Laura," said Phineas, standing with his hat in his hand,—"good night, Miss Effingham." Then he was alone,—quite alone. Would it not be well for him to go down to the bottom of the garden, and fling himself into the quiet river, so that there might be an end of him? Or would it not be better still that he should create for himself some quiet river of life, away from London, away from politics, away from lords, and titled ladies, and fashionable squares, and the parties given by dukes, and the disappointments incident to a small man in attempting to make for himself a career among big men? There had frequently been in the mind of this young man an idea that there was something almost false in his own position,—that his life was a pretence, and that he would ultimately be subject to that ruin which always comes, sooner or later, on things which are false; and now as he wandered alone about Lady Glencora's gardens, this feeling was very strong within his bosom, and robbed him altogether of the honour and glory of having been one of the Duke of Omnium's guests.

CHAPTER LXV. The Cabinet Minister at Killaloe

Phineas did not throw himself into the river from the Duke's garden; and was ready, in spite of Violet Effingham, to start for Ireland with Mr. Monk at the end of the first week in August. The close of that season in London certainly was not a happy period of his life. Violet had spoken to him after such a fashion that he could not bring himself not to believe her. She had given him no hint whether it was likely or unlikely that she and Lord Chiltern would be reconciled; but she had convinced him that he could not be allowed to take Lord Chiltern's place. "A woman cannot transfer her heart," she had said. Phineas was well aware that many women do transfer their hearts; but he had gone to this woman too soon after the wrench which her love had received; he had been too sudden with his proposal for a transfer; and the punishment for such ill judgment must be that success would now be impossible to him. And yet how could he have waited, feeling that Miss Effingham, if she were at all like other girls whom he had known, might have promised herself to some other lover before she would return within his reach in the succeeding spring? But she was not like some other girls. Ah;—he knew that now, and repented him of his haste.

But he was ready for Mr. Monk on the 7th of August, and they started together. Something less than twenty hours took them from London to Killaloe, and during four or five of those twenty hours Mr. Monk was unfitted for any conversation by the uncomfortable feelings incidental to the passage from Holyhead to Kingstown. Nevertheless, there was a great deal of conversation between them during the journey. Mr. Monk had almost made up his mind to leave the Cabinet. "It is sad to me to have to confess it," he said, "but the truth is that my old rival, Turnbull, is right. A man who begins his political life as I began mine, is not the man of whom a Minister should be formed. I am inclined to think that Ministers of Government require almost as much education in their trade as shoemakers or tallow-chandlers. I doubt whether you can make a good public servant of a man simply because he has got the ear of the House of Commons."

"Then you mean to say," said Phineas, "that we are altogether wrong from beginning to end, in our way of arranging these things?"

"I do not say that at all. Look at the men who have been leading statesmen since our present mode of government was formed,—from the days in which it was forming itself, say from Walpole down, and you will find that all who have been of real use had early training as public servants."

"Are we never to get out of the old groove?"

"Not if the groove is good," said Mr. Monk, "Those who have been efficient as ministers sucked in their efficacy with their mother's milk. Lord Brock did so, and Lord de Terrier, and Mr. Mildmay. They seated themselves in office chairs the moment they left college. Mr. Gresham was in office before he was eight-and-twenty. The Duke of St. Bungay was at work as a Private Secretary when he was three-and-twenty. You, luckily for yourself, have done the same."

"And regret it every hour of my life."

"You have no cause for regret, but it is not so with me. If there be any man unfitted by his previous career for office, it is he who has become, or who has endeavoured to become, a popular politician,—an exponent, if I may say so, of public opinion. As far as I can see, office is offered to such men with one view only,—that of clipping their wings."

"And of obtaining their help."

"It is the same thing. Help from Turnbull would mean the withdrawal of all power of opposition from him. He could not give other help for any long term, as the very fact of his accepting power and patronage would take from him his popular leadership. The masses outside require to have their minister as the Queen has hers; but the same man cannot be minister to both. If the people's minister chooses to change his master, and to take the Queen's shilling, something of temporary relief may be gained by government in the fact that the other place will for a time be vacant. But there are candidates enough for such places, and the vacancy is not a vacancy long. Of course the Crown has this pull, that it pays wages, and the people do not."

"I do not think that that influenced you," said Phineas.

"It did not influence me. To you I will make bold to state so much positively, though it would be foolish, perhaps, to do so to others. I did not go for the shilling, though I am so poor a man that the shilling is more to me than it would be to almost any man in the House. I took the shilling, much doubting, but guided in part by this, that I was ashamed of being afraid to take it. They told me,—Mr. Mildmay and the Duke,—that I could earn it to the benefit of the country. I have not earned it, and the country has not been benefited,—unless it be for the good of the country that my voice in the House should be silenced. If I believe that, I ought to hold my tongue without taking a salary for holding it. I have made a mistake, my friend.

Such mistakes made at my time of life cannot be wholly rectified; but, being convinced of my error, I must do the best in my power to put myself right again."

There was a bitterness in all this to Phineas himself of which he could not but make plaint to his companion. "The truth is," he said, "that a man in office must be a slave, and that slavery is distasteful."

"There I think you are wrong. If you mean that you cannot do joint work with other men altogether after your own fashion the same may be said of all work. If you had stuck to the Bar you must have pleaded your causes in conformity with instructions from the attorneys."

"I should have been guided by my own lights in advising those attorneys."

"I cannot see that you suffer anything that ought to go against the grain with you. You are beginning young, and it is your first adopted career. With me it is otherwise. If by my telling you this I shall have led you astray, I shall regret my openness with you. Could I begin again, I would willingly begin as you began."

It was a great day in Killaloe, that on which Mr. Monk arrived with Phineas at the doctor's house. In London, perhaps, a bishop inspires more awe than a Cabinet Minister. In Killaloe, where a bishop might be seen walking about every day, the mitred dignitary of the Church, though much loved, was thought of, I fear, but lightly; whereas a Cabinet Minister coming to stay in the house of a townsman was a thing to be wondered at, to be talked about, to be afraid of, to be a fruitful source of conversation for a year to come. There were many in Killaloe, especially among the elder ladies, who had shaken their heads and expressed the saddest doubts when young Phineas Finn had first become a Parliament man. And though by degrees they had been half brought round, having been driven to acknowledge that he had been wonderfully successful as a Parliament man, still they had continued to shake their heads among themselves, and to fear something in the future,—until he appeared at his old home leading a Cabinet Minister by the hand. There was such assurance in this that even old Mrs. Callaghan, at the brewery, gave way, and began to say all manner of good things, and to praise the doctor's luck in that he had a son gifted with parts so excellent. There was a great desire to see the Cabinet Minister in the flesh, to be with him when he ate and drank, to watch the gait and countenance of the man, and to drink water from this fountain of state lore which had been so wonderfully brought among them by their young townsman. Mrs. Finn was aware that it behoved her to be chary of her invitations, but the lady from the brewery had said such good things of Mrs. Finn's black swan, that she carried her point, and was invited to meet the Cabinet Minister at dinner on the day after his arrival.

Mrs. Flood Jones and her daughter were invited also to be of the party. When Phineas had been last at Killaloe, Mrs. Flood Jones, as the reader may remember, had remained with her daughter at Floodborough,—feeling it to be her duty to keep her daughter away from the danger of an unrequited attachment. But it seemed that her purpose was changed now, or that she no longer feared the danger,—for both Mary and her mother were now again living in Killaloe, and Mary was at the doctor's house as much as ever.

A day or two before the coming of the god and the demigod to the little town, Barbara Finn and her friend had thus come to understand each other as they walked along the Shannon side. "I am sure, my dear, that he is engaged to nobody," said Barbara Finn.

"And I am sure, my dear," said Mary, "that I do not care whether he is or is not."

"What do you mean, Mary?"

"I mean what I say. Why should I care? Five years ago I had a foolish dream, and now I am awake again. Think how old I have got to be!"

"Yes;—you are twenty-three. What has that to do with it?"

"It has this to do with it;—that I am old enough to know better. Mamma and I quite understand each other. She used to be angry with him, but she has got over all that foolishness now. It always made me so vexed;—the idea of being angry with a man because,—because—! You know one can't talk about it, it is so foolish. But that is all over now."

"Do you mean to say you don't care for him, Mary? Do you remember what you used to swear to me less than two years ago?"

"I remember it all very well, and I remember what a goose I was. As for caring for him, of course I do,—because he is your brother, and because I have known him all my life. But if he were going to be married to-morrow, you would see that it would make no difference to me."

Barbara Finn walked on for a couple of minutes in silence before she replied. "Mary," she said at last, "I don't believe a word of it."

"Very well;—then all that I shall ask of you is, that we may not talk about him any more. Mamma believes it, and that is enough for me." Nevertheless, they did talk about Phineas during the whole of that day, and very often talked about him afterwards, as long as Mary remained at Killaloe.

There was a large dinner party at the doctor's on the day after Mr. Monk's arrival. The bishop was not there, though he was on terms sufficiently friendly with the doctor's family to have been invited on so grand an occasion; but he was not there, because Mrs. Finn was determined that she would be taken out to dinner by a Cabinet Minister in the face of all her friends. She was aware that had the bishop been there, she must have taken the bishop's arm. And though there would have been glory in that, the other glory was more to her taste. It was the first time in her life that she had ever seen a Cabinet Minister, and I think that she was a little disappointed at finding him so like other middle-aged gentlemen. She had hoped that Mr. Monk would have assumed something of the dignity of his position; but he assumed nothing. Now the bishop, though he was a very mild man, did assume something by the very facts of his apron and knee-breeches.

"I am sure, sir, it is very good of you to come and put up with our humble way of living," said Mrs. Finn to her guest, as they sat down at table. And yet she had resolved that she would not make any speech of the kind,—that she would condescend to no apology,—that she would bear herself as though a Cabinet Minister dined with her at least once a year. But when the moment came, she broke down, and made this apology with almost abject meekness, and then hated herself because she had done so.

"My dear madam," said Mr. Monk, "I live myself so much like a hermit that your house is a palace of luxury to me." Then he felt that he had made a foolish speech, and he also hated himself. He found it very difficult to talk to his hostess upon any subject, until by chance he mentioned his young friend Phineas. Then her tongue was unloosed. "Your son, madam," he said, "is going with me to Limerick and back to Dublin. It is a shame, I know, taking him so soon away from home, but I should not know how to get on without him."

"Oh, Mr. Monk, it is such a blessing for him, and such an honour for us, that you should be so good to him." Then the mother spoke out all her past fears and all her present hopes, and acknowledged the great glory which it was to her to have a son sitting in Parliament, holding an office with a stately name and a great salary, and blessed with the friendship of such a man as Mr. Monk. After that Mr. Monk got on better with her.

"I don't know any young man," said he, "in whose career I have taken so strong an interest."

"He was always good," said Mrs. Finn, with a tear forcing itself into the corner of each eye. "I am his mother, and of course I ought not to say so,—not in this way; but it is true, Mr. Monk." And then the poor lady was obliged to raise her handkerchief and wipe away the drops.

Phineas on this occasion had taken out to dinner the mother of his devoted Mary, Mrs. Flood Jones. "What a pleasure it must be to the doctor and Mrs. Finn to see you come back in this way," said Mrs. Flood Jones.

"With all my bones unbroken?" said he, laughing.

"Yes; with all your bones unbroken. You know, Phineas, when we first heard that you were to sit in Parliament, we were afraid that you might break a rib or two,—since you choose to talk about the breaking of bones."

"Yes, I know. Everybody thought I should come to grief; but nobody felt so sure of it as I did myself."

"But you have not come to grief."

"I am not out of the wood yet, you know, Mrs. Flood Jones. There is plenty of possibility for grief in my way still."

"As far as I can understand it, you are out of the wood. All that your friends here want to see now is, that you should marry some nice English girl, with a little money, if possible. Rumours have reached us, you know."

"Rumours always lie," said Phineas.

"Sometimes they do, of course; and I am not going to ask any indiscreet questions. But that is what we all hope. Mary was saying, only the other day, that if you were once married, we should all feel quite safe about you. And you know we all take the most lively interest in your welfare. It is not every day that a man from County Clare gets on as you have done, and therefore we are bound to think of you." Thus Mrs. Flood Jones signified to Phineas Finn that she had forgiven him the thoughtlessness of his early youth,—even though there had been something of treachery in that thoughtlessness to her own daughter; and showed him, also, that whatever Mary's feelings might have been once, they were not now of a nature to trouble her. "Of course you will marry?" said Mrs. Flood Jones.

"I should think very likely not," said Phineas, who perhaps looked farther into the mind of the lady than the lady intended.

"Oh, do," said the lady. "Every man should marry as soon as he can, and especially a man in your position."

When the ladies met together in the drawing-room after dinner, it was impossible but that they should discuss Mr. Monk. There was Mrs. Callaghan from the brewery there, and old Lady Blood, of Bloodstone,—who on ordinary occasions would hardly admit that she was on dining-out terms with any one in Killaloe except the bishop, but who had found it impossible to decline to meet a Cabinet Minister,—and there was Mrs. Stackpoole from Sixmiletown, a far-away cousin of the Finns, who hated Lady Blood with a true provincial hatred.

"I don't see anything particularly uncommon in him, after all," said Lady Blood.

"I think he is very nice indeed," said Mrs. Flood Jones.

"So very quiet, my dear, and just like other people," said Mrs. Callaghan, meaning to pronounce a strong eulogium on the Cabinet Minister.

"Very like other people indeed," said Lady Blood.

"And what would you expect, Lady Blood?" said Mrs. Stackpoole. "Men and women in London walk upon two legs, just as they do in Ennis." Now Lady Blood herself had been born and bred in Ennis, whereas Mrs. Stackpoole had come from Limerick, which is a much more considerable town, and therefore there was a satire in this allusion to the habits of the men of Ennis which Lady Blood understood thoroughly.

"My dear Mrs. Stackpoole, I know how the people walk in London quite as well as you do." Lady Blood had once passed three months in London while Sir Patrick had been alive, whereas Mrs. Stackpoole had never done more than visit the metropolis for a day or two.

"Oh, no doubt," said Mrs. Stackpoole; "but I never can understand what it is that people expect. I suppose Mr. Monk ought to have come with his stars on the breast of his coat, to have pleased Lady Blood."

"My dear Mrs. Stackpoole, Cabinet Ministers don't have stars," said Lady Blood.

"I never said they did," said Mrs. Stackpoole.

"He is so nice and gentle to talk to," said Mrs. Finn. "You may say what you will, but men who are high up do very often give themselves airs. Now I must say that this friend of my son's does not do anything of that kind."

"Not the least," said Mrs. Callaghan.

"Quite the contrary," said Mrs. Stackpoole.

"I dare say he is a wonderful man," said Lady Blood. "All I say is, that I didn't hear anything wonderful come out of his mouth; and as for people in Ennis walking on two legs, I have seen donkeys in Limerick doing just the same thing." Now it was well known that Mrs. Stackpoole had two sons living in Limerick, as to neither of whom was it expected that he would set the Shannon on fire. After this little speech there was no further mention of Mr. Monk, as it became necessary that all the good-nature of Mrs. Finn and all the tact of Mrs. Flood Jones and all the energy of Mrs. Callaghan should be used, to prevent the raging of an internecine battle between Mrs. Stackpoole and Lady Blood.

CHAPTER LXVI. Victrix

Mr. Monk's holiday programme allowed him a week at Killaloe, and from thence he was to go to Limerick, and from Limerick to Dublin, in order that, at both places, he might be entertained at a public dinner and make a speech about tenant-right. Foreseeing that Phineas might commit himself if he attended these meetings, Mr. Monk had counselled him to remain at Killaloe. But Phineas had refused to subject himself to such cautious abstinence. Mr. Monk had come to Ireland as his friend, and he would see him through his travels. "I shall not, probably, be asked to speak," said Phineas, "and if I am asked, I need not say more than a few words. And what if I did speak out?"

"You might find it disadvantageous to you in London."

"I must take my chance of that. I am not going to tie myself down for ever and ever for the sake of being Under-Secretary to the Colonies." Mr. Monk said very much to him on the subject,—was constantly saying very much to him about it; but in spite of all that Mr. Monk said, Phineas did make the journey to Limerick and Dublin.

He had not, since his arrival at Killaloe, been a moment alone with Mary Flood Jones till the evening before he started with Mr. Monk. She had kept out of his way successfully, though she had constantly been with him in company, and was beginning to plume herself on the strength and valour of her conduct. But her self-praise had in it nothing of joy, and her glory was very sad. Of course she would care for him no more,—more especially as it was so very evident that he cared not at all for her. But the very fact of her keeping out of his way, made her acknowledge to herself that her position was very miserable. She had declared to her mother that she might certainly go to Killaloe with safety,—that it would be better for her to put herself in the way of meeting him as an old friend,—that the idea of the necessity of shutting herself up because of his approach, was the one thing that gave her real pain. Therefore her mother had brought her to Killaloe and she had met him; but her fancied security had deserted her, and she found herself to be miserable, hoping for something she did not know what, still dreaming of possibilities, feeling during every moment of his presence with her that some special conduct was necessary on her part. She could not make further confession to her mother and ask to be carried back to Floodborough; but she knew that she was very wretched at Killaloe.

As for Phineas, he had felt that his old friend was very cold to him. He was in that humour with reference to Violet Effingham which seemed especially to require consolation. He knew now that all hope was over there. Violet Effingham could never be his wife. Even were she not to marry Lord Chiltern for the next five years, she would not, during those five years, marry any other man. Such was our hero's conviction; and, suffering under this conviction, he was in want of the comfort of feminine sympathy. Had Mary known all this, and had it suited her to play such a part, I think she might have had Phineas at her feet before he had been a week at home. But she had kept aloof from him and had heard nothing of his sorrows. As a natural consequence of this, Phineas was more in love with her than ever.

On the evening before he started with Mr. Monk for Limerick, he managed to be alone with her for a few minutes. Barbara may probably have assisted in bringing about this arrangement, and had, perhaps, been guilty of some treachery,—sisters in such circumstances will sometimes be very treacherous to their friends. I feel sure, however, that Mary herself was quite innocent of any guile in the matter. "Mary," Phineas said to her suddenly, "it seems to me that you have avoided me purposely ever since I have been at home." She smiled and blushed, and stammered and said nothing. "Has there been any reason for it, Mary?"

"No reason at all that I know of," she said.

"We used to be such great friends."

"That was before you were a great man, Phineas. It must necessarily be different now. You know so many people now, and people of such a different sort, that of course I fall a little into the background."

"When you talk in that way, Mary, I know that you are laughing at me."

"Indeed, indeed I am not."

"I believe there is no one in the whole world," he said, after a pause, "whose friendship is more to me than yours is. I think of it so often, Mary. Say that when we come back it shall be between us as it used to be." Then he put out his hand for hers, and she could not help giving it to him. "Of course there will be people," he said, "who talk nonsense, and one cannot help it; but I will not put up with it from you."

"I did not mean to talk nonsense, Phineas!" Then there came some one across them, and the conversation was ended; but the sound of his voice remained on her ears, and she could not help but remember that he had declared that her friendship was dearer to him than the friendship of any one else.

Phineas went with Mr. Monk first to Limerick and then to Dublin, and found himself at both places to be regarded as a hero only second to the great hero. At both places the one subject of debate was tenant-right;—could anything be done to make it profitable for men with capital to put their capital into Irish land? The fertility of the soil was questioned by no one,—nor the sufficiency of external circumstances, such as railroads and the like;—nor the abundance of labour;—nor even security for the wealth to be produced. The only difficulty was in this, that the men who were to produce the wealth had no guarantee that it would be theirs when it was created. In England and elsewhere such guarantees were in existence. Might it not be possible to introduce them into Ireland? That was the question which Mr. Monk had in hand; and in various speeches which he made both before and after the dinners given to him, he pledged himself to keep it well in hand when Parliament should meet. Of course Phineas spoke also. It was impossible that he should be silent when his friend and leader was pouring out his eloquence. Of course he spoke, and of course he pledged himself. Something like the old pleasures of the debating society returned to him, as standing upon a platform before a listening multitude, he gave full vent to his words. In the House of Commons, of late he had been so cabined, cribbed, and confined by office as to have enjoyed nothing of this. Indeed, from the commencement of his career, he had fallen so thoroughly into the decorum of Government ways, as to have missed altogether the delights of that wild irresponsible oratory of which Mr. Monk had spoken to him so often. He had envied men below the gangway, who, though supporting the Government on main questions, could get up on their legs whenever the House was full enough to make it worth their while, and say almost whatever they pleased. There was that Mr. Robson, who literally did say just what came uppermost; and the thing that came uppermost was often ill-natured, often unbecoming the gravity of the House, was always startling; but men listened to him and liked him to speak. But Mr. Robson had—married a woman with money. Oh, why,—why, had not Violet Effingham been kinder to him? He might even yet, perhaps, marry a woman with money. But he could not bring himself to do so unless he loved her.

The upshot of the Dublin meeting was that he also positively pledged himself to support during the next session of Parliament a bill advocating tenant-right. "I am sorry you went so far as that," Mr. Monk said to him almost as soon as the meeting was over. They were standing on the pier at Kingstown, and Mr. Monk was preparing to return to England.

"And why not I as far as you?"

"Because I had thought about it, and I do not think that you have. I am prepared to resign my office to-morrow; and directly that I can see Mr. Gresham and explain to him what I have done, I shall offer to do so."

"He won't accept your resignation."

"He must accept it, unless he is prepared to instruct the Irish Secretary to bring in such a bill as I can support."

"I shall be exactly in the same boat."

"But you ought not to be in the same boat;—nor need you. My advice to you is to say nothing about it till you get back to London, and then speak to Lord Cantrip. Tell him that you will not say anything on the subject in the House, but that in the event of there being a division you hope to be allowed to vote as on an open question. It may be that I shall get Gresham's assent, and if so we shall be all right. If I do not, and if they choose to make it a point with you, you must resign also."

"Of course I shall," said Phineas.

"But I do not think they will. You have been too useful, and they will wish to avoid the weakness which comes to a ministry from changing its team. Good-bye, my dear fellow; and remember this,—my last word of advice to you is to stick by the ship. I am quite sure it is a career which will suit you. I did not begin it soon enough."

Phineas was rather melancholy as he returned alone to Killaloe. It was all very well to bid him stick to the ship, and he knew as well as any one could tell him how material the ship was to him; but there are circumstances in which a man cannot stick to his ship,—cannot stick, at least, to this special Government ship. He knew that whither Mr. Monk went, in this session, he must follow. He had considerable hope that when Mr. Monk explained his purpose to the Prime Minister, the Prime Minister would feel himself obliged to give way. In that case Phineas would not only be able to keep his office, but would have such an opportunity of making a speech in Parliament as circumstances had never yet given to him. When he was again at home he said nothing to his father or to the Killaloeians as to the danger of his position. Of what use would it be to make his mother and sisters miserable, or to incur the useless counsels of the doctor? They seemed to think his speech at Dublin very fine, and were never tired of talking of what Mr. Monk and Phineas were going to do; but the idea had not come home to them that if Mr. Monk or Phineas chose to do anything on their own account, they must give up the places which they held under the Crown.

It was September when Phineas found himself back at Killaloe, and he was due to be at his office in London in November. The excitement of Mr. Monk's company was now over, and he had nothing to do but to receive pouches full of official papers from the Colonial Office, and study all the statistics which came within his reach in reference to the proposed new law for tenant-right. In the meantime Mary was still living with her mother at Killaloe, and still kept herself somewhat aloof from the man she loved. How could it be possible for him not to give way in such circumstances as those?

One day he found himself talking to her about himself, and speaking to her of his own position with more frankness than he ever used with his own family. He had begun by reminding her of that conversation which they had had before he went away with Mr. Monk, and by reminding her also that she had promised to return to her old friendly ways with him.

"Nay, Phineas; there was no promise," she said.

"And are we not to be friends?"

"I only say that I made no particular promise. Of course we are friends. We have always been friends."

"What would you say if you heard that I had resigned my office and given up my seat?" he asked. Of course she expressed her surprise, almost her horror, at such an idea, and then he told her everything. It took long in the telling, because it was necessary that he should explain to her the working of the system which made it impossible for him, as a member of the Government, to entertain an opinion of his own.

"And do you mean that you would lose your salary?" she asked.

"Certainly I should."

"Would not that be very dreadful?"

He laughed as he acknowledged that it would be dreadful. "It is very dreadful, Mary, to have nothing to eat and drink. But what is a man to do? Would you recommend me to say that black is white?"

"I am sure you will never do that."

"You see, Mary, it is very nice to be called by a big name and to have a salary, and it is very comfortable to be envied by one's friends and enemies;—but there are drawbacks. There is this especial drawback." Then he paused for a moment before he went on.

"What especial drawback, Phineas?"

"A man cannot do what he pleases with himself. How can a man marry, so circumstanced as I am?"

She hesitated for a moment, and then she answered him,—"A man may be very happy without marrying, I suppose."

He also paused for many moments before he spoke again, and she then made a faint attempt to escape from him. But before she succeeded he had asked her a question which arrested her. "I wonder whether you would listen to me if I were to tell you a history?" Of course she listened, and the history he told her was the tale of his love for Violet Effingham.

"And she has money of her own?" Mary asked.

"Yes;—she is rich. She has a large fortune."

"Then, Mr. Finn, you must seek some one else who is equally blessed."

"Mary, that is untrue,—that is ill-natured. You do not mean that. Say that you do not mean it. You have not believed that I loved Miss Effingham because she was rich."

"But you have told me that you could love no one who is not rich."

"I have said nothing of the kind. Love is involuntary. It does not often run in a yoke with prudence. I have told you my history as far as it is concerned with Violet Effingham. I did love her very dearly."

"Did love her, Mr. Finn?"

"Yes;—did love her. Is there any inconstancy in ceasing to love when one is not loved? Is there inconstancy in changing one's love, and in loving again?"

"I do not know," said Mary, to whom the occasion was becoming so embarrassing that she no longer was able to reply with words that had a meaning in them.

"If there be, dear, I am inconstant." He paused, but of course she had not a syllable to say. "I have changed my love. But I could not speak of a new passion till I had told the story of that which has passed away. You have heard it all now, Mary. Can you try to love me, after that?" It had come at last,—the thing for which she had been ever wishing. It had come in spite of her imprudence, and in spite of her prudence. When she had heard him to the end she was not a whit angry with him,—she was not in the least aggrieved,—because he had been lost to her in his love for this Miss Effingham, while she had been so nearly lost by her love for him. For women such episodes in the lives of their lovers have an excitement which is almost pleasurable, whereas each man is anxious to hear his lady swear that until he appeared upon the scene her heart had been fancy free. Mary, upon the whole, had liked the story,—had thought that it had been finely told, and was well pleased with the final catastrophe. But, nevertheless, she was not prepared with her reply. "Have you no answer to give me, Mary?" he said, looking up into her eyes. I am afraid that he did not doubt what would be her answer,—as it would be good that all lovers should do. "You must vouchsafe me some word, Mary."

When she essayed to speak she found that she was dumb. She could not get her voice to give her the assistance of a single word. She did not cry, but there was a motion as of sobbing in her throat which impeded all utterance. She was as happy as earth,—as heaven could make her; but she did not know how to tell him that she was happy. And yet she longed to tell it, that he might know how thankful she was to him for his goodness. He still sat looking at her, and now by degrees he had got her hand in his. "Mary," he said, "will you be my wife,—my own wife?"

When half an hour had passed, they were still together, and now she had found the use of her tongue. "Do whatever you like best," she said. "I do not care which you do. If you came to me to-morrow and told me you had no income, it would make no difference. Though to love you and to have your love is all the world to me,—though it makes all the difference between misery and happiness,—I would sooner give up that than be a clog on you." Then he took her in his arms and kissed her. "Oh, Phineas!" she said, "I do love you so entirely!"

"My own one!"

"Yes; your own one. But if you had known it always! Never mind. Now you are my own,—are you not?"

"Indeed yes, dearest."

"Oh, what a thing it is to be victorious at last."

"What on earth are you two doing here these two hours together?" said Barbara, bursting into the room.

"What are we doing?" said Phineas.

"Yes;—what are you doing?"

"Nothing in particular," said Mary.

"Nothing at all in particular," said Phineas. "Only this,—that we have engaged ourselves to marry each other. It is quite a trifle,—is it not, Mary?"

"Oh, Barbara!" said the joyful girl, springing forward into her friend's arms; "I do believe I am the happiest creature on the face of this earth!"

CHAPTER LXVII. Job's Comforters

 Before Phineas had returned to London his engagement with Mary Flood Jones was known to all his family, was known to Mrs. Flood Jones, and was indeed known generally to all Killaloe. That other secret of his, which had reference to the probability of his being obliged to throw up his office, was known only to Mary herself. He thought that he had done all that honour required of him in telling her of his position before he had proposed;—so that she might on that ground refuse him if she were so minded. And yet he had known very well that such prudence on her part was not to be expected. If she loved him, of course she would say so when she was asked. And he had known that she loved him. "There may be delay, Mary," he said to her as he was going; "nay, there must be delay, if I am obliged to resign."

"I do not care a straw for delay if you will be true to me," she said.

"Do you doubt my truth, dearest?"

"Not in the least. I will swear by it as the one thing that is truest in the world."

"You may, dearest. And if this should come to pass I must go to work and put my shoulder to the wheel, and earn an income for you by my old profession before I can make you my wife. With such a motive before me I know that I shall earn an income." And thus they parted. Mary, though of course she would have preferred that her future husband should remain in his high office, that he should be a member of Parliament and an Under-Secretary of State, admitted no doubt into her mind to disturb her happiness; and Phineas, though he had many misgivings as to the prudence of what he had done, was not the less strong in his resolution of constancy and endurance. He would throw up his position, resign his seat, and go to work at the Bar instantly, if he found that his independence as a man required him to do so. And, above all, let come what might, he would be true to Mary Flood Jones.

December was half over before he saw Lord Cantrip. "Yes,—yes;" said Lord Cantrip, when the Under-Secretary began to tell his story; "I saw what you were about. I wish I had been at your elbow."

"If you knew the country as I know it, you would be as eager about it as I am."

"Then I can only say that I am very glad that I do not know the country as you know it. You see, Finn, it's my idea that if a man wants to make himself useful he should stick to some special kind of work. With you it's a thousand pities that you should not do so."

"You think, then, I ought to resign?"

"I don't say anything about that. As you wish it, of course I'll speak to Gresham. Monk, I believe, has resigned already."

"He has written to me, and told me so," said Phineas.

"I always felt afraid of him for your sake, Finn. Mr. Monk is a clever man, and as honest a man as any in the House, but I always thought that he was a dangerous friend for you. However, we will see. I will speak to Gresham after Christmas. There is no hurry about it."

When Parliament met the first great subject of interest was the desertion of Mr. Monk from the Ministry. He at once took his place below the gangway, sitting as it happened exactly in front of Mr. Turnbull, and there he made his explanation. Some one opposite asked a question whether a certain right honourable gentleman had not left the Cabinet. Then Mr. Gresham replied that to his infinite regret his right honourable friend, who lately presided at the Board of Trade, had resigned; and he went on to explain that this resignation had, according to his ideas, been quite unnecessary. His right honourable friend entertained certain ideas about Irish tenant-right, as to which he himself and his right honourable friend the Secretary for Ireland could not exactly pledge themselves to be in unison with him; but he had thought that the motion might have rested at any rate over this session. Then Mr. Monk explained, making his first great speech on Irish tenant-right. He found himself obliged to advocate some immediate measure for giving security to the Irish farmer; and as he could not do so as a member of the Cabinet, he was forced to resign the honour of that position. He said something also as to the great doubt which had ever weighed on his own mind as to the inexpediency of a man at his time of life submitting himself for the first time to the trammels of office. This called up Mr. Turnbull, who took the opportunity of saying that he now agreed cordially with his old friend for the first time since that old friend had listened to the blandishments of the ministerial seducer, and that he welcomed his old friend back to those independent benches with great satisfaction. In this way the debate was very exciting. Nothing was said which made it then necessary for Phineas to get upon his legs or to declare himself; but he perceived that the time would rapidly come in which he must do so. Mr. Gresham, though he strove to speak with gentle words, was evidently very angry with the late President of the Board of Trade; and, moreover, it was quite clear that a bill would be introduced by Mr. Monk himself, which Mr. Gresham was determined to oppose. If all this came to pass and there should be a close division, Phineas felt that his fate would be sealed. When he again spoke to Lord Cantrip on the subject, the Secretary of State shrugged his shoulders and shook his head. "I can only advise you," said Lord Cantrip, "to forget all that took place in Ireland. If you will do so, nobody else will remember it." "As if it were possible to forget such things," he said in the letter which he wrote to Mary that night. "Of course I shall go now. If it were not for your sake, I should not in the least regret it."

He had been with Madame Goesler frequently in the winter, and had discussed with her so often the question of his official position that she had declared that she was coming at last to understand the mysteries of an English Cabinet. "I think you are quite right, my friend," she said,—"quite right. What—you are to be in Parliament and say that this black thing is white, or that this white thing is black, because you like to take your salary! That cannot be honest!" Then, when he came to talk to her of money,—that he must give up Parliament itself, if he gave up his place,—she offered to lend him money. "Why should you not treat me as a friend?" she said. When he pointed out to her that there would never come a time in which he could pay such money back, she stamped her foot and told him that he had better leave her. "You have high principle," she said, "but not principle sufficiently high to understand that this thing could be done between you and me without disgrace to either of us." Then Phineas assured her with tears in his eyes that such an arrangement was impossible without disgrace to him.

But he whispered to this new friend no word of the engagement with his dear Irish Mary. His Irish life, he would tell himself, was a thing quite apart and separate from his life in England. He said not a word about Mary Flood Jones to any of those with whom he lived in London. Why should he, feeling as he did that it would so soon be necessary that he should disappear from among them? About Miss Effingham he had said much to Madame Goesler. She had asked him whether he had abandoned all hope. "That affair, then, is over?" she had said.

"Yes;—it is all over now."

"And she will marry the red-headed, violent lord?"

"Heaven knows. I think she will. But she is exactly the girl to remain unmarried if she takes it into her head that the man she likes is in any way unfitted for her."

"Does she love this lord?"

"Oh yes;—there is no doubt of that." And Phineas, as he made this acknowledgment, seemed to do so without much inward agony of soul. When he had been last in London he could not speak of Violet and Lord Chiltern together without showing that his misery was almost too much for him.

At this time he received some counsel from two friends. One was Laurence Fitzgibbon, and the other was Barrington Erle. Laurence had always been true to him after a fashion, and had never resented his intrusion at the Colonial Office. "Phineas, me boy," he said, "if all this is thrue, you're about up a tree."

"It is true that I shall support Monk's motion."

"Then, me boy, you're up a tree as far as office goes. A place like that niver suited me, because, you see, that poker of a young lord expected so much of a man; but you don't mind that kind of thing, and I thought you were as snug as snug."

"Troubles will come, you see, Laurence."

"Bedad, yes. It's all throubles, I think, sometimes. But you've a way out of all your throubles."

"What way?"

"Pop the question to Madame Max. The money's all thrue, you know."

"I don't doubt the money in the least," said Phineas.

"And it's my belief she'll take you without a second word. Anyways, thry it, Phinny, my boy. That's my advice." Phineas so far agreed with his friend Laurence that he thought it possible that Madame Goesler might accept him were he to propose marriage to her. He knew, of course, that that mode of escape from his difficulties was out of the question for him, but he could not explain this to Laurence Fitzgibbon.

"I am sorry to hear that you have taken up a bad cause," said Barrington Erle to him.

"It is a pity;—is it not?"

"And the worst of it is that you'll sacrifice yourself and do no good to the cause. I never knew a man break away in this fashion, and not feel afterwards that he had done it all for nothing."

"But what is a man to do, Barrington? He can't smother his convictions."

"Convictions! There is nothing on earth that I'm so much afraid of in a young member of Parliament as convictions. There are ever so many rocks against which men get broken. One man can't keep his temper. Another can't hold his tongue. A third can't say a word unless he has been priming himself half a session. A fourth is always thinking of himself, and wanting more than he can get. A fifth is idle, and won't be there when he's wanted. A sixth is always in the way. A seventh lies so that you never can trust him. I've had to do with them all, but a fellow with convictions is the worst of all."

"I don't see how a fellow is to help himself," said Phineas. "When a fellow begins to meddle with politics they will come."

"Why can't you grow into them gradually as your betters and elders have done before you? It ought to be enough for any man, when he begins, to know that he's a Liberal. He understands which side of the House he's to vote, and who is to lead him. What's the meaning of having a leader to a party, if it's not that? Do you think that you and Mr. Monk can go and make a government between you?"

"Whatever I think, I'm sure he doesn't."

"I'm not so sure of that. But look here, Phineas, I don't care two straws about Monk's going. I always thought that Mildmay and the Duke were wrong when they asked him to join. I knew he'd go over the traces,—unless, indeed, he took his money and did nothing for it, which is the way with some of those Radicals. I look upon him as gone."

"He has gone."

"The devil go along with him, as you say in Ireland. But don't you be such a fool as to ruin yourself for a crotchet of Monk's. It isn't too late yet for you to hold back. To tell you the truth, Gresham has said a word to me about it already. He is most anxious that you should stay, but of course you can't stay and vote against us."

"Of course I cannot."

"I look upon you, you know, as in some sort my own child. I've tried to bring other fellows forward who seemed to have something in them, but I have never succeeded as I have with you. You've hit the thing off, and have got the ball at your foot. Upon my honour, in the whole course of my experience I have never known such good fortune as yours."

"And I shall always remember how it began, Barrington," said Phineas, who was greatly moved by the energy and solicitude of his friend.

"But, for God's sake, don't go and destroy it all by such mad perversity as this. They mean to do something next session. Morrison is going to take it up." Sir Walter Morrison was at this time Secretary for Ireland. "But of course we can't let a fellow like Monk take the matter into his own hands just when he pleases. I call it d—d treachery."

"Monk is no traitor, Barrington."

"Men will have their own opinions about that. It's generally understood that when a man is asked to take a seat in the Cabinet he is expected to conform with his colleagues, unless something very special turns up. But I am speaking of you now, and not of Monk. You are not a man of fortune. You cannot afford to make ducks and drakes. You are excellently placed, and you have plenty of time to hark back, if you'll only listen to reason. All that Irish stump balderdash will never be thrown in your teeth by us, if you will just go on as though it had never been uttered."

Phineas could only thank his friend for his advice, which was at least disinterested, and was good of its kind, and tell him that he would think of it. He did think of it very much. He almost thought that, were it to do again, he would allow Mr. Monk to go upon his tour alone, and keep himself from the utterance of anything that so good a judge as Erle could call stump balderdash. As he sat in his arm-chair in his room at the Colonial Office, with despatch-boxes around him, and official papers spread before him,—feeling himself to be one of those who in truth managed and governed the affairs of this great nation, feeling also that if he relinquished his post now he could never regain it,—he did wish that he had been a little less in love with independence, a little quieter in his boastings that no official considerations should ever silence his tongue. But all this was too late now. He knew that his skin was not thick enough to bear the arrows of those archers who would bend their bows against him if he should now dare to vote against Mr. Monk's motion. His own party might be willing to forgive and forget; but there would be others who would read those reports, and would appear in the House with the odious tell-tale newspapers in their hands.

Then he received a letter from his father. Some good-natured person had enlightened the doctor as to the danger in which his son was placing himself. Dr. Finn, who in his own profession was a very excellent and well-instructed man, had been so ignorant of Parliamentary tactics, as to have been proud at his son's success at the Irish meetings. He had thought that Phineas was carrying on his trade as a public speaker with proper energy and continued success. He had cared nothing himself for tenant-right, and had acknowledged to Mr. Monk that he could not understand in what it was that the farmers were wronged. But he knew that Mr. Monk was a Cabinet Minister, and he thought that Phineas was earning his salary. Then there came some one who undeceived him, and the paternal bosom of the doctor was dismayed. "I don't mean to interfere," he said in his letter, "but I can hardly believe that you really intend to resign your place. Yet I am told that you must do so if you go on with this matter. My dear boy, pray think about it. I cannot imagine you are disposed to lose all that you have won for nothing." Mary also wrote to him. Mrs. Finn had been talking to her, and Mary had taught herself to believe that after the many sweet conversations she had had with a man so high in office as Phineas, she really did understand something about the British

Government. Mrs. Finn had interrogated Mary, and Mary had been obliged to own that it was quite possible that Phineas would be called upon to resign.

"But why, my dear? Heaven and earth! Resign two thousand a year!"

"That he may maintain his independence," said Mary proudly.

"Fiddlestick!" said Mrs. Finn. "How is he to maintain you, or himself either, if he goes on in that way? I shouldn't wonder if he didn't get himself all wrong, even now." Then Mrs. Finn began to cry; and Mary could only write to her lover, pointing out to him how very anxious all his friends were that he should do nothing in a hurry. But what if the thing were done already! Phineas in his great discomfort went to seek further counsel from Madame Goesler. Of all his counsellors, Madame Goesler was the only one who applauded him for what he was about to do.

"But, after all, what is it you give up? Mr. Gresham may be out to-morrow, and then where will be your place?"

"There does not seem to be much chance of that at present."

"Who can tell? Of course I do not understand,—but it was only the other day when Mr. Mildmay was there, and only the day before that when Lord de Terrier was there, and again only the day before that when Lord Brock was there." Phineas endeavoured to make her understand that of the four Prime Ministers whom she had named, three were men of the same party as himself, under whom it would have suited him to serve. "I would not serve under any man if I were an English gentleman in Parliament," said Madame Goesler.

"What is a poor fellow to do?" said Phineas, laughing.

"A poor fellow need not be a poor fellow unless he likes," said Madame Goesler. Immediately after this Phineas left her, and as he went along the street he began to question himself whether the prospects of his own darling Mary were at all endangered by his visits to Park Lane; and to reflect what sort of a blackguard he would be,—a blackguard of how deep a dye,—were he to desert Mary and marry Madame Max Goesler. Then he also asked himself as to the nature and quality of his own political honesty if he were to abandon Mary in order that he might maintain his parliamentary independence. After all, if it should ever come to pass that his biography should be written, his biographer would say very much more about the manner in which he kept his seat in Parliament than of the manner in which he kept his engagement with Miss Mary Flood Jones. Half a dozen people who knew him and her might think ill of him for his conduct to Mary, but the world would not condemn him! And when he thundered forth his liberal eloquence from below the gangway as an independent member, having the fortune of his charming wife to back him, giving excellent dinners at the same time in Park Lane, would not the world praise him very loudly?

When he got to his office he found a note from Lord Brentford inviting him to dine in Portman Square.

CHAPTER LXVIII. The Joint Attack

The note from Lord Brentford surprised our hero not a little. He had had no communication with the Earl since the day on which he had been so savagely scolded about the duel, when the Earl had plainly told him that his conduct had been as bad as it could be. Phineas had not on that account become at all ashamed of his conduct in reference to the duel, but he had conceived that any reconciliation between him and the Earl had been out of the question. Now there had come a civilly-worded invitation, asking him to dine with the offended nobleman. The note had been written by Lady Laura, but it had purported to come from Lord Brentford himself. He sent back word to say that he should be happy to have the honour of dining with Lord Brentford.

Parliament at this time had been sitting nearly a month, and it was already March. Phineas had heard nothing of Lady Laura, and did not even know that she was in London till he saw her handwriting. He did not know that she had not gone back to her husband, and that she had remained with her father all the winter at Saulsby. He had also heard that Lord Chiltern had been at Saulsby. All the world had been talking of the separation of Mr. Kennedy from his wife, one half of the world declaring that his wife, if not absolutely false to him, had neglected all her duties; and the other half asserting that Mr. Kennedy's treatment of his wife had been so bad that no woman could possibly have lived with him. There had even been a rumour that Lady Laura had gone off with a lover from the Duke of Omnium's garden party, and some indiscreet tongue had hinted that a certain unmarried Under-Secretary of State was missing at the same time. But Lord Chiltern upon this had shown his teeth with so strong a propensity to do some real biting, that no one had ventured to repeat that rumour. Its untruth was soon established by the fact that Lady Laura Kennedy was living with her father at Saulsby. Of Mr. Kennedy, Phineas had as yet seen nothing since he had been up in town. That gentleman, though a member of the Cabinet, had not been in London at the opening of the session, nor had he attended the Cabinet meetings during the recess. It had been stated in the newspapers that he was ill, and stated in private that he could not bear to show himself since his wife had left him. At last, however, he came to London, and Phineas saw him in the House. Then, when the first meeting of the Cabinet was summoned after his return, it became known that he also had resigned his office. There was nothing said about his resignation in the House. He had resigned on the score of ill-health, and that very worthy peer, Lord Mount Thistle, formerly Sir Marmaduke Morecombe, came back to the Duchy of Lancaster in his place. A

Prime Minister sometimes finds great relief in the possession of a serviceable stick who can be made to go in and out as occasion may require; only it generally happens that the stick will expect some reward when he is made to go out. Lord Mount Thistle immediately saw his way to a viscount's coronet, when he was once more summoned to the august councils of the Ministers.

A few days after this had been arranged, in the interval between Lord Brentford's invitation and Lord Brentford's dinner, Phineas encountered Mr. Kennedy so closely in one of the passages of the House that it was impossible that they should not speak to each other, unless they were to avoid each other as people do who have palpably quarrelled. Phineas saw that Mr. Kennedy was hesitating, and therefore took the bull by the horns. He greeted his former friend in a friendly fashion, shaking him by the hand, and then prepared to pass on. But Mr. Kennedy, though he had hesitated at first, now detained his brother member. "Finn," he said, "if you are not engaged I should like to speak to you for a moment." Phineas was not engaged, and allowed himself to be led out arm-in-arm by the late Chancellor of the Duchy into Westminster Hall. "Of course you know what a terrible thing has happened to me," said Mr. Kennedy.

"Yes;—I have heard of it," said Phineas.

"Everybody has heard of it. That is one of the terrible cruelties of such a blow."

"All those things are very bad of course. I was very much grieved,—because you have both been intimate friends of mine."

"Yes,—yes; we were. Do you ever see her now?"

"Not since last July,—at the Duke's party, you know."

"Ah, yes; the morning of that day was the last on which I spoke to her. It was then she left me."

"I am going to dine with Lord Brentford to-morrow, and I dare say she will be there."

"Yes;—she is in town. I saw her yesterday in her father's carriage. I think that she had no cause to leave me."

"Of course I cannot say anything about that."

"I think she had no cause to leave me." Phineas as he heard this could not but remember all that Lady Laura had told himself, and thought that no woman had ever had a better reason for leaving her husband. "There were things I did not like, and I said so."

"I suppose that is generally the way," replied Phineas.

"But surely a wife should listen to a word of caution from her husband."

"I fancy they never like it," said Phineas.

"But are we all of us to have all that we like? I have not found it so. Or would it be good for us if we had?" Then he paused; but as Phineas had no further remark to make, he continued speaking after they had walked about a third of the length of the hall. "It is not of my own comfort I am thinking now so much as of her name and her future conduct. Of course it will in every sense be best for her that she should come back to her husband's roof."

"Well; yes;—perhaps it would," said Phineas.

"Has she not accepted that lot for better or for worse?" said Mr. Kennedy, solemnly.

"But incompatibility of temper, you know, is always,—always supposed—. You understand me?"

"It is my intention that she should come back to me. I do not wish to make any legal demand;—at any rate, not as yet. Will you consent to be the bearer of a message from me both to herself and to the Earl?"

Now it seemed to Phineas that of all the messengers whom Mr. Kennedy could have chosen he was the most unsuited to be a Mercury in this cause,—not perceiving that he had been so selected with some craft, in order that Lady Laura might understand that the accusation against her was, at any rate, withdrawn, which had named Phineas as her lover. He paused again before he answered. "Of course," he said, "I should be most willing to be of service, if it were possible. But I do not see how I can speak to the Earl about it. Though I am going to dine with him I don't know why he has asked me;—for he and I are on very bad terms. He heard that stupid story about the duel, and has not spoken to me since."

"I heard that, too," said Mr. Kennedy, frowning blackly as he remembered his wife's duplicity.

"Everybody heard of it. But it has made such a difference between him and me, that I don't think I can meddle. Send for Lord Chiltern, and speak to him."

"Speak to Chiltern! Never! He would probably strike me on the head with his club."

"Call on the Earl yourself."

"I did, and he would not see me."

"Write to him."

"I did, and he sent back my letter unopened."

"Write to her."

"I did;—and she answered me, saying only thus; 'Indeed, indeed, it cannot be so.' But it must be so. The laws of God require it, and the laws of man permit it. I want some one to point out that to them more softly than I could do if I were simply to write to that effect. To the Earl, of course, I cannot write again." The conference ended by a promise from Phineas that he would, if possible, say a word to Lady Laura.

When he was shown into Lord Brentford's drawing-room he found not only Lady Laura there, but her brother. Lord Brentford was not in the room. Barrington Erle was there, and so also were Lord and Lady Cantrip.

"Is not your father going to be here?" he said to Lady Laura, after their first greeting.

"We live in that hope," said she, "and do not at all know why he should be late. What has become of him, Oswald?"

"He came in with me half an hour ago, and I suppose he does not dress as quickly as I do," said Lord Chiltern; upon which Phineas immediately understood that the father and the son were reconciled, and he rushed to the conclusion that Violet and her lover would also soon be reconciled, if such were not already the case. He felt some remnant of a soreness that it should be so, as a man feels where his headache has been when the real ache itself has left him. Then the host came in and made his apologies. "Chiltern kept me standing about," he said, "till the east wind had chilled me through and through. The only charm I recognise in youth is that it is impervious to the east wind." Phineas felt quite sure now that Violet and her lover were reconciled, and he had a distinct feeling of the place where the ache had been. Dear Violet! But, after all, Violet lacked that sweet, clinging, feminine softness which made Mary Flood Jones so pre-eminently the most charming of her sex. The Earl, when he had repeated his general apology, especially to Lady Cantrip, who was the only lady present except his daughter, came up to our hero and shook him kindly by the hand. He took him up to one of the windows and then addressed him in a voice of mock solemnity.

"Stick to the colonies, young man," he said, "and never meddle with foreign affairs;—especially not at Blankenberg."

"Never again, my Lord;—never again."

"And leave all questions of fire-arms to be arranged between the Horse Guards and the War Office. I have heard a good deal about it since I saw you, and I retract a part of what I said. But a duel is a foolish thing,—a very foolish thing.

Come;—here is dinner." And the Earl walked off with Lady Cantrip, and Lord Cantrip walked off with Lady Laura. Barrington Erle followed, and Phineas had an opportunity of saying a word to his friend, Lord Chiltern, as they went down together.

"It's all right between you and your father?"

"Yes;—after a fashion. There is no knowing how long it will last. He wants me to do three things, and I won't do any one of them."

"What are the three?"

"To go into Parliament, to be an owner of sheep and oxen, and to hunt in his own county. I should never attend the first, I should ruin myself with the second, and I should never get a run in the third." But there was not a word said about his marriage.

There were only seven who sat down to dinner, and the six were all people with whom Phineas was or had been on most intimate terms. Lord Cantrip was his official chief, and, since that connection had existed between them, Lady Cantrip had been very gracious to him. She quite understood the comfort which it was to her husband to have under him, as his representative in the House of Commons, a man whom he could thoroughly trust and like, and therefore she had used her woman's arts to bind Phineas to her lord in more than mere official bondage. She had tried her skill also upon Laurence Fitzgibbon,—but altogether in vain. He had eaten her dinners and accepted her courtesies, and had given for them no return whatever. But Phineas had possessed a more grateful mind, and had done all that had been required of him;—had done all that had been required of him till there had come that terrible absurdity in Ireland. "I knew very well what sort of things would happen when they brought such a man as Mr. Monk into the Cabinet," Lady Cantrip had said to her husband.

But though the party was very small, and though the guests were all his intimate friends, Phineas suspected nothing special till an attack was made upon him as soon as the servants had left the room. This was done in the presence of the two ladies, and, no doubt, had been preconcerted. There was Lord Cantrip there, who had already said much to him, and Barrington Erle who had said more even than Lord Cantrip. Lord Brentford, himself a member of the Cabinet, opened the attack by asking whether it was actually true that Mr. Monk meant to go on with his motion. Barrington Erle asserted that Mr. Monk positively would do so. "And Gresham will oppose it?" asked the Earl. "Of course he will," said Barrington. "Of course he will," said Lord Cantrip. "I know what I should think of him if he did not," said Lady Cantrip. "He is the last man in the world to be forced into a thing," said Lady Laura. Then Phineas knew pretty well what was coming on him.

Lord Brentford began again by asking how many supporters Mr. Monk would have in the House. "That depends upon the amount of courage which the Conservatives may have," said Barrington Erle. "If they dare to vote for a thoroughly democratic measure, simply for the sake of turning us out, it is quite on the cards that they may succeed." "But of our own people?" asked Lord Cantrip. "You had better inquire that of Phineas Finn," said Barrington. And then the attack was made.

Our hero had a bad half hour of it, though many words were said which must have gratified him much. They all wanted to keep him,—so Lord Cantrip declared, "except one or two whom I could name, and who are particularly anxious to wear his shoes," said Barrington, thinking that certain reminiscences of Phineas with regard to Mr. Bonteen and others might operate as strongly as any other consideration to make him love his place. Lord Brentford declared that he could not understand it,—that he should find himself lost in amazement if such a man as his young friend allowed himself to be led into the outer wilderness by such an *ignis-fatuus* of light as this. Lord Cantrip laid down the unwritten traditional law of Government officials very plainly. A man in office,—in an office which really imposed upon him as much work as he could possibly do with credit to himself or his cause,—was dispensed from the necessity of a conscience with reference to other matters. It was for Sir Walter Morrison to have a conscience about Irish tenant-right, as no doubt he had,—just as Phineas Finn had a conscience about Canada, and Jamaica, and the Cape. Barrington Erle was very strong about parties in general, and painted the comforts of official position in glowing colours. But I think that the two ladies were more efficacious than even their male relatives in the arguments which they used. "We have been so happy to have you among us," said Lady Cantrip, looking at him with beseeching, almost loving eyes. "Mr. Finn knows," said Lady Laura, "that since he first came into Parliament I have always believed in his success, and I have been very proud to see it." "We shall weep over him, as over a fallen angel, if he leaves us," said Lady Cantrip. "I won't say that I will weep," said Lady Laura, "but I do not know anything of the kind that would so truly make me unhappy."

What was he to say in answer to applications so flattering and so pressing? He would have said nothing, had that been possible, but he felt himself obliged to reply. He replied very weakly,—of course, not justifying himself, but declaring that as he had gone so far he must go further. He must vote for the measure now. Both his chief and Barrington Erle proved, or attempted to prove, that he was wrong in this. Of course he would not speak on the measure, and his vote for his party would probably be allowed to pass without notice. One or two newspapers might perhaps attack him; but what public man cared for such attacks as those? His whole party would hang by him, and in that he would find ample consolation. Phineas could only say that he would think of it;—and this he said in so irresolute a tone of voice that all the men then present believed that he was gained. The two ladies, however, were of a different opinion. "In spite of anything that anybody may say, he will do what he thinks right when the time comes," said Laura to her father afterwards. But then Lady Laura had been in love with him,—was perhaps almost in love with him still. "I'm afraid he is a mule," said Lady Cantrip to her husband. "He's a good mule up a hill with a load on his back," said his lordship. "But with a mule there always comes a time when you can't manage him," said Lady Cantrip. But Lady Cantrip had never been in love with Phineas.

Phineas found a moment, before he left Lord Brentford's house, to say a word to Lady Laura as to the commission that had been given to him. "It can never be," said Lady Laura, shuddering;—"never, never, never!"

"You are not angry with me for speaking?"

"Oh, no—not if he told you."

"He made me promise that I would."

"Tell him it cannot be. Tell him that if he has any instruction to send me as to what he considers to be my duty, I will endeavour to comply, if that duty can be done apart. I will recognize him so far, because of my vow. But not even for the sake of my vow, will I endeavour to live with him. His presence would kill me!"

When Phineas repeated this, or as much of this as he judged to be necessary, to Mr. Kennedy a day or two afterwards, that gentleman replied that in such case he would have no alternative but to seek redress at law. "I have done nothing to my wife," said he, "of which I need be ashamed. It will be sad, no doubt, to have all our affairs bandied about in court, and made the subject of comment in newspapers, but a man must go through that, or worse than that, in the vindication of his rights, and for the performance of his duty to his Maker." That very day Mr. Kennedy went to his lawyer, and desired that steps might be taken for the restitution to him of his conjugal rights.

CHAPTER LXIX. The Temptress

Mr. Monk's bill was read the first time before Easter, and Phineas Finn still held his office. He had spoken to the Prime Minister once on the subject, and had been surprised at that gentleman's courtesy;—for Mr. Gresham had the reputation of being unconciliatory in his manners, and very prone to resent anything like desertion from that allegiance which was due to himself as the leader of his party. "You had better stay where you are and take no step that may be irretrievable, till you have quite made up your mind," said Mr. Gresham.

"I fear I have made up my mind," said Phineas.

"Nothing can be done till after Easter," replied the great man, "and there is no knowing how things may go then. I strongly recommend you to stay with us. If you can do this it will be only necessary that you shall put your resignation in Lord Cantrip's hands before you speak or vote against us. See Monk and talk it over with him." Mr. Gresham possibly imagined that Mr. Monk might be moved to abandon his bill, when he saw what injury he was about to do.

At this time Phineas received the following letter from his darling Mary:—

Floodborough,
Thursday.

DEAREST PHINEAS,

We have just got home from Killaloe, and mean to remain here all through the summer. After leaving your sisters this house seems so desolate; but I shall have the more time to think of you. I have been reading Tennyson, as you told me, and I fancy that I could in truth be a Mariana here, if it were not that I am so quite certain that you will come;—and that makes all the difference in the world in a moated grange. Last night I sat at the window and tried to realise what I should feel if you were to tell me that you did not want me; and I got myself into such an ecstatic state of mock melancholy that I cried for half an hour. But when one has such a real living joy at the back of one's romantic melancholy, tears are very pleasant;—they water and do not burn.

I must tell you about them all at Killaloe. They certainly are very unhappy at the idea of your resigning. Your father says very little, but I made him own that to act as you are acting for the sake of principle is very grand. I would not leave him till he had said so, and he did say it. Dear Mrs. Finn does not understand it as well, but she will do so. She complains mostly for my sake, and when I tell her that I will wait twenty years if it is necessary, she tells me I do not know what waiting means. But I will,—and will be happy, and will never really think myself a Mariana. Dear, dear, dear Phineas, indeed I won't. The girls are half sad and half proud. But I am wholly proud, and know that you are doing just what you ought to do. I shall think more of you as a man who might have been a Prime Minister than if you were really sitting in the Cabinet like Lord Cantrip. As for mamma, I cannot make her quite understand it. She merely says that no young man who is going to be married ought to resign anything. Dear mamma;—sometimes she does say such odd things.

You told me to tell you everything, and so I have. I talk to some of the people here, and tell them what they might do if they had tenant-right. One old fellow, Mike Dufferty,—I don't know whether you remember him,—asked if he would have to pay the rent all the same. When I said certainly he would, then he shook his head. But as you said once, when we want to do good to people one has no right to expect that they should understand it. It is like baptizing little infants.

I got both your notes;—seven words in one, Mr. Under-Secretary, and nine in the other! But the one little word at the end was worth a whole sheet full of common words. How nice it is to write letters without paying postage, and to send them about the world with a grand name in the corner. When Barney brings me one he always looks as if he didn't know whether it was a love letter or an order to go to Botany Bay. If he saw the inside of them, how short they are, I don't think he'd think much of you as a lover nor yet as an Under-Secretary.

But I think ever so much of you as both;—I do, indeed; and I am not scolding you a bit. As long as I can have two or three dear, sweet, loving words, I shall be as happy as a queen. Ah, if you knew it all! But you never can know it all. A man has so many other things to learn that he cannot understand it.

Good-bye, dear, dear, dearest man. Whatever you do I shall be quite sure you have done the best.

Ever your own, with all the love of her heart,   MARY F. JONES.

This was very nice. Such a man as was Phineas Finn always takes a delight which he cannot express even to himself in the receipt of such a letter as this. There is nothing so flattering as the warm expression of the confidence of a woman's love, and Phineas thought that no woman ever expressed this more completely than did his Mary. Dear, dearest Mary. As for giving her up, as for treachery to one so trusting, so sweet, so well beloved, that was out of the question. But nevertheless the truth came home to him more clearly day by day, that he of all men was the last

who ought to have given himself up to such a passion. For her sake he ought to
have abstained. So he told himself now. For her sake he ought to have kept aloof
from her;—and for his own sake he ought to have kept aloof from Mr. Monk. That
very day, with Mary's letter in his pocket, he went to the livery stables and
explained that he would not keep his horse any longer. There was no difficulty
about the horse. Mr. Howard Macleod of the Treasury would take him from that
very hour. Phineas, as he walked away, uttered a curse upon Mr. Howard Macleod.
Mr. Howard Macleod was just beginning the glory of his life in London, and he,
Phineas Finn, was bringing his to an end.

With Mary's letter in his pocket he went up to Portman Square. He had again got
into the habit of seeing Lady Laura frequently, and was often with her brother, who
now again lived at his father's house. A letter had reached Lord Brentford, through
his lawyer, in which a demand was made by Mr. Kennedy for the return of his
wife. She was quite determined that she would never go back to him; and there had
come to her a doubt whether it would not be expedient that she should live abroad
so as to be out of the way of persecution from her husband. Lord Brentford was in
great wrath, and Lord Chiltern had once or twice hinted that perhaps he had better
"see" Mr. Kennedy. The amenities of such an interview, as this would be, had up to
the present day been postponed; and, in a certain way, Phineas had been used as a
messenger between Mr. Kennedy and his wife's family.

"I think it will end," she said, "in my going to Dresden, and settling myself there.
Papa will come to me when Parliament is not sitting."

"It will be very dull."

"Dull! What does dulness amount to when one has come to such a pass as this?
When one is in the ruck of fortune, to be dull is very bad; but when misfortune
comes, simple dulness is nothing. It sounds almost like relief."

"It is so hard that you should be driven away." She did not answer him for a while,
and he was beginning to think of his own case also. Was it not hard that he too
should be driven away? "It is odd enough that we should both be going at the same
time."

"But you will not go?"

"I think I shall. I have resolved upon this,—that if I give up my place, I will give
up my seat too. I went into Parliament with the hope of office, and how can I
remain there when I shall have gained it and then have lost it?"

"But you will stay in London, Mr. Finn?"

"I think not. After all that has come and gone I should not be happy here, and I
should make my way easier and on cheaper terms in Dublin. My present idea is

that I shall endeavour to make a practice over in my own country. It will be hard work beginning at the bottom;—will it not?"

"And so unnecessary."

"Ah, Lady Laura,—if it only could be avoided! But it is of no use going through all that again."

"How much we would both of us avoid if we could only have another chance!" said Lady Laura. "If I could only be as I was before I persuaded myself to marry a man whom I never loved, what a paradise the earth would be to me! With me all regrets are too late."

"And with me as much so."

"No, Mr. Finn. Even should you resign your office, there is no reason why you should give up your seat."

"Simply that I have no income to maintain me in London."

She was silent for a few moments, during which she changed her seat so as to come nearer to him, placing herself on a corner of a sofa close to the chair on which he was seated. "I wonder whether I may speak to you plainly," she said.

"Indeed you may."

"On any subject?"

"Yes;—on any subject."

"I trust you have been able to rid your bosom of all remembrances of Violet Effingham."

"Certainly not of all remembrances, Lady Laura."

"Of all hope, then?"

"I have no such hope."

"And of all lingering desires?"

"Well, yes;—and of all lingering desires. I know now that it cannot be. Your brother is welcome to her."

"Ah;—of that I know nothing. He, with his perversity, has estranged her. But I am sure of this,—that if she do not marry him, she will marry no one. But it is not on account of him that I speak. He must fight his own battles now."

"I shall not interfere with him, Lady Laura."

"Then why should you not establish yourself by a marriage that will make place a matter of indifference to you? I know that it is within your power to do so." Phineas put his hand up to his breastcoat pocket, and felt that Mary's letter,—her precious letter,—was there safe. It certainly was not in his power to do this thing which Lady Laura recommended to him, but he hardly thought that the present was a moment suitable for explaining to her the nature of the impediment which stood in the way of such an arrangement. He had so lately spoken to Lady Laura with an assurance of undying constancy of his love for Miss Effingham, that he could not as yet acknowledge the force of another passion. He shook his head by way of reply. "I tell you that it is so," she said with energy.

"I am afraid not."

"Go to Madame Goesler, and ask her. Hear what she will say."

"Madame Goesler would laugh at me, no doubt."

"Psha! You do not think so. You know that she would not laugh. And are you the man to be afraid of a woman's laughter? I think not."

Again he did not answer her at once, and when he did speak the tone of his voice was altered. "What was it you said of yourself, just now?"

"What did I say of myself?"

"You regretted that you had consented to marry a man,—whom you did not love."

"Why should you not love her? And it is so different with a man! A woman is wretched if she does not love her husband, but I fancy that a man gets on very well without any such feeling. She cannot domineer over you. She cannot expect you to pluck yourself out of your own soil, and begin a new growth altogether in accordance with the laws of her own. It was that which Mr. Kennedy did."

"I do not for a moment think that she would take me, if I were to offer myself."

"Try her," said Lady Laura energetically. "Such trials cost you but little;—we both of us know that!" Still he said nothing of the letter in his pocket. "It is everything that you should go on now that you have once begun. I do not believe in you working at the Bar. You cannot do it. A man who has commenced life as you have done with the excitement of politics, who has known what it is to take a prominent part in the control of public affairs, cannot give it up and be happy at other work. Make her your wife, and you may resign or remain in office just as you choose. Office will be much easier to you than it is now, because it will not be a necessity. Let me at any rate have the pleasure of thinking that one of us can remain here,—that we need not both fall together."

Still he did not tell her of the letter in his pocket. He felt that she moved him,—that she made him acknowledge to himself how great would be the pity of such a failure as would be his. He was quite as much alive as she could be to the fact that work at the Bar, either in London or in Dublin, would have no charms for him now. The prospect of such a life was very dreary to him. Even with the comfort of Mary's love such a life would be very dreary to him. And then he knew,—he thought that he knew,—that were he to offer himself to Madame Goesler he would not in truth be rejected. She had told him that if poverty was a trouble to him he need be no longer poor. Of course he had understood this. Her money was at his service if he should choose to stoop and pick it up. And it was not only money that such a marriage would give him. He had acknowledged to himself more than once that Madame Goesler was very lovely, that she was clever, attractive in every way, and as far as he could see, blessed with a sweet temper. She had a position, too, in the world that would help him rather than mar him. What might he not do with an independent seat in the House of Commons, and as joint owner of the little house in Park Lane? Of all careers which the world could offer to a man the pleasantest would then be within his reach. "You appear to me as a tempter," he said at last to Lady Laura.

"It is unkind of you to say that, and ungrateful. I would do anything on earth in my power to help you."

"Nevertheless you are a tempter."

"I know how it ought to have been," she said, in a low voice. "I know very well how it ought to have been. I should have kept myself free till that time when we met on the braes of Loughlinter, and then all would have been well with us."

"I do not know how that might have been," said Phineas, hoarsely.

"You do not know! But I know. Of course you have stabbed me with a thousand daggers when you have told me from time to time of your love for Violet. You have been very cruel,—needlessly cruel. Men are so cruel! But for all that I have known that I could have kept you,—had it not been too late when you spoke to me. Will you not own as much as that?"

"Of course you would have been everything to me. I should never have thought of Violet then."

"That is the only kind word you have said to me from that day to this. I try to comfort myself in thinking that it would have been so. But all that is past and gone, and done. I have had my romance and you have had yours. As you are a man, it is natural that you should have been disturbed by a double image;—it is not so with me."

"And yet you can advise me to offer marriage to a woman,—a woman whom I am to seek merely because she is rich?"

"Yes;—I do so advise you. You have had your romance and must now put up with reality. Why should I so advise you but for the interest that I have in you? Your prosperity will do me no good. I shall not even be here to see it. I shall hear of it only as so many a woman banished out of England hears a distant misunderstood report of what is going on in the country she has left. But I still have regard enough,—I will be bold, and, knowing that you will not take it amiss, will say love enough for you,—to feel a desire that you should not be shipwrecked. Since we first took you in hand between us, Barrington and I, I have never swerved in my anxiety on your behalf. When I resolved that it would be better for us both that we should be only friends, I did not swerve. When you would talk to me so cruelly of your love for Violet, I did not swerve. When I warned you from Loughlinter because I thought there was danger, I did not swerve. When I bade you not to come to me in London because of my husband, I did not swerve. When my father was hard upon you, I did not swerve then. I would not leave him till he was softened. When you tried to rob Oswald of his love, and I thought you would succeed,—for I did think so,—I did not swerve. I have ever been true to you. And now that I must hide myself and go away, and be seen no more, I am true still."

"Laura,—dearest Laura!" he exclaimed.

"Ah, no!" she said, speaking with no touch of anger, but all in sorrow;—"it must not be like that. There is no room for that. Nor do you mean it. I do not think so ill of you. But there may not be even words of affection between us—only such as I may speak to make you know that I am your friend."

"You are my friend," he said, stretching out his hand to her as he turned away his face. "You are my friend, indeed."

"Then do as I would have you do."

He put his hand into his pocket, and had the letter between his fingers with the purport of showing it to her. But at the moment the thought occurred to him that were he to do so, then, indeed, he would be bound for ever. He knew that he was bound for ever,—bound for ever to his own Mary; but he desired to have the privilege of thinking over such bondage once more before he proclaimed it even to his dearest friend. He had told her that she tempted him, and she stood before him now as a temptress. But lest it might be possible that she should not tempt in vain,—that letter in his pocket must never be shown to her. In that case Lady Laura must never hear from his lips the name of Mary Flood Jones.

He left her without any assured purpose;—without, that is, the assurance to her of any fixed purpose. There yet wanted a week to the day on which Mr. Monk's bill was to be read,—or not to be read,—the second time; and he had still that interval before he need decide. He went to his club, and before he dined he strove to write a line to Mary;—but when he had the paper before him he found that it was impossible to do so. Though he did not even suspect himself of an intention to be false, the idea that was in his mind made the effort too much for him. He put the paper away from him and went down and eat his dinner.

It was a Saturday, and there was no House in the evening. He had remained in Portman Square with Lady Laura till near seven o'clock, and was engaged to go out in the evening to a gathering at Mrs. Gresham's house. Everybody in London would be there, and Phineas was resolved that as long as he remained in London he would be seen at places where everybody was seen. He would certainly be at Mrs. Gresham's gathering; but there was an hour or two before he need go home to dress, and as he had nothing to do, he went down to the smoking-room of his club. The seats were crowded, but there was one vacant; and before he had looked about him to scrutinise his neighbourhood, he found that he had placed himself with Bonteen on his right hand and Ratler on his left. There were no two men in all London whom he more thoroughly disliked; but it was too late for him to avoid them now.

They instantly attacked him, first on one side and then on the other. "So I am told you are going to leave us," said Bonteen.

"Who can have been ill-natured enough to whisper such a thing?" replied Phineas.

"The whispers are very loud, I can tell you," said Ratler. "I think I know already pretty nearly how every man in the House will vote, and I have not got your name down on the right side."

"Change it for heaven's sake," said Phineas.

"I will, if you'll tell me seriously that I may," said Ratler.

"My opinion is," said Bonteen, "that a man should be known either as a friend or foe. I respect a declared foe."

"Know me as a declared foe then," said Phineas, "and respect me."

"That's all very well," said Ratler, "but it means nothing. I've always had a sort of fear about you, Finn, that you would go over the traces some day. Of course it's a very grand thing to be independent."

"The finest thing in the world," said Bonteen; "only so d—d useless."

"But a man shouldn't be independent and stick to the ship at the same time. You forget the trouble you cause, and how you upset all calculations."

"I hadn't thought of the calculations," said Phineas.

"The fact is, Finn," said Bonteen, "you are made of clay too fine for office. I've always found it has been so with men from your country. You are the grandest horses in the world to look at out on a prairie, but you don't like the slavery of harness."

"And the sound of a whip over our shoulders sets us kicking;—does it not, Ratler?"

"I shall show the list to Gresham to-morrow," said Ratler, "and of course he can do as he pleases; but I don't understand this kind of thing."

"Don't you be in a hurry," said Bonteen. "I'll bet you a sovereign Finn votes with us yet. There's nothing like being a little coy to set off a girl's charms. I'll bet you a sovereign, Ratler, that Finn goes out into the lobby with you and me against Monk's bill."

Phineas, not being able to stand any more of this most unpleasant raillery, got up and went away. The club was distasteful to him, and he walked off and sauntered for a while about the park. He went down by the Duke of York's column as though he were going to his office, which of course was closed at this hour, but turned round when he got beyond the new public buildings,—buildings which he was never destined to use in their completed state,—and entered the gates of the enclosure, and wandered on over the bridge across the water. As he went his mind was full of thought. Could it be good for him to give up everything for a fair face? He swore to himself that of all women whom he had ever seen Mary was the sweetest and the dearest and the best. If it could be well to lose the world for a woman, it would be well to lose it for her. Violet, with all her skill, and all her strength, and all her grace, could never have written such a letter as that which he still held in his pocket. The best charm of a woman is that she should be soft, and trusting, and generous; and who ever had been more soft, more trusting, and more generous than his Mary? Of course he would be true to her, though he did lose the world.

But to yield such a triumph to the Ratlers and Bonteens whom he left behind him,—to let them have their will over him,—to know that they would rejoice scurrilously behind his back over his downfall! The feeling was terrible to him. The last words which Bonteen had spoken made it impossible to him now not to support his old friend Mr. Monk. It was not only what Bonteen had said, but that the words of Mr. Bonteen so plainly indicated what would be the words of all the other Bonteens. He knew that he was weak in this. He knew that had he been strong, he would have allowed himself to be guided,—if not by the firm decision of his own spirit,—by the counsels of such men as Mr. Gresham and Lord Cantrip, and not by the sarcasms of the Bonteens and Ratlers of official life. But men who sojourn amidst savagery fear the mosquito more than they do the lion. He could not bear to think that he should yield his blood to such a one as Bonteen.

And he must yield his blood, unless he could vote for Mr. Monk's motion, and hold his ground afterwards among them all in the House of Commons. He would at any rate see the session out, and try a fall with Mr. Bonteen when they should be sitting on different benches,—if ever fortune should give him an opportunity. And in the meantime, what should he do about Madame Goesler? What a fate was his to have the handsomest woman in London with thousands and thousands a year at his disposal! For,—so he now swore to himself,—Madame Goesler was the handsomest woman in London, as Mary Flood Jones was the sweetest girl in the world.

He had not arrived at any decision so fixed as to make him comfortable when he went home and dressed for Mrs. Gresham's party. And yet he knew,—he thought that he knew that he would be true to Mary Flood Jones.

CHAPTER LXX. The Prime Minister's House

The rooms and passages and staircases at Mrs. Gresham's house were very crowded when Phineas arrived there. Men of all shades of politics were there, and the wives and daughters of such men; and there was a streak of royalty in one of the saloons, and a whole rainbow of foreign ministers with their stars, and two blue ribbons were to be seen together on the first landing-place, with a stout lady between them carrying diamonds enough to load a pannier. Everybody was there. Phineas found that even Lord Chiltern was come, as he stumbled across his friend on the first foot-ground that he gained in his ascent towards the rooms. "Halloa,—you here?" said Phineas. "Yes, by George!" said the other, "but I am going to escape as soon as possible. I've been trying to make my way up for the last hour, but could never get round that huge promontory there. Laura was more persevering." "Is Kennedy here?" Phineas whispered. "I do not know," said Chiltern, "but she was determined to run the chance."

A little higher up,—for Phineas was blessed with more patience than Lord Chiltern possessed,—he came upon Mr. Monk. "So you are still admitted privately," said Phineas.

"Oh dear yes,—and we have just been having a most friendly conversation about you. What a man he is! He knows everything. He is so accurate; so just in the abstract,—and in the abstract so generous!"

"He has been very generous to me in detail as well as in abstract," said Phineas.

"Ah, yes; I am not thinking of individuals exactly. His want of generosity is to large masses,—to a party, to classes, to a people; whereas his generosity is for mankind at large. He assumes the god, affects to nod, and seems to shake the spheres. But I have nothing against him. He has asked me here to-night, and has talked to me most familiarly about Ireland."

"What do you think of your chance of a second reading?" asked Phineas.

"What do you think of it?—you hear more of those things than I do."

"Everybody says it will be a close division."

"I never expected it," said Mr. Monk.

"Nor I, till I heard what Daubeny said at the first reading. They will all vote for the bill *en masse*,—hating it in their hearts all the time."

"Let us hope they are not so bad as that."

"It is the way with them always. They do all our work for us,—sailing either on one tack or the other. That is their use in creation, that when we split among ourselves, as we always do, they come in and finish our job for us. It must be unpleasant for them to be always doing that which they always say should never be done at all."

"Wherever the gift horse may come from, I shall not look it in the mouth," said Mr. Monk. "There is only one man in the House whom I hope I may not see in the lobby with me, and that is yourself."

"The question is decided now," said Phineas.

"And how is it decided?"

Phineas could not tell his friend that a question of so great magnitude to him had been decided by the last sting which he had received from an insect so contemptible as Mr. Bonteen, but he expressed the feeling as well as he knew how to express it. "Oh, I shall be with you. I know what you are going to say, and I know how good you are. But I could not stand it. Men are beginning already to say things which almost make me get up and kick them. If I can help it, I will give occasion to no man to hint anything to me which can make me be so wretched as I have been to-day. Pray do not say anything more. My idea is that I shall resign to-morrow."

"Then I hope that we may fight the battle side by side," said Mr. Monk, giving him his hand.

"We will fight the battle side by side," replied Phineas.

After that he pushed his way still higher up the stairs, having no special purpose in view, not dreaming of any such success as that of reaching his host or hostess,—merely feeling that it should be a point of honour with him to make a tour through the rooms before he descended the stairs. The thing, he thought, was to be done with courage and patience, and this might, probably, be the last time in his life that he would find himself in the house of a Prime Minister. Just at the turn of the balustrade at the top of the stairs, he found Mr. Gresham in the very spot on which Mr. Monk had been talking with him. "Very glad to see you," said Mr. Gresham. "You, I find, are a persevering man, with a genius for getting upwards."

"Like the sparks," said Phineas.

"Not quite so quickly," said Mr. Gresham.

"But with the same assurance of speedy loss of my little light."

It did not suit Mr. Gresham to understand this, so he changed the subject. "Have you seen the news from America?"

"Yes, I have seen it, but do not believe it," said Phineas.

"Ah, you have such faith in a combination of British colonies, properly backed in Downing Street, as to think them strong against a world in arms. In your place I should hold to the same doctrine,—hold to it stoutly."

"And you do now, I hope, Mr. Gresham?"

"Well,—yes,—I am not down-hearted. But I confess to a feeling that the world would go on even though we had nothing to say to a single province in North America. But that is for your private ear. You are not to whisper that in Downing Street." Then there came up somebody else, and Phineas went on upon his slow course. He had longed for an opportunity to tell Mr. Gresham that he could go to Downing Street no more, but such opportunity had not reached him.

For a long time he found himself stuck close by the side of Miss Fitzgibbon,—Miss Aspasia Fitzgibbon,—who had once relieved him from terrible pecuniary anxiety by paying for him a sum of money which was due by him on her brother's account. "It's a very nice thing to be here, but one does get tired of it," said Miss Fitzgibbon.

"Very tired," said Phineas.

"Of course it is a part of your duty, Mr. Finn. You are on your promotion and are bound to be here. When I asked Laurence to come, he said there was nothing to be got till the cards were shuffled again."

"They'll be shuffled very soon," said Phineas.

"Whatever colour comes up, you'll hold trumps, I know," said the lady. "Some hands always hold trumps." He could not explain to Miss Fitzgibbon that it would never again be his fate to hold a single trump in his hand; so he made another fight, and got on a few steps farther.

He said a word as he went to half a dozen friends,—as friends went with him. He was detained for five minutes by Lady Baldock, who was very gracious and very disagreeable. She told him that Violet was in the room, but where she did not know. "She is somewhere with Lady Laura, I believe; and really, Mr. Finn, I do not like it." Lady Baldock had heard that Phineas had quarrelled with Lord Brentford, but had not heard of the reconciliation. "Really, I do not like it. I am told that Mr. Kennedy is in the house, and nobody knows what may happen."

"Mr. Kennedy is not likely to say anything."

"One cannot tell. And when I hear that a woman is separated from her husband, I always think that she must have been imprudent. It may be uncharitable, but I think it is most safe so to consider."

"As far as I have heard the circumstances, Lady Laura was quite right," said Phineas.

"It may be so. Gentlemen will always take the lady's part,—of course. But I should be very sorry to have a daughter separated from her husband,—very sorry."

Phineas, who had nothing now to gain from Lady Baldock's favour, left her abruptly, and went on again. He had a great desire to see Lady Laura and Violet together, though he could hardly tell himself why. He had not seen Miss Effingham since his return from Ireland, and he thought that if he met her alone he could hardly have talked to her with comfort; but he knew that if he met her with Lady Laura, she would greet him as a friend, and speak to him as though there were no cause for embarrassment between them. But he was so far disappointed, that he suddenly encountered Violet alone. She had been leaning on the arm of Lord Baldock, and Phineas saw her cousin leave her. But he would not be such a coward as to avoid her, especially as he knew that she had seen him. "Oh, Mr. Finn!" she said, "do you see that?"

"See what?"

"Look; There is Mr. Kennedy. We had heard that it was possible, and Laura made me promise that I would not leave her." Phineas turned his head, and saw Mr. Kennedy standing with his back bolt upright against a door-post, with his brow as black as thunder. "She is just opposite to him, where he can see her," said Violet. "Pray take me to her. He will think nothing of you, because I know that you are still friends with both of them. I came away because Lord Baldock wanted to introduce me to Lady Mouser. You know he is going to marry Miss Mouser."

Phineas, not caring much about Lord Baldock and Miss Mouser, took Violet's hand upon his arm, and very slowly made his way across the room to the spot indicated. There they found Lady Laura alone, sitting under the upas-tree influence of her husband's gaze. There was a concourse of people between them, and Mr. Kennedy did not seem inclined to make any attempt to lessen the distance. But Lady Laura had found it impossible to move while she was under her husband's eyes.

"Mr. Finn," she said, "could you find Oswald? I know he is here."

"He has gone," said Phineas. "I was speaking to him downstairs."

"You have not seen my father? He said he would come."

"I have not seen him, but I will search."

"No;—it will do no good. I cannot stay. His carriage is there, I know,—waiting for me." Phineas immediately started off to have the carriage called, and promised to return with as much celerity as he could use. As he went, making his way much quicker through the crowd than he had done when he had no such object for haste, he purposely avoided the door by which Mr. Kennedy had stood. It would have been his nearest way, but his present service, he thought, required that he should keep aloof from the man. But Mr. Kennedy passed through the door and intercepted him in his path.

"Is she going?" he asked.

"Well. Yes. I dare say she may before long. I shall look for Lord Brentford's carriage by-and-by."

"Tell her she need not go because of me. I shall not return. I shall not annoy her here. It would have been much better that a woman in such a plight should not have come to such an assembly."

"You would not wish her to shut herself up."

"I would wish her to come back to the home that she has left, and, if there be any law in the land, she shall be made to do so. You tell her that I say so." Then Mr. Kennedy fought his way down the stairs, and Phineas Finn followed in his wake.

About half an hour afterwards Phineas returned to the two ladies with tidings that the carriage would be at hand as soon as they could be below. "Did he see you?" said Lady Laura.

"Yes, he followed me."

"And did he speak to you?"

"Yes;—he spoke to me."

"And what did he say?" And then, in the presence of Violet, Phineas gave the message. He thought it better that it should be given; and were he to decline to deliver it now, it would never be given. "Whether there be law in the land to protect me or whether there be none, I will never live with him," said Lady Laura. "Is a woman like a head of cattle, that she can be fastened in her crib by force? I will never live with him though all the judges of the land should decide that I must do so."

Phineas thought much of all this as he went to his solitary lodgings. After all, was not the world much better with him than it was with either of those two wretched married beings? And why? He had not, at any rate as yet, sacrificed for money or social gains any of the instincts of his nature. He had been fickle, foolish, vain, uncertain, and perhaps covetous;—but as yet he had not been false. Then he took out Mary's last letter and read it again.

CHAPTER LXXI. Comparing Notes

It would, perhaps, be difficult to decide,—between Lord Chiltern and Miss Effingham,—which had been most wrong, or which had been nearest to the right, in the circumstances which had led to their separation. The old lord, wishing to induce his son to undertake work of some sort, and feeling that his own efforts in this direction were worse than useless, had closeted himself with his intended daughter-in-law, and had obtained from her a promise that she would use her influence with her lover. "Of course I think it right that he should do something," Violet had said. "And he will if you bid him," replied the Earl. Violet expressed a great doubt as to this willingness of obedience; but, nevertheless, she promised to do her best, and she did her best. Lord Chiltern, when she spoke to him, knit his brows with an apparent ferocity of anger which his countenance frequently expressed without any intention of ferocity on his part. He was annoyed, but was not savagely disposed to Violet. As he looked at her, however, he seemed to be very savagely disposed. "What is it you would have me do?" he said.

"I would have you choose some occupation, Oswald."

"What occupation? What is it that you mean? Ought I to be a shoemaker?"

"Not that by preference, I should say; but that if you please." When her lover had frowned at her, Violet had resolved,—had strongly determined, with inward assertions of her own rights,—that she would not be frightened by him.

"You are talking nonsense, Violet. You know that I cannot be a shoemaker."

"You may go into Parliament."

"I neither can, nor would I if I could. I dislike the life."

"You might farm."

"I cannot afford it."

"You might,—might do anything. You ought to do something. You know that you ought. You know that your father is right in what he says."

"That is easily asserted, Violet; but it would, I think, be better that you should take my part than my father's, if it be that you intend to be my wife."

"You know that I intend to be your wife; but would you wish that I should respect my husband?"

"And will you not do so if you marry me?" he asked.

Then Violet looked into his face and saw that the frown was blacker than ever. The great mark down his forehead was deeper and more like an ugly wound than she had ever seen it; and his eyes sparkled with anger; and his face was red as with fiery wrath. If it was so with him when she was no more than engaged to him, how would it be when they should be man and wife? At any rate, she would not fear him,—not now at least. "No, Oswald," she said. "If you resolve upon being an idle man, I shall not respect you. It is better that I should tell you the truth."

"A great deal better," he said.

"How can I respect one whose whole life will be,—will be—?"

"Will be what?" he demanded with a loud shout.

"Oswald, you are very rough with me."

"What do you say that my life will be?"

Then she again resolved that she would not fear him. "It will be discreditable," she said.

"It shall not discredit you," he replied. "I will not bring disgrace on one I have loved so well. Violet, after what you have said, we had better part." She was still proud, still determined, and they did part. Though it nearly broke her heart to see him leave her, she bid him go. She hated herself afterwards for her severity to him; but, nevertheless, she would not submit to recall the words which she had spoken. She had thought him to be wrong, and, so thinking, had conceived it to be her duty and her privilege to tell him what she thought. But she had no wish to lose him;—no wish not to be his wife even, though he should be as idle as the wind. She was so constituted that she had never allowed him or any other man to be master of her heart,—till she had with a full purpose given her heart away. The day before she had resolved to give it to one man, she might, I think, have resolved to give it to another. Love had not conquered her, but had been taken into her service. Nevertheless, she could not now rid herself of her servant, when she found that his services would stand her no longer in good stead. She parted from Lord Chiltern with an assent, with an assured brow, and with much dignity in her gait; but as soon as she was alone she was a prey to remorse. She had declared to the man who was to have been her husband that his life was discreditable,—and, of course, no man would bear such language. Had Lord Chiltern borne it, he would not have been worthy of her love.

She herself told Lady Laura and Lord Brentford what had occurred,—and had told Lady Baldock also. Lady Baldock had, of course, triumphed,—and Violet sought her revenge by swearing that she would regret for ever the loss of so inestimable a gentleman. "Then why have you given him up, my dear?" demanded Lady Baldock. "Because I found that he was too good for me," said Violet. It may be doubtful whether Lady Baldock was not justified, when she declared that her niece was to her a care so harassing that no aunt known in history had ever been so troubled before.

Lord Brentford had fussed and fumed, and had certainly made things worse. He had quarrelled with his son, and then made it up, and then quarrelled again,—swearing that the fault must all be attributed to Chiltern's stubbornness and Chiltern's temper. Latterly, however, by Lady Laura's intervention, Lord Brentford and his son had again been reconciled, and the Earl endeavoured manfully to keep his tongue from disagreeable words, and his face from evil looks, when his son was present. "They will make it up," Lady Laura had said, "if you and I do not attempt to make it up for them. If we do, they will never come together." The Earl was convinced, and did his best. But the task was very difficult to him. How was he to keep his tongue off his son while his son was daily saying things of which any father,—any such father as Lord Brentford,—could not but disapprove? Lord Chiltern professed to disbelieve even in the wisdom of the House of Lords, and on one occasion asserted that it must be a great comfort to any Prime Minister to have three or four old women in the Cabinet. The father, when he heard this, tried to rebuke his son tenderly, strove even to be jocose. It was the one wish of his heart that Violet Effingham should be his daughter-in-law. But even with this wish he found it very hard to keep his tongue off Lord Chiltern.

When Lady Laura discussed the matter with Violet, Violet would always declare that there was no hope. "The truth is," she said on the morning of that day on which they both went to Mrs. Gresham's, "that though we like each other,—love each other, if you choose to say so,—we are not fit to be man and wife."

"And why not fit?"

"We are too much alike. Each is too violent, too headstrong, and too masterful."

"You, as the woman, ought to give way," said Lady Laura.

"But we do not always do just what we ought."

"I know how difficult it is for me to advise, seeing to what a pass I have brought myself."

"Do not say that, dear;—or rather do say it, for we have, both of us, brought ourselves to what you call a pass,—to such a pass that we are like to be able to live together and discuss it for the rest of our lives. The difference is, I take it, that you have not to accuse yourself, and that I have."

"I cannot say that I have not to accuse myself," said Lady Laura. "I do not know that I have done much wrong to Mr. Kennedy since I married him; but in marrying him I did him a grievous wrong."

"And he has avenged himself."

"We will not talk of vengeance. I believe he is wretched, and I know that I am;—and that has come of the wrong that I have done."

"I will make no man wretched," said Violet.

"Do you mean that your mind is made up against Oswald?"

"I mean that, and I mean much more. I say that I will make no man wretched. Your brother is not the only man who is so weak as to be willing to run the hazard."

"There is Lord Fawn."

"Yes, there is Lord Fawn, certainly. Perhaps I should not do him much harm; but then I should do him no good."

"And poor Phineas Finn."

"Yes;—there is Mr. Finn. I will tell you something, Laura. The only man I ever saw in the world whom I have thought for a moment that it was possible that I should like,—like enough to love as my husband,—except your brother, was Mr. Finn."

"And now?"

"Oh;—now; of course that is over," said Violet.

"It is over?"

"Quite over. Is he not going to marry Madame Goesler? I suppose all that is fixed by this time. I hope she will be good to him, and gracious, and let him have his own way, and give him his tea comfortably when he comes up tired from the House; for I confess that my heart is a little tender towards Phineas still. I should not like to think that he had fallen into the hands of a female Philistine."

"I do not think he will marry Madame Goesler."

"Why not?"

"I can hardly tell you;—but I do not think he will. And you loved him once,—eh, Violet?"

"Not quite that, my dear. It has been difficult with me to love. The difficulty with most girls, I fancy, is not to love. Mr. Finn, when I came to measure him in my mind, was not small, but he was never quite tall enough. One feels oneself to be a sort of recruiting sergeant, going about with a standard of inches. Mr. Finn was just half an inch too short. He lacks something in individuality. He is a little too much a friend to everybody."

"Shall I tell you a secret, Violet?"

"If you please, dear; though I fancy it is one I know already."

"He is the only man whom I ever loved," said Lady Laura.

"But it was too late when you learned to love him," said Violet.

"It was too late, when I was so sure of it as to wish that I had never seen Mr. Kennedy. I felt it coming on me, and I argued with myself that such a marriage would be bad for us both. At that moment there was trouble in the family, and I had not a shilling of my own."

"You had paid it for Oswald."

"At any rate, I had nothing;—and he had nothing. How could I have dared to think even of such a marriage?"

"Did he think of it, Laura?"

"I suppose he did."

"You know he did. Did you not tell me before?"

"Well;—yes. He thought of it. I had come to some foolish, half-sentimental resolution as to friendship, believing that he and I could be knit together by some adhesion of fraternal affection that should be void of offence to my husband; and in furtherance of this he was asked to Loughlinter when I went there, just after I had accepted Robert. He came down, and I measured him too, as you have done. I measured him, and I found that he wanted nothing to come up to the height required by my standard. I think I knew him better than you did."

"Very possibly;—but why measure him at all, when such measurement was useless?"

"Can one help such things? He came to me one day as I was sitting up by the Linter. You remember the place, where it makes its first leap."

"I remember it very well."

"So do I. Robert had shown it me as the fairest spot in all Scotland."

"And there this lover of ours sang his song to you?"

"I do not know what he told me then; but I know that I told him that I was engaged; and I felt when I told him so that my engagement was a sorrow to me. And it has been a sorrow from that day to this."

"And the hero, Phineas,—he is still dear to you?"

"Dear to me?"

"Yes. You would have hated me, had he become my husband? And you will hate Madame Goesler when she becomes his wife?"

"Not in the least. I am no dog in the manger. I have even gone so far as almost to wish, at certain moments, that you should accept him."

"And why?"

"Because he has wished it so heartily."

"One can hardly forgive a man for such speedy changes," said Violet.

"Was I not to forgive him;—I, who had turned myself away from him with a fixed purpose the moment that I found that he had made a mark upon my heart? I could not wipe off the mark, and yet I married. Was he not to try to wipe off his mark?"

"It seems that he wiped it off very quickly;—and since that he has wiped off another mark. One doesn't know how many marks he has wiped off. They are like the inn-keeper's score which he makes in chalk. A damp cloth brings them all away, and leaves nothing behind."

"What would you have?"

"There should be a little notch on the stick,—to remember by," said Violet. "Not that I complain, you know. I cannot complain, as I was not notched myself."

"You are silly, Violet."

"In not having allowed myself to be notched by this great champion?"

"A man like Mr. Finn has his life to deal with,—to make the most of it, and to divide it between work, pleasure, duty, ambition, and the rest of it as best he may. If he have any softness of heart, it will be necessary to him that love should bear a part in all these interests. But a man will be a fool who will allow love to be the master of them all. He will be one whose mind is so ill-balanced as to allow him to be the victim of a single wish. Even in a woman passion such as that is evidence of weakness, and not of strength."

"It seems, then, Laura, that you are weak."

"And if I am, does that condemn him? He is a man, if I judge him rightly, who will be constant as the sun, when constancy can be of service."

"You mean that the future Mrs. Finn will be secure?"

"That is what I mean;—and that you or I, had either of us chosen to take his name, might have been quite secure. We have thought it right to refuse to do so."

"And how many more, I wonder?"

"You are unjust, and unkind, Violet. So unjust and unkind that it is clear to me he has just gratified your vanity, and has never touched your heart. What would you have had him do, when I told him that I was engaged?"

"I suppose that Mr. Kennedy would not have gone to Blankenberg with him."

"Violet!"

"That seems to be the proper thing to do. But even that does not adjust things finally;—does it?" Then some one came upon them, and the conversation was brought to an end.

CHAPTER LXXII. Madame Goesler's Generosity

When Phineas Finn left Mr. Gresham's house he had quite resolved what he would do. On the next morning he would tell Lord Cantrip that his resignation was a necessity, and that he would take that nobleman's advice as to resigning at once, or waiting till the day on which Mr. Monk's Irish Bill would be read for the second time.

"My dear Finn, I can only say that I deeply regret it," said Lord Cantrip.

"So do I. I regret to leave office, which I like,—and which indeed I want. I regret specially to leave this office, as it has been a thorough pleasure to me; and I regret, above all, to leave you. But I am convinced that Monk is right, and I find it impossible not to support him."

"I wish that Mr. Monk was at Bath," said Lord Cantrip.

Phineas could only smile, and shrug his shoulders, and say that even though Mr. Monk were at Bath it would not probably make much difference. When he tendered his letter of resignation, Lord Cantrip begged him to withdraw it for a day or two. He would, he said, speak to Mr. Gresham. The debate on the second reading of Mr. Monk's bill would not take place till that day week, and the resignation would be in time if it was tendered before Phineas either spoke or voted against the Government. So Phineas went back to his room, and endeavoured to make himself useful in some work appertaining to his favourite Colonies.

That conversation had taken place on a Friday, and on the following Sunday, early in the day, he left his rooms after a late breakfast,—a prolonged breakfast, during which he had been studying tenant-right statistics, preparing his own speech, and endeavouring to look forward into the future which that speech was to do so much to influence,—and turned his face towards Park Lane. There had been a certain understanding between him and Madame Goesler that he was to call in Park Lane on this Sunday morning, and then declare to her what was his final resolve as to the office which he held. "It is simply to bid her adieu," he said to himself, "for I shall hardly see her again." And yet, as he took off his morning easy coat, and dressed himself for the streets, and stood for a moment before his looking-glass, and saw that his gloves were fresh and that his boots were properly polished, I think there was a care about his person which he would have hardly taken had he been quite assured that he simply intended to say good-bye to the lady whom he was about to visit. But if there were any such conscious feeling, he administered to himself an antidote before he left the house. On returning to the sitting-room he went to a little desk from which he took out the letter from Mary which the reader has seen, and carefully perused every word of it. "She is the best of them all," he said to himself, as he refolded the letter and put it back into his desk. I am not sure that it is well that a man should have any large number from whom to select a best; as, in such circumstances, he is so very apt to change his judgment from hour to hour. The qualities which are the most attractive before dinner sometimes become the least so in the evening.

The morning was warm, and he took a cab. It would not do that he should speak even his last farewell to such a one as Madame Goesler with all the heat and dust of a long walk upon him. Having been so careful about his boots and gloves he might as well use his care to the end. Madame Goesler was a very pretty woman, who spared herself no trouble in making herself as pretty as Nature would allow, on behalf of those whom she favoured with her smiles; and to such a lady some special attention was due by one who had received so many of her smiles as had Phineas. And he felt, too, that there was something special in this very visit. It was to be made by appointment, and there had come to be an understanding between them that Phineas should tell her on this occasion what was his resolution with reference to his future life. I think that he had been very wise in fortifying himself with a further glance at our dear Mary's letter, before he trusted himself within Madame Goesler's door.

Yes;—Madame Goesler was at home. The door was opened by Madame Goesler's own maid, who, smiling, explained that the other servants were all at church. Phineas had become sufficiently intimate at the cottage in Park Lane to be on friendly terms with Madame Goesler's own maid, and now made some little half-familiar remark as to the propriety of his visit during church time. "Madame will not refuse to see you, I am thinking," said the girl, who was a German. "And she is alone?" asked Phineas. "Alone? Yes;—of course she is alone. Who should be with her now?" Then she took him up into the drawing-room; but, when there, he found that Madame Goesler was absent. "She shall be down directly," said the girl. "I shall tell her who is here, and she will come."

It was a very pretty room. It may almost be said that there could be no prettier room in all London. It looked out across certain small private gardens,—which were as bright and gay as money could make them when brought into competition with London smoke,—right on to the park. Outside and inside the window, flowers and green things were so arranged that the room itself almost looked as though it were a bower in a garden. And everything in that bower was rich and rare; and there was nothing there which annoyed by its rarity or was distasteful by its richness. The seats, though they were costly as money could buy, were meant for sitting, and were comfortable as seats. There were books for reading, and the means of reading them. Two or three gems of English art were hung upon the walls, and could be seen backwards and forwards in the mirrors. And there were precious toys lying here and there about the room,—toys very precious, but placed there not because of their price, but because of their beauty. Phineas already knew enough of the art of living to be aware that the woman who had made that room what it was, had charms to add a beauty to everything she touched. What would such a life as his want, if graced by such a companion,—such a life as his might be, if the means which were hers were at his command? It would want one thing, he thought,—the self-respect which he would lose if he were false to the girl who was trusting him with such sweet trust at home in Ireland.

In a very few minutes Madame Goesler was with him, and, though he did not think about it, he perceived that she was bright in her apparel, that her hair was as soft as care could make it, and that every charm belonging to her had been brought into use for his gratification. He almost told himself that he was there in order that he might ask to have all those charms bestowed upon himself. He did not know who had lately come to Park Lane and been a suppliant for the possession of those rich endowments; but I wonder whether they would have been more precious in his eyes had he known that they had so moved the heart of the great Duke as to have induced him to lay his coronet at the lady's feet. I think that had he known that the lady had refused the coronet, that knowledge would have enhanced the value of the prize.

"I am so sorry to have kept you waiting," she said, as she gave him her hand. "I was an owl not to be ready for you when you told me that you would come."

"No;—but a bird of paradise to come to me so sweetly, and at an hour when all the other birds refuse to show the feather of a single wing."

"And you,—you feel like a naughty boy, do you not, in thus coming out on a Sunday morning?"

"Do you feel like a naughty girl?"

"Yes;—just a little so. I do not know that I should care for everybody to hear that I received visitors,—or worse still, a visitor,—at this hour on this day. But then it is so pleasant to feel oneself to be naughty! There is a Bohemian flavour of picnic about it which, though it does not come up to the rich gusto of real wickedness, makes one fancy that one is on the border of that delightful region in which there is none of the constraint of custom,—where men and women say what they like, and do what they like."

"It is pleasant enough to be on the borders," said Phineas.

"That is just it. Of course decency, morality, and propriety, all made to suit the eye of the public, are the things which are really delightful. We all know that, and live accordingly,—as well as we can. I do at least."

"And do not I, Madame Goesler?"

"I know nothing about that, Mr. Finn, and want to ask no questions. But if you do, I am sure you agree with me that you often envy the improper people,—the Bohemians,—the people who don't trouble themselves about keeping any laws except those for breaking which they would be put into nasty, unpleasant prisons. I envy them. Oh, how I envy them!"

"But you are free as air."

"The most cabined, cribbed, and confined creature in the world! I have been fighting my way up for the last four years, and have not allowed myself the liberty of one flirtation;—not often even the recreation of a natural laugh. And now I shouldn't wonder if I don't find myself falling back a year or two, just because I have allowed you to come and see me on a Sunday morning. When I told Lotta that you were coming, she shook her head at me in dismay. But now that you are here, tell me what you have done."

"Nothing as yet, Madame Goesler."

"I thought it was to have been settled on Friday?"

"It was settled,—before Friday. Indeed, as I look back at it all now, I can hardly tell when it was not settled. It is impossible, and has been impossible, that I should do otherwise. I still hold my place, Madame Goesler, but I have declared that I shall give it up before the debate comes on."

"It is quite fixed?"

"Quite fixed, my friend."

"And what next?" Madame Goesler, as she thus interrogated him, was leaning across towards him from the sofa on which she was placed, with both her elbows resting on a small table before her. We all know that look of true interest which the countenance of a real friend will bear when the welfare of his friend is in question. There are doubtless some who can assume it without feeling,—as there are actors who can personate all the passions. But in ordinary life we think that we can trust such a face, and that we know the true look when we see it. Phineas, as he gazed into Madame Goesler's eyes, was sure that the lady opposite him was not acting. She at least was anxious for his welfare, and was making his cares her own. "What next?" said she, repeating her words in a tone that was somewhat hurried.

"I do not know that there will be any next. As far as public life is concerned, there will be no next for me, Madame Goesler."

"That is out of the question," she said. "You are made for public life."

"Then I shall be untrue to my making, I fear. But to speak plainly—"

"Yes; speak plainly. I want to understand the reality."

"The reality is this. I shall keep my seat to the end of the session, as I think I may be of use. After that I shall give it up."

"Resign that too?" she said in a tone of chagrin.

"The chances are, I think, that there will be another dissolution. If they hold their own against Mr. Monk's motion, then they will pass an Irish Reform Bill. After that I think they must dissolve."

"And you will not come forward again?"

"I cannot afford it."

"Psha! Some five hundred pounds or so!"

"And, besides that, I am well aware that my only chance at my old profession is to give up all idea of Parliament. The two things are not compatible for a beginner at the law. I know it now, and have bought my knowledge by a bitter experience."

"And where will you live?"

"In Dublin, probably."

"And you will do,—will do what?"

"Anything honest in a barrister's way that may be brought to me. I hope that I may never descend below that."

"You will stand up for all the blackguards, and try to make out that the thieves did not steal?"

"It may be that that sort of work may come in my way."

"And you will wear a wig and try to look wise?"

"The wig is not universal in Ireland, Madame Goesler."

"And you will wrangle, as though your very soul were in it, for somebody's twenty pounds?"

"Exactly."

"You have already made a name in the greatest senate in the world, and have governed other countries larger than your own—"

"No;—I have not done that. I have governed no country.

"I tell you, my friend, that you cannot do it. It is out of the question. Men may move forward from little work to big work; but they cannot move back and do little work, when they have had tasks which were really great. I tell you, Mr. Finn, that the House of Parliament is the place for you to work in. It is the only place;—that and the abodes of Ministers. Am not I your friend who tell you this?"

"I know that you are my friend."

"And will you not credit me when I tell you this? What do you fear, that you should run away? You have no wife;—no children. What is the coming misfortune that you dread?" She paused a moment as though for an answer, and he felt that now had come the time in which it would be well that he should tell her of his engagement with his own Mary. She had received him very playfully; but now within the last few minutes there had come upon her a seriousness of gesture, and almost a solemnity of tone, which made him conscious that he should in no way trifle with her. She was so earnest in her friendship that he owed it to her to tell her everything. But before he could think of the words in which his tale should be told, she had gone on with her quick questions. "Is it solely about money that you fear?" she said.

"It is simply that I have no income on which to live."

"Have I not offered you money?"

"But, Madame Goesler, you who offer it would yourself despise me if I took it."

"No;—I do deny it." As she said this,—not loudly but with much emphasis,—she came and stood before him where he was sitting. And as he looked at her he could perceive that there was a strength about her of which he had not been aware. She was stronger, larger, more robust physically than he had hitherto conceived. "I do deny it," she said. "Money is neither god nor devil, that it should make one noble and another vile. It is an accident, and, if honestly possessed, may pass from you to me, or from me to you, without a stain. You may take my dinner from me if I give it you, my flowers, my friendship, my,—my,—my everything, but my money! Explain to me the cause of the phenomenon. If I give to you a thousand pounds, now this moment, and you take it, you are base;—but if I leave it you in my will,—and die,—you take it, and are not base. Explain to me the cause of that."

"You have not said it quite all," said Phineas hoarsely.

"What have I left unsaid? If I have left anything unsaid, do you say the rest."

"It is because you are a woman, and young, and beautiful, that no man may take wealth from your hands."

"Oh, it is that!"

"It is that partly,"

"If I were a man you might take it, though I were young and beautiful as the morning?"

"No;—presents of money are always bad. They stain and load the spirit, and break the heart."

"And specially when given by a woman's hand?"

"It seems so to me. But I cannot argue of it. Do not let us talk of it any more."

"Nor can I argue. I cannot argue, but I can be generous,—very generous. I can deny myself for my friend,—can even lower myself in my own esteem for my friend. I can do more than a man can do for a friend. You will not take money from my hand?"

"No, Madame Goesler;—I cannot do that."

"Take the hand then first. When it and all that it holds are your own, you can help yourself as you list." So saying, she stood before him with her right hand stretched out towards him.

What man will say that he would not have been tempted? Or what woman will declare that such temptation should have had no force? The very air of the room in which she dwelt was sweet in his nostrils, and there hovered around her an halo of grace and beauty which greeted all his senses. She invited him to join his lot to hers, in order that she might give to him all that was needed to make his life rich and glorious. How would the Ratlers and the Bonteens envy him when they heard of the prize which had become his! The Cantrips and the Greshams would feel that he was a friend doubly valuable, if he could be won back; and Mr. Monk would greet him as a fitting ally,—an ally strong with the strength which he had before wanted. With whom would he not be equal? Whom need he fear? Who would not praise him? The story of his poor Mary would be known only in a small village, out beyond the Channel. The temptation certainly was very strong.

But he had not a moment in which to doubt. She was standing there with her face turned from him, but with her hand still stretched towards him. Of course he took it. What man so placed could do other than take a woman's hand?

"My friend," he said.

"I will be called friend by you no more," she said. "You must call me Marie, your own Marie, or you must never call me by any name again. Which shall it be, sir?" He paused a moment, holding her hand, and she let it lie there for an instant while she listened. But still she did not look at him. "Speak to me! Tell me! Which shall it be?" Still he paused. "Speak to me. Tell me!" she said again.

"It cannot be as you have hinted to me," he said at last. His words did not come louder than a low whisper; but they were plainly heard, and instantly the hand was withdrawn.

"Cannot be!" she exclaimed. "Then I have betrayed myself."

"No;—Madame Goesler."

"Sir; I say yes! If you will allow me I will leave you. You will, I know, excuse me if I am abrupt to you." Then she strode out of the room, and was no more seen of the eyes of Phineas Finn.

He never afterwards knew how he escaped out of that room and found his way into Park Lane. In after days he had some memory that he remained there, he knew not how long, standing on the very spot on which she had left him; and that at last there grew upon him almost a fear of moving, a dread lest he should be heard, an inordinate desire to escape without the sound of a footfall, without the clicking of a lock. Everything in that house had been offered to him. He had refused it all, and then felt that of all human beings under the sun none had so little right to be standing there as he. His very presence in that drawing-room was an insult to the woman whom he had driven from it.

But at length he was in the street, and had found his way across Piccadilly into the Green Park. Then, as soon as he could find a spot apart from the Sunday world, he threw himself upon the turf; and tried to fix his thoughts upon the thing that he had done. His first feeling, I think, was one of pure and unmixed disappointment;—of disappointment so bitter, that even the vision of his own Mary did not tend to comfort him. How great might have been his success, and how terrible was his failure! Had he taken the woman's hand and her money, had he clenched his grasp on the great prize offered to him, his misery would have been ten times worse the first moment that he would have been away from her. Then, indeed,—it being so that he was a man with a heart within his breast,—there would have been no comfort for him, in his outlooks on any side. But even now, when he had done right,—knowing well that he had done right,—he found that comfort did not come readily within his reach.

CHAPTER LXXIII. Amantium Iræ

Miss Effingham's life at this time was not the happiest in the world. Her lines, as she once said to her friend Lady Laura, were not laid for her in pleasant places. Her residence was still with her aunt, and she had come to find that it was almost impossible any longer to endure Lady Baldock, and quite impossible to escape from Lady Baldock. In former days she had had a dream that she might escape, and live alone if she chose to be alone; that she might be independent in her life, as a man is independent, if she chose to live after that fashion; that she might take her own fortune in her own hand, as the law certainly allowed her to do, and act with it as she might please. But latterly she had learned to understand that all this was not possible for her. Though one law allowed it, another law disallowed it, and the latter law was at least as powerful as the former. And then her present misery was enhanced by the fact that she was now banished from the second home which she had formerly possessed. Hitherto she had always been able to escape from Lady Baldock to the house of her friend, but now such escape was out of the question. Lady Laura and Lord Chiltern lived in the same house, and Violet could not live with them.

Lady Baldock understood all this, and tortured her niece accordingly. It was not premeditated torture. The aunt did not mean to make her niece's life a burden to her, and, so intending, systematically work upon a principle to that effect. Lady Baldock, no doubt, desired to do her duty conscientiously. But the result was torture to poor Violet, and a strong conviction on the mind of each of the two ladies that the other was the most unreasonable being in the world.

The aunt, in these days, had taken it into her head to talk of poor Lord Chiltern. This arose partly from a belief that the quarrel was final, and that, therefore, there would be no danger in aggravating Violet by this expression of pity,—partly from a feeling that it would be better that her niece should marry Lord Chiltern than that she should not marry at all,—and partly, perhaps, from the general principle that, as she thought it right to scold her niece on all occasions, this might be best done by taking an opposite view of all questions to that taken by the niece to be scolded. Violet was supposed to regard Lord Chiltern as having sinned against her, and therefore Lady Baldock talked of "poor Lord Chiltern." As to the other lovers, she had begun to perceive that their conditions were hopeless. Her daughter Augusta had explained to her that there was no chance remaining either for Phineas, or for

Lord Fawn, or for Mr. Appledom. "I believe she will be an old maid, on purpose to
bring me to my grave," said Lady Baldock. When, therefore, Lady Baldock was
told one day that Lord Chiltern was in the house, and was asking to see Miss
Effingham, she did not at once faint away, and declare that they would all be
murdered,—as she would have done some months since. She was perplexed by a
double duty. If it were possible that Violet should relent and be reconciled, then it
would be her duty to save Violet from the claws of the wild beast. But if there was
no such chance, then it would be her duty to poor Lord Chiltern to see that he was
not treated with contumely and ill-humour.

"Does she know that he is here?" Lady Baldock asked her daughter.

"Not yet, mamma."

"Oh dear, oh dear! I suppose she ought to see him. She has given him so much
encouragement!"

"I suppose she will do as she pleases, mamma."

"Augusta, how can you talk in that way? Am I to have no control in my own
house?" It was, however, soon apparent to her that in this matter she was to have
no control.

"Lord Chiltern is down-stairs," said Violet, coming into the room abruptly.

"So Augusta tells me. Sit down, my dear."

"I cannot sit down, aunt,—not just now. I have sent down to say that I would be
with him in a minute. He is the most impatient soul alive, and I must not keep him
waiting."

"And you mean to see him?"

"Certainly I shall see him," said Violet, as she left the room.

"I wonder that any woman should ever take upon herself the charge of a niece!"
said Lady Baldock to her daughter in a despondent tone, as she held up her hands
in dismay. In the meantime, Violet had gone down-stairs with a quick step, and had
then boldly entered the room in which her lover was waiting to receive her.

"I have to thank you for coming to me, Violet," said Lord Chiltern. There was still
in his face something of savagery,—an expression partly of anger and partly of
resolution to tame the thing with which he was angry. Violet did not regard the
anger half so keenly as she did that resolution of taming. An angry lord, she
thought, she could endure, but she could not bear the idea of being tamed by any
one.

"Why should I not come?" she said. "Of course I came when I was told that you were here. I do not think that there need be a quarrel between us, because we have changed our minds."

"Such changes make quarrels," said he.

"It shall not do so with me, unless you choose that it shall," said Violet. "Why should we be enemies,—we who have known each other since we were children? My dearest friends are your father and your sister. Why should we be enemies?"

"I have come to ask you whether you think that I have ill-used you?"

"Ill-used me! Certainly not. Has any one told you that I have accused you?"

"No one has told me so."

"Then why do you ask me?"

"Because I would not have you think so,—if I could help it. I did not intend to be rough with you. When you told me that my life was disreputable—"

"Oh, Oswald, do not let us go back to that. What good will it do?"

"But you said so."

"I think not."

"I believe that that was your word,—the harshest word that you could use in all the language."

"I did not mean to be harsh. If I used it, I will beg your pardon. Only let there be an end of it. As we think so differently about life in general, it was better that we should not be married. But that is settled, and why should we go back to words that were spoken in haste, and which are simply disagreeable?"

"I have come to know whether it is settled."

"Certainly. You settled it yourself, Oswald. I told you what I thought myself bound to tell you. Perhaps I used language which I should not have used. Then you told me that I could not be your wife;—and I thought you were right, quite right."

"I was wrong, quite wrong," he said impetuously. "So wrong, that I can never forgive myself, if you do not relent. I was such a fool, that I cannot forgive myself my folly. I had known before that I could not live without you; and when you were mine, I threw you away for an angry word."

"It was not an angry word," she said.

"Say it again, and let me have another chance to answer it."

"I think I said that idleness was not,—respectable, or something like that, taken out of a copy-book probably. But you are a man who do not like rebukes, even out of copy-books. A man so thin-skinned as you are must choose for himself a wife with a softer tongue than mine."

"I will choose none other!" he said. But still he was savage in his tone and in his gestures. "I made my choice long since, as you know well enough. I do not change easily. I cannot change in this. Violet, say that you will be my wife once more, and I will swear to work for you like a coal-heaver."

"My wish is that my husband,—should I ever have one,—should work, not exactly as a coal-heaver."

"Come, Violet," he said,—and now the look of savagery departed from him, and there came a smile over his face, which, however, had in it more of sadness than of hope or joy,—"treat me fairly,—or rather, treat me generously if you can. I do not know whether you ever loved me much."

"Very much,—years ago, when you were a boy."

"But not since? If it be so, I had better go. Love on one side only is a poor affair at best."

"A very poor affair."

"It is better to bear anything than to try and make out life with that. Some of you women never want to love any one."

"That was what I was saying of myself to Laura but the other day. With some women it is so easy. With others it is so difficult, that perhaps it never comes to them."

"And with you?"

"Oh, with me—. But it is better in these matters to confine oneself to generalities. If you please, I will not describe myself personally. Were I to do so, doubtless I should do it falsely."

"You love no one else, Violet?"

"That is my affair, my lord."

"By heavens, and it is mine too. Tell me that you do, and I will go away and leave you at once. I will not ask his name, and I will trouble you no more. If it is not so, and if it is possible that you should forgive me—"

"Forgive you! When have I been angry with you?"

"Answer me my question, Violet."

"I will not answer you your question,—not that one."

"What question will you answer?"

"Any that may concern yourself and myself. None that may concern other people."

"You told me once that you loved me."

"This moment I told you that I did so,—years ago."

"But now?"

"That is another matter."

"Violet, do you love me now?"

"That is a point-blank question at any rate," she said.

"And you will answer it?"

"I must answer it,—I suppose."

"Well, then?"

"Oh, Oswald, what a fool you are! Love you! of course I love you. If you can understand anything, you ought to know that I have never loved any one else;—that after what has passed between us, I never shall love any one else. I do love you. There. Whether you throw me away from you, as you did the other day,—with great scorn, mind you,—or come to me with sweet, beautiful promises, as you do now, I shall love you all the same. I cannot be your wife, if you will not have me; can I? When you run away in your tantrums because I quote something out of the copy-book, I can't run after you. It would not be pretty. But as for loving you, if you doubt that, I tell you, you are a—fool." As she spoke the last words she pouted out her lips at him, and when he looked into her face he saw that her eyes were full of tears. He was standing now with his arm round her waist, so that it was not easy for him to look into her face.

"I am a fool," he said.

"Yes;—you are; but I don't love you the less on that account."

"I will never doubt it again."

"No;—do not; and, for me, I will not say another word, whether you choose to heave coals or not. You shall do as you please. I meant to be very wise;—I did indeed."

"You are the grandest girl that ever was made."

"I do not want to be grand at all, and I never will be wise any more. Only do not frown at me and look savage." Then she put up her hand to smooth his brow. "I am half afraid of you still, you know. There. That will do. Now let me go, that I may tell my aunt. During the last two months she has been full of pity for poor Lord Chiltern."

"It has been poor Lord Chiltern with a vengeance!" said he.

"But now that we have made it up, she will be horrified again at all your wickednesses. You have been a turtle dove lately;—now you will be an ogre again. But, Oswald, you must not be an ogre to me."

As soon as she could get quit of her lover, she did tell her tale to Lady Baldock. "You have accepted him again!" said her aunt, holding up her hands. "Yes,—I have accepted him again," replied Violet. "Then the responsibility must be on your own shoulders," said her aunt; "I wash my hands of it." That evening, when she discussed the matter with her daughter, Lady Baldock spoke of Violet and Lord Chiltern, as though their intended marriage were the one thing in the world which she most deplored.

CHAPTER LXXIV. The Beginning of the End

The day of the debate had come, and Phineas Finn was still sitting in his room at the Colonial Office. But his resignation had been sent in and accepted, and he was simply awaiting the coming of his successor. About noon his successor came, and he had the gratification of resigning his arm-chair to Mr. Bonteen. It is generally understood that gentlemen leaving offices give up either seals or a portfolio. Phineas had been put in possession of no seal and no portfolio; but there was in the room which he had occupied a special arm-chair, and this with much regret he surrendered to the use and comfort of Mr. Bonteen. There was a glance of triumph in his enemy's eyes, and an exultation in the tone of his enemy's voice, which were very bitter to him. "So you are really going?" said Mr. Bonteen. "Well; I dare say it is all very proper. I don't quite understand the thing myself, but I have no doubt you are right." "It isn't easy to understand; is it?" said Phineas, trying to laugh. But Mr. Bonteen did not feel the intended satire, and poor Phineas found it useless to attempt to punish the man he hated. He left him as quickly as he could, and went to say a few words of farewell to his late chief.

"Good-bye, Finn," said Lord Cantrip. "It is a great trouble to me that we should have to part in this way."

"And to me also, my lord. I wish it could have been avoided."

"You should not have gone to Ireland with so dangerous a man as Mr. Monk. But it is too late to think of that now."

"The milk is spilt; is it not?"

"But these terrible rendings asunder never last very long," said Lord Cantrip, "unless a man changes his opinions altogether. How many quarrels and how many reconciliations we have lived to see! I remember when Gresham went out of office, because he could not sit in the same room with Mr. Mildmay, and yet they became the fastest of political friends. There was a time when Plinlimmon and the Duke could not stable their horses together at all; and don't you remember when Palliser was obliged to give up his hopes of office because he had some bee in his bonnet?" I think, however, that the bee in Mr. Palliser's bonnet to which Lord Cantrip was alluding made its buzzing audible on some subject that was not exactly political. "We shall have you back again before long, I don't doubt. Men who can really do their work are too rare to be left long in the comfort of the benches below the gangway." This was very kindly said, and Phineas was flattered and comforted. He could not, however, make Lord Cantrip understand the whole truth. For him the dream of a life of politics was over for ever. He had tried it, and had succeeded beyond his utmost hopes; but, in spite of his success, the ground had crumbled to pieces beneath his feet, and he knew that he could never recover the niche in the world's gallery which he was now leaving.

That same afternoon he met Mr. Gresham in one of the passages leading to the House, and the Prime Minister put his arm through that of our hero as they walked together into the lobby. "I am sorry that we are losing you," said Mr. Gresham.

"You may be sure that I am sorry to be so lost," said Phineas.

"These things will occur in political life," said the leader; "but I think that they seldom leave rancour behind them when the purpose is declared, and when the subject of disagreement is marked and understood. The defalcation which creates angry feeling is that which has to be endured without previous warning,—when a man votes against his party,—or a set of men, from private pique or from some cause which is never clear." Phineas, when he heard this, knew well how terribly this very man had been harassed, and driven nearly wild, by defalcation, exactly of that nature which he was attempting to describe. "No doubt you and Mr. Monk think you are right," continued Mr. Gresham.

"We have given strong evidence that we think so," said Phineas. "We give up our places, and we are, both of us, very poor men."

"I think you are wrong, you know, not so much in your views on the question itself—which, to tell the truth, I hardly understand as yet."

"We will endeavour to explain them."

"And will do so very clearly, no doubt. But I think that Mr. Monk was wrong in desiring, as a member of a Government, to force a measure which, whether good or bad, the Government as a body does not desire to initiate,—at any rate, just now."

"And therefore he resigned," said Phineas.

"Of course. But it seems to me that he failed to comprehend the only way in which a great party can act together, if it is to do any service in this country. Don't for a moment think that I am blaming him or you."

"I am nobody in this matter," said Phineas.

"I can assure you, Mr. Finn, that we have not regarded you in that light, and I hope that the time may come when we may be sitting together again on the same bench."

Neither on the Treasury bench nor on any other in that House was he to sit again after this fashion! That was the trouble which was crushing his spirit at this moment, and not the loss of his office! He knew that he could not venture to think of remaining in London as a member of Parliament with no other income than that which his father could allow him, even if he could again secure a seat in Parliament. When he had first been returned for Loughshane he had assured his friends that his duty as a member of the House of Commons would not be a bar to his practice in the Courts. He had now been five years a member, and had never once made an attempt at doing any part of a barrister's work. He had gone altogether into a different line of life, and had been most successful;—so successful that men told him, and women more frequently than men, that his career had been a miracle of success. But there had been, as he had well known from the first, this drawback in the new profession which he had chosen, that nothing in it could be permanent. They who succeed in it, may probably succeed again; but then the success is intermittent, and there may be years of hard work in opposition, to which, unfortunately, no pay is assigned. It is almost imperative, as he now found, that they who devote themselves to such a profession should be men of fortune. When he had commenced his work,—at the period of his first return for Loughshane,—he had had no thought of mending his deficiency in this respect by a rich marriage. Nor had it ever occurred to him that he would seek a marriage for that purpose. Such an idea would have been thoroughly distasteful to him. There had been no stain of premeditated mercenary arrangement upon him at any time. But circumstances had so fallen out with him, that as he won his spurs in Parliament, as he became known, and was placed first in one office and then in another, prospects of love and money together were opened to him, and he ventured on, leaving Mr. Low and the law behind him,—because these prospects were so alluring. Then had come Mr. Monk and Mary Flood Jones,—and everything around him had collapsed.

Everything around him had collapsed,—with, however, a terrible temptation to him to inflate his sails again, at the cost of his truth and his honour. The temptation would have affected him not at all, had Madame Goesler been ugly, stupid, or personally disagreeable. But she was, he thought, the most beautiful woman he had ever seen, the most witty, and in many respects the most charming. She had offered to give him everything that she had, so to place him in the world that opposition would be more pleasant to him than office, to supply every want, and had done so in a manner that had gratified all his vanity. But he had refused it all, because he was bound to the girl at Floodborough. My readers will probably say that he was not a true man unless he could do this without a regret. When Phineas thought of it all, there were many regrets.

But there was at the same time a resolve on his part, that if any man had ever loved the girl he promised to love, he would love Mary Flood Jones. A thousand times he had told himself that she had not the spirit of Lady Laura, or the bright wit of Violet Effingham, or the beauty of Madame Goesler. But Mary had charms of her own that were more valuable than them all. Was there one among the three who had trusted him as she trusted him,—or loved him with the same satisfied devotion? There were regrets, regrets that were heavy on his heart;—for London, and Parliament, and the clubs, and Downing Street, had become dear to him. He liked to think of himself as he rode in the park, and was greeted by all those whose greeting was the most worth having. There were regrets,—sad regrets. But the girl whom he loved better than the parks and the clubs,—better even than Westminster and Downing Street, should never know that they had existed.

These thoughts were running through his mind even while he was listening to Mr. Monk, as he propounded his theory of doing justice to Ireland. This might probably be the last great debate in which Phineas would be able to take a part, and he was determined that he would do his best in it. He did not intend to speak on this day, if, as was generally supposed, the House would be adjourned before a division could be obtained. But he would remain on the alert and see how the thing went. He had come to understand the forms of the place, and was as well-trained a young member of Parliament as any there. He had been quick at learning a lesson that is not easily learned, and knew how things were going, and what were the proper moments for this question or that form of motion. He could anticipate a count-out, understood the tone of men's minds, and could read the gestures of the House. It was very little likely that the debate should be over to-night. He knew that; and as the present time was the evening of Tuesday, he resolved at once that he would speak as early as he could on the following Thursday. What a pity it was, that with one who had learned so much, all his learning should be in vain!

At about two o'clock, he himself succeeded in moving the adjournment of the debate. This he did from a seat below the gangway, to which he had removed himself from the Treasury bench. Then the House was up, and he walked home with Mr. Monk. Mr. Monk, since he had been told positively by Phineas that he had resolved upon resigning his office, had said nothing more of his sorrow at his friend's resolve, but had used him as one political friend uses another, telling him all his thoughts and all his hopes as to this new measure of his, and taking counsel with him as to the way in which the fight should be fought. Together they had counted over the list of members, marking these men as supporters, those as opponents, and another set, now more important than either, as being doubtful. From day to day those who had been written down as doubtful were struck off that third list, and put in either the one or the other of those who were either supporters or opponents. And their different modes of argument were settled between these two allied orators, how one should take this line and the other that. To Mr. Monk this was very pleasant. He was quite assured now that opposition was more congenial to his spirit, and more fitting for him than office. There was no doubt to him as to his future sitting in Parliament, let the result of this contest be what it might. The work which he was now doing, was the work for which he had been training himself all his life. While he had been forced to attend Cabinet Councils from week to week, he had been depressed. Now he was exultant. Phineas seeing and understanding all this, said but little to his friend of his own prospects. As long as this pleasant battle was raging, he could fight in it shoulder to shoulder with the man he loved. After that there would be a blank.

"I do not see how we are to fail to have a majority after Daubeny's speech to-night," said Mr. Monk, as they walked together down Parliament Street through the bright moonlight.

"He expressly said that he only spoke for himself," said Phineas.

"But we know what that means. He is bidding for office, and of course those who want office with him will vote as he votes. We have already counted those who would go into office, but they will not carry the whole party."

"It will carry enough of them."

"There are forty or fifty men on his side of the House, and as many perhaps on ours," said Mr. Monk, "who have no idea of any kind on any bill, and who simply follow the bell, whether into this lobby or that. Argument never touches them. They do not even look to the result of a division on their own interests, as the making of any calculation would be laborious to them. Their party leader is to them a Pope whom they do not dream of doubting. I never can quite make up my mind whether it is good or bad that there should be such men in Parliament."

"Men who think much want to speak often," said Phineas.

"Exactly so,—and of speaking members, God knows that we have enough. And I suppose that these purblind sheep do have some occult weight that is salutary. They enable a leader to be a leader, and even in that way they are useful. We shall get a division on Thursday."

"I understand that Gresham has consented to that."

"So Ratler told me. Palliser is to speak, and Barrington Erle. And they say that Robson is going to make an onslaught specially on me. We shall get it over by one o'clock."

"And if we beat them?" asked Phineas.

"It will depend on the numbers. Everybody who has spoken to me about it, seems to think that they will dissolve if there be a respectable majority against them."

"Of course he will dissolve," said Phineas, speaking of Mr. Gresham; "what else can he do?"

"He is very anxious to carry his Irish Reform Bill first, if he can do so. Good-night, Phineas. I shall not be down to-morrow as there is nothing to be done. Come to me on Thursday, and we will go to the House together."

On the Wednesday Phineas was engaged to dine with Mr. Low. There was a dinner party in Bedford Square, and Phineas met half-a-dozen barristers and their wives,—men to whom he had looked up as successful pundits in the law some five or six years ago, but who since that time had almost learned to look up to him. And now they treated him with that courteousness of manner which success in life always begets. There was a judge there who was very civil to him; and the judge's wife whom he had taken down to dinner was very gracious to him. The judge had got his prize in life, and was therefore personally indifferent to the fate of ministers; but the judge's wife had a brother who wanted a County Court from Lord De Terrier, and it was known that Phineas was giving valuable assistance towards the attainment of this object. "I do think that you and Mr. Monk are so right," said the judge's wife. Phineas, who understood how it came to pass that the judge's wife should so cordially approve his conduct, could not help thinking how grand a thing it would be for him to have a County Court for himself.

When the guests were gone he was left alone with Mr. and Mrs. Low, and remained awhile with them, there having been an understanding that they should have a last chat together over the affairs of our hero. "Do you really mean that you will not stand again?" asked Mrs. Low.

"I do mean it. I may say that I cannot do so. My father is hardly so well able to help me as he was when I began this game, and I certainly shall not ask him for money to support a canvass."

"It's a thousand pities," said Mrs. Low.

"I really had begun to think that you would make it answer," said Mr. Low.

"In one way I have made it answer. For the last three years I have lived upon what I have earned, and I am not in debt. But now I must begin the world again. I am afraid I shall find the drudgery very hard."

"It is hard no doubt," said the barrister, who had gone through it all, and was now reaping the fruits of it. "But I suppose you have not forgotten what you learned?"

"Who can say? I dare say I have. But I did not mean the drudgery of learning, so much as the drudgery of looking after work;—of expecting briefs which perhaps will never come. I am thirty years old now, you know."

"Are you indeed?" said Mrs. Low,—who knew his age to a day. "How the time passes. I'm sure I hope you'll get on, Mr. Finn. I do indeed."

"I am sure he will, if he puts his shoulder to it," said Mr. Low.

Neither the lawyer nor his wife repeated any of those sententious admonitions, which had almost become rebukes, and which had been so common in their mouths. The fall with which they had threatened Phineas Finn had come upon him, and they were too generous to remind him of their wisdom and sagacity. Indeed, when he got up to take his leave, Mrs. Low, who probably might not see him again for years, was quite affectionate in her manners to him, and looked as if she were almost minded to kiss him as she pressed his hand. "We will come and see you," she said, "when you are Master of the Rolls in Dublin."

"We shall see him before then thundering at us poor Tories in the House," said Mr. Low. "He will be back again sooner or later." And so they parted.

CHAPTER LXXV. P. P. C.

On the Thursday morning before Phineas went to Mr. Monk, a gentleman called upon him at his lodgings. Phineas requested the servant to bring up the gentleman's name, but tempted perhaps by a shilling the girl brought up the gentleman instead. It was Mr. Quintus Slide from the office of the "Banner of the People."

"Mr. Finn," said Quintus, with his hand extended, "I have come to offer you the calumet of peace." Phineas certainly desired no such calumet. But to refuse a man's hand is to declare active war after a fashion which men do not like to adopt except on deliberation. He had never cared a straw for the abuse which Mr. Slide had poured upon him, and now he gave his hand to the man of letters. But he did not sit down, nor did he offer a seat to Mr. Slide. "I know that as a man of sense who knows the world, you will accept the calumet of peace," continued Mr. Slide.

"I don't know why I should be asked particularly to accept war or peace," said Phineas.

"Well, Mr. Finn,—I don't often quote the Bible; but those who are not for us must be against us. You will agree to that. Now that you've freed yourself from the iniquities of that sink of abomination in Downing Street, I look upon you as a man again."

"Upon my word you are very kind."

"As a man and also a brother. I suppose you know that I've got the *Banner* into my own 'ands now." Phineas was obliged to explain that he had not hitherto been made acquainted with this great literary and political secret. "Oh dear, yes, altogether so. We've got rid of old Rusty as I used to call him. He wouldn't go the pace, and so we stripped him. He's doing the *West of England Art Journal* now, and he 'angs out down at Bristol."

"I hope he'll succeed, Mr. Slide."

"He'll earn his wages. He's a man who will always earn his wages, but nothing more. Well, now, Mr. Finn, I will just offer you one word of apology for our little severities."

"Pray do nothing of the kind."

"Indeed I shall. Dooty is dooty. There was some things printed which were a little rough, but if one isn't a little rough there ain't no flavour. Of course I wrote 'em. You know my 'and, I dare say."

"I only remember that there was some throwing of mud."

"Just so. But mud don't break any bones; does it? When you turned against us I had to be down on you, and I was down upon you;—that's just about all of it. Now you're coming among us again, and so I come to you with a calumet of peace."

"But I am not coming among you."

"Yes you are, Finn, and bringing Monk with you." It was now becoming very disagreeable, and Phineas was beginning to perceive that it would soon be his turn to say something rough. "Now I'll tell you what my proposition is. If you'll do us two leaders a week through the session, you shall have a cheque for L16 on the last day of every month. If that's not honester money than what you got in Downing Street, my name is not Quintus Slide."

"Mr. Slide," said Phineas,—and then he paused.

"If we are to come to business, drop the Mister. It makes things go so much easier."

"We are not to come to business, and I do not want things to go easy. I believe you said some things of me in your newspaper that were very scurrilous."

"What of that? If you mind that sort of thing—"

"I did not regard it in the least. You are quite welcome to continue it. I don't doubt but you will continue it. But you are not welcome to come here afterwards."

"Do you mean to turn me out?"

"Just that. You printed a heap of lies—"

"Lies, Mr. Finn! Did you say lies, sir?"

"I said lies;—lies;—lies!" And Phineas walked over at him as though he were going to pitch him instantly out of the window. "You may go and write as many more as you like. It is your trade, and you must do it or starve. But do not come to me again." Then he opened the door and stood with it in his hand.

"Very well, sir. I shall know how to punish this."

"Exactly. But if you please you'll go and do your punishment at the office of the *Banner*,—unless you like to try it here. You want to kick me and spit at me, but you will prefer to do it in print."

"Yes, sir," said Quintus Slide. "I shall prefer to do it in print,—though I must own that the temptation to adopt the manual violence of a ruffian is great, very great, very great indeed." But he resisted the temptation and walked down the stairs, concocting his article as he went.

Mr. Quintus Slide did not so much impede the business of his day but what Phineas was with Mr. Monk by two, and in his place in the House when prayers were read at four. As he sat in his place, conscious of the work that was before him, listening to the presentation of petitions, and to the formal reading of certain notices of motions, which with the asking of sundry questions occupied over half an hour, he looked back and remembered accurately his own feelings on a certain night on which he had intended to get up and address the House. The ordeal before him had then been so terrible, that it had almost obliterated for the moment his senses of hearing and of sight. He had hardly been able to perceive what had been going on around him, and had vainly endeavoured to occupy himself in recalling to his memory the words which he wished to pronounce. When the time for pronouncing them had come, he had found himself unable to stand upon his legs. He smiled as he recalled all this in his memory, waiting impatiently for the moment in which he might rise. His audience was assured to him now, and he did not fear it. His opportunity for utterance was his own, and even the Speaker could not deprive him of it. During these minutes he thought not at all of the words that he was to say. He had prepared his matter but had prepared no words. He knew that words would come readily enough to him, and that he had learned the task of turning his thoughts quickly into language while standing with a crowd of listeners around him,—as a practised writer does when seated in his chair. There was no violent beating at his heart now, no dimness of the eyes, no feeling that the ground was turning round under his feet. If only those weary vain questions would get themselves all asked, so that he might rise and begin the work of the night. Then there came the last thought as the House was hushed for his rising. What was the good of it all, when he would never have an opportunity of speaking there again?

But not on that account would he be slack in his endeavour now. He would be listened to once at least, not as a subaltern of the Government but as the owner of a voice prominent in opposition to the Government. He had been taught by Mr. Monk that that was the one place in the House in which a man with a power of speaking could really enjoy pleasure without alloy. He would make the trial,—once, if never again. Things had so gone with him that the rostrum was his own, and a House crammed to overflowing was there to listen to him. He had given up his place in order that he might be able to speak his mind, and had become aware that many intended to listen to him while he spoke. He had observed that the rows of strangers were thick in the galleries, that peers were standing in the passages, and that over the reporter's head, the ribbons of many ladies were to be seen through the bars of their cage. Yes;—for this once he would have an audience.

He spoke for about an hour, and while he was speaking he knew nothing about himself, whether he was doing it well or ill. Something of himself he did say soon after he had commenced,—not quite beginning with it, as though his mind had been laden with the matter. He had, he said, found himself compelled to renounce his happy allegiance to the First Lord of the Treasury, and to quit the pleasant company in which, humble as had been his place, he had been allowed to sit and act, by his unfortunate conviction in this great subject. He had been told, he said, that it was a misfortune in itself for one so young as he to have convictions. But his Irish birth and Irish connection had brought this misfortune of his country so closely home to him that he had found the task of extricating himself from it to be impossible. Of what further he said, speaking on that terribly unintelligible subject, a tenant-right proposed for Irish farmers, no English reader will desire to know much. Irish subjects in the House of Commons are interesting or are dull, are debated before a crowded audience composed of all who are leaders in the great world of London, or before empty benches, in accordance with the importance of the moment and the character of the debate. For us now it is enough to know that to our hero was accorded that attention which orators love,—which will almost make an orator if it can be assured. A full House with a promise of big type on the next morning would wake to eloquence the propounder of a Canadian grievance, or the mover of an Indian budget.

Phineas did not stir out of the House till the division was over, having agreed with Mr. Monk that they two would remain through it all and hear everything that was to be said. Mr. Gresham had already spoken, and to Mr. Palliser was confided the task of winding up the argument for the Government. Mr. Robson spoke also, greatly enlivening the tedium of the evening, and to Mr. Monk was permitted the privilege of a final reply. At two o'clock the division came, and the Ministry were beaten by a majority of twenty-three. "And now," said Mr. Monk, as he again walked home with Phineas, "the pity is that we are not a bit nearer tenant-right than we were before."

"But we are nearer to it."

"In one sense, yes. Such a debate and such a majority will make men think. But no;—think is too high a word; as a rule men don't think. But it will make them believe that there is something in it. Many who before regarded legislation on the subject as chimerical, will now fancy that it is only dangerous, or perhaps not more than difficult. And so in time it will come to be looked on as among the things possible, then among the things probable;—and so at last it will be ranged in the list of those few measures which the country requires as being absolutely needed. That is the way in which public opinion is made."

"It is no loss of time," said Phineas, "to have taken the first great step in making it."

"The first great step was taken long ago," said Mr. Monk,—"taken by men who were looked upon as revolutionary demagogues, almost as traitors, because they took it. But it is a great thing to take any step that leads us onwards."

Two days after this Mr. Gresham declared his intention of dissolving the House because of the adverse division which had been produced by Mr. Monk's motion, but expressed a wish to be allowed to carry an Irish Reform Bill through Parliament before he did so. He explained how expedient this would be, but declared at the same time that if any strong opposition were made, he would abandon the project. His intention simply was to pass with regard to Ireland a measure which must be passed soon, and which ought to be passed before a new election took place. The bill was ready, and should be read for the first time on the next night, if the House were willing. The House was willing, though there were very many recalcitrant Irish members. The Irish members made loud opposition, and then twitted Mr. Gresham with his promise that he would not go on with his bill, if opposition were made. But, nevertheless, he did go on, and the measure was hurried through the two Houses in a week. Our hero who still sat for Loughshane, but who was never to sit for Loughshane again, gave what assistance he could to the Government, and voted for the measure which deprived Loughshane for ever of its parliamentary honours.

"And very dirty conduct I think it was," said Lord Tulla, when he discussed the subject with his agent. "After being put in for the borough twice, almost free of expense, it was very dirty." It never occurred to Lord Tulla that a member of Parliament might feel himself obliged to vote on such a subject in accordance with his judgment.

This Irish Reform Bill was scrambled through the two Houses, and then the session was over. The session was over, and they who knew anything of the private concerns of Mr. Phineas Finn were aware that he was about to return to Ireland, and did not intend to reappear on the scene which had known him so well for the last five years. "I cannot tell you how sad it makes me," said Mr. Monk.

"And it makes me sad too," said Phineas. "I try to shake off the melancholy, and tell myself from day to day that it is unmanly. But it gets the better of me just at present."

"I feel quite certain that you will come back among us again," said Mr. Monk.

"Everybody tells me so; and yet I feel quite certain that I shall never come back,—never come back with a seat in Parliament. As my old tutor, Low, has told me scores of times, I began at the wrong end. Here I am, thirty years of age, and I have not a shilling in the world, and I do not know how to earn one."

"Only for me you would still be receiving ever so much a year, and all would be pleasant," said Mr. Monk.

"But how long would it have lasted? The first moment that Daubeny got the upper hand I should have fallen lower than I have fallen now. If not this year, it would have been the next. My only comfort is in this,—that I have done the thing myself, and have not been turned out." To the very last, however, Mr. Monk continued to express his opinion that Phineas would come back, declaring that he had known no instance of a young man who had made himself useful in Parliament, and then had been allowed to leave it in early life.

Among those of whom he was bound to take a special leave, the members of the family of Lord Brentford were, of course, the foremost. He had already heard of the reconciliation of Miss Effingham and Lord Chiltern, and was anxious to offer his congratulation to both of them. And it was essential to him that he should see Lady Laura. To her he wrote a line, saying how much he hoped that he should be able to bid her adieu, and a time was fixed for his coming at which she knew that she would meet him alone. But, as chance ruled it, he came upon the two lovers together, and then remembered that he had hardly ever before been in the same room with both of them at the same time.

"Oh, Mr. Finn, what a beautiful speech you made. I read every word of it," said Violet.

"And I didn't even look at it, old fellow," said Chiltern, getting up and putting his arm on the other's shoulder in a way that was common with him when he was quite intimate with the friend near him.

"Laura went down and heard it," said Violet. "I could not do that, because I was tied to my aunt. You can't conceive how dutiful I am during this last month."

"And is it to be in a month, Chiltern?" said Phineas.

"She says so. She arranges everything,—in concert with my father. When I threw up the sponge, I simply asked for a long day. 'A long day, my lord,' I said. But my father and Violet between them refused me any mercy."

"You do not believe him," said Violet.

"Not a word. If I did he would want to see me on the coast of Flanders again, I don't doubt. I have come to congratulate you both."

"Thank you, Mr. Finn," said Violet, taking his hand with hearty kindness. "I should not have been quite happy without one nice word from you."

"I shall try and make the best of it," said Chiltern. "But, I say, you'll come over and ride Bonebreaker again. He's down there at the 'Bull,' and I've taken a little box close by. I can't stand the governor's county for hunting."

"And will your wife go down to Willingford?"

"Of course she will, and ride to hounds a great deal closer than I can ever do. Mind you come, and if there's anything in the stable fit to carry you, you shall have it."

Then Phineas had to explain that he had come to bid them farewell, and that it was not at all probable that he should ever be able to see Willingford again in the hunting season. "I don't suppose that I shall make either of you quite understand it, but I have got to begin again. The chances are that I shall never see another foxhound all my life."

"Not in Ireland!" exclaimed Lord Chiltern.

"Not unless I should have to examine one as a witness. I have nothing before me but downright hard work; and a great deal of that must be done before I can hope to earn a shilling."

"But you are so clever," said Violet. "Of course it will come quickly."

"I do not mean to be impatient about it, nor yet unhappy," said Phineas. "Only hunting won't be much in my line."

"And will you leave London altogether?" Violet asked.

"Altogether. I shall stick to one club,—Brooks's; but I shall take my name off all the others."

"What a deuce of a nuisance!" said Lord Chiltern.

"I have no doubt you will be very happy," said Violet; "and you'll be a Lord Chancellor in no time. But you won't go quite yet."

"Next Sunday."

"You will return. You must be here for our wedding;—indeed you must. I will not be married unless you do."

Even this, however, was impossible. He must go on Sunday, and must return no more. Then he made his little farewell speech, which he could not deliver without some awkward stuttering. He would think of her on the day of her marriage, and pray that she might be happy. And he would send her a little trifle before he went, which he hoped she would wear in remembrance of their old friendship.

"She shall wear it, whatever it is, or I'll know the reason why," said Chiltern.

"Hold your tongue, you rough bear!" said Violet. "Of course I'll wear it. And of course I'll think of the giver. I shall have many presents, but few that I will think of so much." Then Phineas left the room, with his throat so full that he could not speak another word.

"He is still broken-hearted about you," said the favoured lover as soon as his rival had left the room.

"It is not that," said Violet. "He is broken-hearted about everything. The whole world is vanishing away from him. I wish he could have made up his mind to marry that German woman with all the money." It must be understood, however, that Phineas had never spoken a word to any one as to the offer which the German woman had made to him.

It was on the morning of the Sunday on which he was to leave London that he saw Lady Laura. He had asked that it might be so, in order that he might then have nothing more upon his mind. He found her quite alone, and he could see by her eyes that she had been weeping. As he looked at her, remembering that it was not yet six years since he had first been allowed to enter that room, he could not but perceive how very much she was altered in appearance. Then she had been three-and-twenty, and had not looked to be a day older. Now she might have been taken to be nearly forty, so much had her troubles preyed upon her spirit, and eaten into the vitality of her youth. "So you have come to say good-bye," she said, smiling as she rose to meet him.

"Yes, Lady Laura;—to say good-bye. Not for ever, I hope, but probably for long."

"No, not for ever. At any rate, we will not think so." Then she paused; but he was silent, sitting with his hat dangling in his two hands, and his eyes fixed upon the floor. "Do you know, Mr. Finn," she continued, "that sometimes I am very angry with myself about you."

"Then it must be because you have been too kind to me."

"It is because I fear that I have done much to injure you. From the first day that I knew you,—do you remember, when we were talking here, in this very room, about the beginning of the Reform Bill;—from that day I wished that you should come among us and be one of us."

"I have been with you, to my infinite satisfaction,—while it lasted."

"But it has not lasted, and now I fear that it has done you harm."

"Who can say whether it has been for good or evil? But of this I am sure you will be certain,—that I am very grateful to you for all the goodness you have shown me." Then again he was silent.

She did not know what it was that she wanted, but she did desire some expression from his lips that should be warmer than an expression of gratitude. An expression of love,—of existing love,—she would have felt to be an insult, and would have treated it as such. Indeed, she knew that from him no such insult could come. But she was in that morbid, melancholy state of mind which requires the excitement of more than ordinary sympathy, even though that sympathy be all painful; and I think that she would have been pleased had he referred to the passion for herself which he had once expressed. If he would have spoken of his love, and of her mistake, and have made some half-suggestion as to what might have been their lives had things gone differently,—though she would have rebuked him even for that,—still it would have comforted her. But at this moment, though he remembered much that had passed between them, he was not even thinking of the Braes of Linter. All that had taken place four years ago;—and there had been so many other things since which had moved him even more than that! "You have heard what I have arranged for myself?" she said at last.

"Your father has told me that you are going to Dresden."

"Yes;—he will accompany me,—coming home of course for Parliament. It is a sad break-up, is it not? But the lawyer says that if I remain here I may be subject to very disagreeable attempts from Mr. Kennedy to force me to go back again. It is odd, is it not, that he should not understand how impossible it is?"

"He means to do his duty."

"I believe so. But he becomes more stern every day to those who are with him. And then, why should I remain here? What is there to tempt me? As a woman separated from her husband I cannot take an interest in those things which used to charm me. I feel that I am crushed and quelled by my position, even though there is no disgrace in it."

"No disgrace, certainly," said Phineas.

"But I am nobody,—or worse than nobody."

"And I also am going to be a nobody," said Phineas, laughing.

"Ah; you are a man and will get over it, and you have many years before you will begin to be growing old. I am growing old already. Yes, I am. I feel it, and know it, and see it. A woman has a fine game to play; but then she is so easily bowled out, and the term allowed to her is so short."

"A man's allowance of time may be short too," said Phineas.

"But he can try his hand again." Then there was another pause. "I had thought, Mr. Finn, that you would have married," she said in her very lowest voice.

"You knew all my hopes and fears about that."

"I mean that you would have married Madame Goesler."

"What made you think that, Lady Laura?"

"Because I saw that she liked you, and because such a marriage would have been so suitable. She has all that you want. You know what they say of her now?"

"What do they say?"

"That the Duke of Omnium offered to make her his wife, and that she refused him for your sake."

"There is nothing that people won't say;—nothing on earth," said Phineas. Then he got up and took his leave of her. He also wanted to part from her with some special expression of affection, but he did not know how to choose his words. He had wished that some allusion should be made, not to the Braes of Linter, but to the close confidence which had so long existed between them; but he found that the language to do this properly was wanting to him. Had the opportunity arisen he would have told her now the whole story of Mary Flood Jones; but the opportunity did not come, and he left her, never having mentioned the name of his Mary or having hinted at his engagement to any one of his friends in London. "It is better so," he said to himself. "My life in Ireland is to be a new life, and why should I mix two things together that will be so different?"

He was to dine at his lodgings, and then leave them for good at eight o'clock. He had packed up everything before he went to Portman Square, and he returned home only just in time to sit down to his solitary mutton chop. But as he sat down he saw a small note addressed to himself lying on the table among the crowd of books, letters, and papers, of which he had still to make disposal. It was a very small note in an envelope of a peculiar tint of pink, and he knew the handwriting well. The blood mounted all over his face as he took it up, and he hesitated for a moment before he opened it. It could not be that the offer should be repeated to him. Slowly, hardly venturing at first to look at the enclosure, he opened it, and the words which it contained were as follows:—

Sunday morning.

I learn that you are going to-day, and I write a word which you will receive just as you are departing. It is to say merely this,—that when I left you the other day I was angry, not with you, but with myself. Let me wish you all good wishes and that prosperity which I know you will deserve, and which I think you will win.

Yours very truly, M. M. G.

Should he put off his journey and go to her this very evening and claim her as his friend? The question was asked and answered in a moment. Of course he would not go to her. Were he to do so there would be only one possible word for him to say, and that word should certainly never be spoken. But he wrote to her a reply, shorter even than her own short note.

Thanks, dear friend. I do not doubt but that you and I understand each other thoroughly, and that each trusts the other for good wishes and honest intentions.

Always yours, P. F.

I write these as I am starting.

When he had written this, he kept it till the last moment in his hand, thinking that he would not send it. But as he slipped into the cab, he gave the note to his late landlady to post.

At the station Bunce came to him to say a word of farewell, and Mrs. Bunce was on his arm.

"Well done, Mr. Finn, well done," said Bunce. "I always knew there was a good drop in you."

"You always told me I should ruin myself in Parliament, and so I have," said Phineas.

"Not at all. It takes a deal to ruin a man if he's got the right sperrit. I've better hopes of you now than ever I had in the old days when you used to be looking out for Government place;—and Mr. Monk has tried that too. I thought he would find the iron too heavy for him." "God bless you, Mr. Finn," said Mrs. Bunce with her handkerchief up to her eyes. "There's not one of 'em I ever had as lodgers I've cared about half as much as I did for you." Then they shook hands with him through the window, and the train was off.

CHAPTER LXXVI. Conclusion

We are told that it is a bitter moment with the Lord Mayor when he leaves the Mansion House and becomes once more Alderman Jones, of No. 75, Bucklersbury. Lord Chancellors going out of office have a great fall though they take pensions with them for their consolation. And the President of the United States when he leaves the glory of the White House and once more becomes a simple citizen must feel the change severely. But our hero, Phineas Finn, as he turned his back upon the scene of his many successes, and prepared himself for permanent residence in his own country, was, I think, in a worse plight than any of the reduced divinities to whom I have alluded. They at any rate had known that their fall would come. He, like Icarus, had flown up towards the sun, hoping that his wings of wax would bear him steadily aloft among the gods. Seeing that his wings were wings of wax, we must acknowledge that they were very good. But the celestial lights had been too strong for them, and now, having lived for five years with lords and countesses, with Ministers and orators, with beautiful women and men of fashion, he must start again in a little lodging in Dublin, and hope that the attorneys of that litigious city might be good to him. On his journey home he made but one resolution. He would make the change, or attempt to make it, with manly strength. During his last month in London he had allowed himself to be sad, depressed, and melancholy. There should be an end of all that now. Nobody at home should see that he was depressed. And Mary, his own Mary, should at any rate have no cause to think that her love and his own engagement had ever been the cause to him of depression. Did he not value her love more than anything in the world? A thousand times he told himself that he did.

She was there in the old house at Killaloe to greet him. Her engagement was an affair known to all the county, and she had no idea that it would become her to be coy in her love. She was in his arms before he had spoken to his father and mother, and had made her little speech to him,—very inaudibly indeed,—while he was covering her sweet face with kisses. "Oh, Phineas, I am so proud of you; and I think you are so right, and I am so glad you have done it." Again he covered her face with kisses. Could he ever have had such satisfaction as this had he allowed Madame Goesler's hand to remain in his?

On the first night of his arrival he sat for an hour downstairs with his father talking over his plans. He felt,—he could not but feel,—that he was not the hero now that he had been when he was last at Killaloe,—when he had come thither with a Cabinet Minister under his wing. And yet his father did his best to prevent the growth of any such feeling. The old doctor was not quite as well off as he had been when Phineas first started with his high hopes for London. Since that day he had abandoned his profession and was now living on the fruits of his life's labour. For the last two years he had been absolved from the necessity of providing an income for his son, and had probably allowed himself to feel that no such demand upon him would again be made. Now, however, it was necessary that he should do so. Could his son manage to live on two hundred a-year? There would then be four hundred a-year left for the wants of the family at home. Phineas swore that he could fight his battle on a hundred and fifty, and they ended the argument by splitting the difference. He had been paying exactly the same sum of money for the rooms he had just left in London; but then, while he held those rooms, his income had been two thousand a-year. Tenant-right was a very fine thing, but could it be worth such a fall as this?

"And about dear Mary?" said the father.

"I hope it may not be very long," said Phineas.

"I have not spoken to her about it, but your mother says that Mrs. Flood Jones is very averse to a long engagement."

"What can I do? She would not wish me to marry her daughter with no other income than an allowance made by you."

"Your mother says that she has some idea that you and she might live together;—that if they let Floodborough you might take a small house in Dublin. Remember, Phineas, I am not proposing it myself."

Then Phineas bethought himself that he was not even yet so low in the world that he need submit himself to terms dictated to him by Mrs. Flood Jones. "I am glad that you do not propose it, sir."

"Why so, Phineas?"

"Because I should have been obliged to oppose the plan even if it had come from you. Mothers-in-law are never a comfort in a house."

"I never tried it myself," said the doctor.

"And I never will try it. I am quite sure that Mary does not expect any such thing, and that she is willing to wait. If I can shorten the term of waiting by hard work, I will do so." The decision to which Phineas had come on this matter was probably made known to Mrs. Flood Jones after some mild fashion by old Mrs. Finn. Nothing more was said to Phineas about a joint household; but he was quite able to perceive from the manner of the lady towards him that his proposed mother-in-law wished him to understand that he was treating her daughter very badly. What did it signify? None of them knew the story of Madame Goesler, and of course none of them would know it. None of them would ever hear how well he had behaved to his little Mary.

But Mary did know it all before he left her to go up to Dublin. The two lovers allowed themselves,—or were allowed by their elders, one week of exquisite bliss together; and during this week, Phineas told her, I think, everything. He told her everything as far as he could do so without seeming to boast of his own successes. How is a man not to tell such tales when he has on his arm, close to him, a girl who tells him her little everything of life, and only asks for his confidence in return? And then his secrets are so precious to her and so sacred, that he feels as sure of her fidelity as though she were a very goddess of faith and trust. And the temptation to tell is so great. For all that he has to tell she loves him the better and still the better. A man desires to win a virgin heart, and is happy to know,—or at least to believe,—that he has won it. With a woman every former rival is an added victim to the wheels of the triumphant chariot in which she is sitting. "All these has he known and loved, culling sweets from each of them. But now he has come to me, and I am the sweetest of them all." And so Mary was taught to believe of Laura and of Violet and of Madame Goesler,—that though they had had charms to please, her lover had never been so charmed as he was now while she was hanging to his breast. And I think that she was right in her belief. During those lovely summer evening walks along the shores of Lough Derg, Phineas was as happy as he had ever been at any moment of his life.

"I shall never be impatient,—never," she said to him on the last evening. "All I want is that you should write to me."

"I shall want more than that, Mary."

"Then you must come down and see me. When you do come they will be happy, happy days for me. But of course we cannot be married for the next twenty years."

"Say forty, Mary."

"I will say anything that you like;—you will know what I mean just as well. And, Phineas, I must tell you one thing,—though it makes me sad to think of it, and will make me sad to speak of it."

"I will not have you sad on our last night, Mary."

"I must say it. I am beginning to understand how much you have given up for me."

"I have given up nothing for you."

"If I had not been at Killaloe when Mr. Monk was here, and if we had not,—had not,—oh dear, if I had not loved you so very much, you might have remained in London, and that lady would have been your wife."

"Never!" said Phineas stoutly.

"Would she not? She must not be your wife now, Phineas. I am not going to pretend that I will give you up."

"That is unkind, Mary."

"Oh, well; you may say what you please. If that is unkind, I am unkind. It would kill me to lose you."

Had he done right? How could there be a doubt about it? How could there be a question about it? Which of them had loved him, or was capable of loving him as Mary loved him? What girl was ever so sweet, so gracious, so angelic, as his own Mary? He swore to her that he was prouder of winning her than of anything he had ever done in all his life, and that of all the treasures that had ever come in his way she was the most precious. She went to bed that night the happiest girl in all Connaught, although when she parted from him she understood that she was not to see him again till Christmas-Eve.

But she did see him again before the summer was over, and the manner of their meeting was in this wise. Immediately after the passing of that scrambled Irish Reform Bill, Parliament, as the reader knows, was dissolved. This was in the early days of June, and before the end of July the new members were again assembled at Westminster. This session, late in summer, was very terrible; but it was not very long, and then it was essentially necessary. There was something of the year's business which must yet be done, and the country would require to know who were to be the Ministers of the Government. It is not needed that the reader should be troubled any further with the strategy of one political leader or of another, or that more should be said of Mr. Monk and his tenant-right. The House of Commons had offended Mr. Gresham by voting in a majority against him, and Mr. Gresham had punished the House of Commons by subjecting it to the expense and nuisance of a new election. All this is constitutional, and rational enough to Englishmen, though it may be unintelligible to strangers. The upshot on the present occasion was that the Ministers remained in their places and that Mr. Monk's bill, though it had received the substantial honour of a second reading, passed away for the present into the limbo of abortive legislation.

All this would not concern us at all, nor our poor hero much, were it not that the great men with whom he had been for two years so pleasant a colleague, remembered him with something of affectionate regret. Whether it began with Mr. Gresham or with Lord Cantrip, I will not say;—or whether Mr. Monk, though now a political enemy, may have said a word that brought about the good deed. Be that as it may, just before the summer session was brought to a close Phineas received the following letter from Lord Cantrip:—

Downing Street,
August 4, 186—.

MY DEAR MR. FINN,—

Mr. Gresham has been talking to me, and we both think that possibly a permanent Government appointment may be acceptable to you. We have no doubt, that should this be the case, your services would be very valuable to the country. There is a vacancy for a poor-law inspector at present in Ireland, whose residence I believe should be in Cork. The salary is a thousand a-year. Should the appointment suit you, Mr. Gresham will be most happy to nominate you to the office. Let me have a line at your early convenience.

Believe me,
Most sincerely yours,   CANTRIP.

He received the letter one morning in Dublin, and within three hours he was on his route to Killaloe. Of course he would accept the appointment, but he would not even do that without telling Mary of his new prospect. Of course he would accept the appointment. Though he had been as yet barely two months in Dublin, though he had hardly been long enough settled to his work to have hoped to be able to see in which way there might be a vista open leading to success, still he had fancied that he had seen that success was impossible. He did not know how to begin,—and men were afraid of him, thinking that he was unsteady, arrogant, and prone to failure. He had not seen his way to the possibility of a guinea.

"A thousand a-year!" said Mary Flood Jones, opening her eyes wide with wonder at the golden future before them.

"It is nothing very great for a perpetuity," said Phineas.

"Oh, Phineas; surely a thousand a-year will be very nice."

"It will be certain," said Phineas, "and then we can be married to-morrow."

"But I have been making up my mind to wait ever so long," said Mary.

"Then your mind must be unmade," said Phineas.

What was the nature of the reply to Lord Cantrip the reader may imagine, and thus we will leave our hero an Inspector of Poor Houses in the County of Cork.